Message from
Hidenori Kusaka

I received quite a lot of responses when I wrote about *Pokémon GO* in the author comment for *X•Y* volume 3. I was writing about how difficult it was to complete the Pokédex. It really is hard work. There have been updates of Kanto, Johto, Hoenn, Sinnoh, Unova, and Kalos. So far, the only Pokédex I've managed to complete is Kanto. I would at least like to complete the Johto Pokédex. Where are you, Corsola? (To be continued...)

Message from
Satoshi Yamamoto

The *X•Y* arc has entered the second half of the story. There are so many scenes leading up to the climax that I'd like to draw as the cover illustration. I can't make up my mind. I had several candidates for the cover illustration of this volume too, but as you can see, I ended up with this illustration. If you look at the final product, it seems like Xerneas is shaped like a *Y* and Yveltal is shaped like an *X*, but that is a complete coincidence (*laugh*).

Hidenori Kusaka is the writer for *Pokémon Adventures*. Running continuously for over 20 years, *Pokémon Adventures* is the only manga series to completely cover all the *Pokémon* games and has become one of the most popular series of all time. In addition to writing manga, he also edits children's books and plans mixed-media projects for Shogakukan's children's magazines. He uses the Pokémon Electrode as his author portrait.

Satoshi Yamamoto is the artist for *Pokémon Adventures*, which he began working on in 2001, starting with volume 10. Yamamoto launched his manga career in 1993 with the horror-action title *Kimen Senshi*, which ran in Shogakukan's *Weekly Shonen Sunday* magazine, followed by the series *Kaze no Denshosha*. Yamamoto's favorite manga creators/artists include FUJIKO F FUJIO (*Doraemon*), Yukinobu Hoshino (*2001 Nights*), and Katsuhiro Otomo (*Akira*). He loves films, monsters, detective novels, and punk rock music. He uses the Pokémon Swalot as his artist portrait.

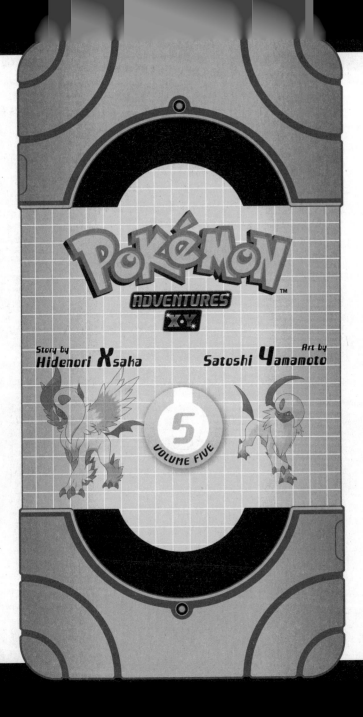

POKÉMON™ ADVENTURES X·Y

Story by
Hidenori Kusaka

Art by
Satoshi Yamamoto

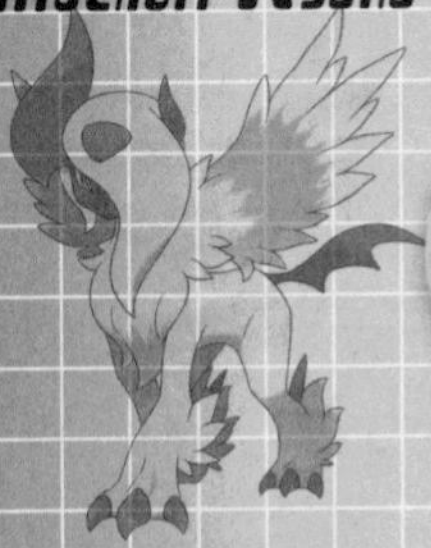

5
VOLUME FIVE

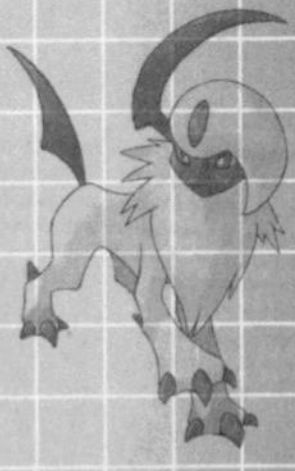

The Story Thus Far...

A story about young people entrusted with Pokédexes by the world's leading Pokémon researchers. Together with their Pokémon, they travel, do battle, and evolve!

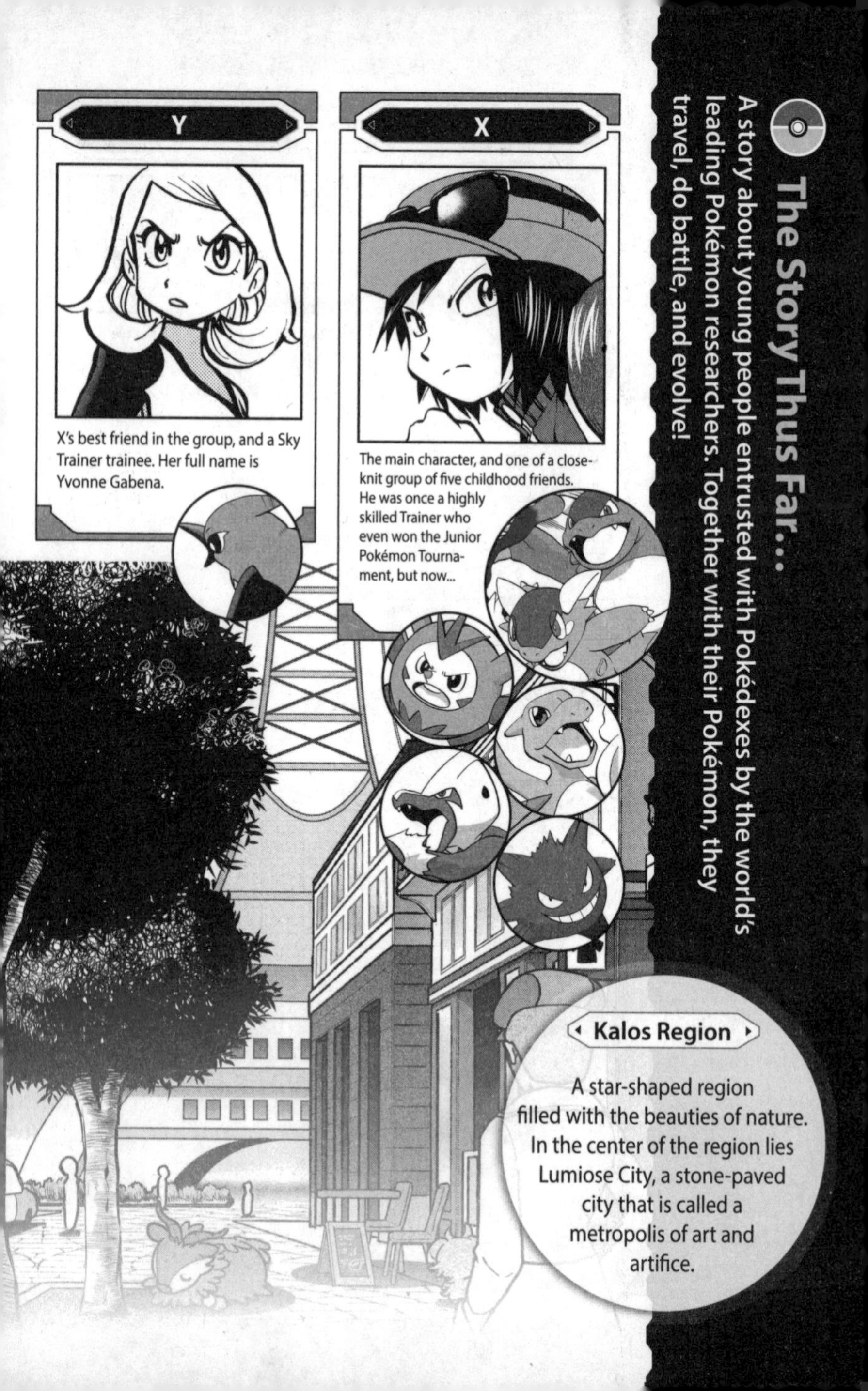

X

The main character, and one of a close-knit group of five childhood friends. He was once a highly skilled Trainer who even won the Junior Pokémon Tournament, but now...

Y

X's best friend in the group, and a Sky Trainer trainee. Her full name is Yvonne Gabena.

Kalos Region

A star-shaped region filled with the beauties of nature. In the center of the region lies Lumiose City, a stone-paved city that is called a metropolis of art and artifice.

THE STORY THUS FAR

The Kalos region, Vaniville Town—four close childhood friends are trying to get the reclusive X out of his room when the Legendary Pokémon Yveltal and Xerneas suddenly appear. Then they are all attacked by a mysterious group wearing red suits who try to steal the Mega Ring that X wears on his arm like a bracelet. After Korrina's Key Stone is stolen, Lysandre gains the power to Mega Evolve. X decides to confront Lysandre, who is wielding a Mega Gyarados. The Gym Leaders gather to stop the Ultimate Weapon from being activated, but they are too late. Now, Xerneas calls out to them to place the Ultimate Weapon inside a Poké Ball.

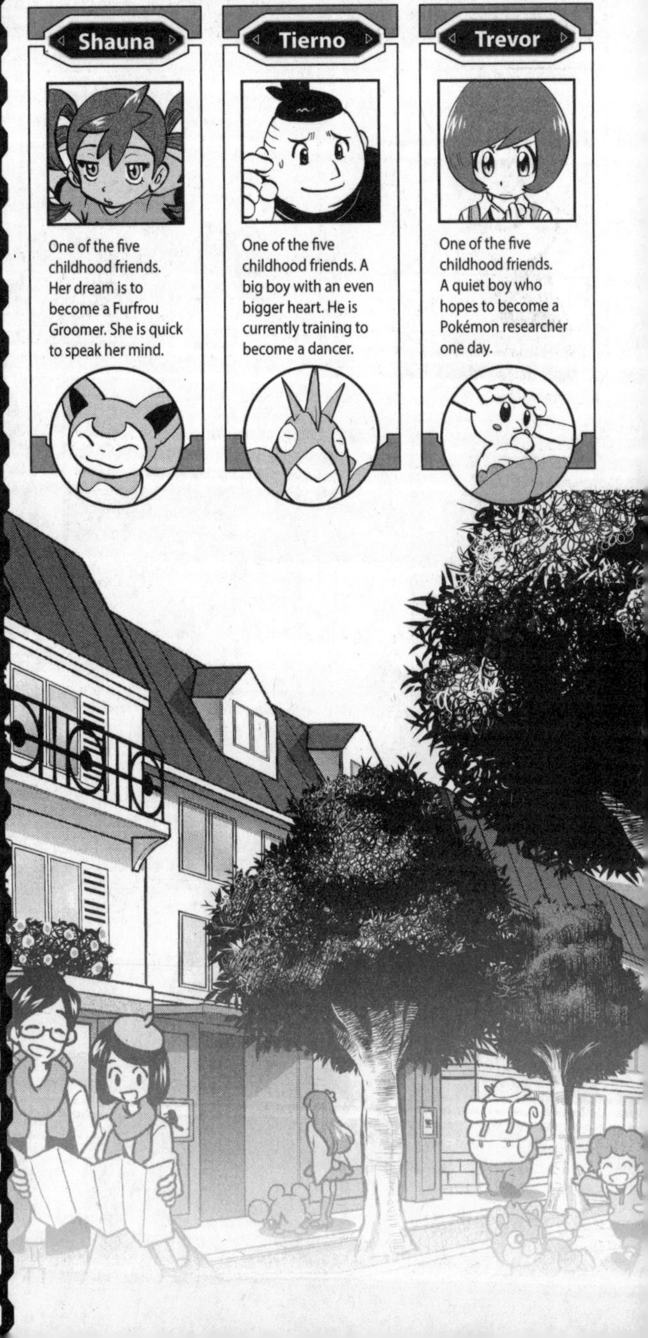
Shauna
One of the five childhood friends. Her dream is to become a Furfrou Groomer. She is quick to speak her mind.
Tierno
One of the five childhood friends. A big boy with an even bigger heart. He is currently training to become a dancer.
Trevor
One of the five childhood friends. A quiet boy who hopes to become a Pokémon researcher one day.

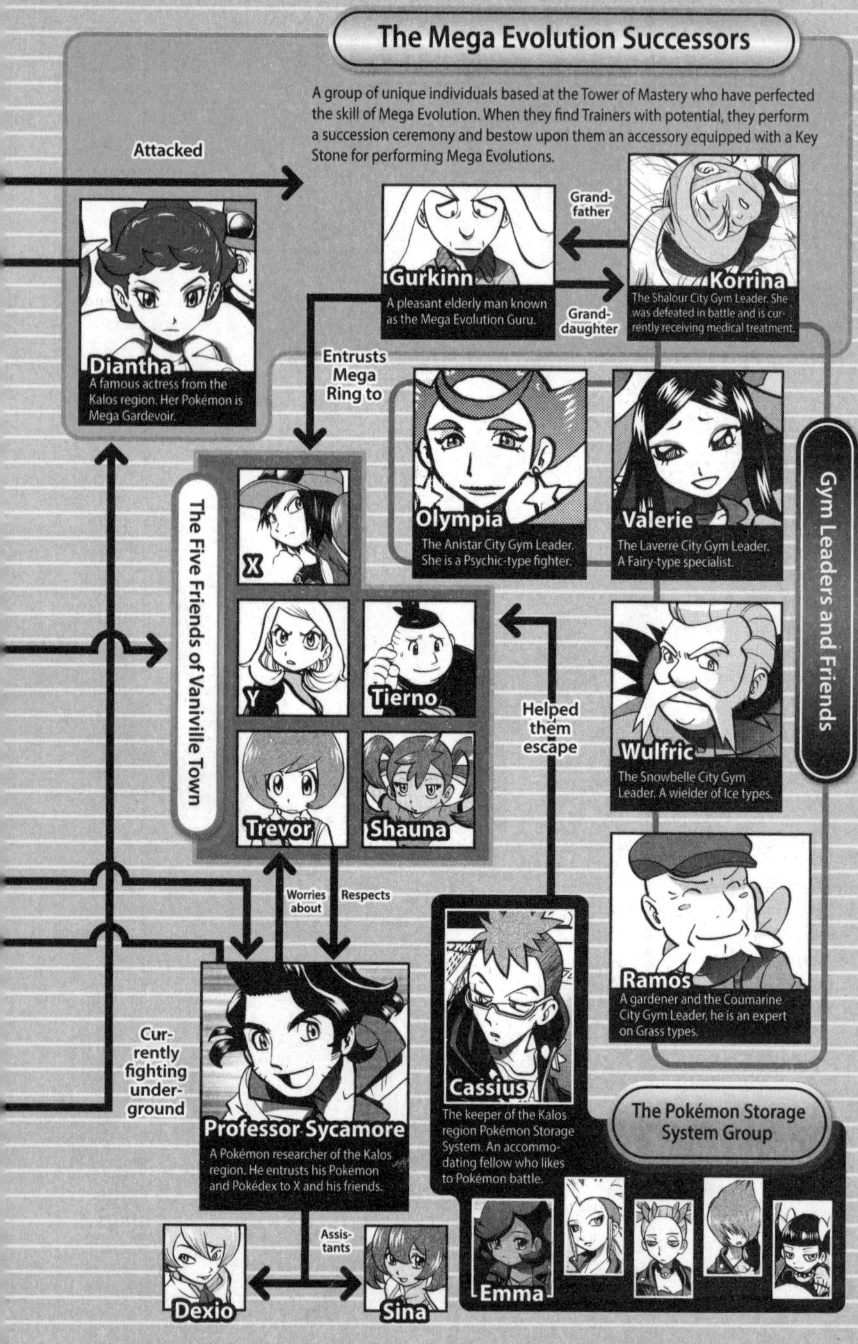
The Mega Evolution Successors
A group of unique individuals based at the Tower of Mastery who have perfected the skill of Mega Evolution. When they find Trainers with potential, they perform a succession ceremony and bestow upon them an accessory equipped with a Key Stone for performing Mega Evolutions.
Attacked
Diantha
A famous actress from the Kalos region. Her Pokémon is Mega Gardevoir.
Gurkinn
A pleasant elderly man known as the Mega Evolution Guru.
Grand-father
Grand-daughter
Korrina
The Shalour City Gym Leader. She was defeated in battle and is currently receiving medical treatment.
Entrusts Mega Ring to
Olympia
The Anistar City Gym Leader. She is a Psychic-type fighter.
Valerie
The Laverre City Gym Leader. A Fairy-type specialist.
Gym Leaders and Friends
The Five Friends of Vaniville Town
X
Y
Tierno
Trevor
Shauna
Helped them escape
Wulfric
The Snowbelle City Gym Leader. A wielder of Ice types.
Worries about
Respects
Ramos
A gardener and the Coumarine City Gym Leader, he is an expert on Grass types.
Cur-rently fighting under-ground
Professor Sycamore
A Pokémon researcher of the Kalos region. He entrusts his Pokémon and Pokédex to X and his friends.
Cassius
The keeper of the Kalos region Pokémon Storage System. An accommodating fellow who likes to Pokémon battle.
The Pokémon Storage System Group
Assis-tants
Dexio
Sina
Emma

Character Correlation Chart

Track the connections between the people revolving around X.

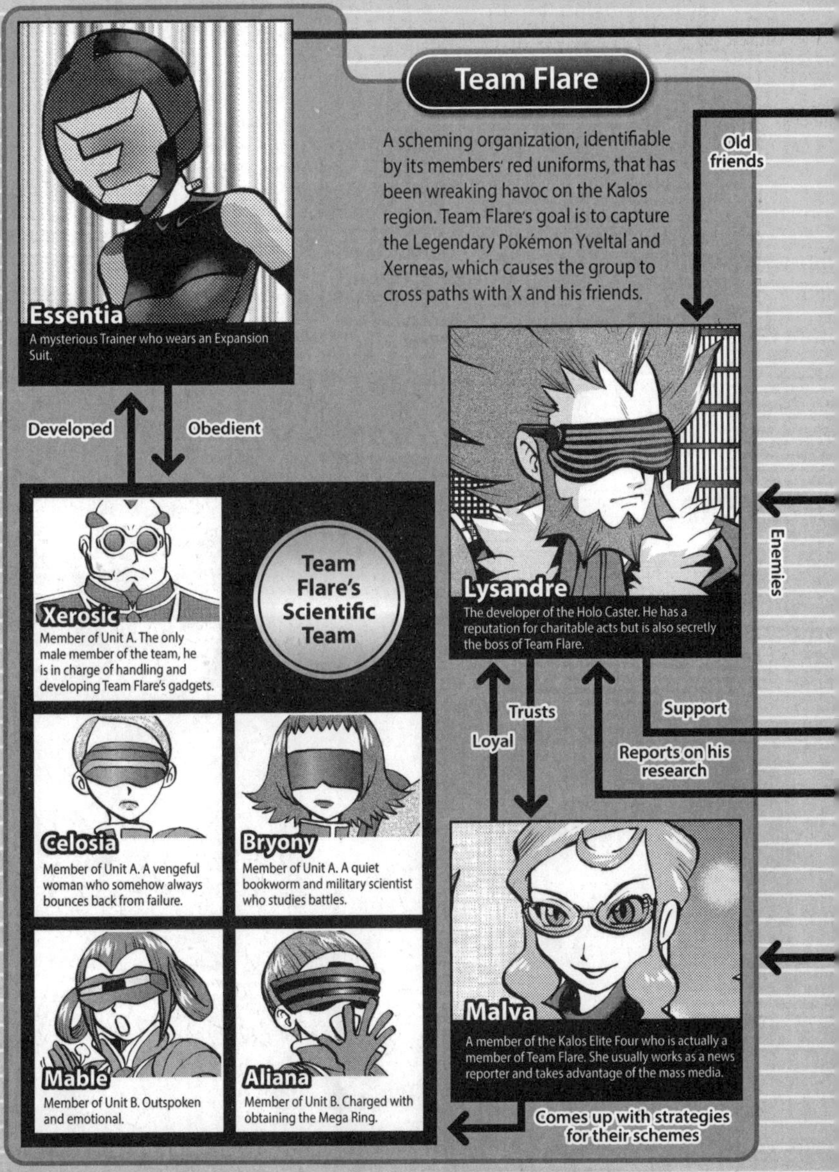

Team Flare
A scheming organization, identifiable by its members' red uniforms, that has been wreaking havoc on the Kalos region. Team Flare's goal is to capture the Legendary Pokémon Yveltal and Xerneas, which causes the group to cross paths with X and his friends.
Essentia
A mysterious Trainer who wears an Expansion Suit.
Developed
Obedient
Old friends
Lysandre
The developer of the Holo Caster. He has a reputation for charitable acts but is also secretly the boss of Team Flare.
Enemies
Team Flare's Scientific Team
Xerosic
Member of Unit A. The only male member of the team, he is in charge of handling and developing Team Flare's gadgets.
Celosia
Member of Unit A. A vengeful woman who somehow always bounces back from failure.
Bryony
Member of Unit A. A quiet bookworm and military scientist who studies battles.
Mable
Member of Unit B. Outspoken and emotional.
Aliana
Member of Unit B. Charged with obtaining the Mega Ring.
Trusts
Loyal
Support
Reports on his research
Malva
A member of the Kalos Elite Four who is actually a member of Team Flare. She usually works as a news reporter and takes advantage of the mass media.
Comes up with strategies for their schemes

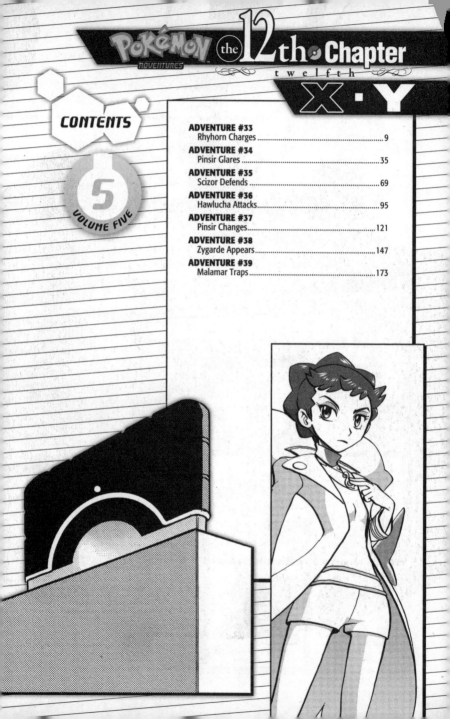

Pokémon Adventures the 12th Chapter twelfth X·Y

CONTENTS

5 VOLUME FIVE

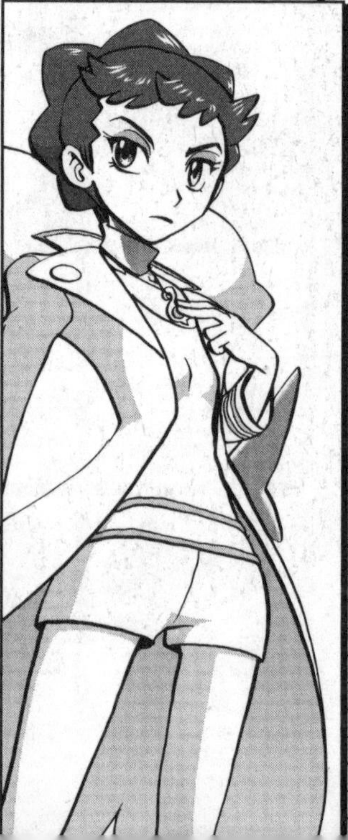

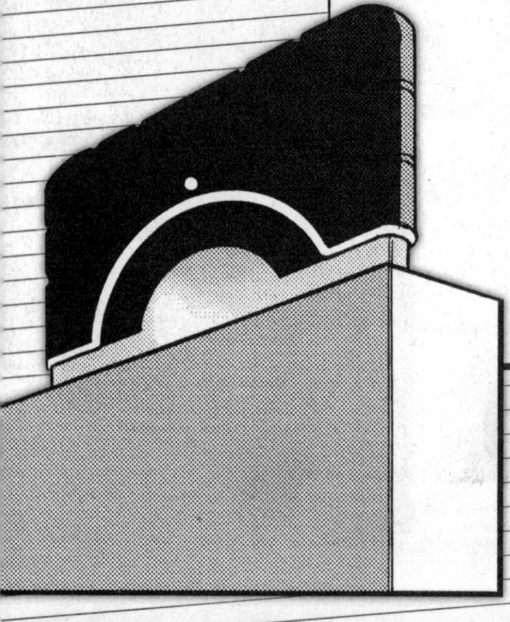

Adventure #33
Rhyhorn Charges

X●Y

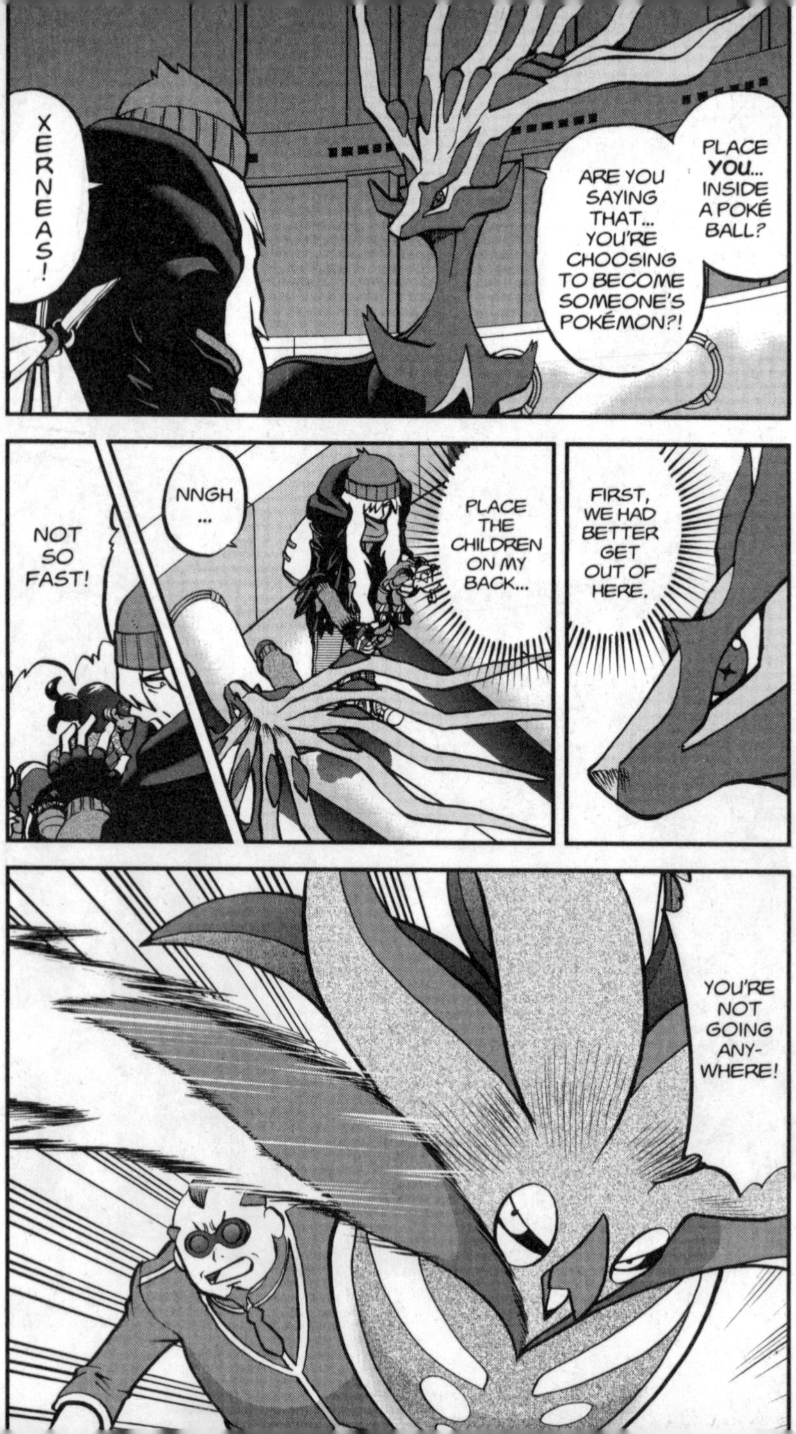
PLACE **YOU**... INSIDE A POKÉ BALL?
ARE YOU SAYING THAT... YOU'RE CHOOSING TO BECOME SOMEONE'S POKÉMON?!
XERNEAS!
FIRST, WE HAD BETTER GET OUT OF HERE.
PLACE THE CHILDREN ON MY BACK...
NNGH...
NOT SO FAST!
YOU'RE NOT GOING ANY-WHERE!

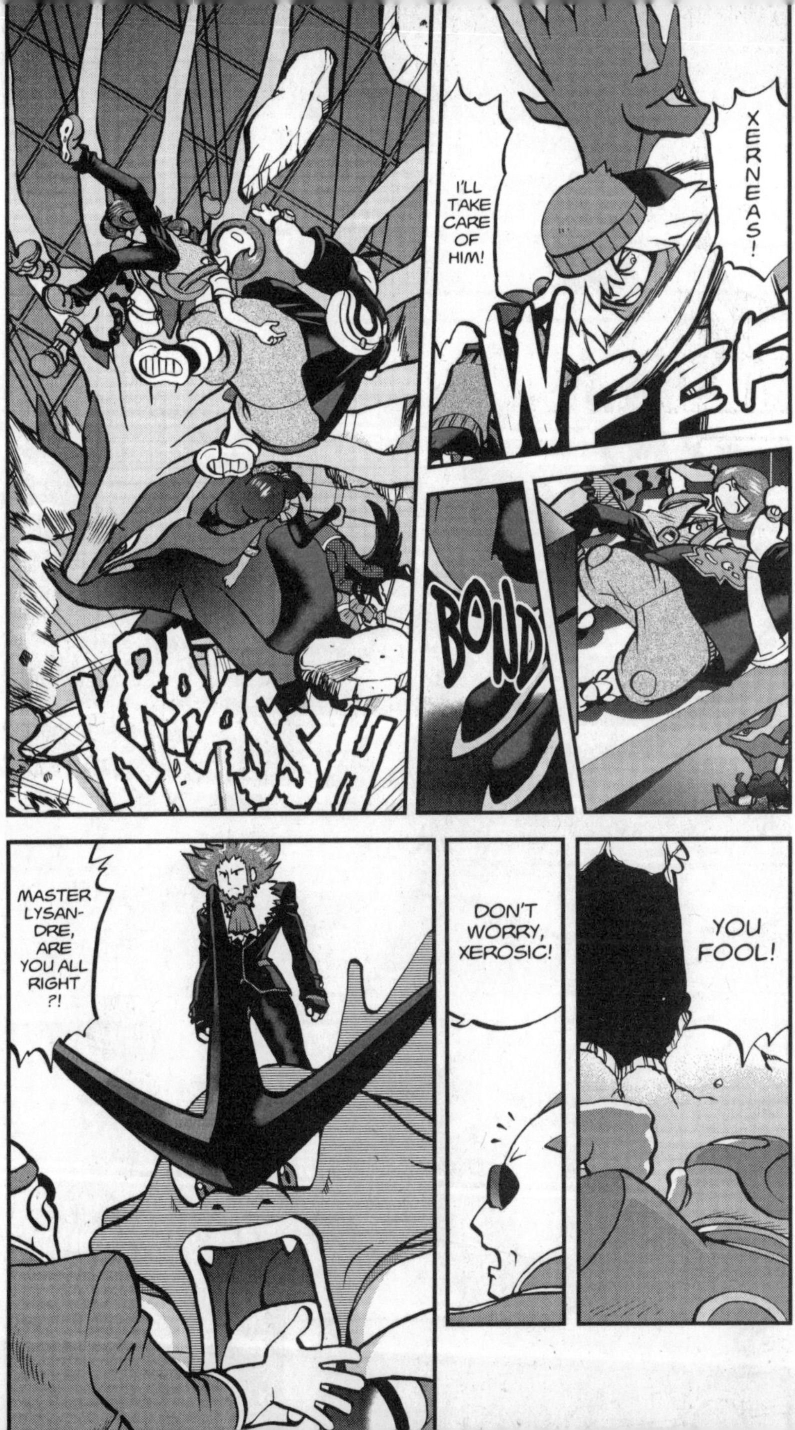

XERNEAS!
I'LL TAKE CARE OF HIM!
WFFF
BOND
KRASSH
YOU FOOL!
DON'T WORRY, XEROSIC!
MASTER LYSANDRE, ARE YOU ALL RIGHT?!

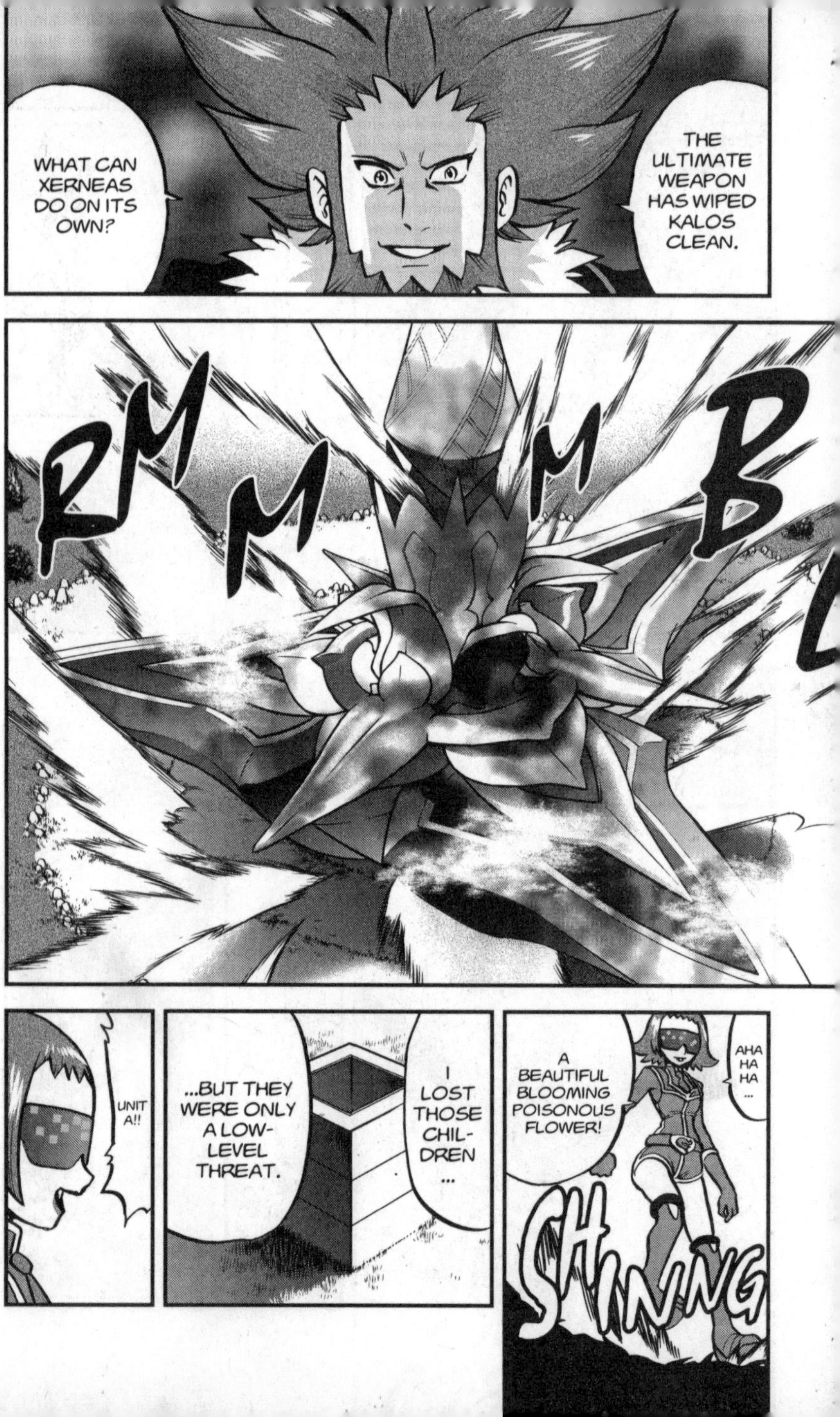
THE ULTIMATE WEAPON HAS WIPED KALOS CLEAN.
WHAT CAN XERNEAS DO ON ITS OWN?
RMMMB
AHA HA HA ...
A BEAUTIFUL BLOOMING POISONOUS FLOWER!
SHINNG
I LOST THOSE CHIL-DREN ...
...BUT THEY WERE ONLY A LOW-LEVEL THREAT.
UNIT A!!

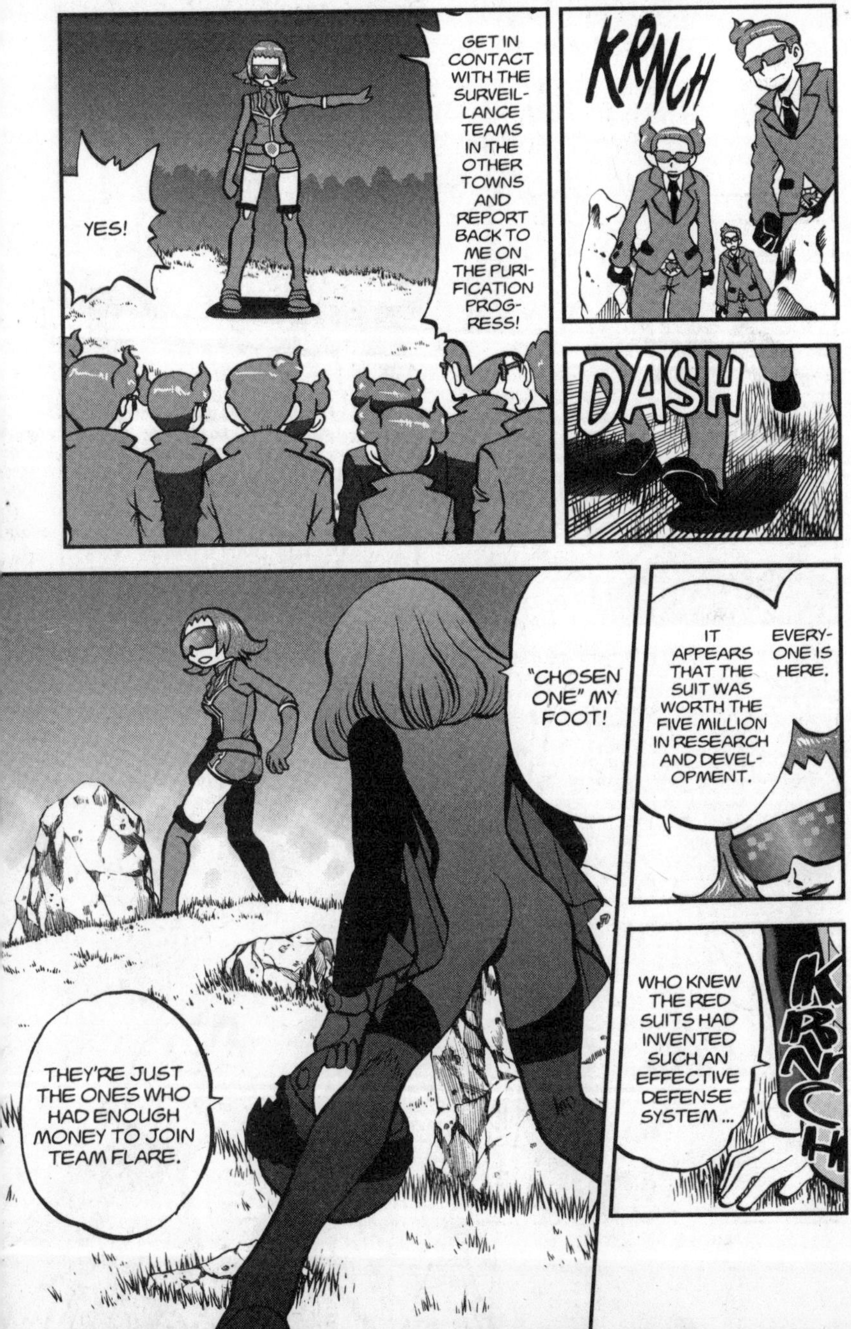
KRNCH
DASH
GET IN CONTACT WITH THE SURVEIL-LANCE TEAMS IN THE OTHER TOWNS AND REPORT BACK TO ME ON THE PURI-FICATION PROG-RESS!
YES!
EVERY-ONE IS HERE.
IT APPEARS THAT THE SUIT WAS WORTH THE FIVE MILLION IN RESEARCH AND DEVEL-OPMENT.
KRNCH
WHO KNEW THE RED SUITS HAD INVENTED SUCH AN EFFECTIVE DEFENSE SYSTEM ...
"CHOSEN ONE" MY FOOT!
THEY'RE JUST THE ONES WHO HAD ENOUGH MONEY TO JOIN TEAM FLARE.

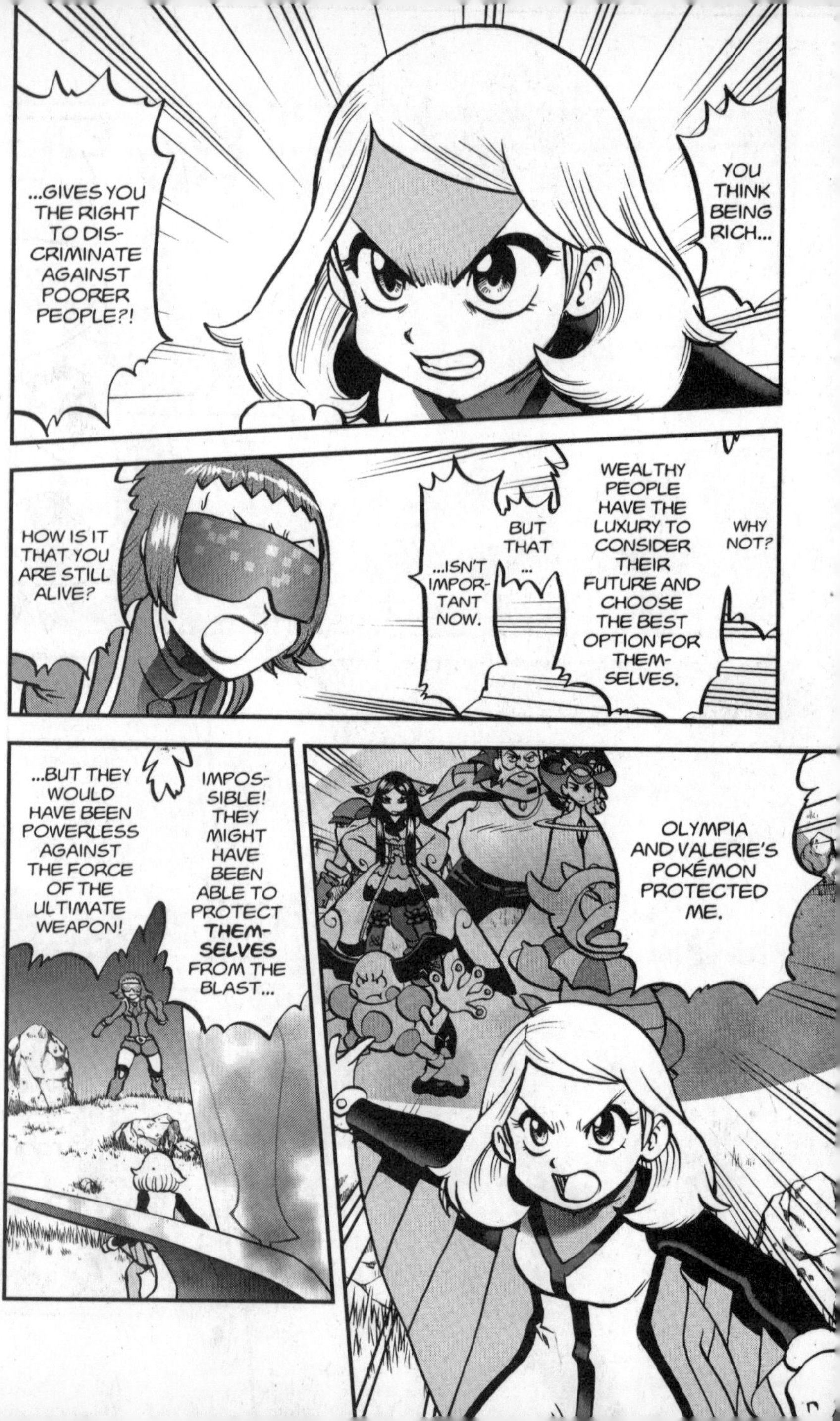
YOU THINK BEING RICH...
...GIVES YOU THE RIGHT TO DIS-CRIMINATE AGAINST POORER PEOPLE?!
WHY NOT?
WEALTHY PEOPLE HAVE THE LUXURY TO CONSIDER THEIR FUTURE AND CHOOSE THE BEST OPTION FOR THEM-SELVES.
BUT THAT...
...ISN'T IMPOR-TANT NOW.
HOW IS IT THAT YOU ARE STILL ALIVE?
OLYMPIA AND VALERIE'S POKÉMON PROTECTED ME.
IMPOS-SIBLE! THEY MIGHT HAVE BEEN ABLE TO PROTECT **THEM-SELVES** FROM THE BLAST...
...BUT THEY WOULD HAVE BEEN POWERLESS AGAINST THE FORCE OF THE ULTIMATE WEAPON!

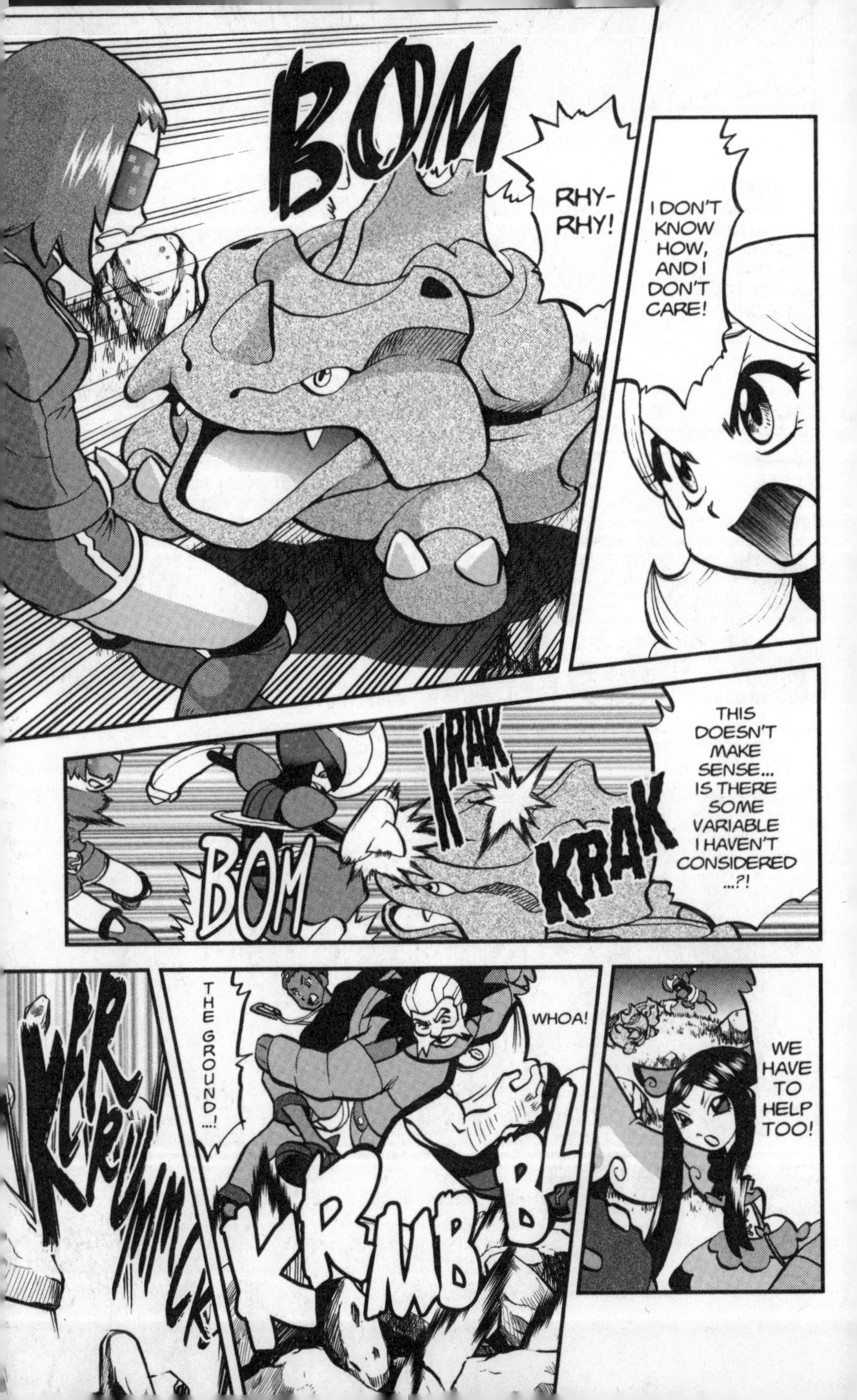
I DON'T KNOW HOW, AND I DON'T CARE!
BOM
RHY-RHY!
THIS DOESN'T MAKE SENSE... IS THERE SOME VARIABLE I HAVEN'T CONSIDERED ...?!
KRAK
KRAK
BOM
WE HAVE TO HELP TOO!
WHOA!
THE GROUND...!
KRMBBL
KRRUMMMCK!

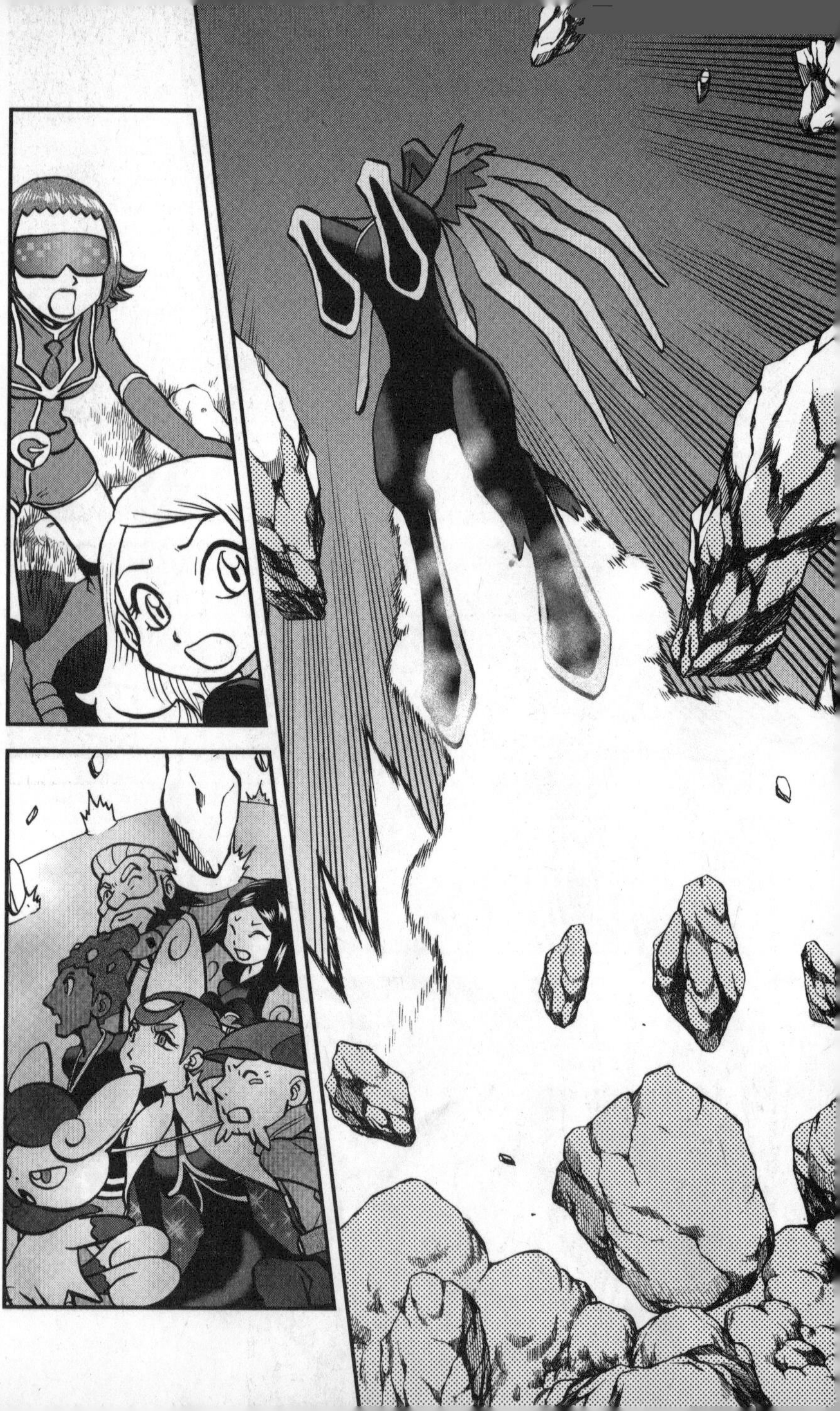

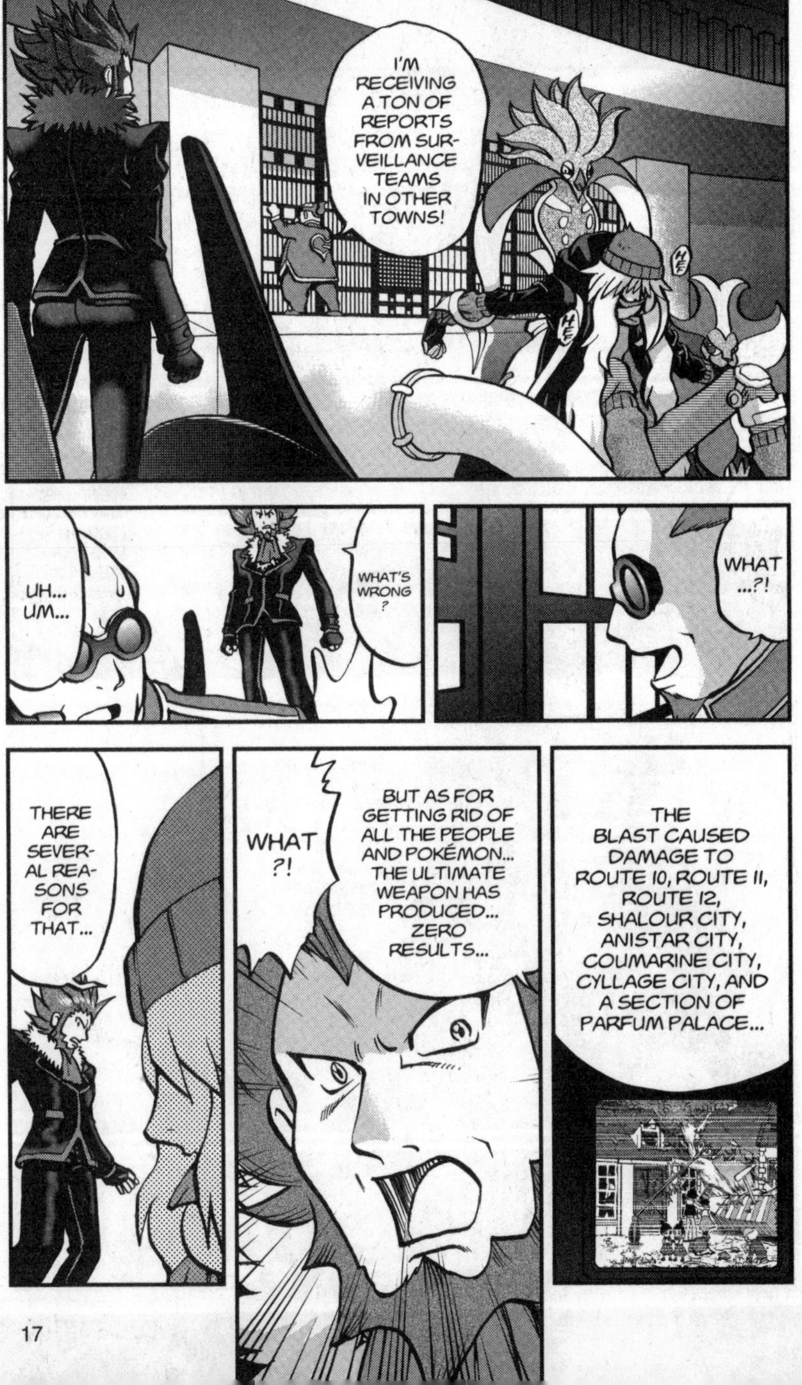
I'M RECEIVING A TON OF REPORTS FROM SUR-VEILLANCE TEAMS IN OTHER TOWNS!
HEF
HEF
WHAT ...?!
WHAT'S WRONG ?
UH... UM...
THE BLAST CAUSED DAMAGE TO ROUTE 10, ROUTE 11, ROUTE 12, SHALOUR CITY, ANISTAR CITY, COUMARINE CITY, CYLLAGE CITY, AND A SECTION OF PARFUM PALACE...
BUT AS FOR GETTING RID OF ALL THE PEOPLE AND POKÉMON... THE ULTIMATE WEAPON HAS PRODUCED... ZERO RESULTS...
WHAT ?!
THERE ARE SEVER-AL REA-SONS FOR THAT...

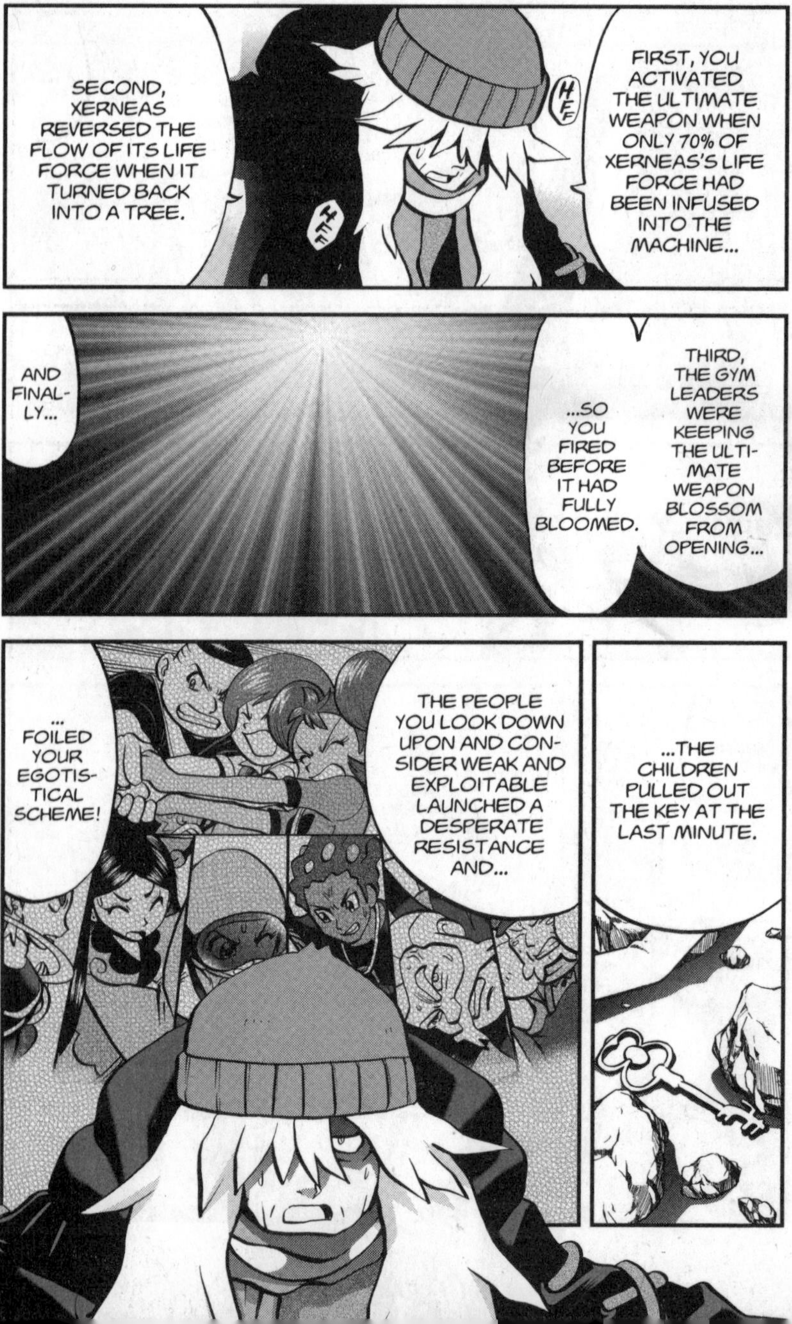
FIRST, YOU ACTIVATED THE ULTIMATE WEAPON WHEN ONLY 70% OF XERNEAS'S LIFE FORCE HAD BEEN INFUSED INTO THE MACHINE...
HFF
HFF
SECOND, XERNEAS REVERSED THE FLOW OF ITS LIFE FORCE WHEN IT TURNED BACK INTO A TREE.
THIRD, THE GYM LEADERS WERE KEEPING THE ULTIMATE WEAPON BLOSSOM FROM OPENING...
...SO YOU FIRED BEFORE IT HAD FULLY BLOOMED.
AND FINALLY...
...THE CHILDREN PULLED OUT THE KEY AT THE LAST MINUTE.
THE PEOPLE YOU LOOK DOWN UPON AND CONSIDER WEAK AND EXPLOITABLE LAUNCHED A DESPERATE RESISTANCE AND...
... FOILED YOUR EGOTISTICAL SCHEME!

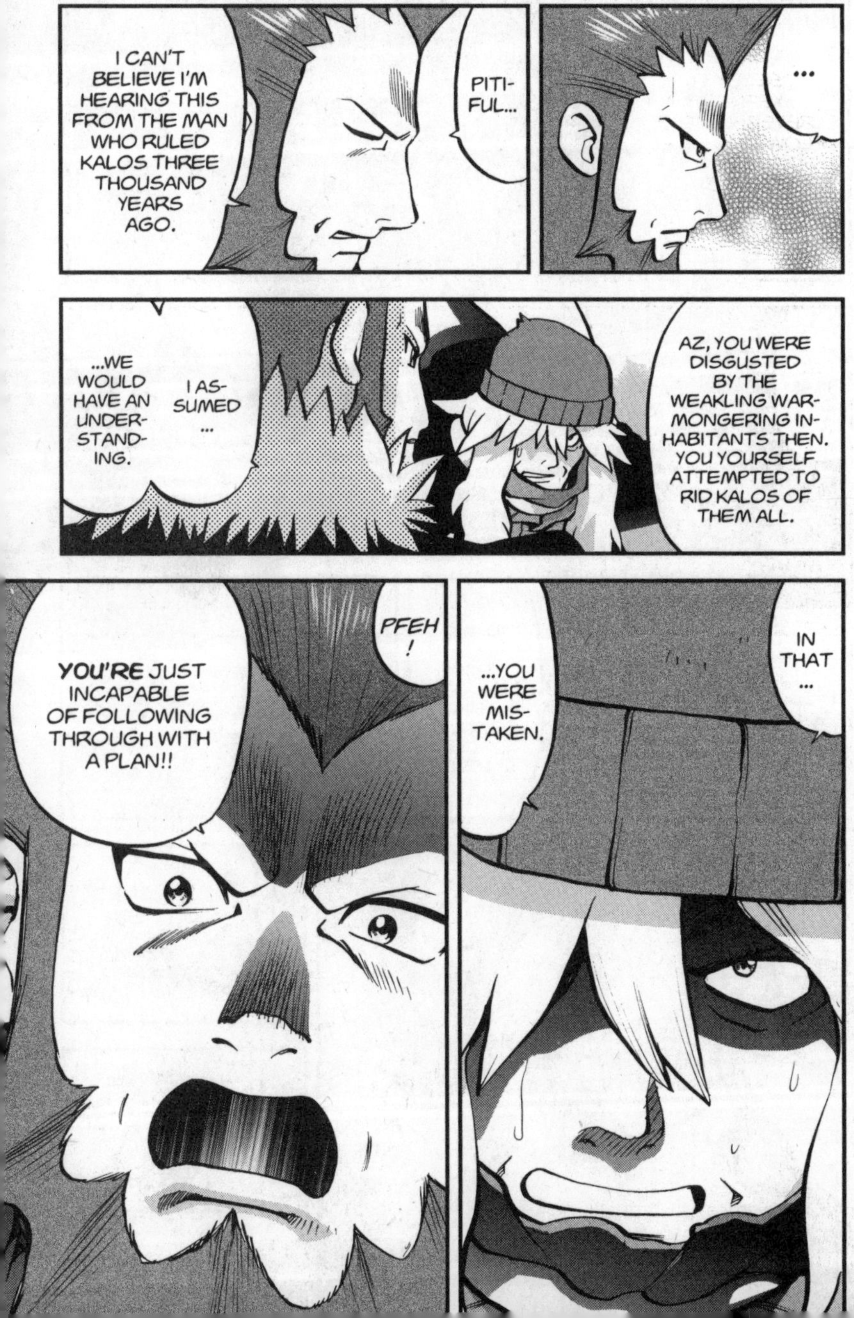
...
PITIFUL...
I CAN'T BELIEVE I'M HEARING THIS FROM THE MAN WHO RULED KALOS THREE THOUSAND YEARS AGO.
AZ, YOU WERE DISGUSTED BY THE WEAKLING WARMONGERING INHABITANTS THEN. YOU YOURSELF ATTEMPTED TO RID KALOS OF THEM ALL.
I ASSUMED...
...WE WOULD HAVE AN UNDERSTANDING.
IN THAT...
...YOU WERE MISTAKEN.
PFEH!
YOU'RE JUST INCAPABLE OF FOLLOWING THROUGH WITH A PLAN!!

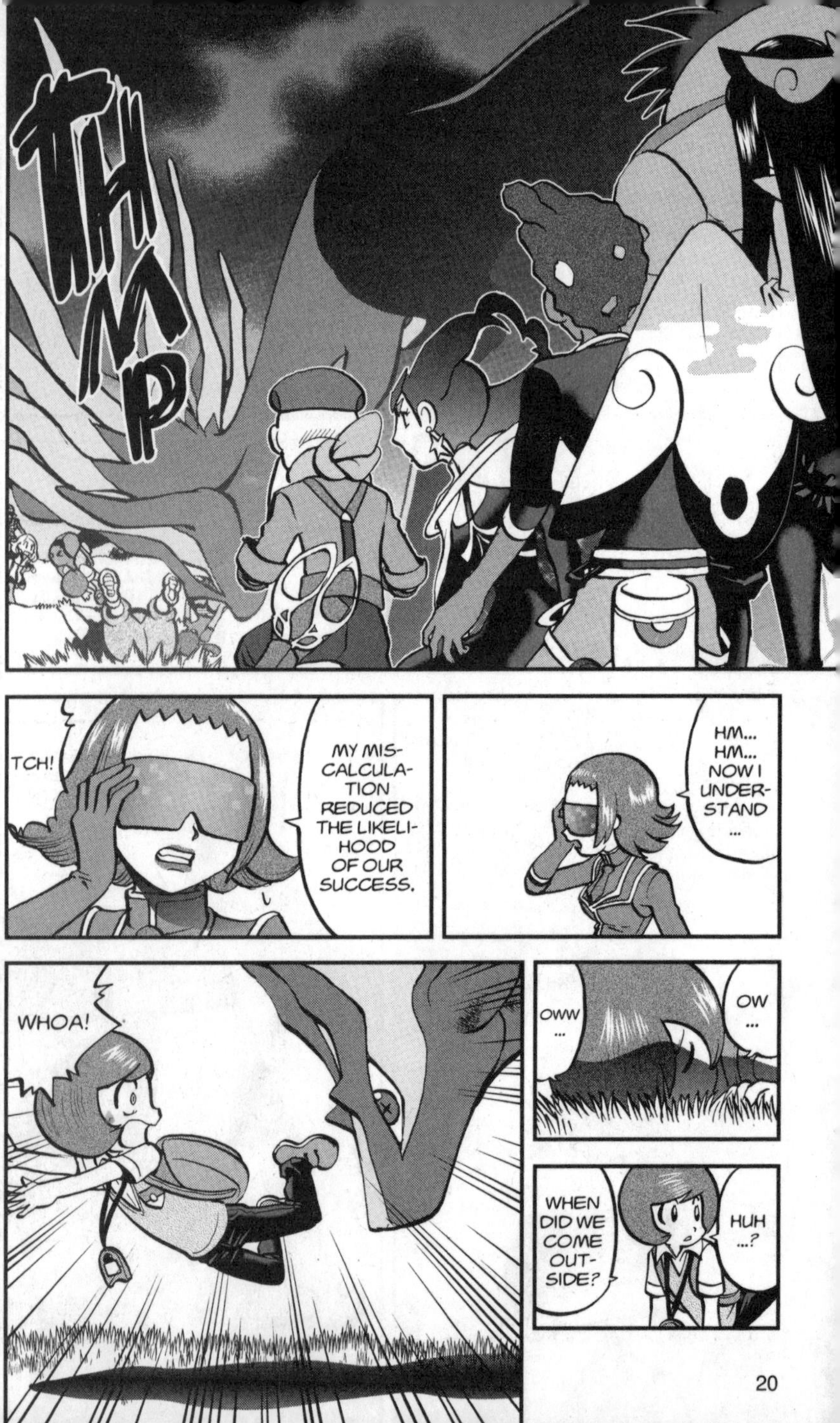
THMP
HM... HM... NOW I UNDERSTAND ...
MY MISCALCULATION REDUCED THE LIKELIHOOD OF OUR SUCCESS.
TCH!
OW ...
OWW ...
HUH ...?
WHEN DID WE COME OUTSIDE?
WHOA!

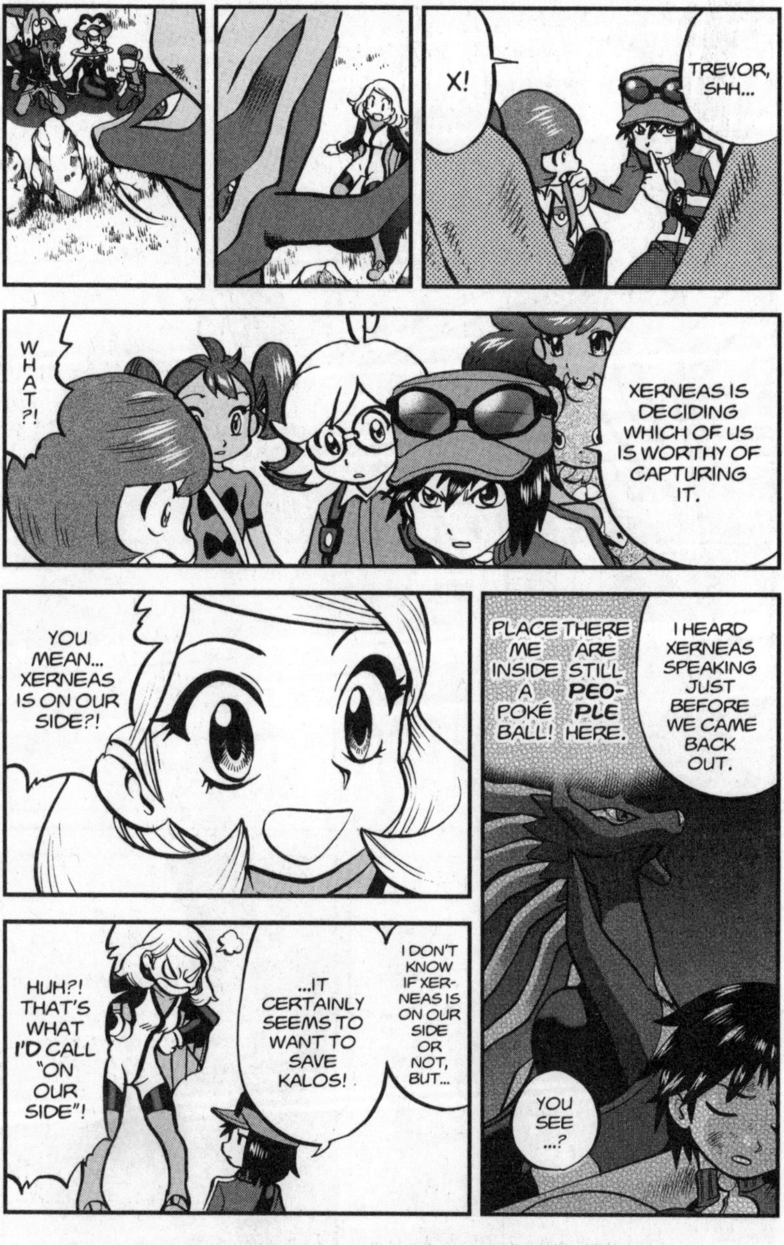
X!
TREVOR, SHH...
XERNEAS IS DECIDING WHICH OF US IS WORTHY OF CAPTURING IT.
WHAT?!
I HEARD XERNEAS SPEAKING JUST BEFORE WE CAME BACK OUT.
THERE ARE STILL **PEOPLE** HERE.
PLACE ME INSIDE A POKÉ BALL!
YOU SEE ...?
YOU MEAN... XERNEAS IS ON OUR SIDE?!
I DON'T KNOW IF XERNEAS IS ON OUR SIDE OR NOT, BUT...
...IT CERTAINLY SEEMS TO WANT TO SAVE KALOS!
HUH?! THAT'S WHAT **I'D** CALL "ON OUR SIDE"!

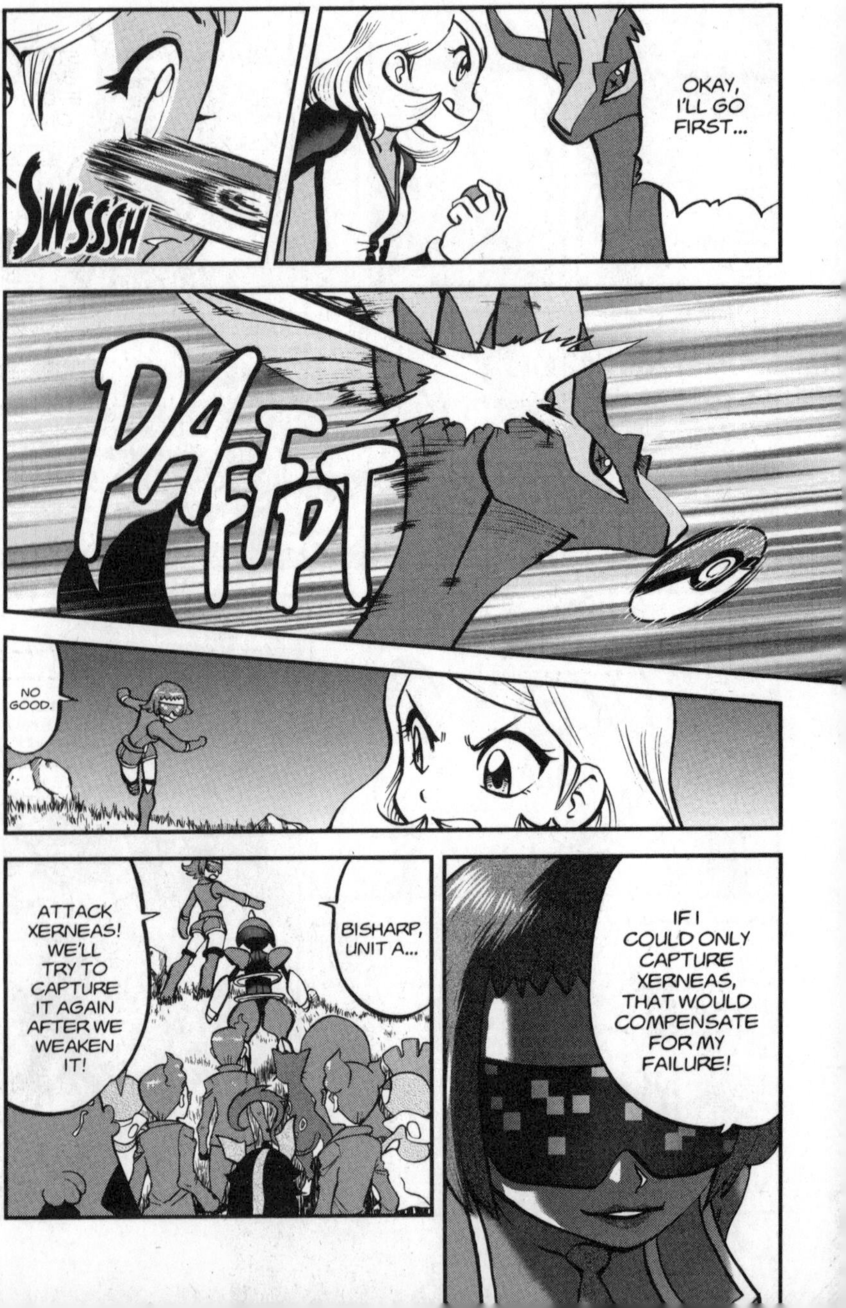
OKAY, I'LL GO FIRST...
SWSSSH
PAFFPT
NO GOOD.
IF I COULD ONLY CAPTURE XERNEAS, THAT WOULD COMPENSATE FOR MY FAILURE!
BISHARP, UNIT A...
ATTACK XERNEAS! WE'LL TRY TO CAPTURE IT AGAIN AFTER WE WEAKEN IT!

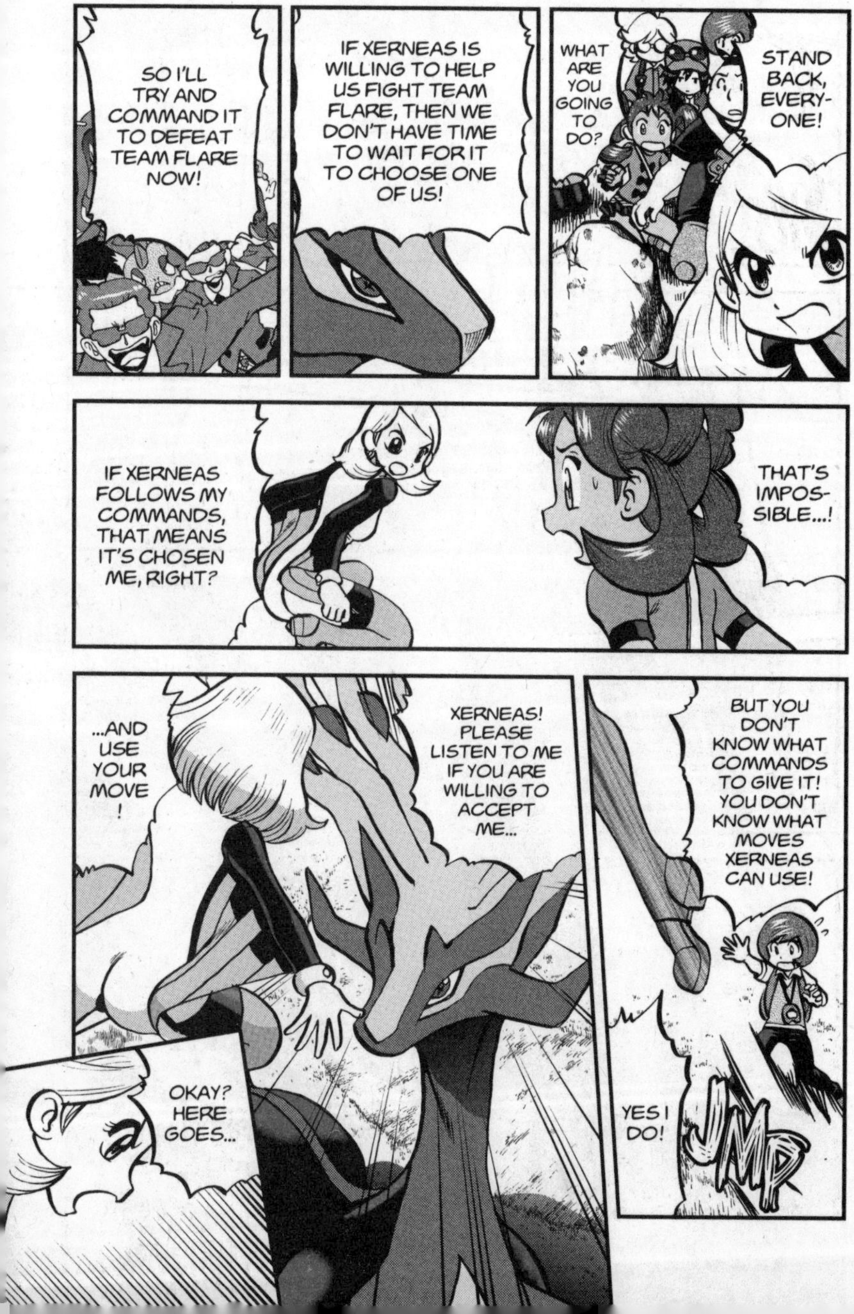
STAND BACK, EVERY-ONE!
WHAT ARE YOU GOING TO DO?
IF XERNEAS IS WILLING TO HELP US FIGHT TEAM FLARE, THEN WE DON'T HAVE TIME TO WAIT FOR IT TO CHOOSE ONE OF US!
SO I'LL TRY AND COMMAND IT TO DEFEAT TEAM FLARE NOW!
THAT'S IMPOS-SIBLE...!
IF XERNEAS FOLLOWS MY COMMANDS, THAT MEANS IT'S CHOSEN ME, RIGHT?
BUT YOU DON'T KNOW WHAT COMMANDS TO GIVE IT! YOU DON'T KNOW WHAT MOVES XERNEAS CAN USE!
YES I DO!
JMP
XERNEAS! PLEASE LISTEN TO ME IF YOU ARE WILLING TO ACCEPT ME...
...AND USE YOUR MOVE!
OKAY? HERE GOES...

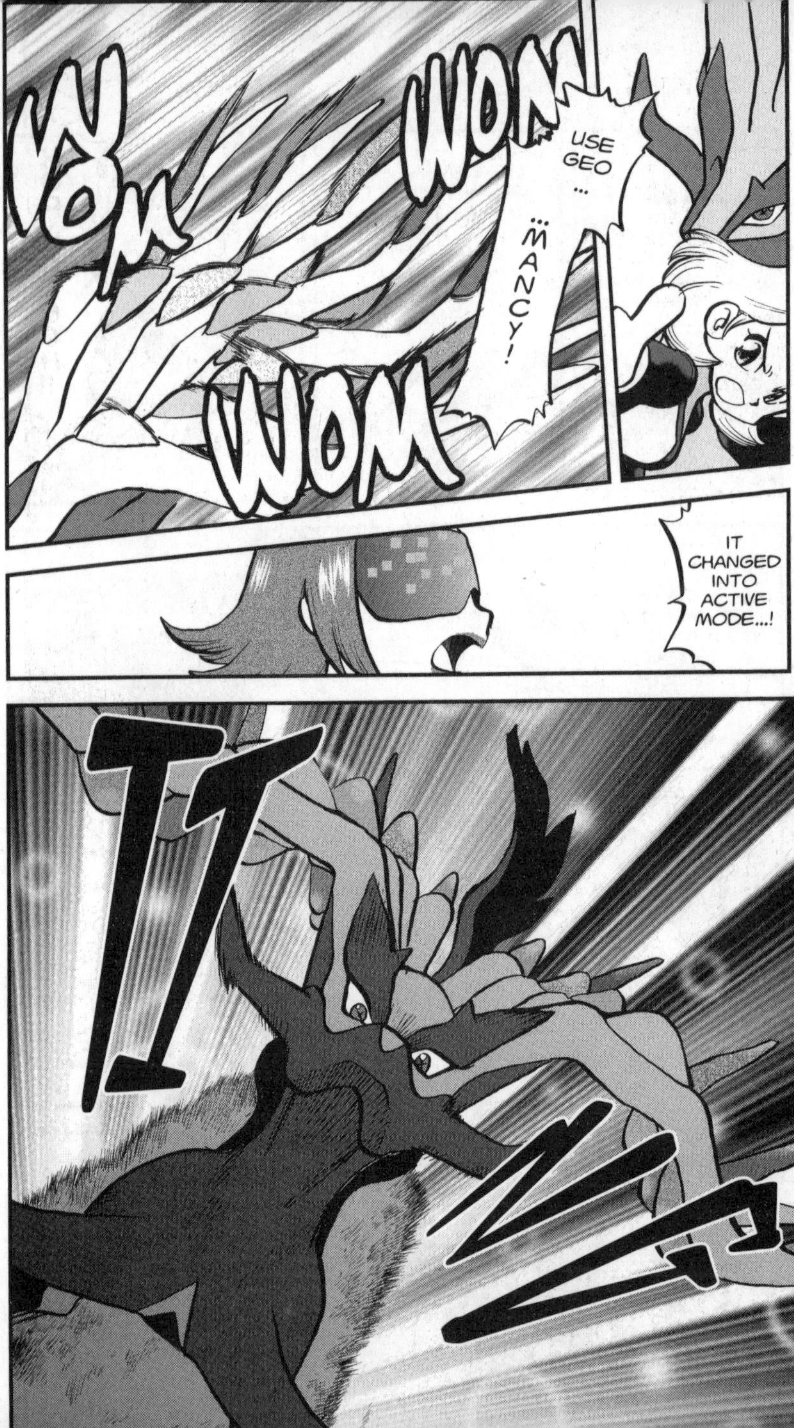
WOM
USE GEO... ...MANCY!
WOM
WOM
IT CHANGED INTO ACTIVE MODE...!

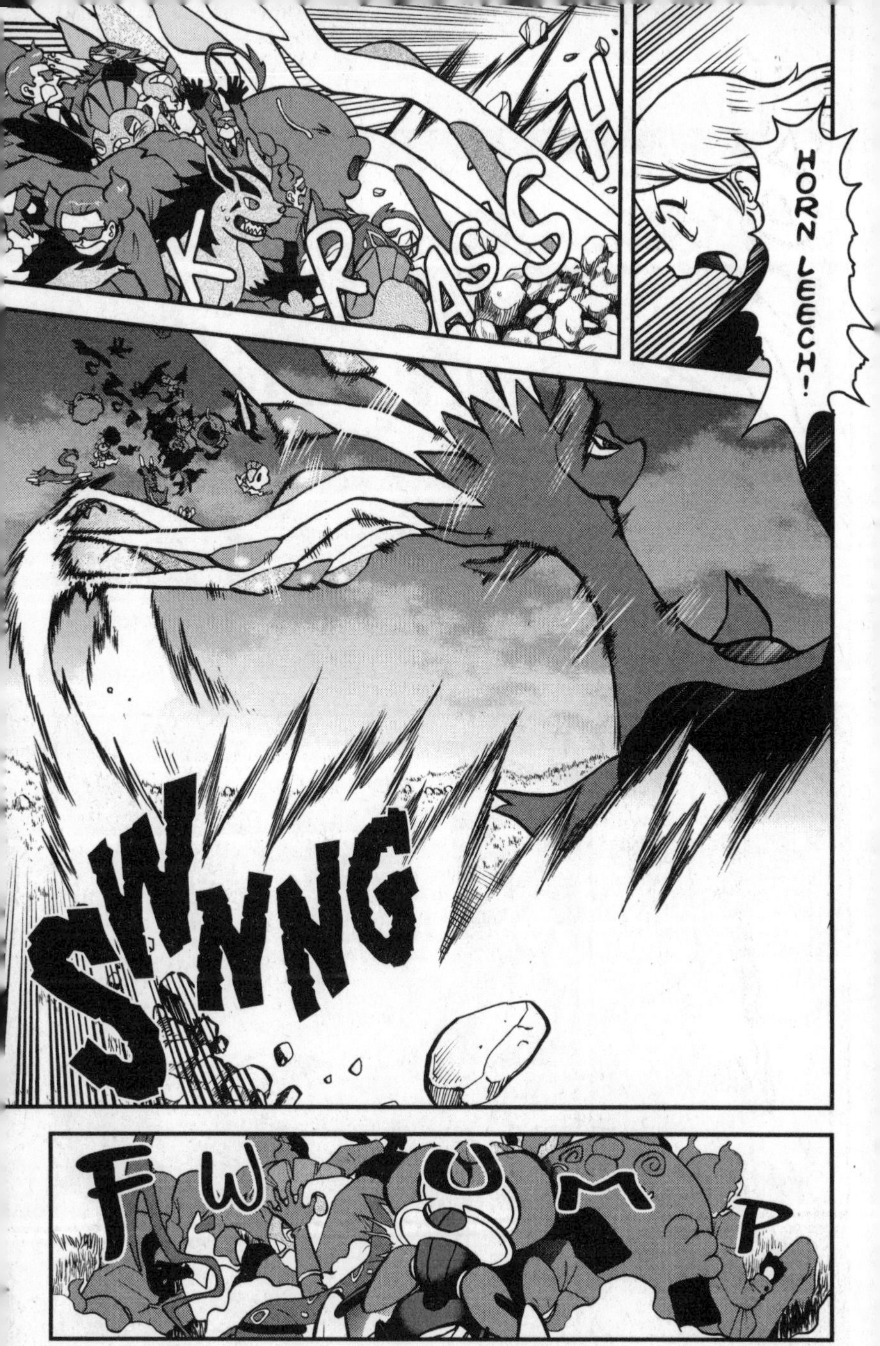
HORN LEECH!
KRASSH
SWNNG
FWUMP

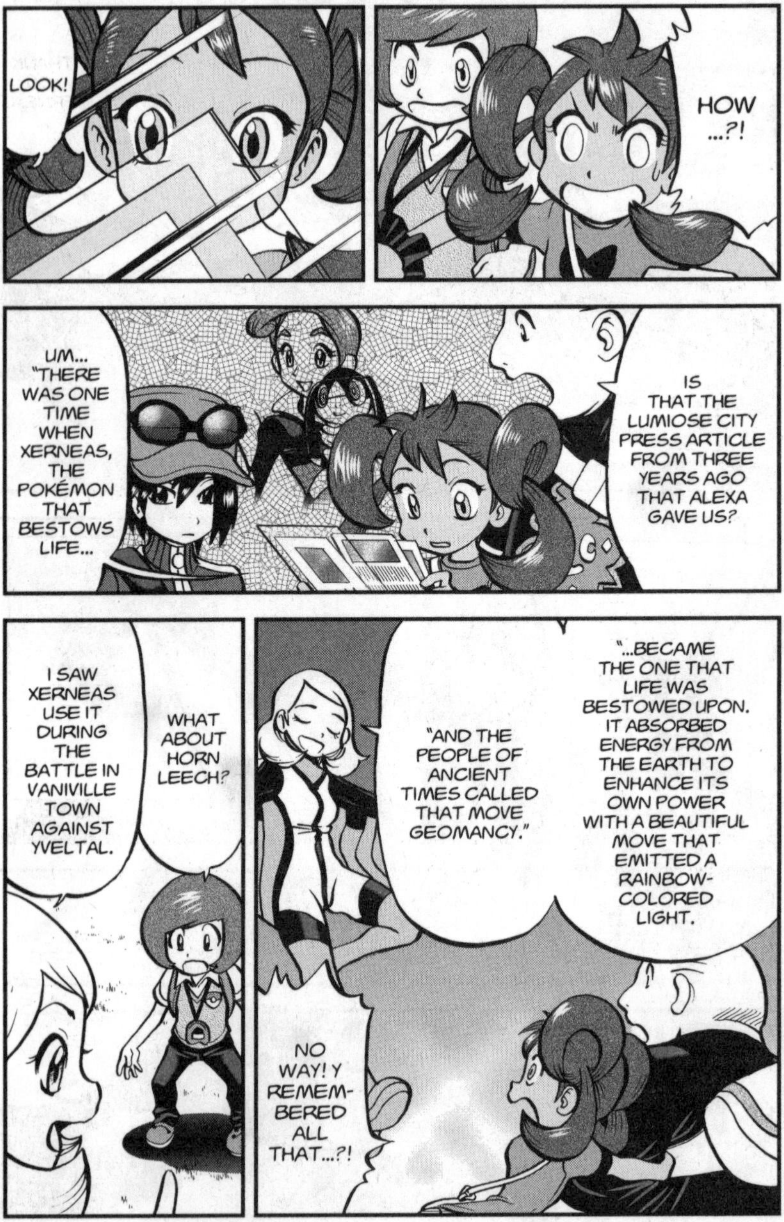
HOW ...?!
LOOK!
IS THAT THE LUMIOSE CITY PRESS ARTICLE FROM THREE YEARS AGO THAT ALEXA GAVE US?
UM... "THERE WAS ONE TIME WHEN XERNEAS, THE POKÉMON THAT BESTOWS LIFE...
"...BECAME THE ONE THAT LIFE WAS BESTOWED UPON. IT ABSORBED ENERGY FROM THE EARTH TO ENHANCE ITS OWN POWER WITH A BEAUTIFUL MOVE THAT EMITTED A RAINBOW-COLORED LIGHT.
"AND THE PEOPLE OF ANCIENT TIMES CALLED THAT MOVE GEOMANCY."
NO WAY! Y REMEMBERED ALL THAT...?!
WHAT ABOUT HORN LEECH?
I SAW XERNEAS USE IT DURING THE BATTLE IN VANIVILLE TOWN AGAINST YVELTAL.

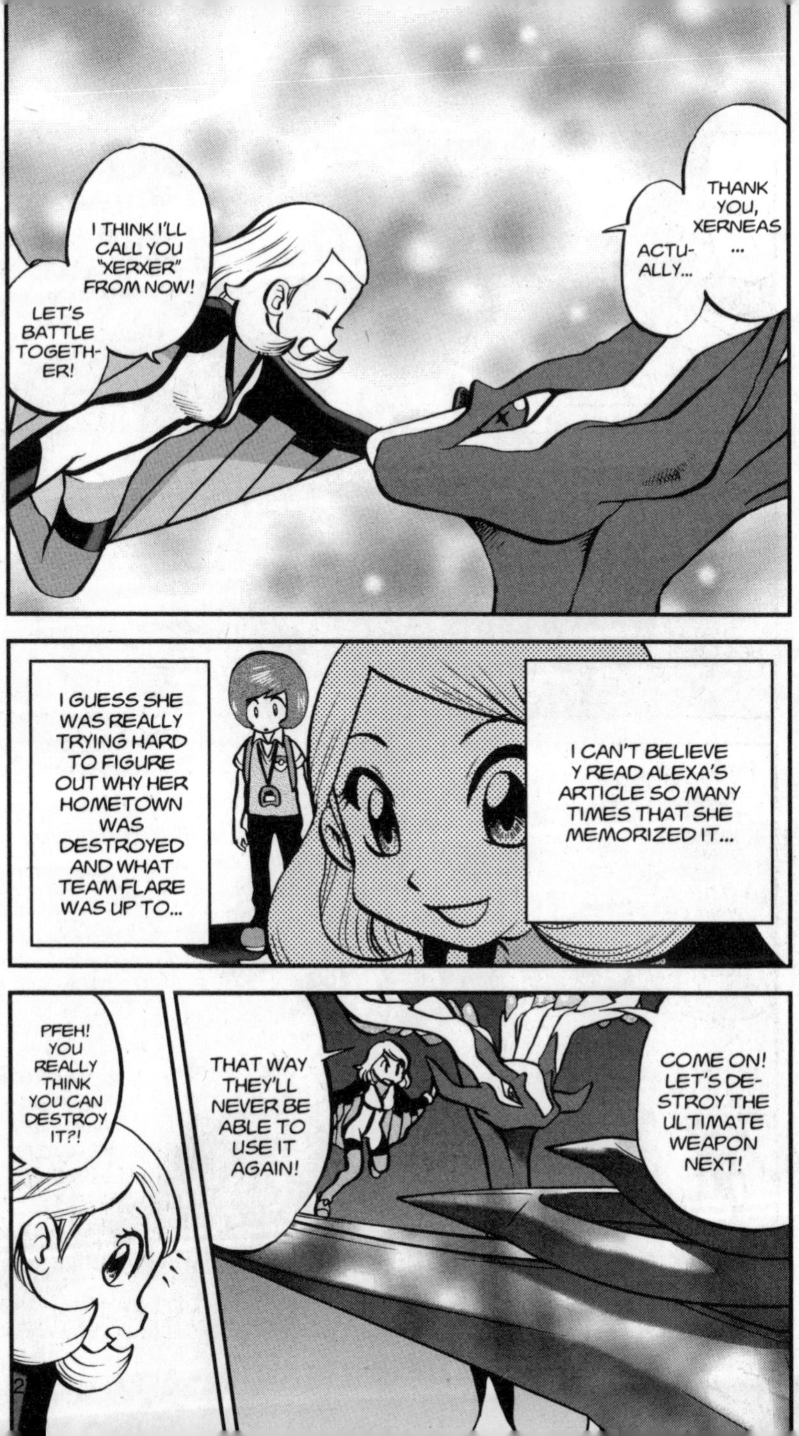
THANK YOU, XERNEAS ...
ACTU-ALLY...
I THINK I'LL CALL YOU "XERXER" FROM NOW!
LET'S BATTLE TOGETH-ER!
I CAN'T BELIEVE Y READ ALEXA'S ARTICLE SO MANY TIMES THAT SHE MEMORIZED IT...
I GUESS SHE WAS REALLY TRYING HARD TO FIGURE OUT WHY HER HOMETOWN WAS DESTROYED AND WHAT TEAM FLARE WAS UP TO...
COME ON! LET'S DE-STROY THE ULTIMATE WEAPON NEXT!
THAT WAY THEY'LL NEVER BE ABLE TO USE IT AGAIN!
PFEH! YOU REALLY THINK YOU CAN DESTROY IT?!

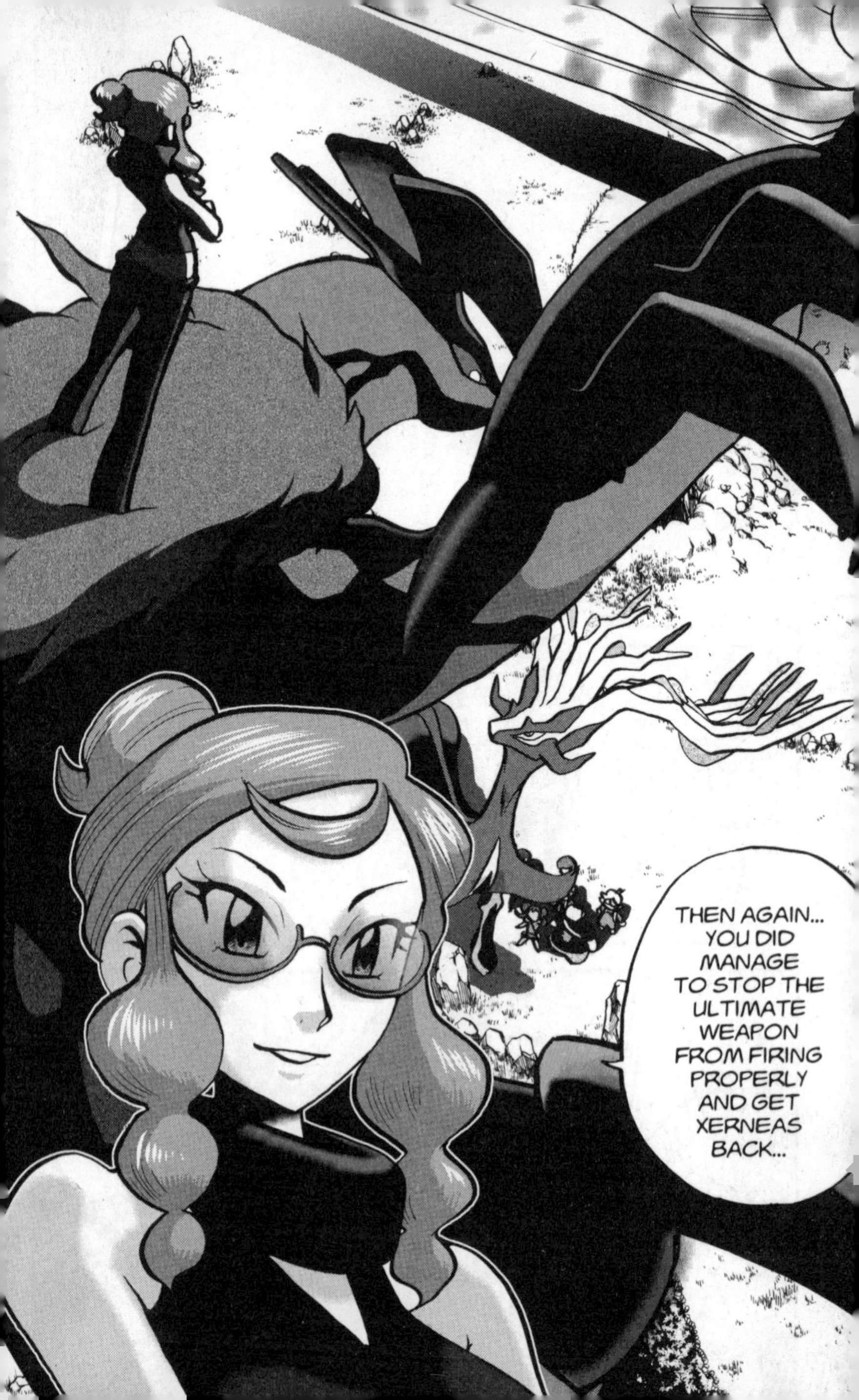
THEN AGAIN... YOU DID MANAGE TO STOP THE ULTIMATE WEAPON FROM FIRING PROPERLY AND GET XERNEAS BACK...

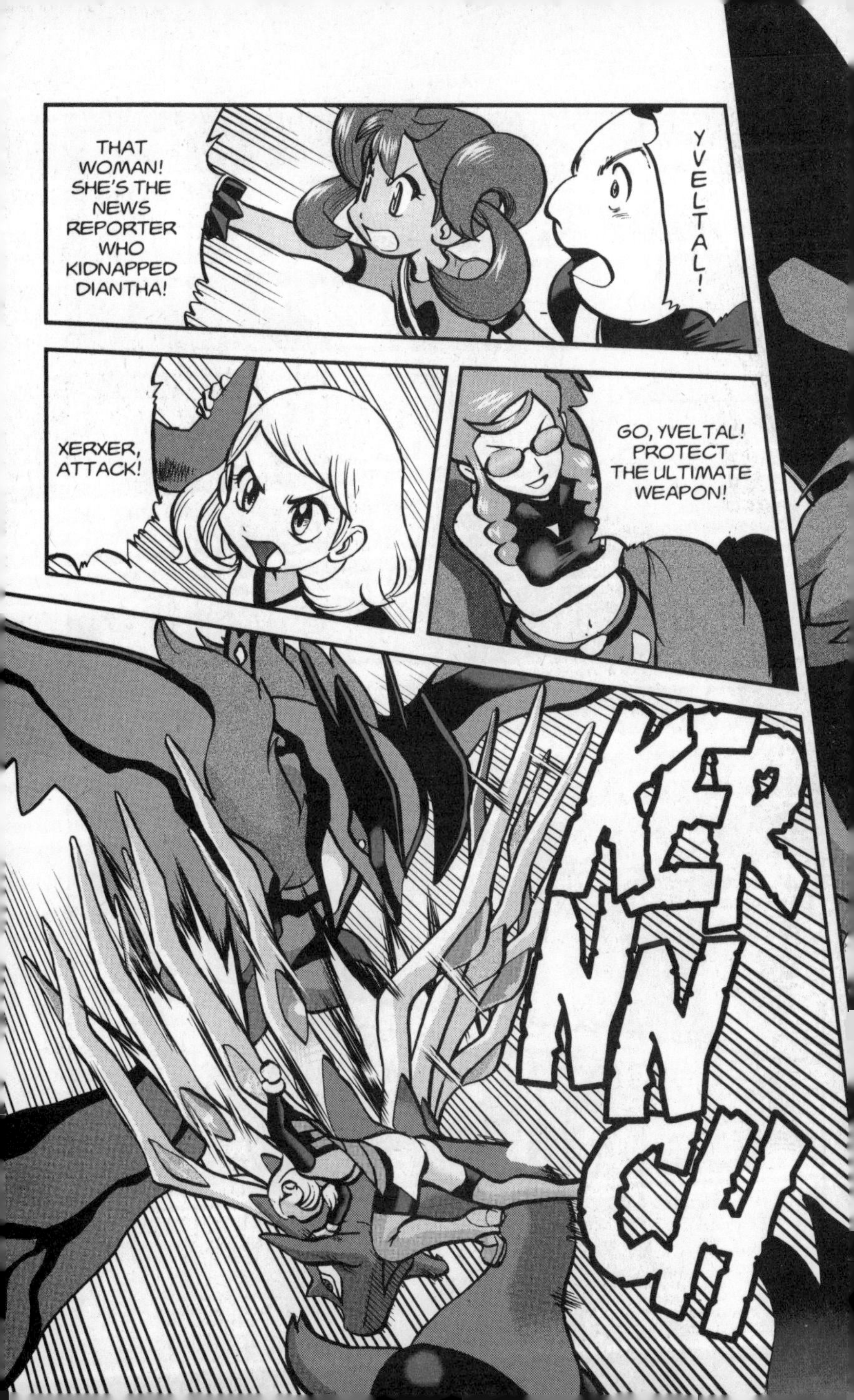
YVELTAL!
THAT WOMAN! SHE'S THE NEWS REPORTER WHO KIDNAPPED DIANTHA!
GO, YVELTAL! PROTECT THE ULTIMATE WEAPON!
XERXER, ATTACK!
KERNNCH

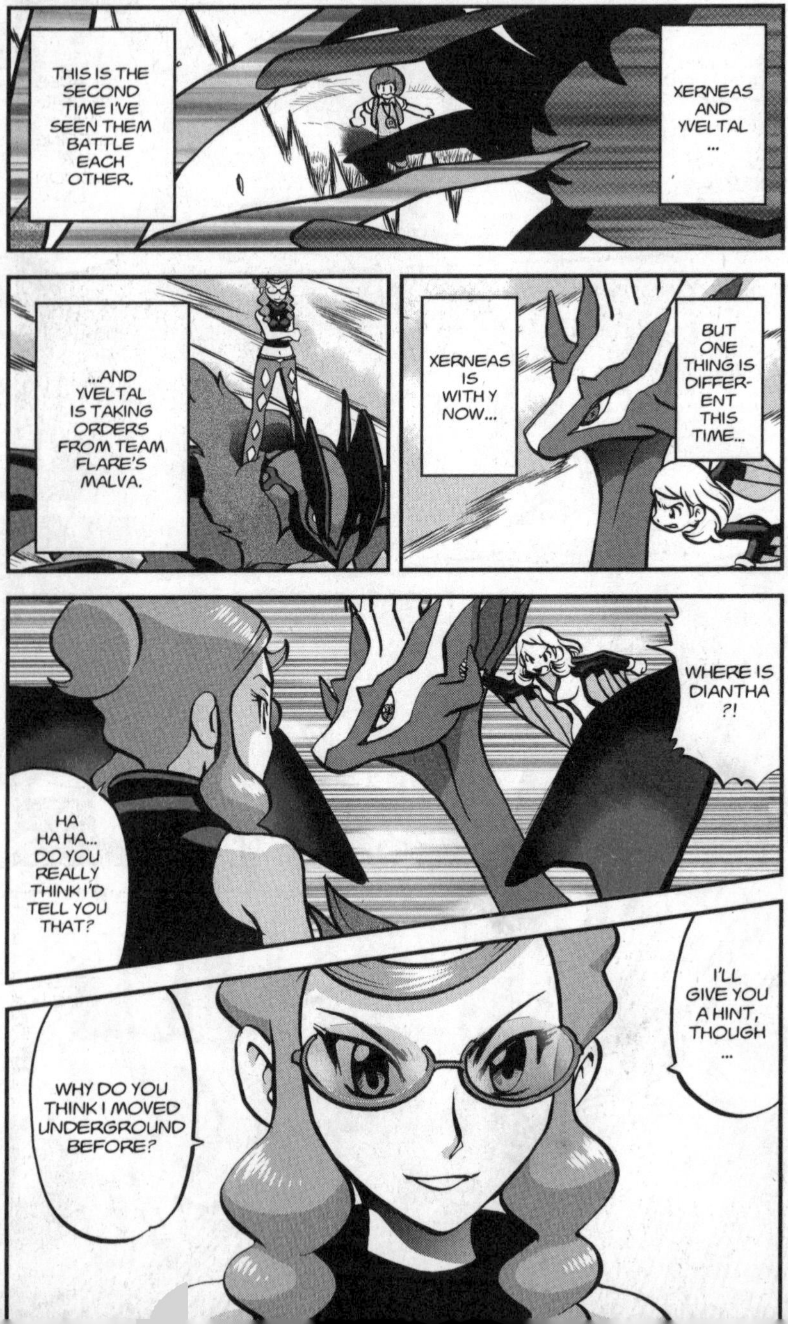
XERNEAS AND YVELTAL ...
THIS IS THE SECOND TIME I'VE SEEN THEM BATTLE EACH OTHER.
BUT ONE THING IS DIFFER-ENT THIS TIME...
XERNEAS IS WITH Y NOW...
...AND YVELTAL IS TAKING ORDERS FROM TEAM FLARE'S MALVA.
WHERE IS DIANTHA ?!
HA HA HA... DO YOU REALLY THINK I'D TELL YOU THAT?
I'LL GIVE YOU A HINT, THOUGH ...
WHY DO YOU THINK I MOVED UNDERGROUND BEFORE?

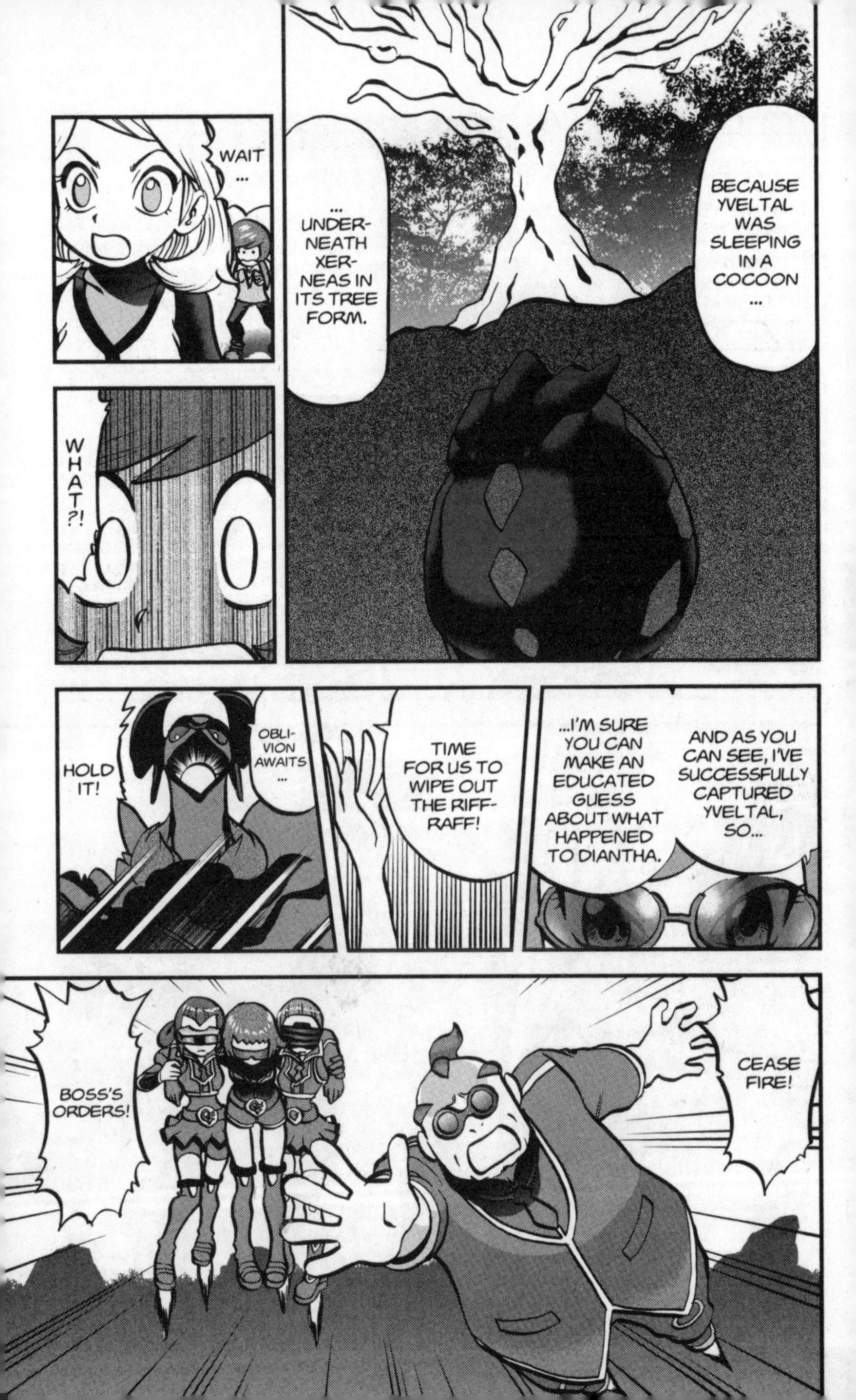

BECAUSE YVELTAL WAS SLEEPING IN A COCOON...
...UNDERNEATH XERNEAS IN ITS TREE FORM.
WAIT...
WHAT?!
AND AS YOU CAN SEE, I'VE SUCCESSFULLY CAPTURED YVELTAL, SO...
...I'M SURE YOU CAN MAKE AN EDUCATED GUESS ABOUT WHAT HAPPENED TO DIANTHA.
TIME FOR US TO WIPE OUT THE RIFF-RAFF!
OBLIVION AWAITS...
HOLD IT!
CEASE FIRE!
BOSS'S ORDERS!

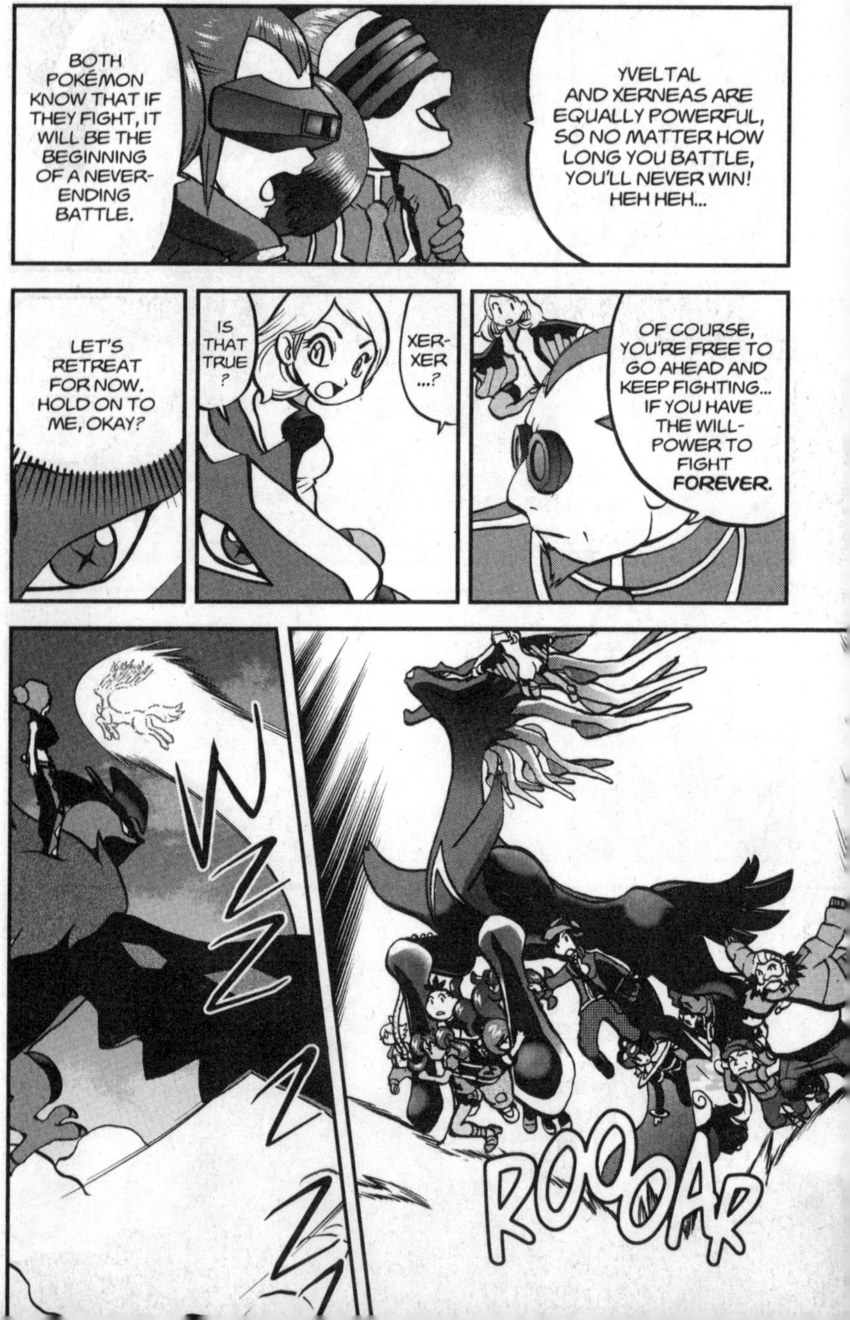
YVELTAL AND XERNEAS ARE EQUALLY POWERFUL, SO NO MATTER HOW LONG YOU BATTLE, YOU'LL NEVER WIN! HEH HEH...
BOTH POKÉMON KNOW THAT IF THEY FIGHT, IT WILL BE THE BEGINNING OF A NEVER-ENDING BATTLE.
OF COURSE, YOU'RE FREE TO GO AHEAD AND KEEP FIGHTING... IF YOU HAVE THE WILL-POWER TO FIGHT **FOREVER.**
XER-XER ...?
IS THAT TRUE ?
LET'S RETREAT FOR NOW. HOLD ON TO ME, OKAY?
ROOOAR

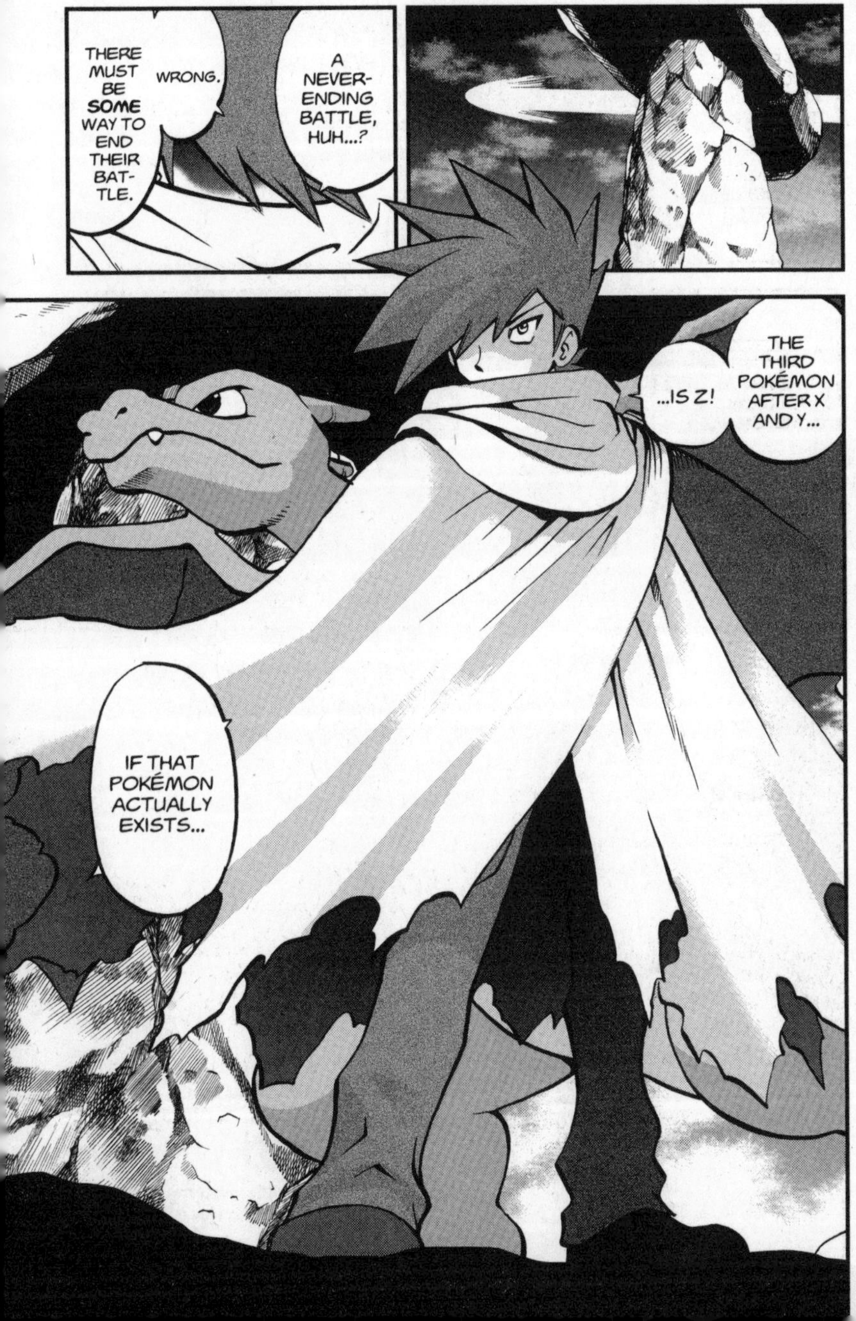
A NEVER-ENDING BATTLE, HUH...?
WRONG.
THERE MUST BE **SOME** WAY TO END THEIR BATTLE.
THE THIRD POKÉMON AFTER X AND Y...
...IS Z!
IF THAT POKÉMON ACTUALLY EXISTS...

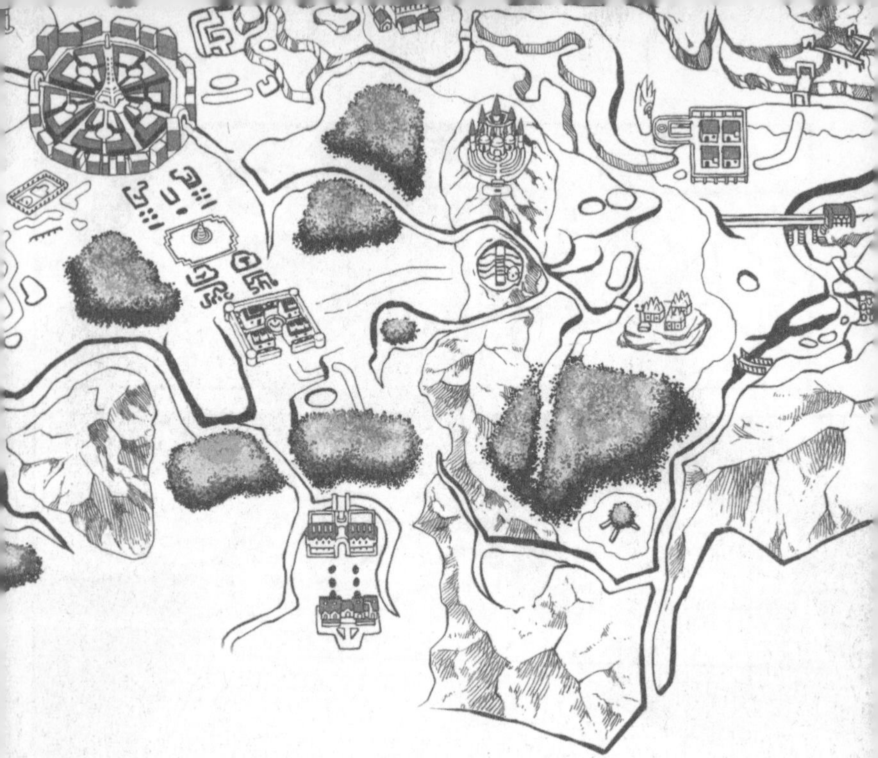

Current Location

Geosenge Town

A town lined with mysterious stones and encircled by strange ruins of old.

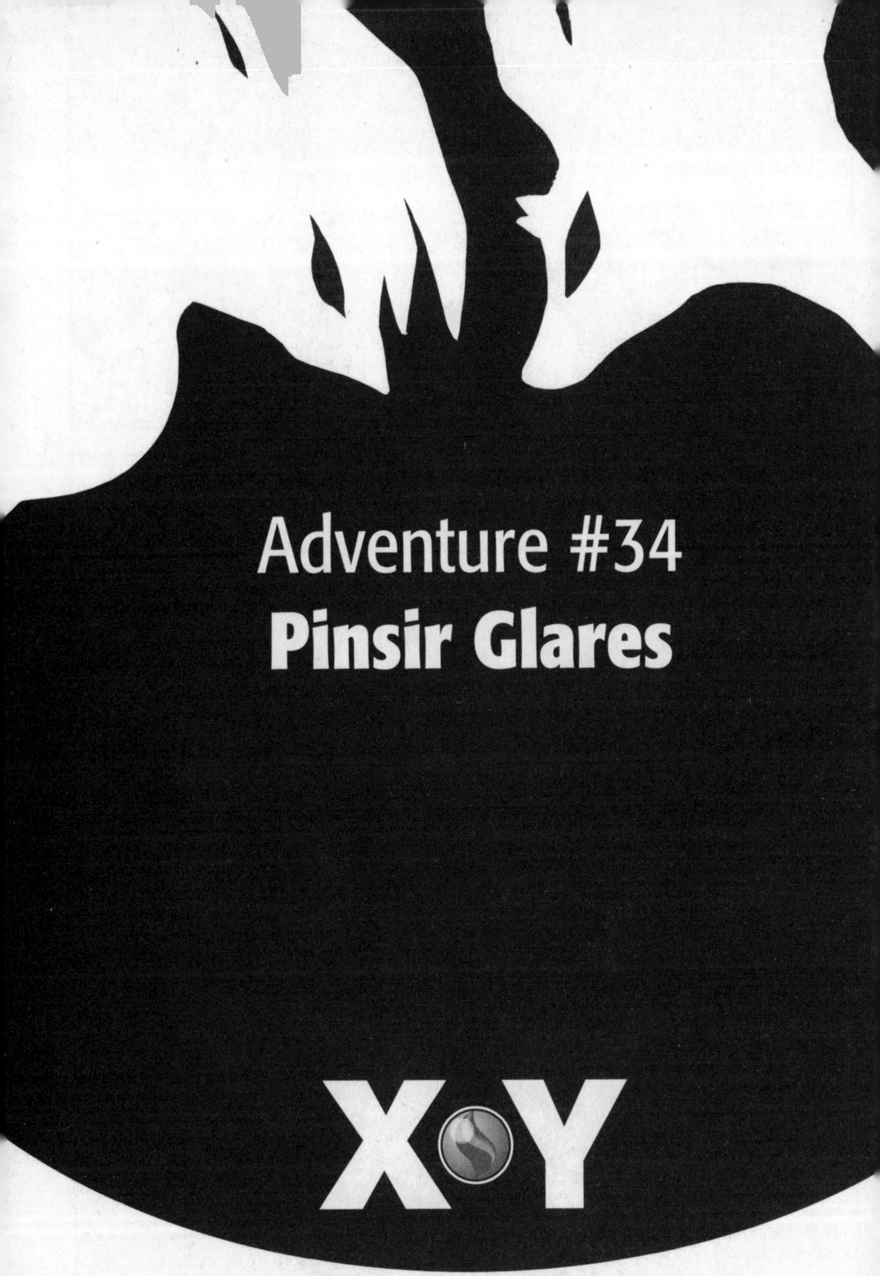

Adventure #34
Pinsir Glares

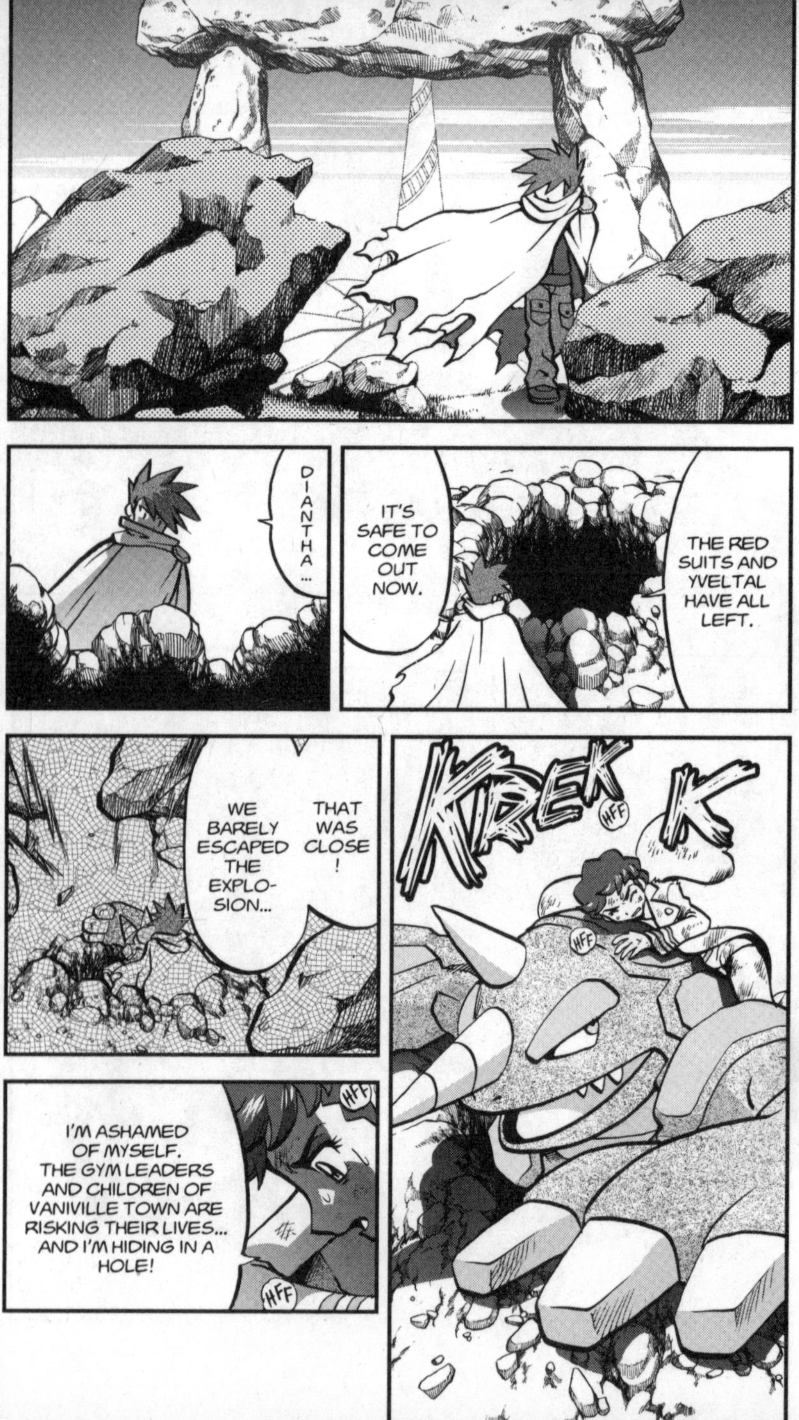
THE RED SUITS AND YVELTAL HAVE ALL LEFT.
IT'S SAFE TO COME OUT NOW.
DIANTHA...
KREK K
HFF
HFF
THAT WAS CLOSE!
WE BARELY ESCAPED THE EXPLOSION...
HFF
I'M ASHAMED OF MYSELF. THE GYM LEADERS AND CHILDREN OF VANIVILLE TOWN ARE RISKING THEIR LIVES... AND I'M HIDING IN A HOLE!
HFF

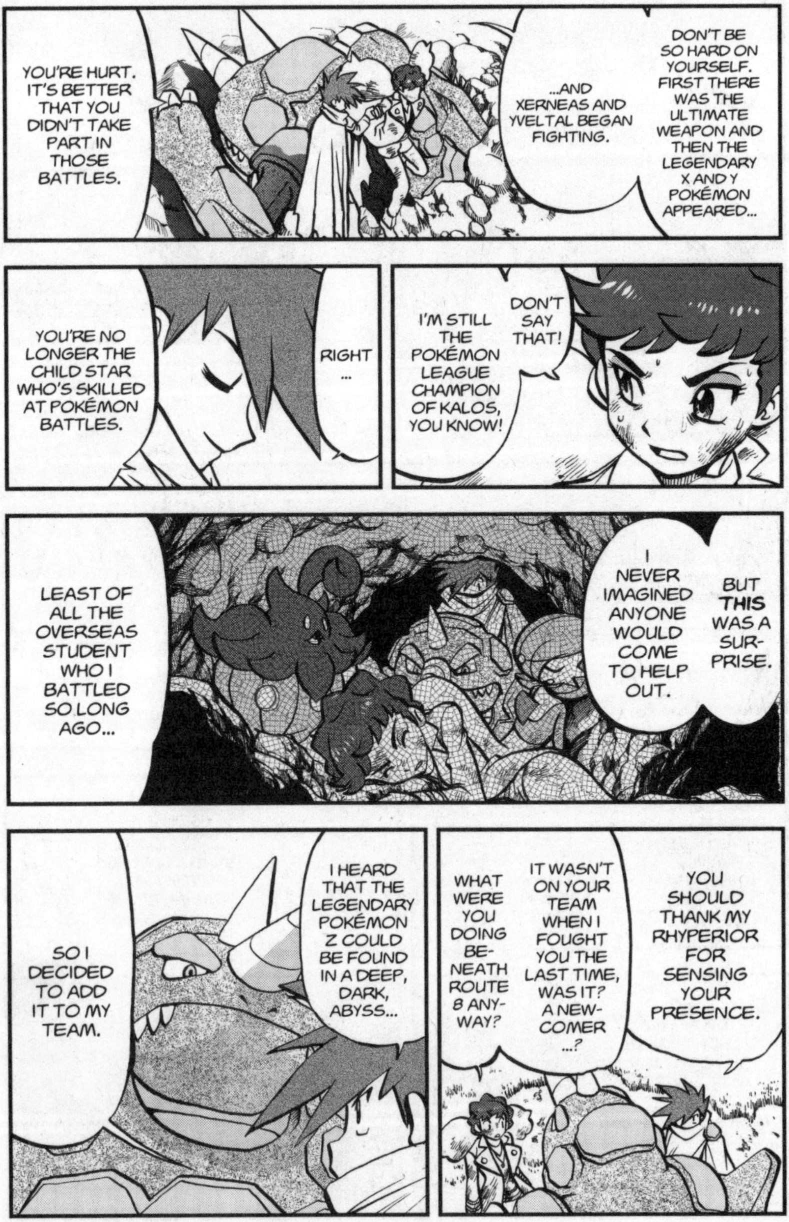
DON'T BE SO HARD ON YOURSELF. FIRST THERE WAS THE ULTIMATE WEAPON AND THEN THE LEGENDARY X AND Y POKÉMON APPEARED...
...AND XERNEAS AND YVELTAL BEGAN FIGHTING.
YOU'RE HURT. IT'S BETTER THAT YOU DIDN'T TAKE PART IN THOSE BATTLES.
DON'T SAY THAT!
I'M STILL THE POKÉMON LEAGUE CHAMPION OF KALOS, YOU KNOW!
RIGHT...
YOU'RE NO LONGER THE CHILD STAR WHO'S SKILLED AT POKÉMON BATTLES.
BUT **THIS** WAS A SURPRISE.
I NEVER IMAGINED ANYONE WOULD COME TO HELP OUT.
LEAST OF ALL THE OVERSEAS STUDENT WHO I BATTLED SO LONG AGO...
YOU SHOULD THANK MY RHYPERIOR FOR SENSING YOUR PRESENCE.
IT WASN'T ON YOUR TEAM WHEN I FOUGHT YOU THE LAST TIME, WAS IT? A NEWCOMER ...?
WHAT WERE YOU DOING BENEATH ROUTE 8 ANYWAY?
I HEARD THAT THE LEGENDARY POKÉMON Z COULD BE FOUND IN A DEEP, DARK, ABYSS...
SO I DECIDED TO ADD IT TO MY TEAM.

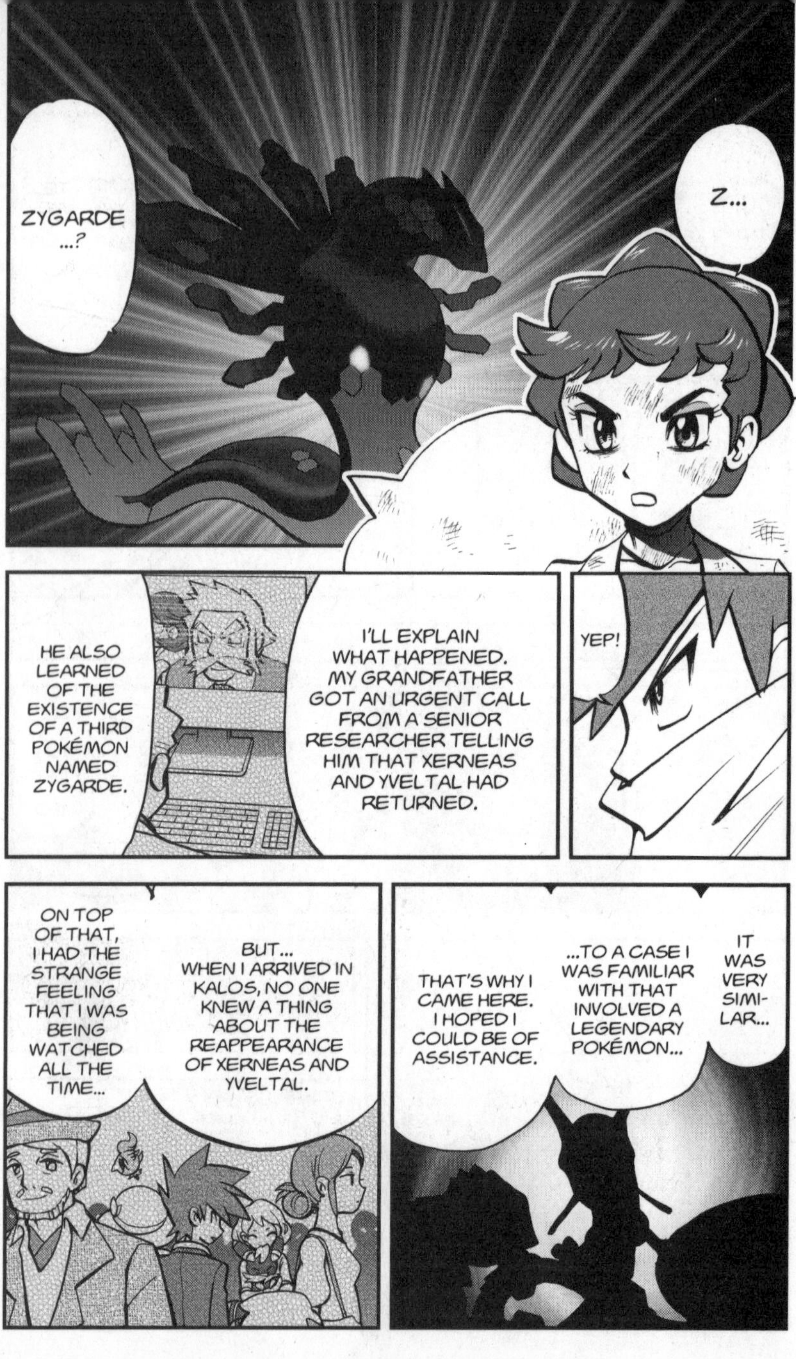
Z...
ZYGARDE ...?
YEP!
I'LL EXPLAIN WHAT HAPPENED. MY GRANDFATHER GOT AN URGENT CALL FROM A SENIOR RESEARCHER TELLING HIM THAT XERNEAS AND YVELTAL HAD RETURNED.
HE ALSO LEARNED OF THE EXISTENCE OF A THIRD POKÉMON NAMED ZYGARDE.
IT WAS VERY SIMI-LAR...
...TO A CASE I WAS FAMILIAR WITH THAT INVOLVED A LEGENDARY POKÉMON...
THAT'S WHY I CAME HERE. I HOPED I COULD BE OF ASSISTANCE.
BUT... WHEN I ARRIVED IN KALOS, NO ONE KNEW A THING ABOUT THE REAPPEARANCE OF XERNEAS AND YVELTAL.
ON TOP OF THAT, I HAD THE STRANGE FEELING THAT I WAS BEING WATCHED ALL THE TIME...

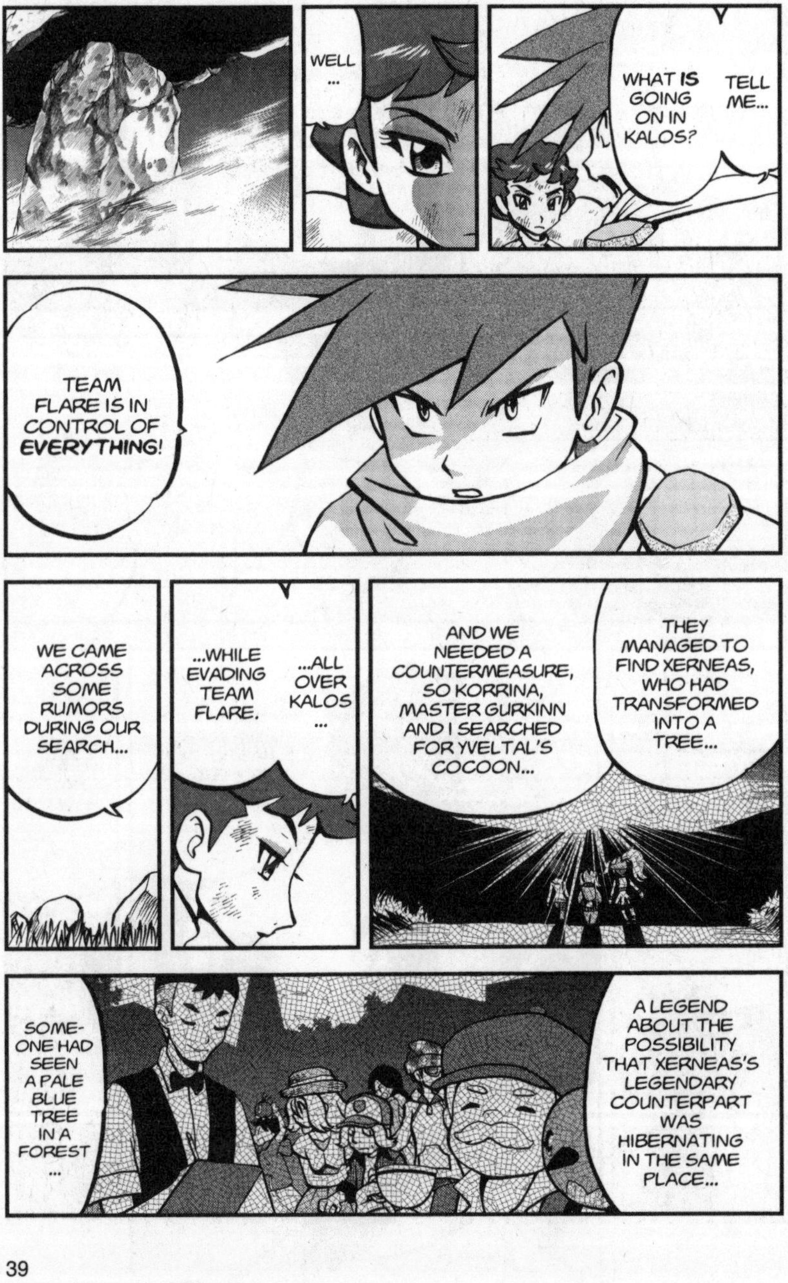
TELL ME...
WHAT IS GOING ON IN KALOS?
WELL ...
TEAM FLARE IS IN CONTROL OF EVERYTHING!
THEY MANAGED TO FIND XERNEAS, WHO HAD TRANSFORMED INTO A TREE...
AND WE NEEDED A COUNTERMEASURE, SO KORRINA, MASTER GURKINN AND I SEARCHED FOR YVELTAL'S COCOON...
...ALL OVER KALOS ...
...WHILE EVADING TEAM FLARE.
WE CAME ACROSS SOME RUMORS DURING OUR SEARCH...
A LEGEND ABOUT THE POSSIBILITY THAT XERNEAS'S LEGENDARY COUNTERPART WAS HIBERNATING IN THE SAME PLACE...
SOME-ONE HAD SEEN A PALE BLUE TREE IN A FOREST ...

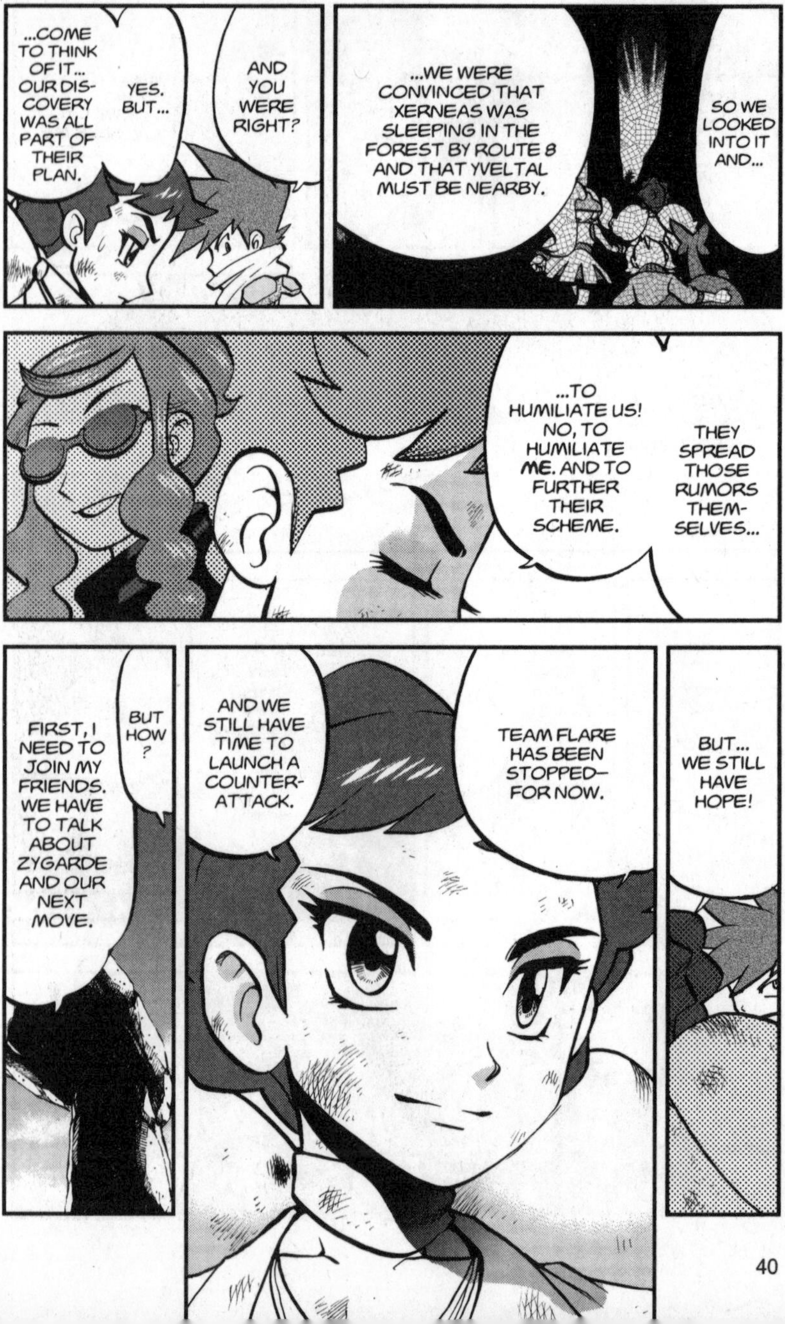
SO WE LOOKED INTO IT AND...
...WE WERE CONVINCED THAT XERNEAS WAS SLEEPING IN THE FOREST BY ROUTE 8 AND THAT YVELTAL MUST BE NEARBY.
AND YOU WERE RIGHT?
YES. BUT...
...COME TO THINK OF IT... OUR DISCOVERY WAS ALL PART OF THEIR PLAN.
THEY SPREAD THOSE RUMORS THEMSELVES...
...TO HUMILIATE US! NO, TO HUMILIATE ME. AND TO FURTHER THEIR SCHEME.
BUT... WE STILL HAVE HOPE!
TEAM FLARE HAS BEEN STOPPED—FOR NOW.
AND WE STILL HAVE TIME TO LAUNCH A COUNTER-ATTACK.
BUT HOW?
FIRST, I NEED TO JOIN MY FRIENDS. WE HAVE TO TALK ABOUT ZYGARDE AND OUR NEXT MOVE.

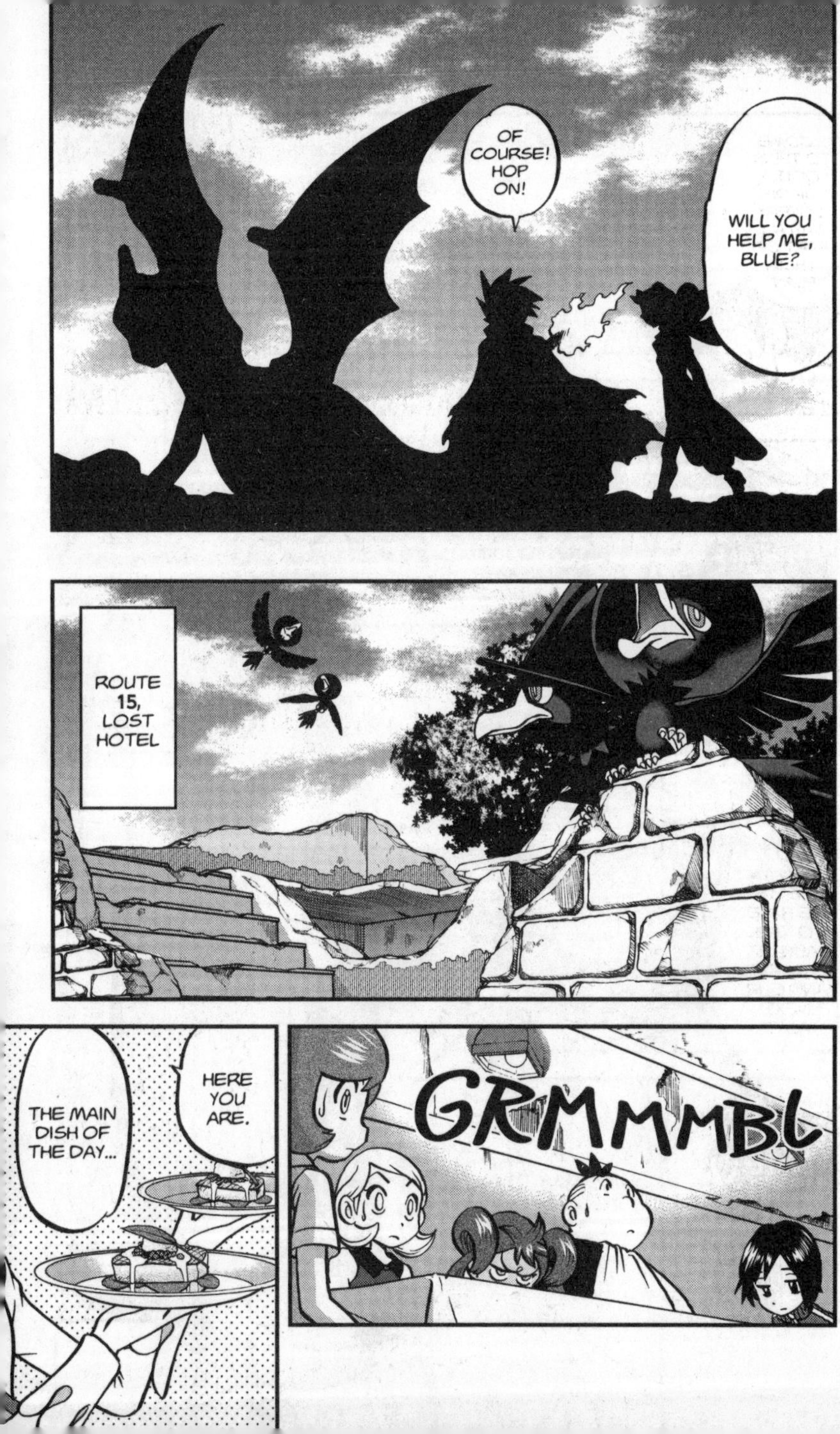
WILL YOU HELP ME, BLUE?
OF COURSE! HOP ON!
ROUTE 15, LOST HOTEL
GRMMMBL
HERE YOU ARE.
THE MAIN DISH OF THE DAY...

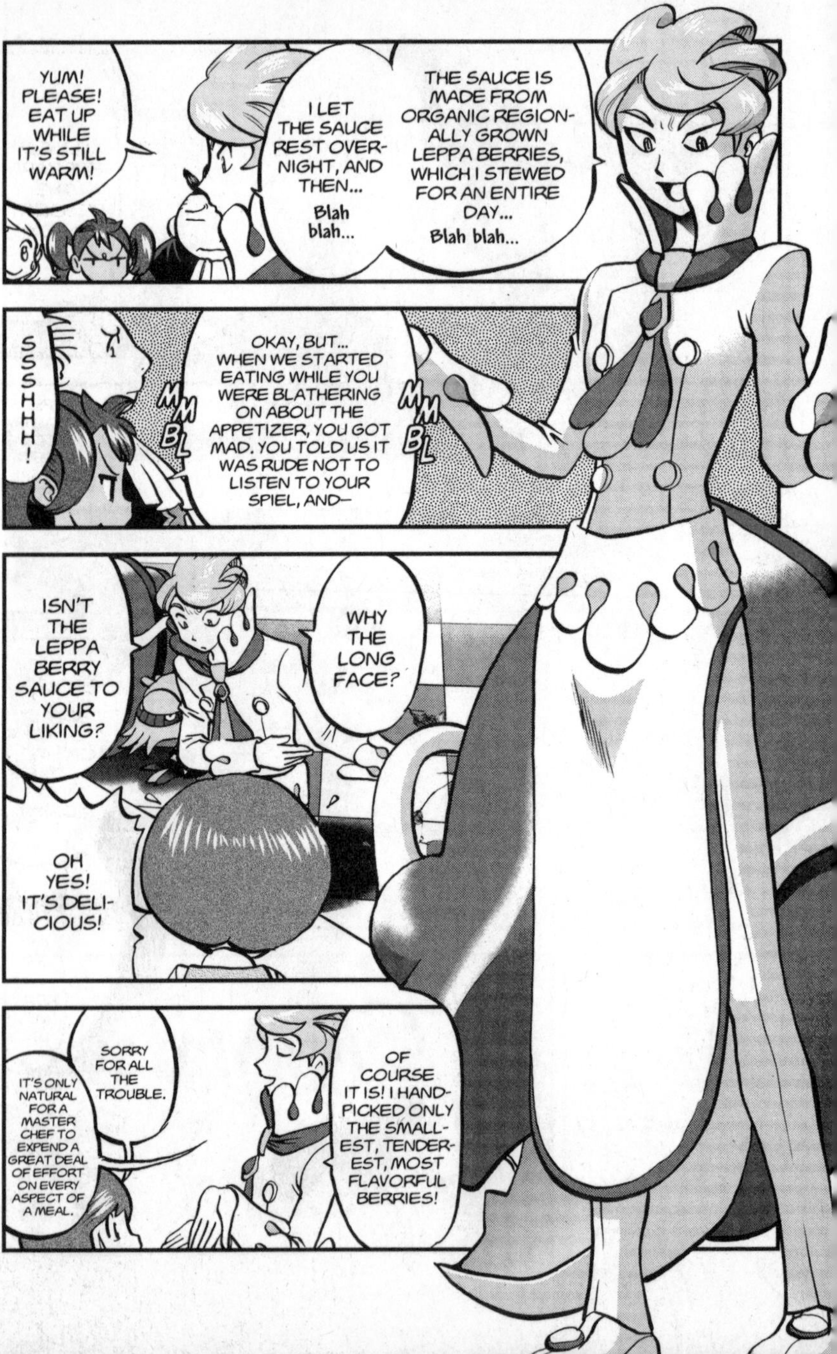
THE SAUCE IS MADE FROM ORGANIC REGION-ALLY GROWN LEPPA BERRIES, WHICH I STEWED FOR AN ENTIRE DAY... Blah blah...
I LET THE SAUCE REST OVER-NIGHT, AND THEN... Blah blah...
YUM! PLEASE! EAT UP WHILE IT'S STILL WARM!
MMBL
OKAY, BUT... WHEN WE STARTED EATING WHILE YOU WERE BLATHERING ON ABOUT THE APPETIZER, YOU GOT MAD. YOU TOLD US IT WAS RUDE NOT TO LISTEN TO YOUR SPIEL, AND—
MMBL
SSSHHH!
WHY THE LONG FACE?
ISN'T THE LEPPA BERRY SAUCE TO YOUR LIKING?
OH YES! IT'S DELI-CIOUS!
OF COURSE IT IS! I HAND-PICKED ONLY THE SMALL-EST, TENDER-EST, MOST FLAVORFUL BERRIES!
SORRY FOR ALL THE TROUBLE.
IT'S ONLY NATURAL FOR A MASTER CHEF TO EXPEND A GREAT DEAL OF EFFORT ON EVERY ASPECT OF A MEAL.

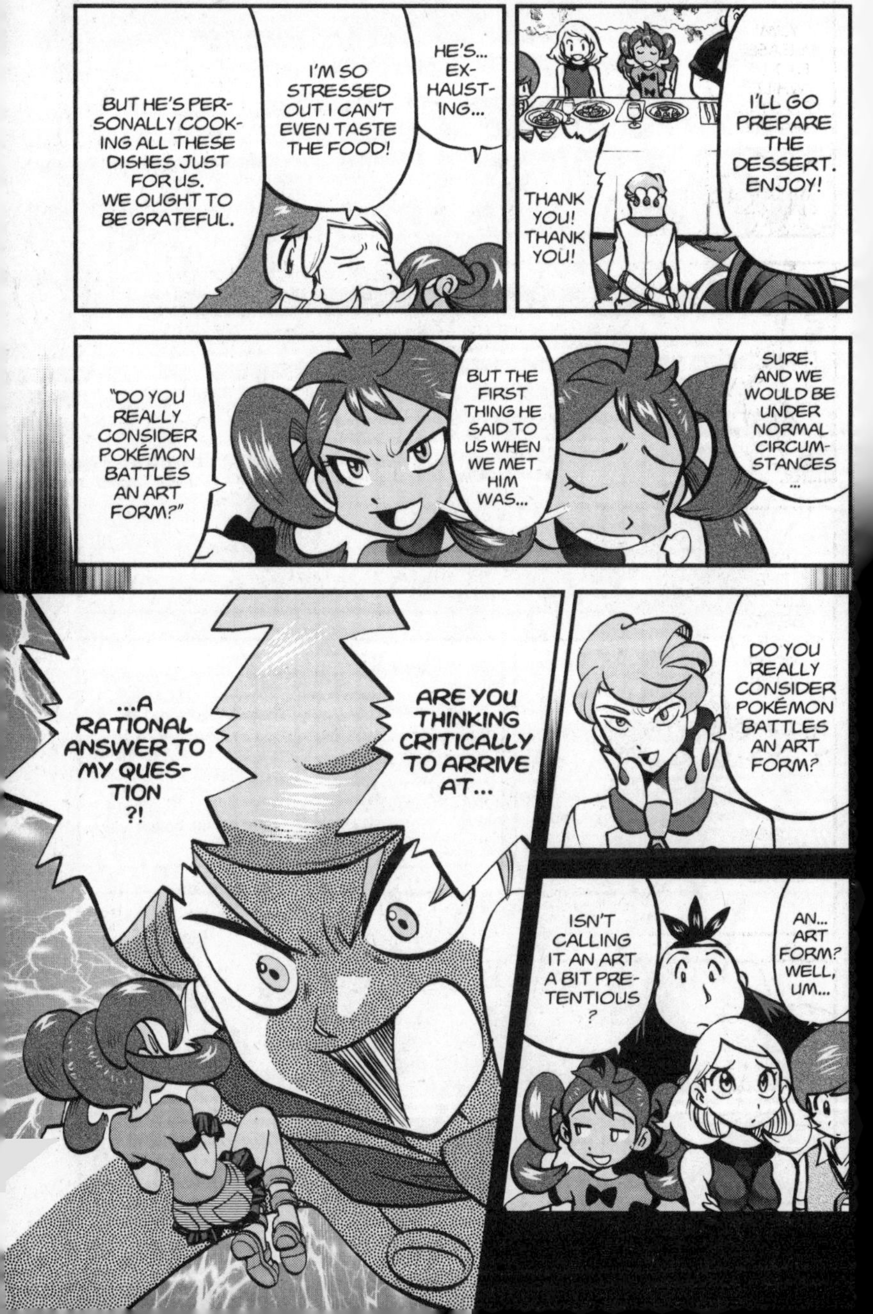
I'LL GO PREPARE THE DESSERT. ENJOY!
THANK YOU! THANK YOU!
HE'S... EX-HAUSTING...
I'M SO STRESSED OUT I CAN'T EVEN TASTE THE FOOD!
BUT HE'S PERSONALLY COOKING ALL THESE DISHES JUST FOR US. WE OUGHT TO BE GRATEFUL.
SURE. AND WE WOULD BE UNDER NORMAL CIRCUMSTANCES...
BUT THE FIRST THING HE SAID TO US WHEN WE MET HIM WAS...
"DO YOU REALLY CONSIDER POKÉMON BATTLES AN ART FORM?"
DO YOU REALLY CONSIDER POKÉMON BATTLES AN ART FORM?
AN... ART FORM? WELL, UM...
ISN'T CALLING IT AN ART A BIT PRETENTIOUS?
ARE YOU THINKING CRITICALLY TO ARRIVE AT...
...A RATIONAL ANSWER TO MY QUESTION?!

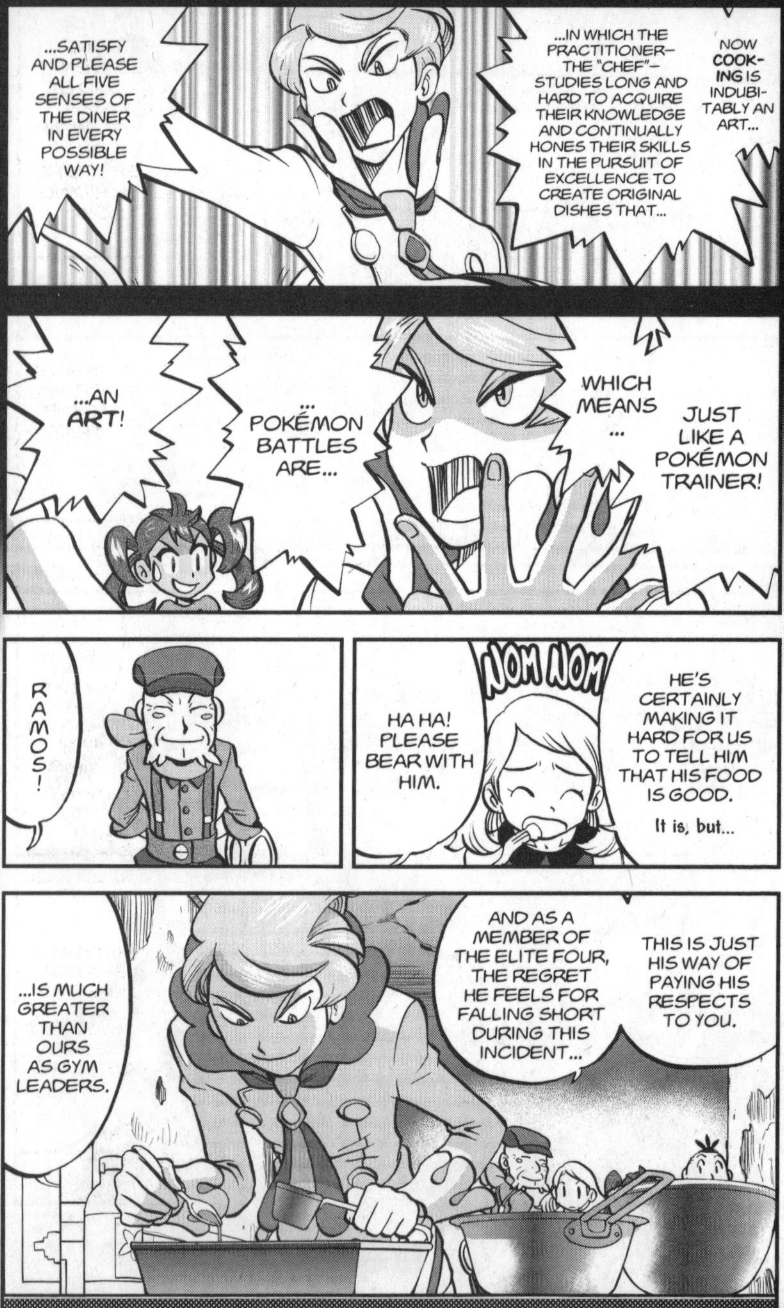
NOW COOKING IS INDUBITABLY AN ART...
...IN WHICH THE PRACTITIONER—THE "CHEF"—STUDIES LONG AND HARD TO ACQUIRE THEIR KNOWLEDGE AND CONTINUALLY HONES THEIR SKILLS IN THE PURSUIT OF EXCELLENCE TO CREATE ORIGINAL DISHES THAT...
...SATISFY AND PLEASE ALL FIVE SENSES OF THE DINER IN EVERY POSSIBLE WAY!
JUST LIKE A POKÉMON TRAINER!
WHICH MEANS ...
... POKÉMON BATTLES ARE...
...AN ART!
NOM NOM
HE'S CERTAINLY MAKING IT HARD FOR US TO TELL HIM THAT HIS FOOD IS GOOD.
It is, but...
HA HA! PLEASE BEAR WITH HIM.
RAMOS!
THIS IS JUST HIS WAY OF PAYING HIS RESPECTS TO YOU.
AND AS A MEMBER OF THE ELITE FOUR, THE REGRET HE FEELS FOR FALLING SHORT DURING THIS INCIDENT...
...IS MUCH GREATER THAN OURS AS GYM LEADERS.

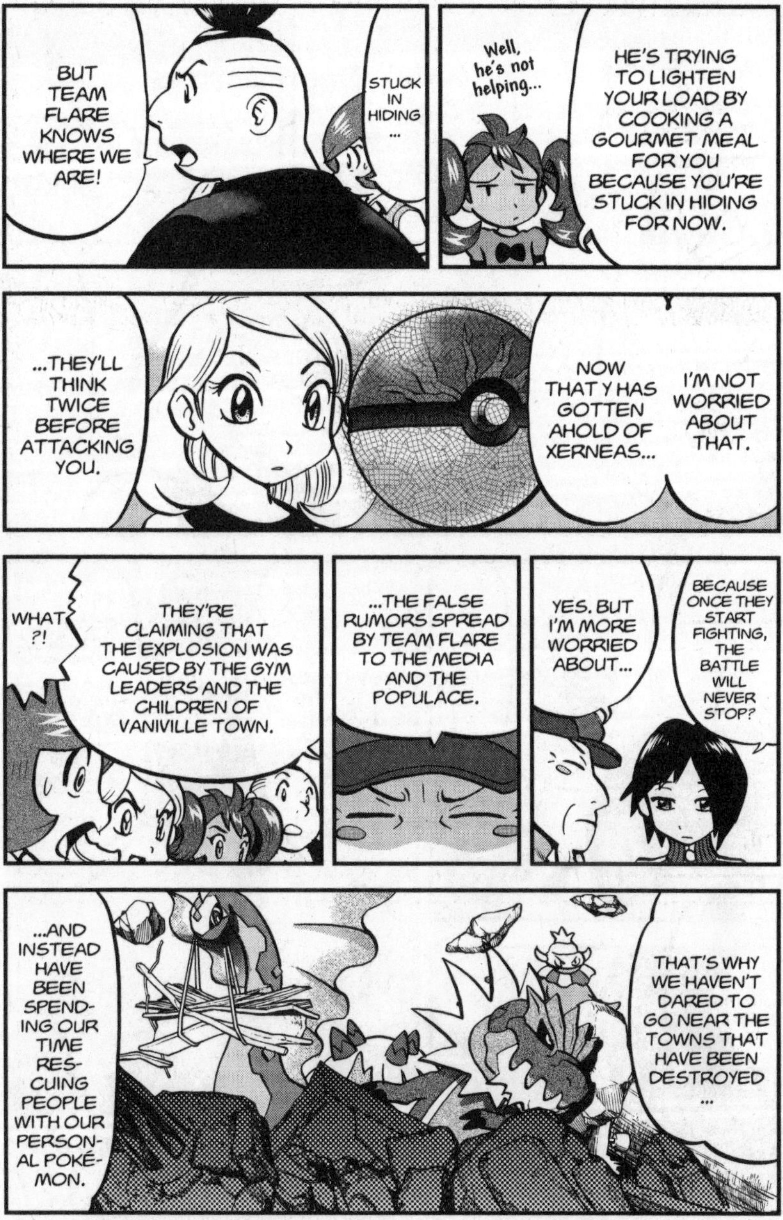
HE'S TRYING TO LIGHTEN YOUR LOAD BY COOKING A GOURMET MEAL FOR YOU BECAUSE YOU'RE STUCK IN HIDING FOR NOW.
Well, he's not helping...
STUCK IN HIDING ...
BUT TEAM FLARE KNOWS WHERE WE ARE!
I'M NOT WORRIED ABOUT THAT.
NOW THAT Y HAS GOTTEN AHOLD OF XERNEAS...
...THEY'LL THINK TWICE BEFORE ATTACKING YOU.
BECAUSE ONCE THEY START FIGHTING, THE BATTLE WILL NEVER STOP?
YES. BUT I'M MORE WORRIED ABOUT...
...THE FALSE RUMORS SPREAD BY TEAM FLARE TO THE MEDIA AND THE POPULACE.
THEY'RE CLAIMING THAT THE EXPLOSION WAS CAUSED BY THE GYM LEADERS AND THE CHILDREN OF VANIVILLE TOWN.
WHAT?!
THAT'S WHY WE HAVEN'T DARED TO GO NEAR THE TOWNS THAT HAVE BEEN DESTROYED...
...AND INSTEAD HAVE BEEN SPENDING OUR TIME RESCUING PEOPLE WITH OUR PERSONAL POKÉMON.

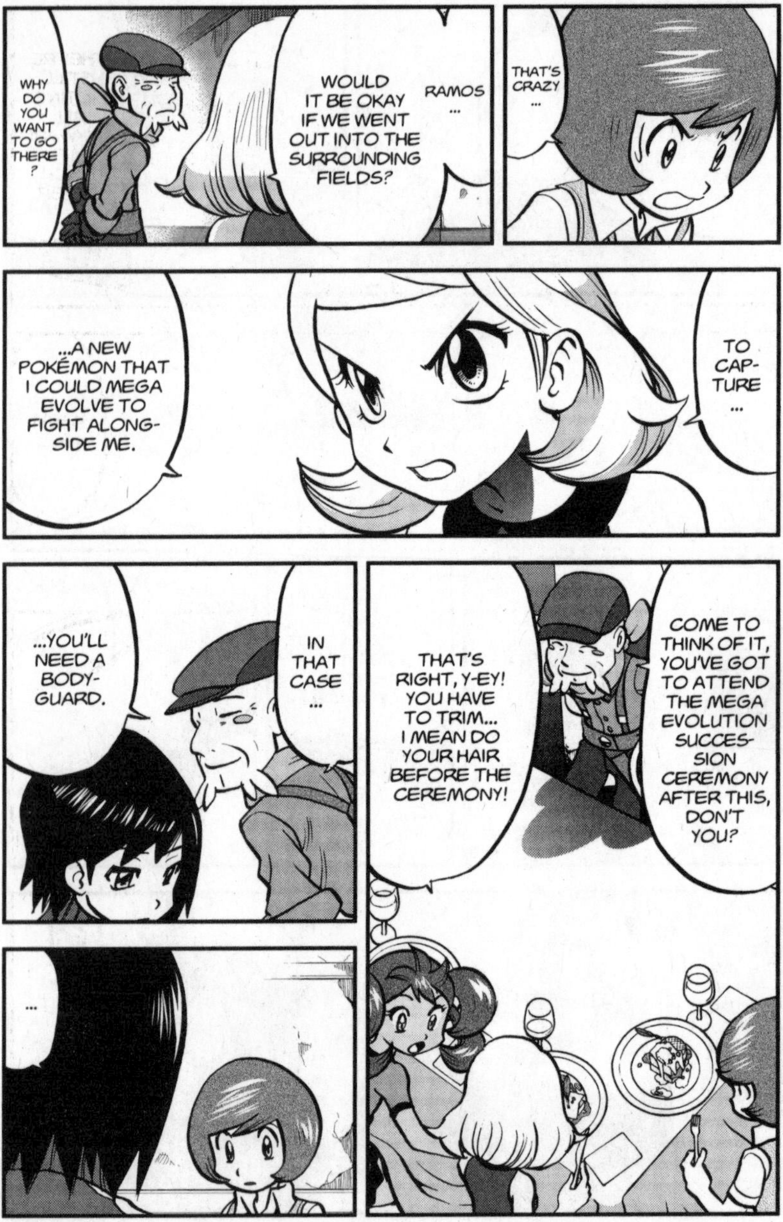
THAT'S CRAZY ...
RAMOS ...
WOULD IT BE OKAY IF WE WENT OUT INTO THE SURROUNDING FIELDS?
WHY DO YOU WANT TO GO THERE?
TO CAP-TURE ...
...A NEW POKÉMON THAT I COULD MEGA EVOLVE TO FIGHT ALONG-SIDE ME.
COME TO THINK OF IT, YOU'VE GOT TO ATTEND THE MEGA EVOLUTION SUCCES-SION CEREMONY AFTER THIS, DON'T YOU?
THAT'S RIGHT, Y-EY! YOU HAVE TO TRIM... I MEAN DO YOUR HAIR BEFORE THE CEREMONY!
IN THAT CASE ...
...YOU'LL NEED A BODY-GUARD.
...

THEY'RE STILL ACTING ALL AWKWARD WITH EACH OTHER.

Y HASN'T CHEWED OUT X FOR ACTING ON HIS OWN LIKE SHE USUALLY DOES... SO X DOESN'T KNOW WHAT TO EXPECT AND HOW TO BEHAVE...

...THINKING?

WHAT IS Y...

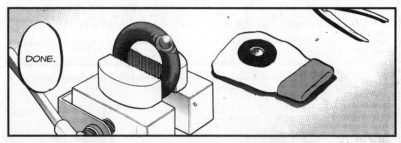

DONE.

OH!

AH! RIGHT ON TIME!

NOK NOK

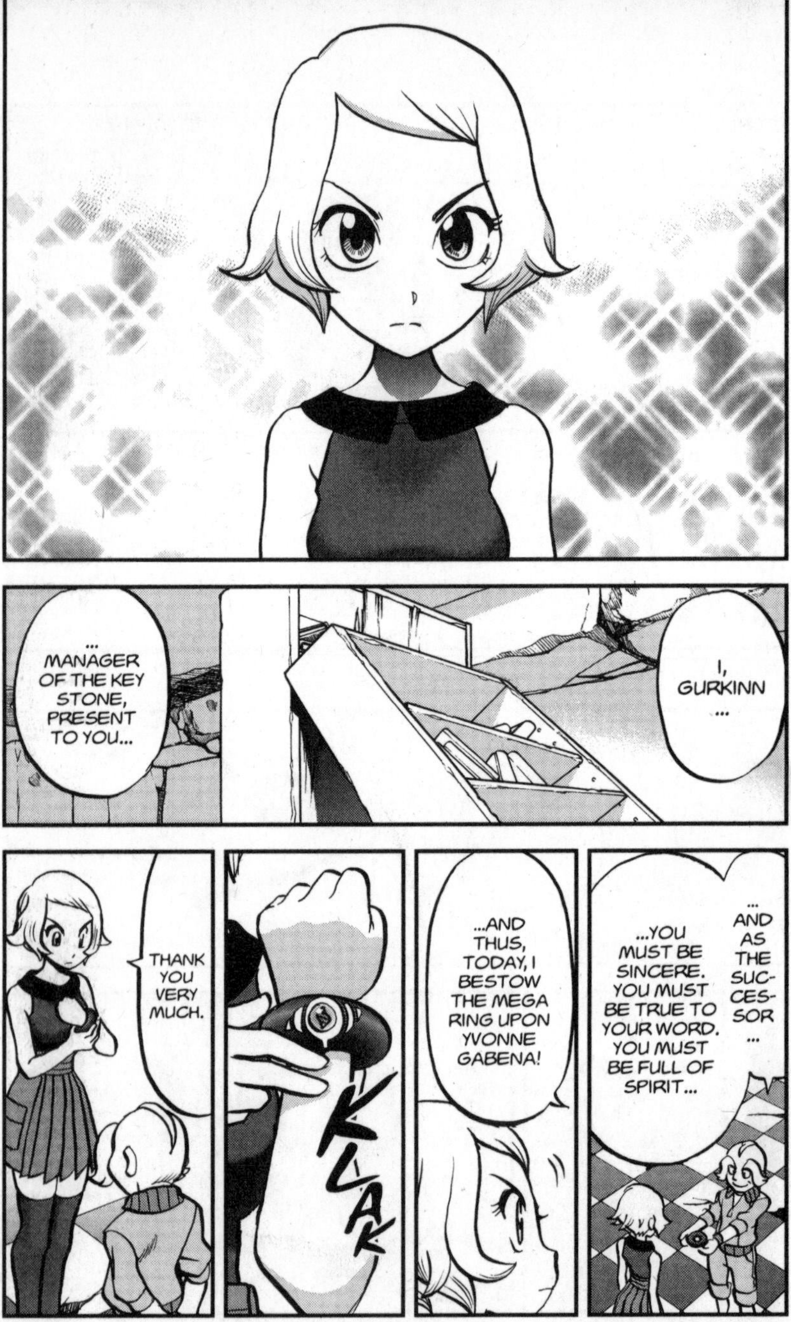
I, GURKINN ...
... MANAGER OF THE KEY STONE, PRESENT TO YOU...
... AND AS THE SUC-CES-SOR ...
...YOU MUST BE SINCERE. YOU MUST BE TRUE TO YOUR WORD. YOU MUST BE FULL OF SPIRIT...
...AND THUS, TODAY, I BESTOW THE MEGA RING UPON YVONNE GABENA!
KLAK
THANK YOU VERY MUCH.

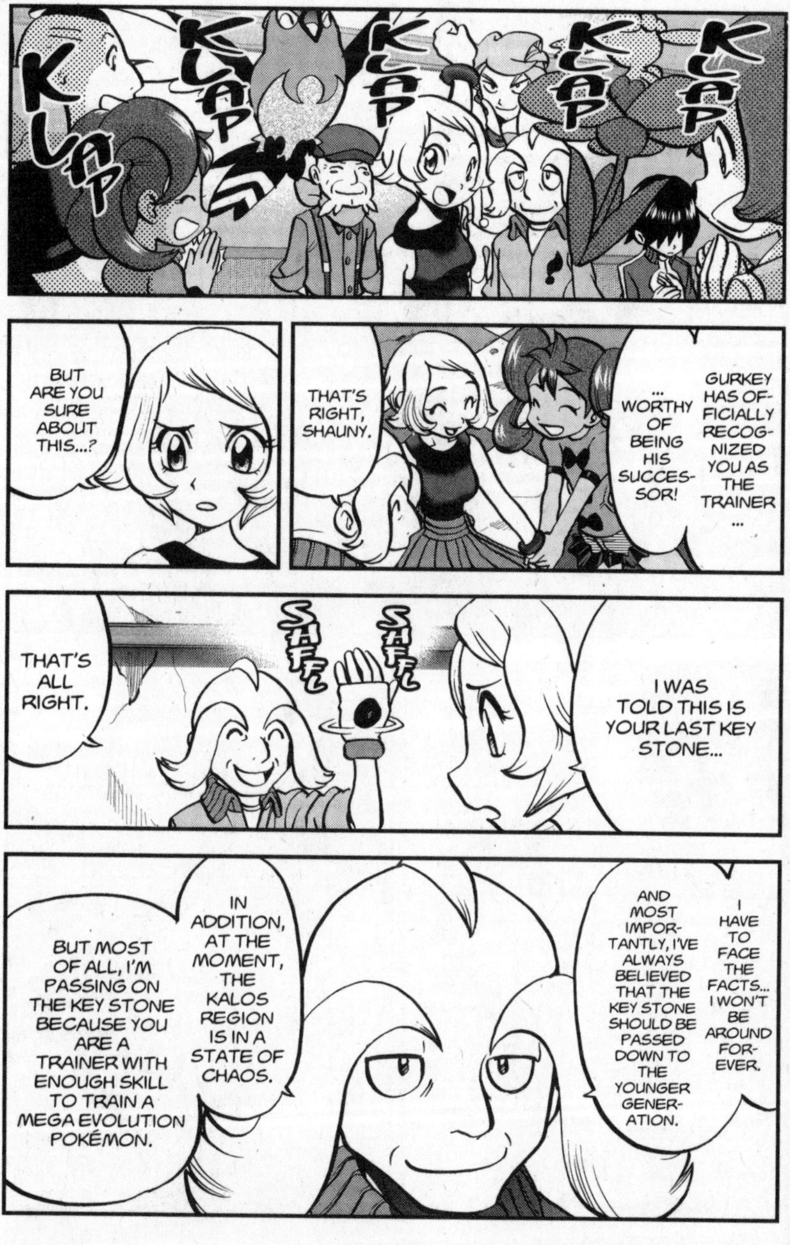
KLAP
KLAP
KLAP
KLAP
KLAP
GURKEY HAS OFFICIALLY RECOGNIZED YOU AS THE TRAINER...
...WORTHY OF BEING HIS SUCCESSOR!
THAT'S RIGHT, SHAUNY.
BUT ARE YOU SURE ABOUT THIS...?
I WAS TOLD THIS IS YOUR LAST KEY STONE...
SHFFL
SHFFL
THAT'S ALL RIGHT.
I HAVE TO FACE THE FACTS... I WON'T BE AROUND FOREVER.
AND MOST IMPORTANTLY, I'VE ALWAYS BELIEVED THAT THE KEY STONE SHOULD BE PASSED DOWN TO THE YOUNGER GENERATION.
IN ADDITION, AT THE MOMENT, THE KALOS REGION IS IN A STATE OF CHAOS.
BUT MOST OF ALL, I'M PASSING ON THE KEY STONE BECAUSE YOU ARE A TRAINER WITH ENOUGH SKILL TO TRAIN A MEGA EVOLUTION POKÉMON.

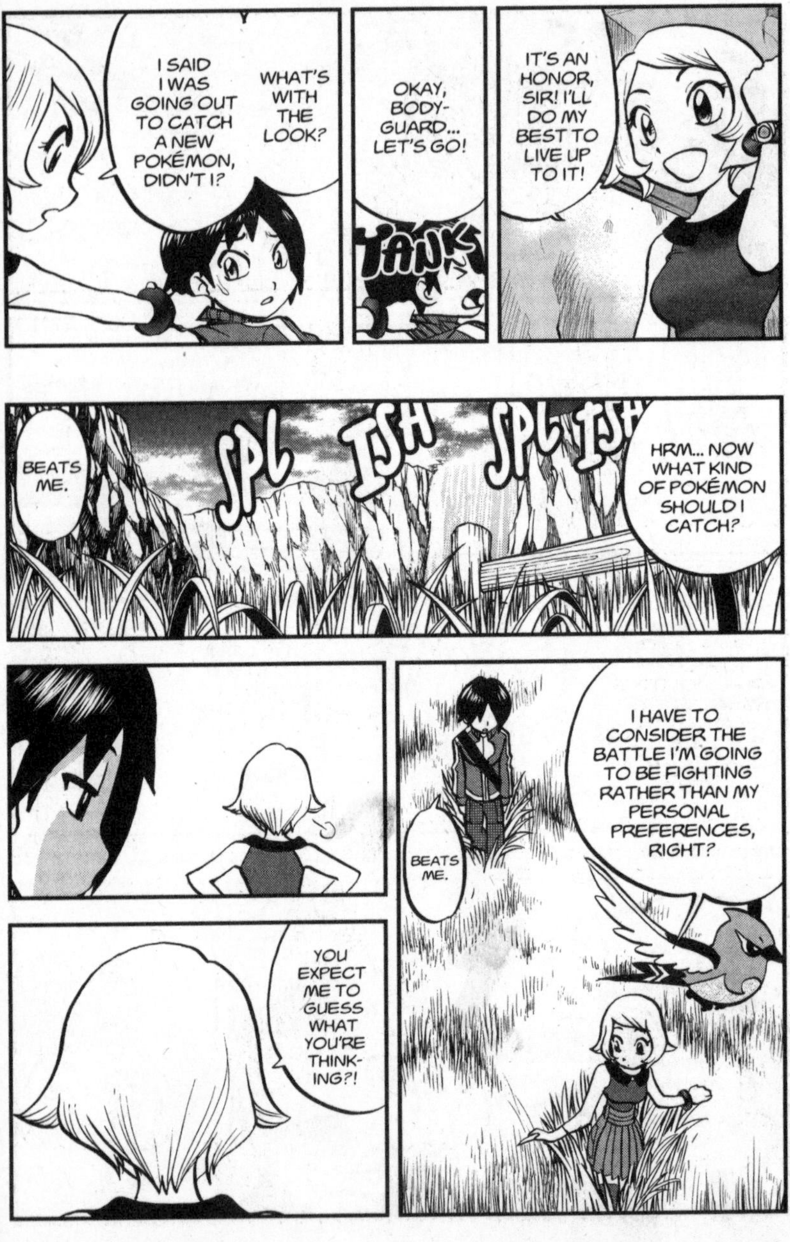

IT'S AN HONOR, SIR! I'LL DO MY BEST TO LIVE UP TO IT!
OKAY, BODY-GUARD... LET'S GO!
YANK
WHAT'S WITH THE LOOK?
I SAID I WAS GOING OUT TO CATCH A NEW POKÉMON, DIDN'T I?
HRM... NOW WHAT KIND OF POKÉMON SHOULD I CATCH?
SPLISH
SPLISH
BEATS ME.
I HAVE TO CONSIDER THE BATTLE I'M GOING TO BE FIGHTING RATHER THAN MY PERSONAL PREFERENCES, RIGHT?
BEATS ME.
YOU EXPECT ME TO GUESS WHAT YOU'RE THINKING?!

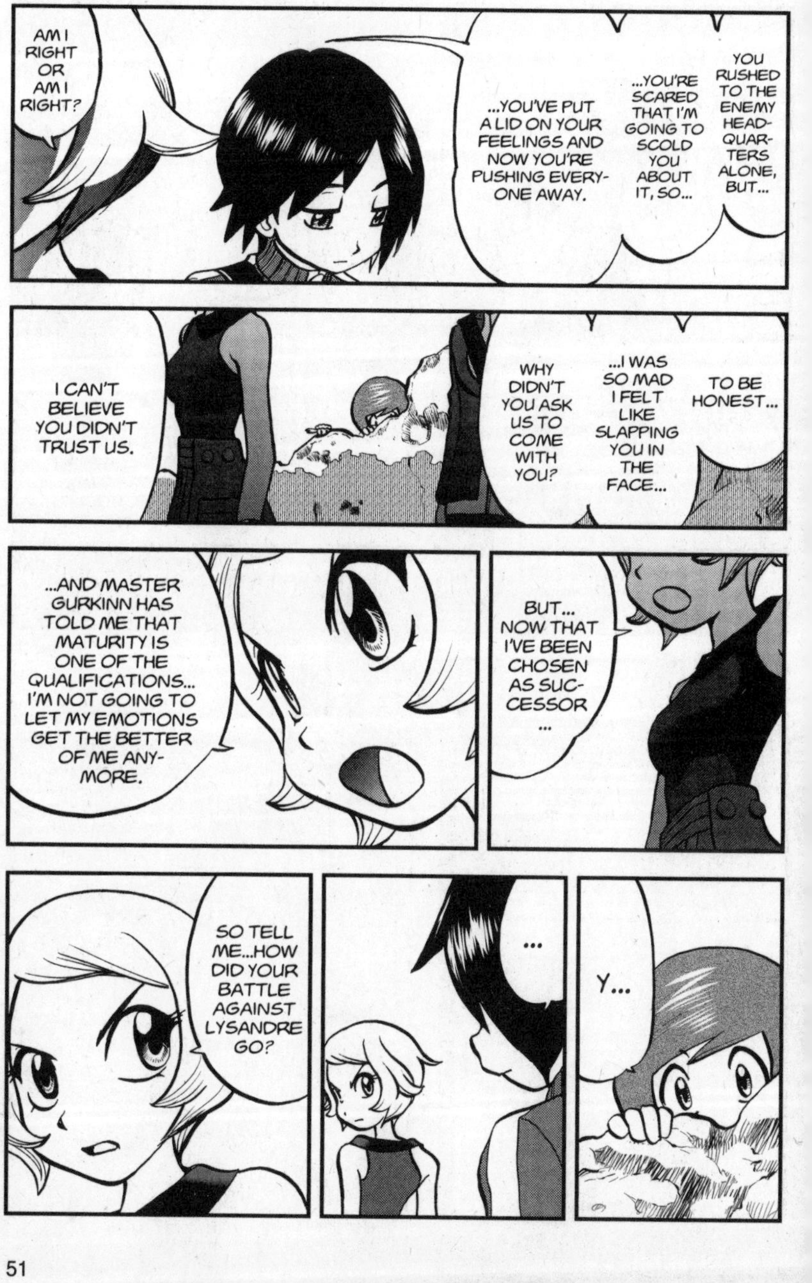
YOU RUSHED TO THE ENEMY HEADQUARTERS ALONE, BUT...
...YOU'RE SCARED THAT I'M GOING TO SCOLD YOU ABOUT IT, SO...
...YOU'VE PUT A LID ON YOUR FEELINGS AND NOW YOU'RE PUSHING EVERYONE AWAY.
AM I RIGHT OR AM I RIGHT?
TO BE HONEST...
...I WAS SO MAD I FELT LIKE SLAPPING YOU IN THE FACE...
WHY DIDN'T YOU ASK US TO COME WITH YOU?
I CAN'T BELIEVE YOU DIDN'T TRUST US.
BUT... NOW THAT I'VE BEEN CHOSEN AS SUCCESSOR...
...AND MASTER GURKINN HAS TOLD ME THAT MATURITY IS ONE OF THE QUALIFICATIONS... I'M NOT GOING TO LET MY EMOTIONS GET THE BETTER OF ME ANYMORE.
Y...
...
SO TELL ME...HOW DID YOUR BATTLE AGAINST LYSANDRE GO?

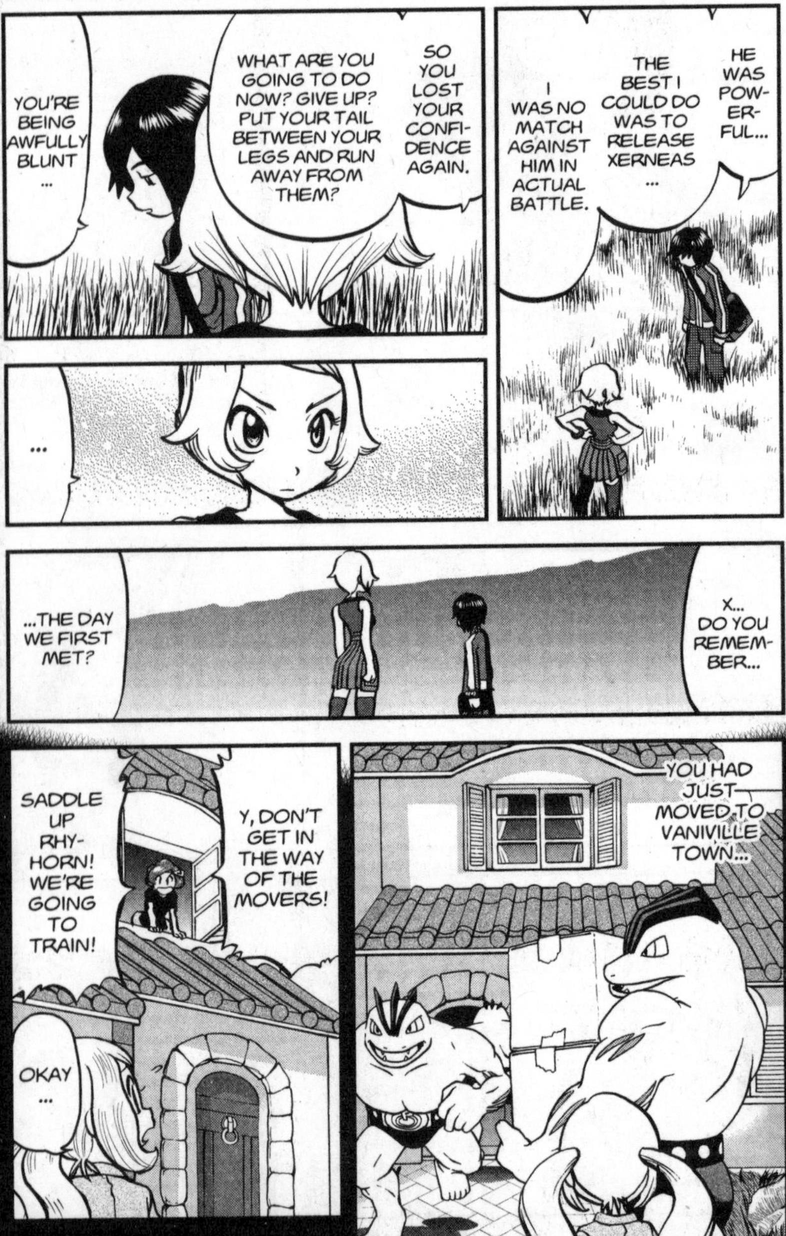
HE WAS POWER-FUL...
THE BEST I COULD DO WAS TO RELEASE XERNEAS ...
I WAS NO MATCH AGAINST HIM IN ACTUAL BATTLE.
SO YOU LOST YOUR CONFI-DENCE AGAIN.
WHAT ARE YOU GOING TO DO NOW? GIVE UP? PUT YOUR TAIL BETWEEN YOUR LEGS AND RUN AWAY FROM THEM?
YOU'RE BEING AWFULLY BLUNT ...
...
X... DO YOU REMEM-BER...
...THE DAY WE FIRST MET?
YOU HAD JUST MOVED TO VANIVILLE TOWN...
Y, DON'T GET IN THE WAY OF THE MOVERS!
SADDLE UP RHY-HORN! WE'RE GOING TO TRAIN!
OKAY ...

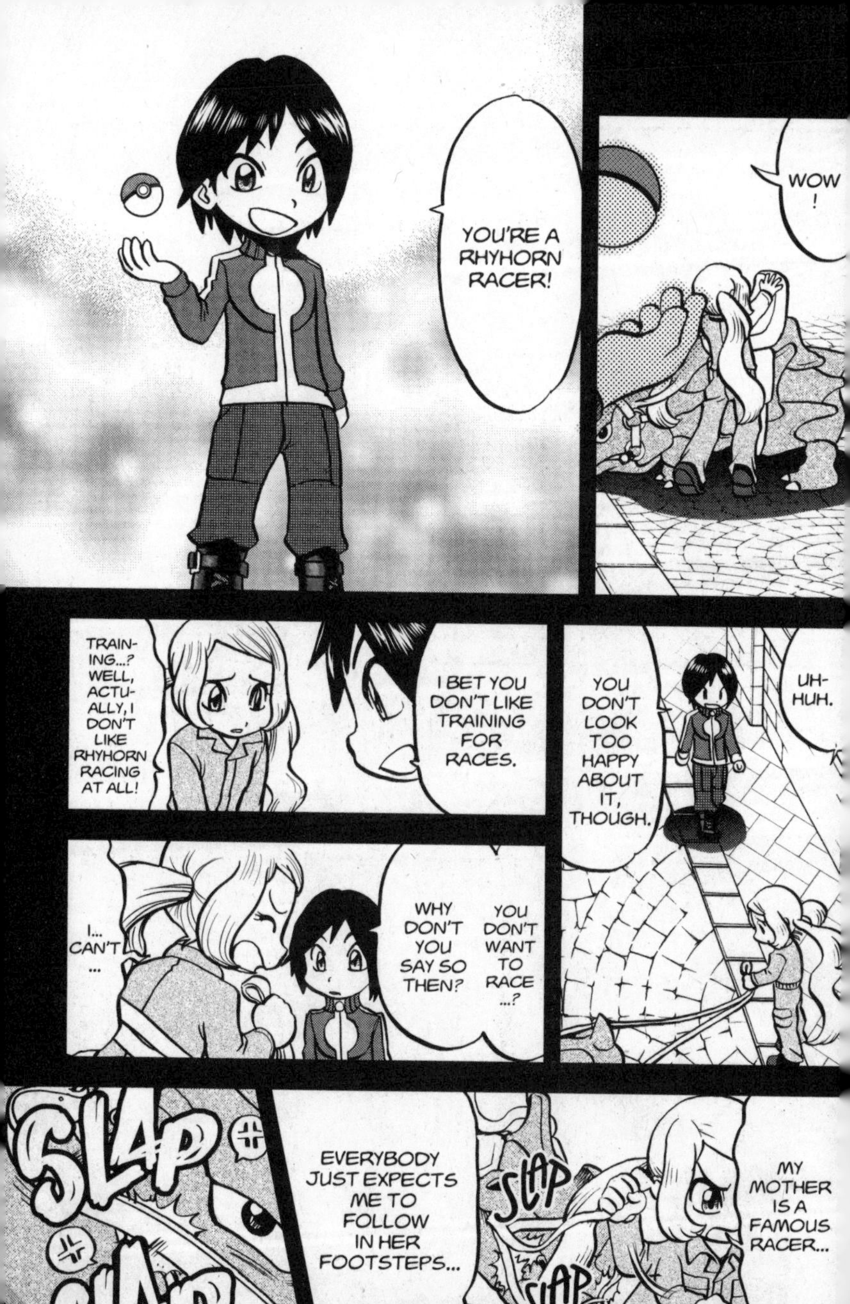
WOW!
YOU'RE A RHYHORN RACER!
UH-HUH.
YOU DON'T LOOK TOO HAPPY ABOUT IT, THOUGH.
I BET YOU DON'T LIKE TRAINING FOR RACES.
TRAINING...? WELL, ACTUALLY, I DON'T LIKE RHYHORN RACING AT ALL!
YOU DON'T WANT TO RACE...?
WHY DON'T YOU SAY SO THEN?
I... CAN'T...
MY MOTHER IS A FAMOUS RACER...
SLAP
SLAP
EVERYBODY JUST EXPECTS ME TO FOLLOW IN HER FOOTSTEPS...
SLAP

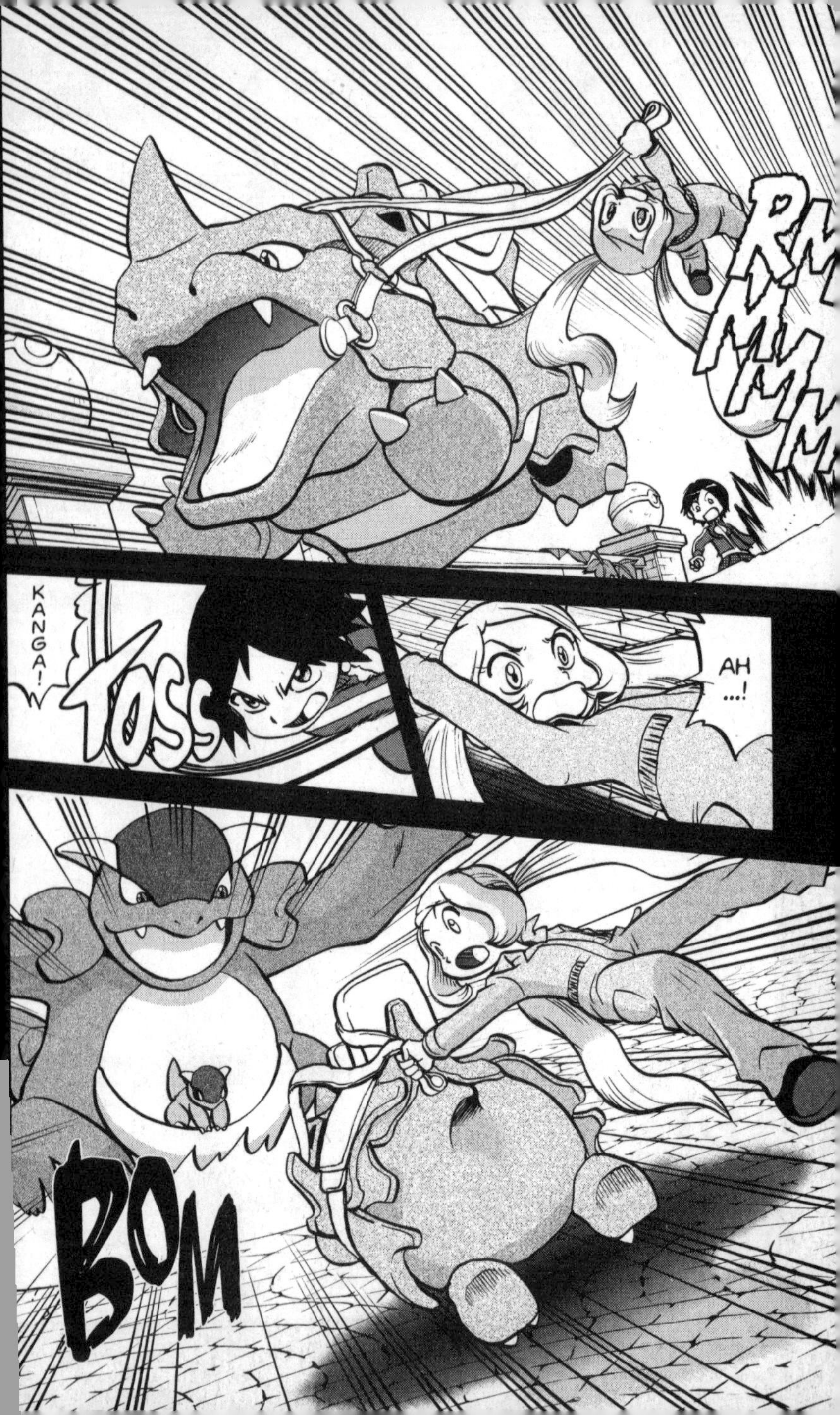
RMMMM
AH ...!
KANGA!
TOSS
BOM

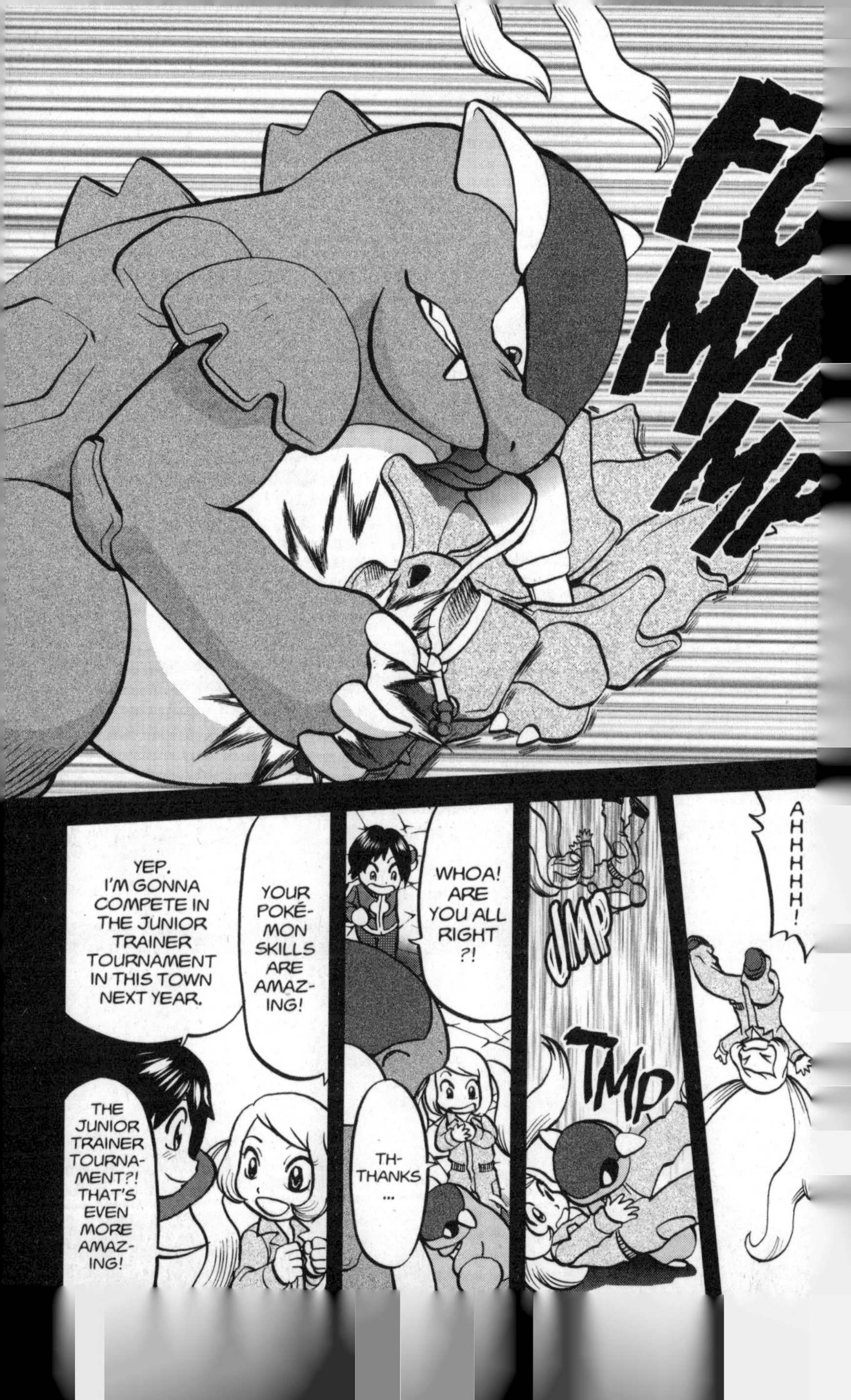
FUMMMP
AHHHHHH!
JMP
TMP
WHOA! ARE YOU ALL RIGHT ?!
TH-THANKS...
YOUR POKÉ-MON SKILLS ARE AMAZ-ING!
YEP. I'M GONNA COMPETE IN THE JUNIOR TRAINER TOURNAMENT IN THIS TOWN NEXT YEAR.
THE JUNIOR TRAINER TOURNA-MENT?! THAT'S EVEN MORE AMAZ-ING!

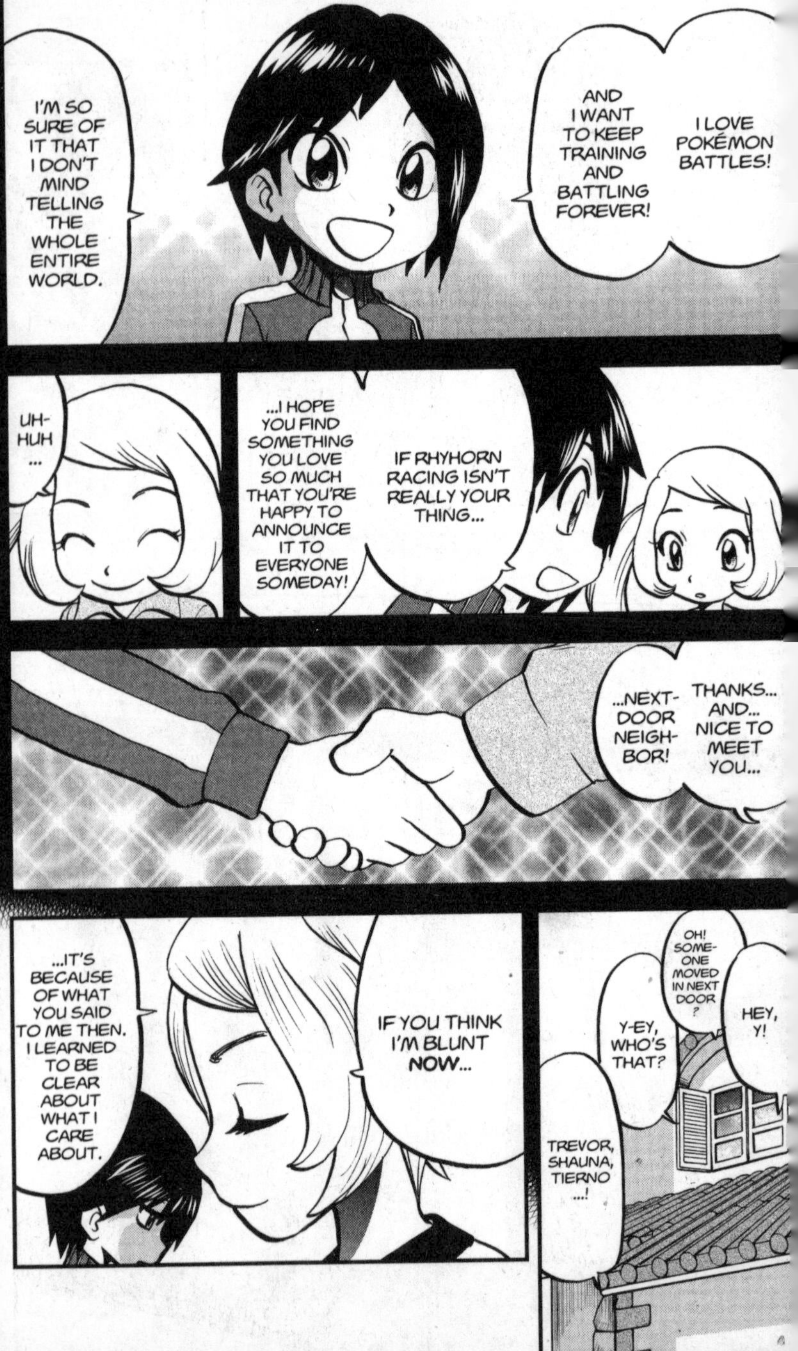
I LOVE POKÉMON BATTLES!
AND I WANT TO KEEP TRAINING AND BATTLING FOREVER!
I'M SO SURE OF IT THAT I DON'T MIND TELLING THE WHOLE ENTIRE WORLD.
IF RHYHORN RACING ISN'T REALLY YOUR THING...
...I HOPE YOU FIND SOMETHING YOU LOVE SO MUCH THAT YOU'RE HAPPY TO ANNOUNCE IT TO EVERYONE SOMEDAY!
UH-HUH...
THANKS... AND... NICE TO MEET YOU...
...NEXT-DOOR NEIGHBOR!
HEY, Y!
OH! SOME-ONE MOVED IN NEXT DOOR?
Y-EY, WHO'S THAT?
TREVOR, SHAUNA, TIERNO...!
IF YOU THINK I'M BLUNT **NOW**...
...IT'S BECAUSE OF WHAT YOU SAID TO ME THEN. I LEARNED TO BE CLEAR ABOUT WHAT I CARE ABOUT.

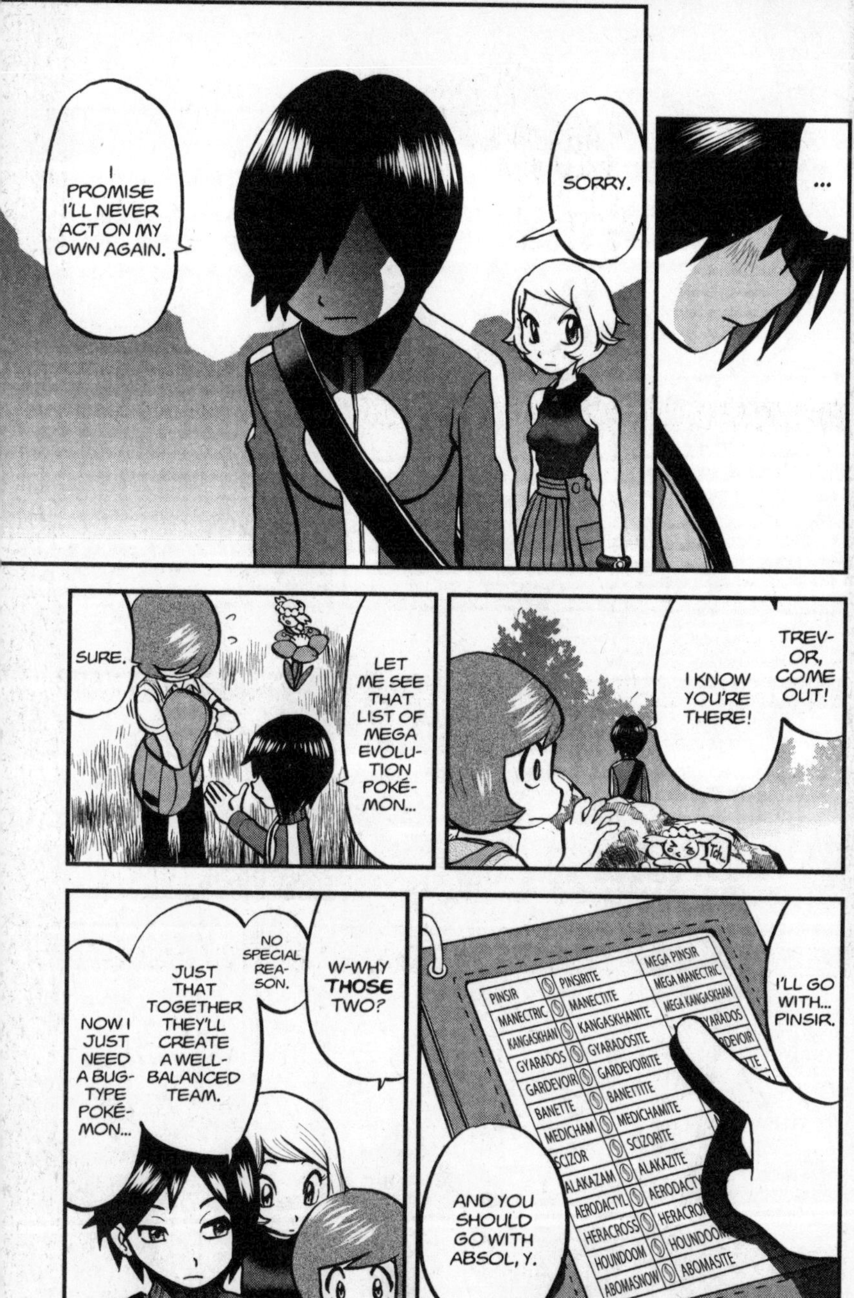
...
SORRY.
I PROMISE I'LL NEVER ACT ON MY OWN AGAIN.
TREV-OR, COME OUT!
I KNOW YOU'RE THERE!
Tch.
LET ME SEE THAT LIST OF MEGA EVOLUTION POKÉMON...
SURE.
I'LL GO WITH... PINSIR.
MEGA PINSIR
PINSIR PINSIRITE
MEGA MANECTRIC
MANECTRIC MANECTITE
MEGA KANGASKHAN
KANGASKHAN KANGASKHANITE
GYARADOS GYARADOSITE
GARDEVOIR GARDEVOIRITE
BANETTE BANETTITE
MEDICHAM MEDICHAMITE
SCIZOR SCIZORITE
ALAKAZAM ALAKAZITE
HOUNDOOM
ABOMASNOW ABOMASITE
AND YOU SHOULD GO WITH ABSOL, Y.
W-WHY THOSE TWO?
NO SPECIAL REA-SON.
JUST THAT TOGETHER THEY'LL CREATE A WELL-BALANCED TEAM.
NOW I JUST NEED A BUG-TYPE POKÉMON...

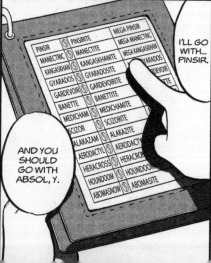

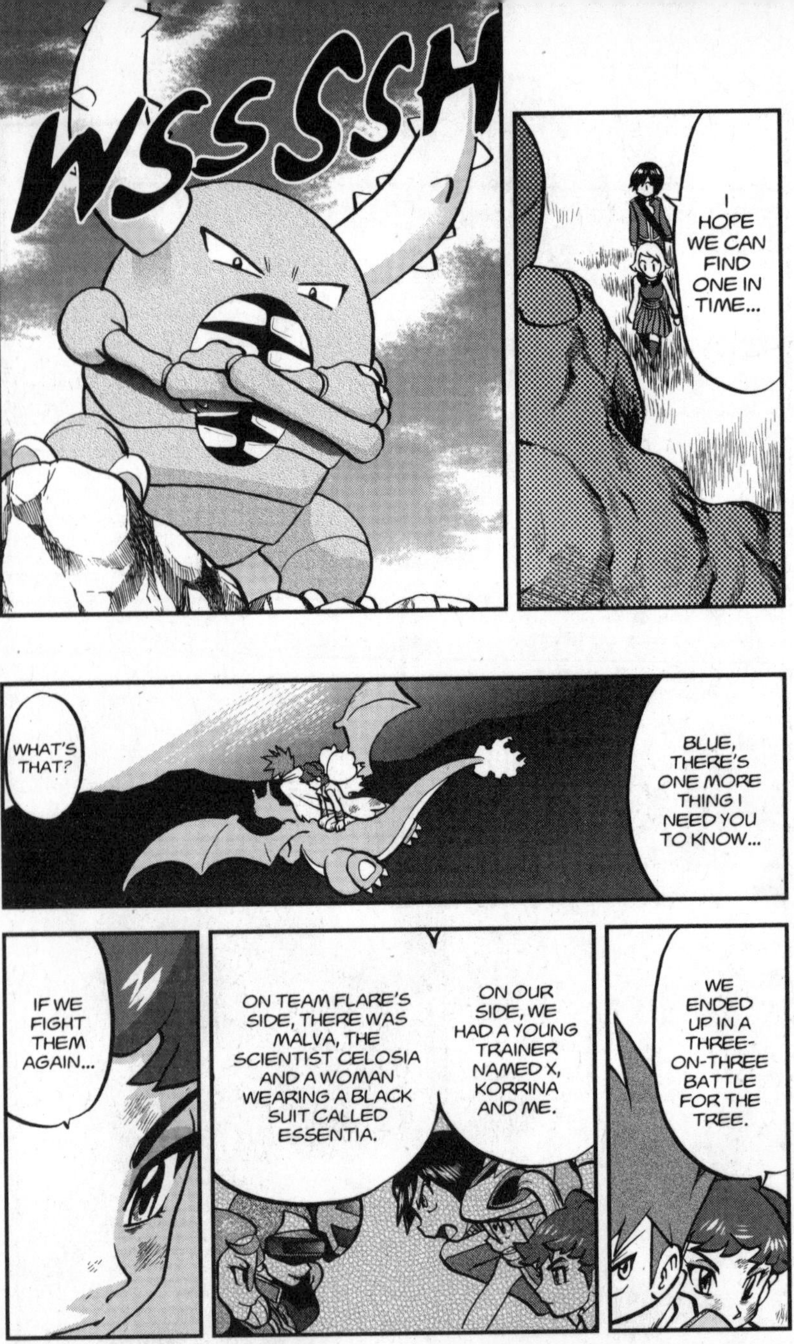
I HOPE WE CAN FIND ONE IN TIME...
WSSSSH
BLUE, THERE'S ONE MORE THING I NEED YOU TO KNOW...
WHAT'S THAT?
WE ENDED UP IN A THREE-ON-THREE BATTLE FOR THE TREE.
ON OUR SIDE, WE HAD A YOUNG TRAINER NAMED X, KORRINA AND ME.
ON TEAM FLARE'S SIDE, THERE WAS MALVA, THE SCIENTIST CELOSIA AND A WOMAN WEARING A BLACK SUIT CALLED ESSENTIA.
IF WE FIGHT THEM AGAIN...

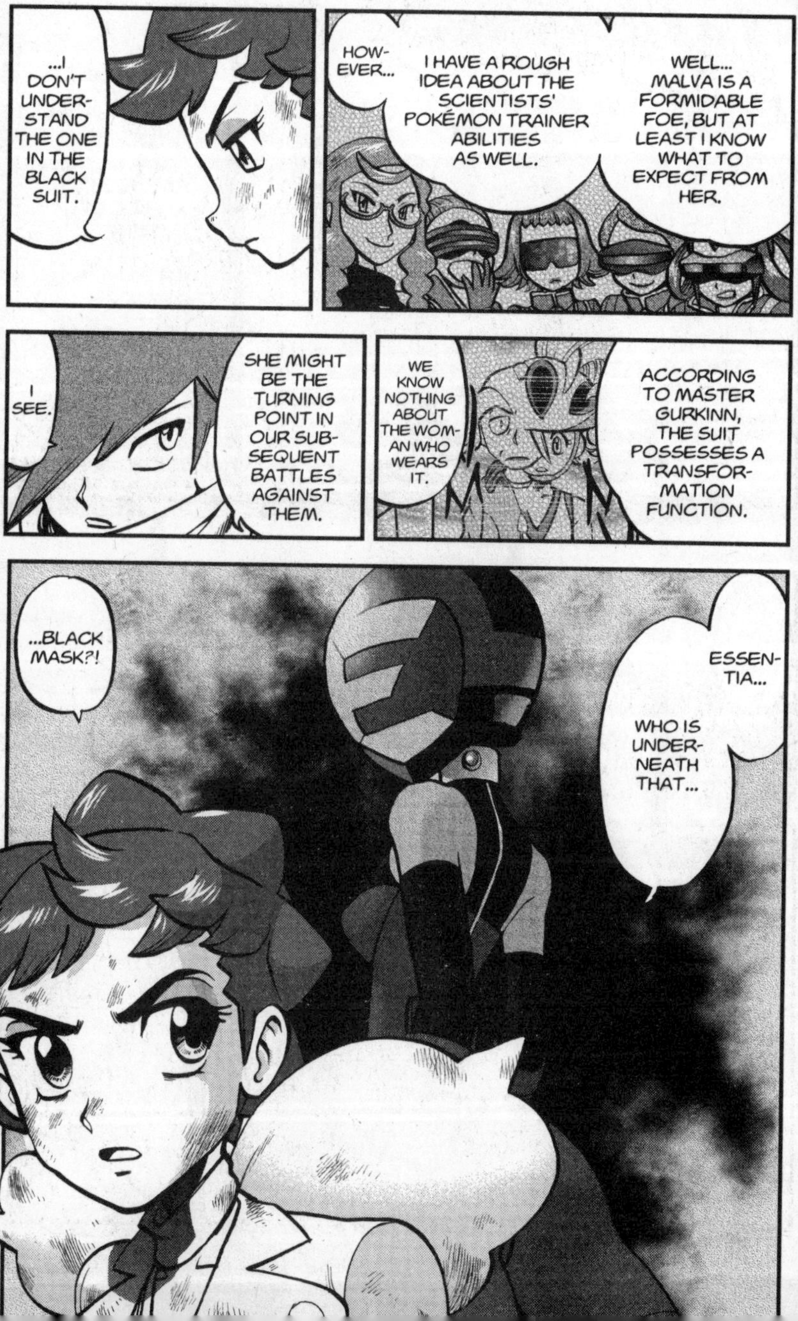
WELL... MALVA IS A FORMIDABLE FOE, BUT AT LEAST I KNOW WHAT TO EXPECT FROM HER.
I HAVE A ROUGH IDEA ABOUT THE SCIENTISTS' POKÉMON TRAINER ABILITIES AS WELL.
HOW-EVER...
...I DON'T UNDER-STAND THE ONE IN THE BLACK SUIT.
ACCORDING TO MASTER GURKINN, THE SUIT POSSESSES A TRANSFOR-MATION FUNCTION.
WE KNOW NOTHING ABOUT THE WOM-AN WHO WEARS IT.
SHE MIGHT BE THE TURNING POINT IN OUR SUB-SEQUENT BATTLES AGAINST THEM.
I SEE.
ESSEN-TIA...
WHO IS UNDER-NEATH THAT...
...BLACK MASK?!

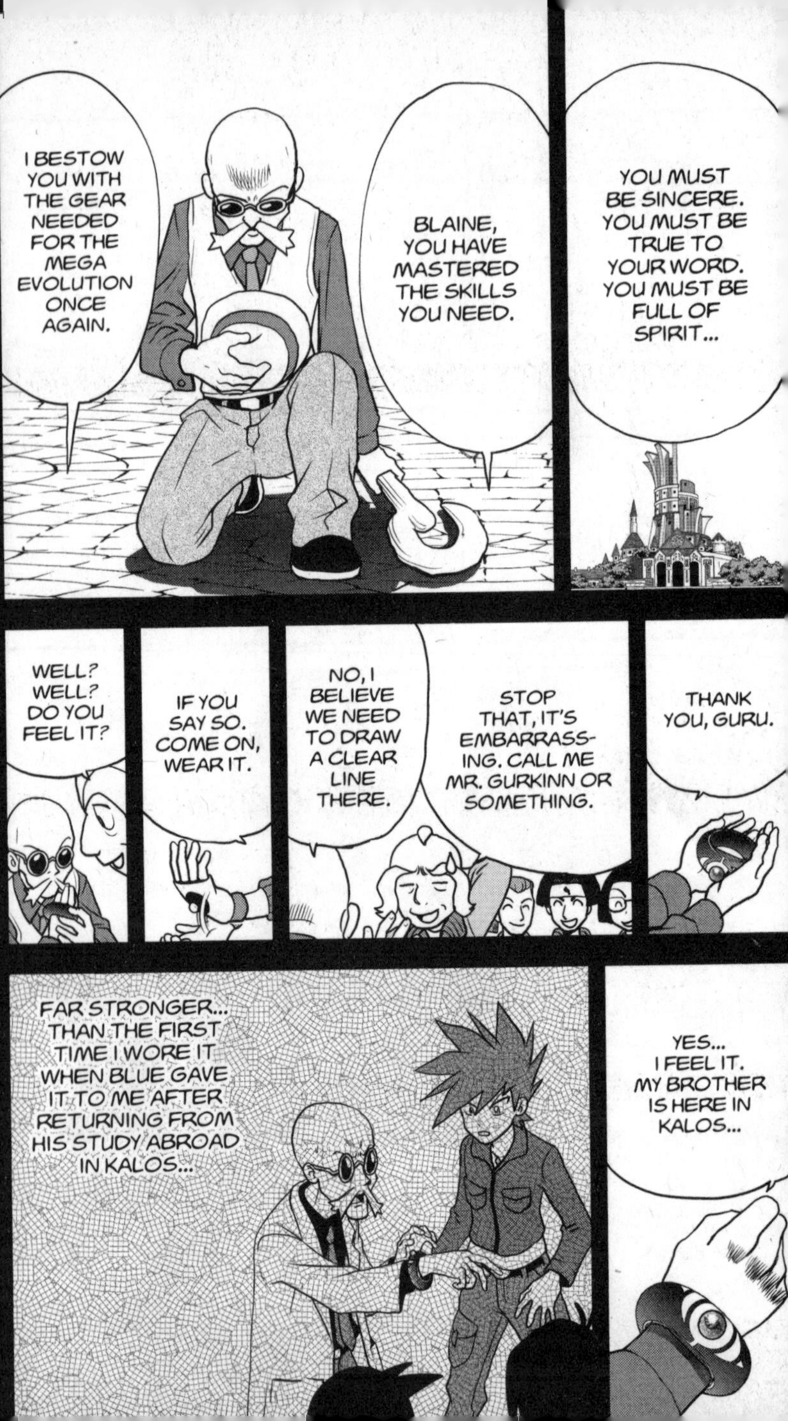
YOU MUST BE SINCERE. YOU MUST BE TRUE TO YOUR WORD. YOU MUST BE FULL OF SPIRIT...
BLAINE, YOU HAVE MASTERED THE SKILLS YOU NEED.
I BESTOW YOU WITH THE GEAR NEEDED FOR THE MEGA EVOLUTION ONCE AGAIN.
THANK YOU, GURU.
STOP THAT, IT'S EMBARRASS-ING. CALL ME MR. GURKINN OR SOMETHING.
NO, I BELIEVE WE NEED TO DRAW A CLEAR LINE THERE.
IF YOU SAY SO. COME ON, WEAR IT.
WELL? WELL? DO YOU FEEL IT?
YES... I FEEL IT. MY BROTHER IS HERE IN KALOS...
FAR STRONGER... THAN THE FIRST TIME I WORE IT WHEN BLUE GAVE IT TO ME AFTER RETURNING FROM HIS STUDY ABROAD IN KALOS...

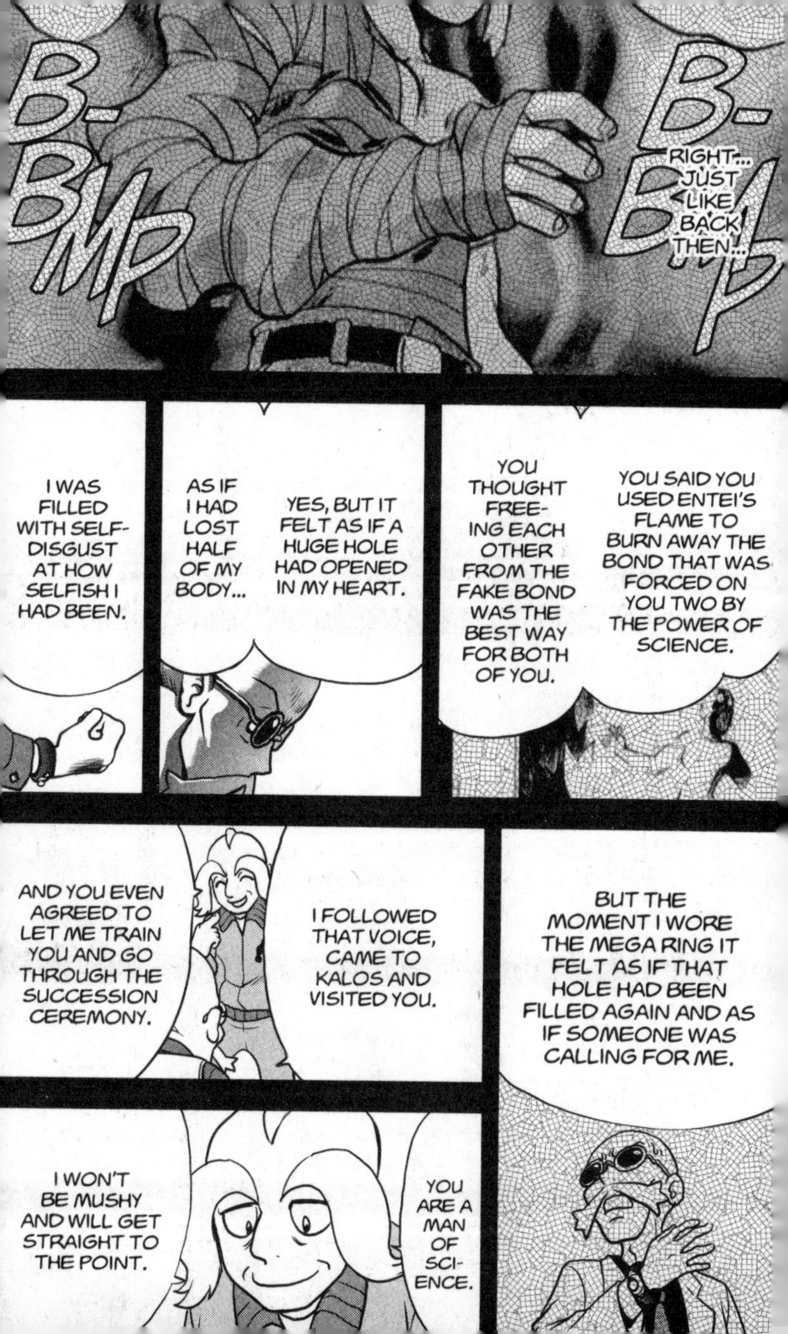
B-BMP
RIGHT... JUST LIKE BACK THEN...
B-BMP
YOU SAID YOU USED ENTEI'S FLAME TO BURN AWAY THE BOND THAT WAS FORCED ON YOU TWO BY THE POWER OF SCIENCE.
YOU THOUGHT FREE-ING EACH OTHER FROM THE FAKE BOND WAS THE BEST WAY FOR BOTH OF YOU.
YES, BUT IT FELT AS IF A HUGE HOLE HAD OPENED IN MY HEART.
AS IF I HAD LOST HALF OF MY BODY...
I WAS FILLED WITH SELF-DISGUST AT HOW SELFISH I HAD BEEN.
BUT THE MOMENT I WORE THE MEGA RING IT FELT AS IF THAT HOLE HAD BEEN FILLED AGAIN AND AS IF SOMEONE WAS CALLING FOR ME.
I FOLLOWED THAT VOICE, CAME TO KALOS AND VISITED YOU.
AND YOU EVEN AGREED TO LET ME TRAIN YOU AND GO THROUGH THE SUCCESSION CEREMONY.
YOU ARE A MAN OF SCI-ENCE.
I WON'T BE MUSHY AND WILL GET STRAIGHT TO THE POINT.

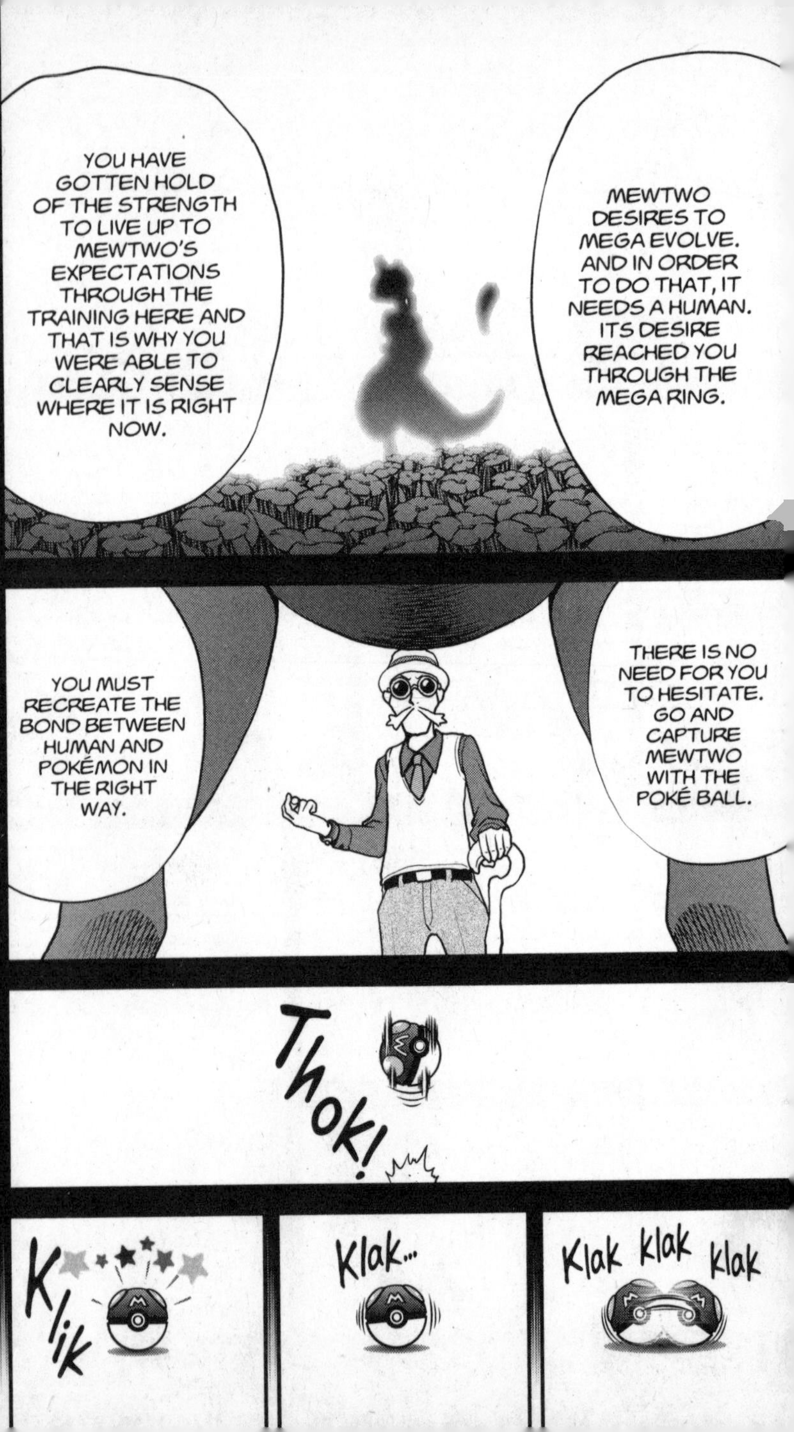
MEWTWO DESIRES TO MEGA EVOLVE. AND IN ORDER TO DO THAT, IT NEEDS A HUMAN. ITS DESIRE REACHED YOU THROUGH THE MEGA RING.
YOU HAVE GOTTEN HOLD OF THE STRENGTH TO LIVE UP TO MEWTWO'S EXPECTATIONS THROUGH THE TRAINING HERE AND THAT IS WHY YOU WERE ABLE TO CLEARLY SENSE WHERE IT IS RIGHT NOW.
THERE IS NO NEED FOR YOU TO HESITATE. GO AND CAPTURE MEWTWO WITH THE POKÉ BALL.
YOU MUST RECREATE THE BOND BETWEEN HUMAN AND POKÉMON IN THE RIGHT WAY.
Thok!
Klak klak klak
Klak...
Klik

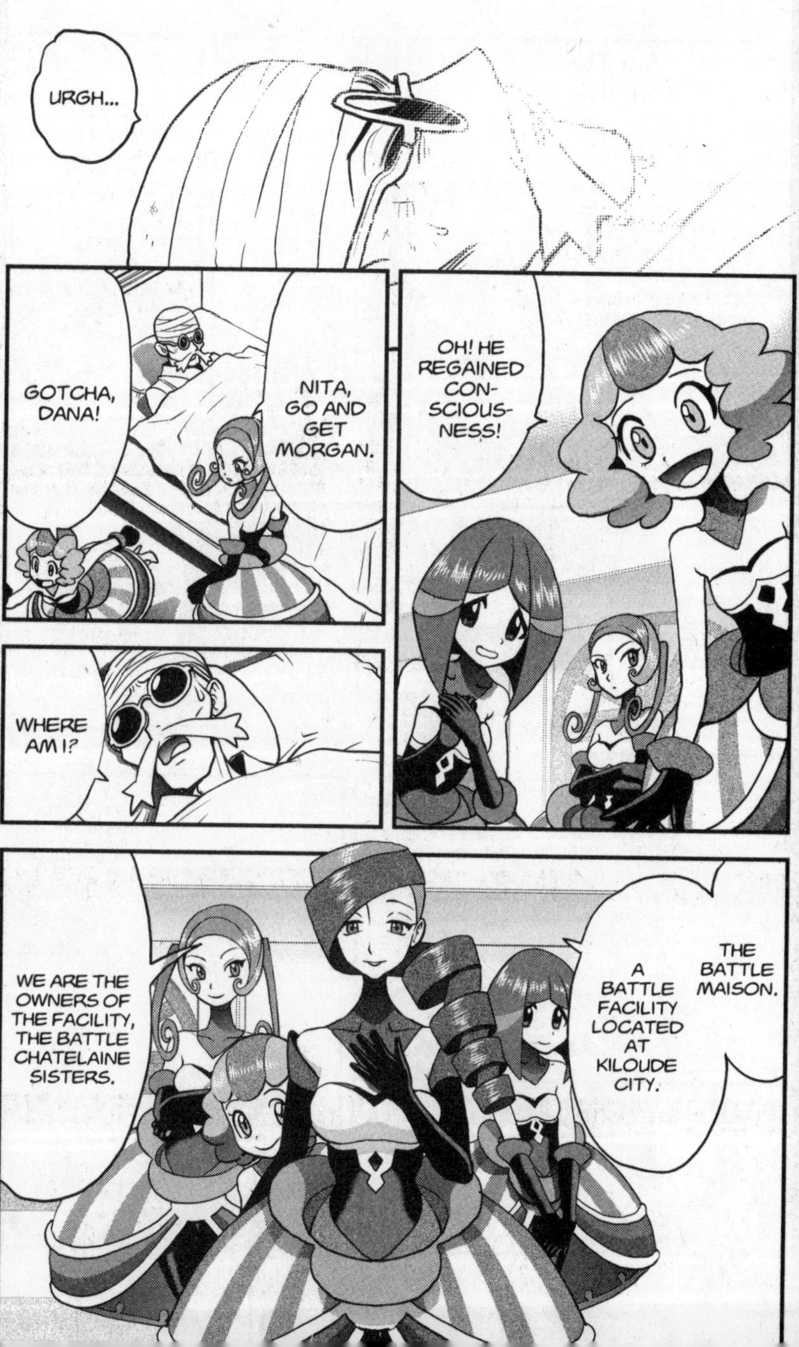
URGH...
OH! HE REGAINED CONSCIOUSNESS!
NITA, GO AND GET MORGAN.
GOTCHA, DANA!
WHERE AM I?
THE BATTLE MAISON.
A BATTLE FACILITY LOCATED AT KILOUDE CITY.
WE ARE THE OWNERS OF THE FACILITY, THE BATTLE CHATELAINE SISTERS.

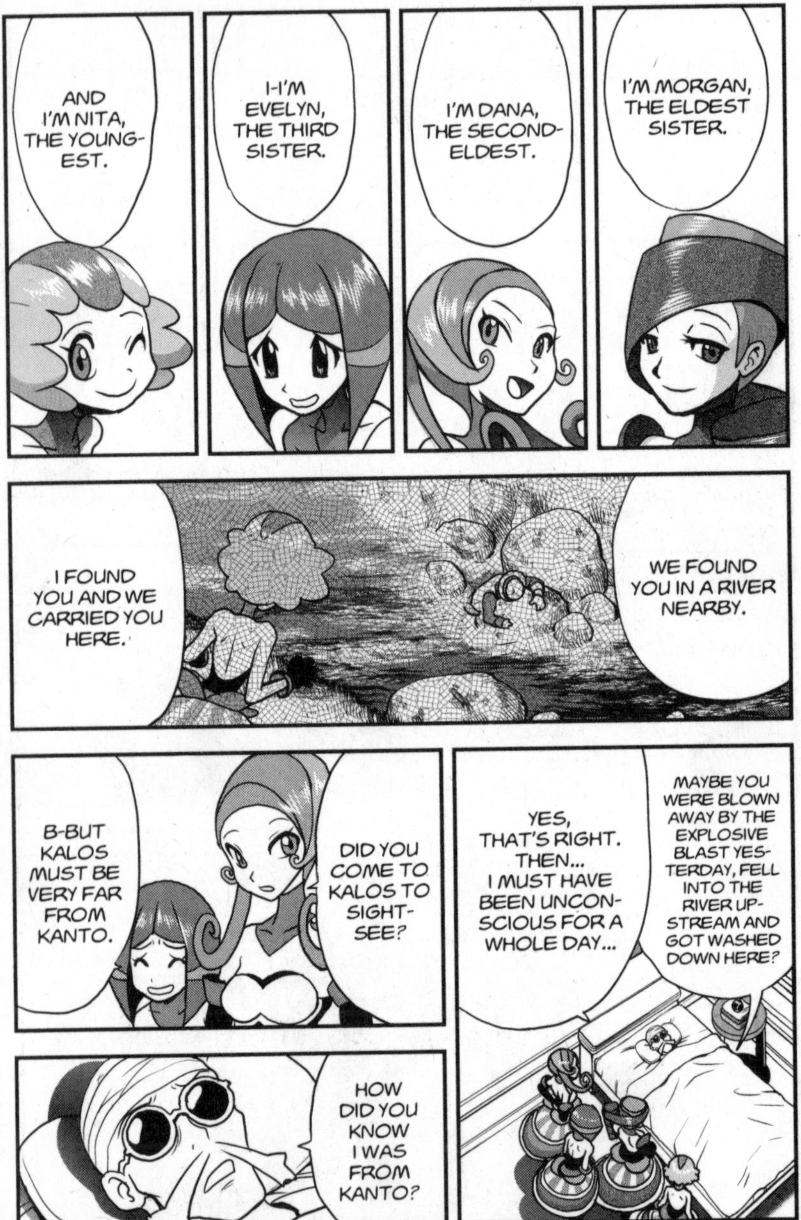
I'M MORGAN, THE ELDEST SISTER.
I'M DANA, THE SECOND-ELDEST.
I-I'M EVELYN, THE THIRD SISTER.
AND I'M NITA, THE YOUNG-EST.
WE FOUND YOU IN A RIVER NEARBY.
I FOUND YOU AND WE CARRIED YOU HERE.
MAYBE YOU WERE BLOWN AWAY BY THE EXPLOSIVE BLAST YES-TERDAY, FELL INTO THE RIVER UP-STREAM AND GOT WASHED DOWN HERE?
YES, THAT'S RIGHT. THEN... I MUST HAVE BEEN UNCON-SCIOUS FOR A WHOLE DAY...
DID YOU COME TO KALOS TO SIGHT-SEE?
B-BUT KALOS MUST BE VERY FAR FROM KANTO.
HOW DID YOU KNOW I WAS FROM KANTO?

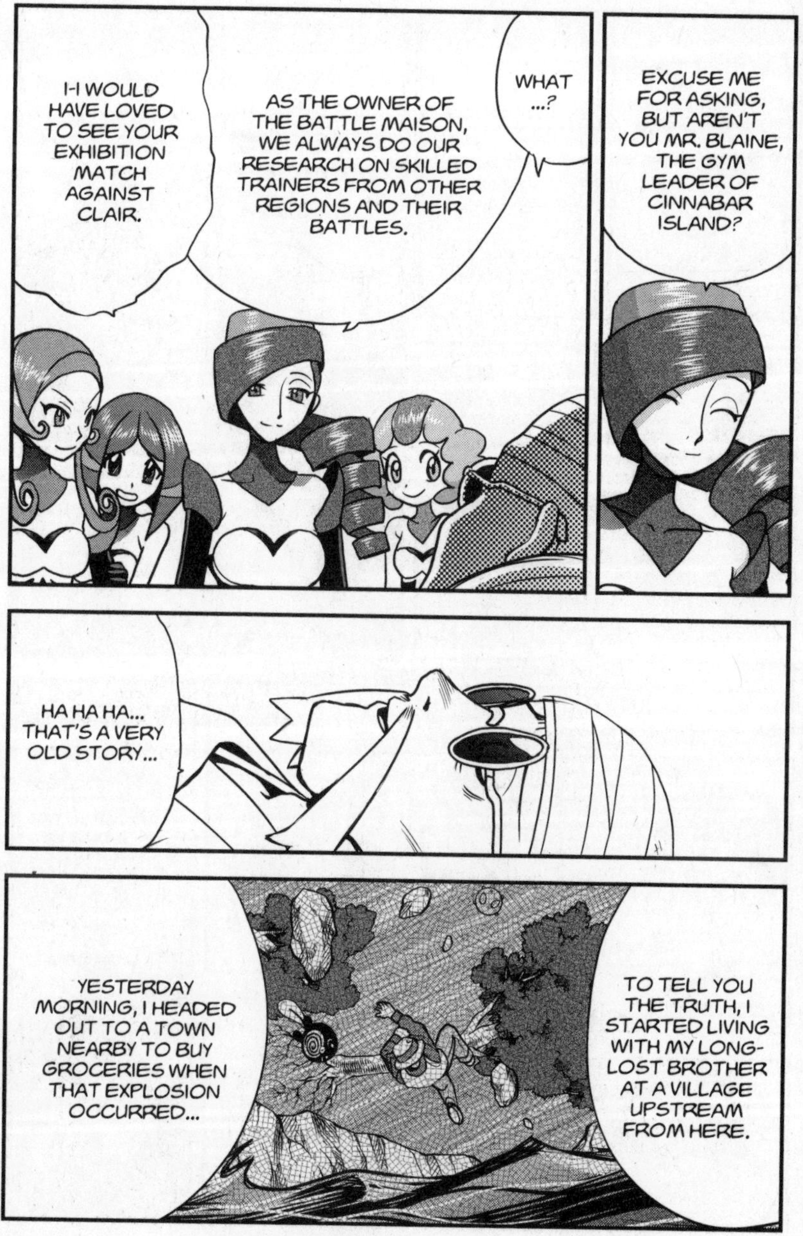
EXCUSE ME FOR ASKING, BUT AREN'T YOU MR. BLAINE, THE GYM LEADER OF CINNABAR ISLAND?
WHAT ...?
AS THE OWNER OF THE BATTLE MAISON, WE ALWAYS DO OUR RESEARCH ON SKILLED TRAINERS FROM OTHER REGIONS AND THEIR BATTLES.
I-I WOULD HAVE LOVED TO SEE YOUR EXHIBITION MATCH AGAINST CLAIR.
HA HA HA... THAT'S A VERY OLD STORY...
TO TELL YOU THE TRUTH, I STARTED LIVING WITH MY LONG-LOST BROTHER AT A VILLAGE UPSTREAM FROM HERE.
YESTERDAY MORNING, I HEADED OUT TO A TOWN NEARBY TO BUY GROCERIES WHEN THAT EXPLOSION OCCURRED...

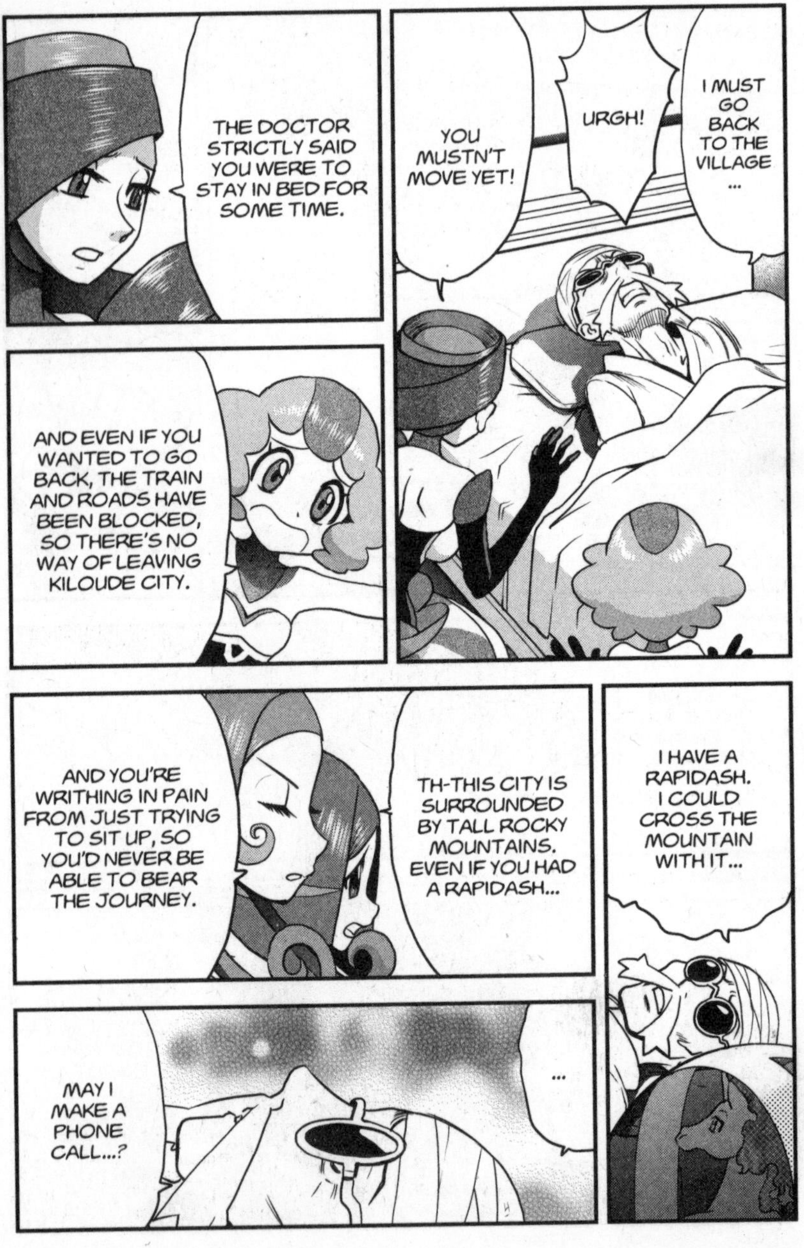
I MUST GO BACK TO THE VILLAGE ...
URGH!
YOU MUSTN'T MOVE YET!
THE DOCTOR STRICTLY SAID YOU WERE TO STAY IN BED FOR SOME TIME.
AND EVEN IF YOU WANTED TO GO BACK, THE TRAIN AND ROADS HAVE BEEN BLOCKED, SO THERE'S NO WAY OF LEAVING KILOUDE CITY.
I HAVE A RAPIDASH. I COULD CROSS THE MOUNTAIN WITH IT...
TH-THIS CITY IS SURROUNDED BY TALL ROCKY MOUNTAINS. EVEN IF YOU HAD A RAPIDASH...
AND YOU'RE WRITHING IN PAIN FROM JUST TRYING TO SIT UP, SO YOU'D NEVER BE ABLE TO BEAR THE JOURNEY.
...
MAY I MAKE A PHONE CALL...?

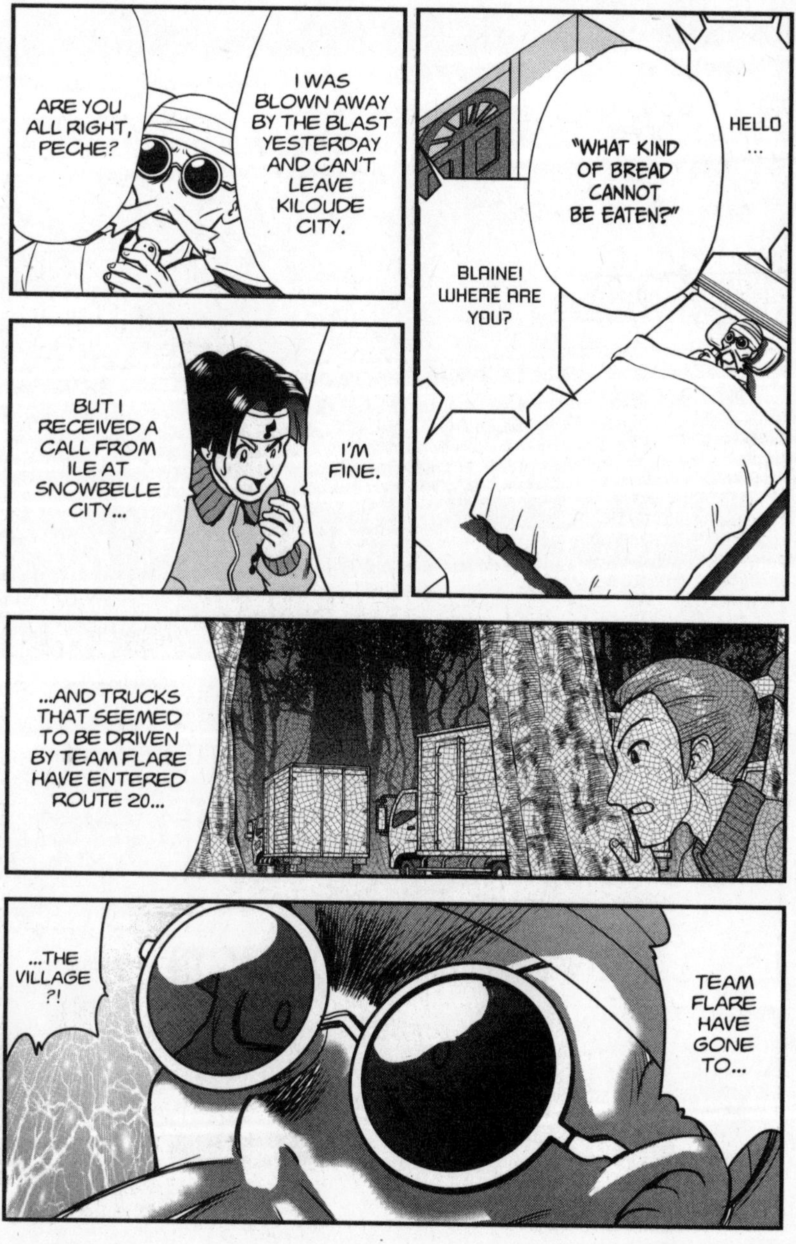
HELLO ...
"WHAT KIND OF BREAD CANNOT BE EATEN?"
BLAINE! WHERE ARE YOU?
I WAS BLOWN AWAY BY THE BLAST YESTERDAY AND CAN'T LEAVE KILOUDE CITY.
ARE YOU ALL RIGHT, PECHE?
I'M FINE.
BUT I RECEIVED A CALL FROM ILE AT SNOWBELLE CITY...
...AND TRUCKS THAT SEEMED TO BE DRIVEN BY TEAM FLARE HAVE ENTERED ROUTE 20...
TEAM FLARE HAVE GONE TO...
...THE VILLAGE ?!

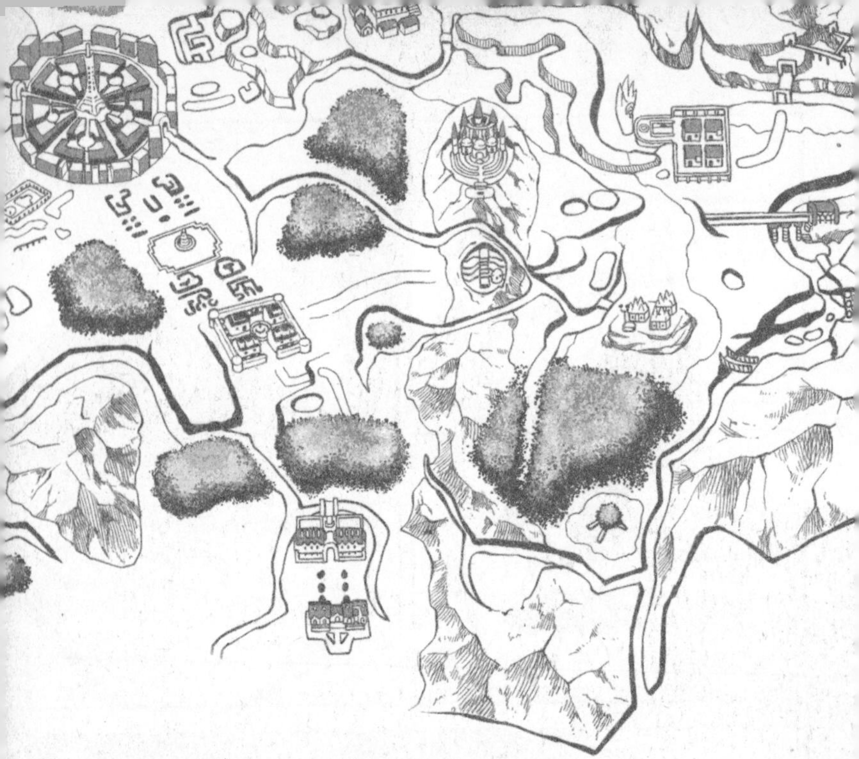

Current Location

Route 15
Brun Way

This path has become a popular hangout for the wild and directionless kids of Lumiose City.

▼

Lost Hotel

This once-famous hotel clings to the shade of its former glory after tragedy left it in ruins.

Adventure #35
Scizor Defends

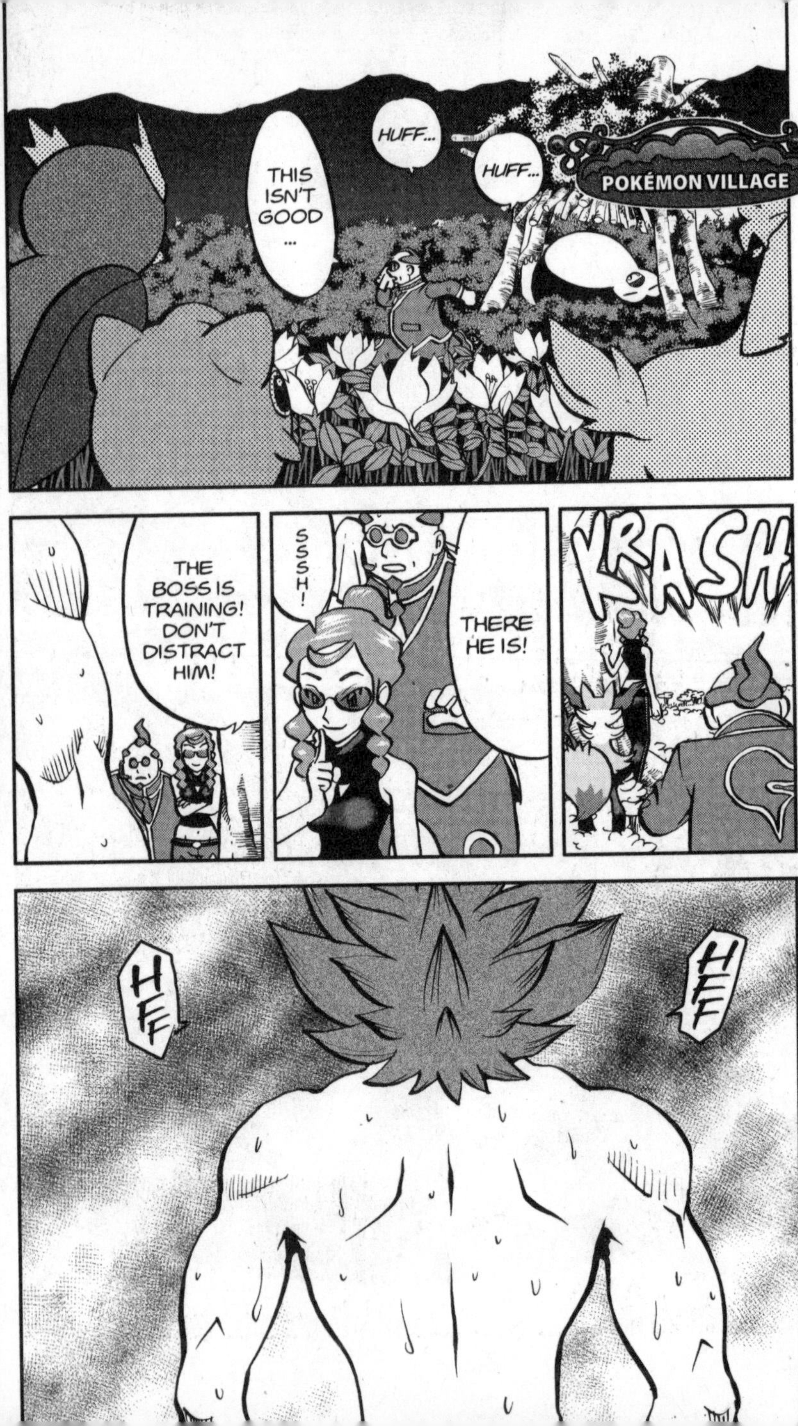
POKÉMON VILLAGE
HUFF...
HUFF...
THIS ISN'T GOOD ...
KRASH
THERE HE IS!
SSSH!
THE BOSS IS TRAINING! DON'T DISTRACT HIM!
HFF
HFF

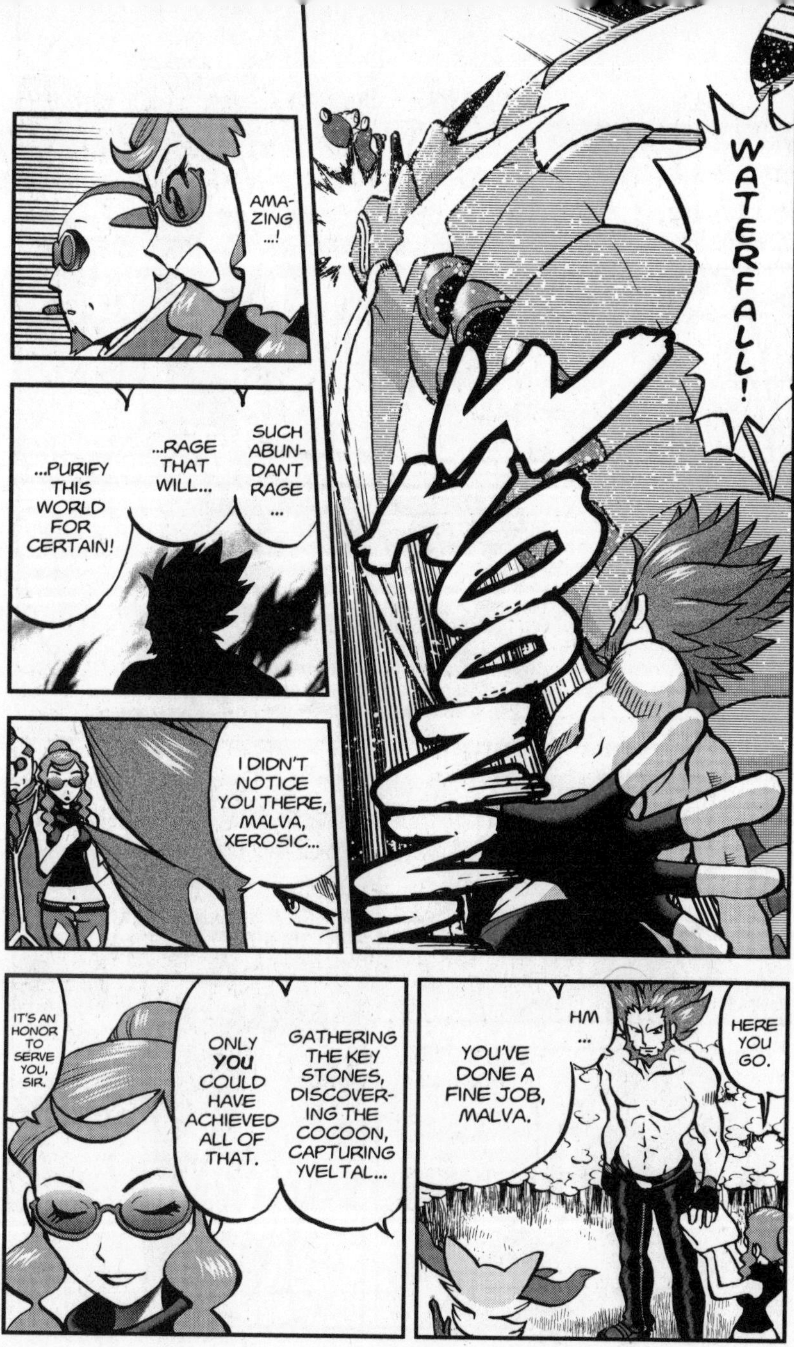
WATERFALL!
AMA-ZING ...!
SUCH ABUN-DANT RAGE ...
...RAGE THAT WILL...
...PURIFY THIS WORLD FOR CERTAIN!
I DIDN'T NOTICE YOU THERE, MALVA, XEROSIC...
HERE YOU GO.
HM ...
YOU'VE DONE A FINE JOB, MALVA.
GATHERING THE KEY STONES, DISCOVER-ING THE COCOON, CAPTURING YVELTAL...
ONLY **YOU** COULD HAVE ACHIEVED ALL OF THAT.
IT'S AN HONOR TO SERVE YOU, SIR.

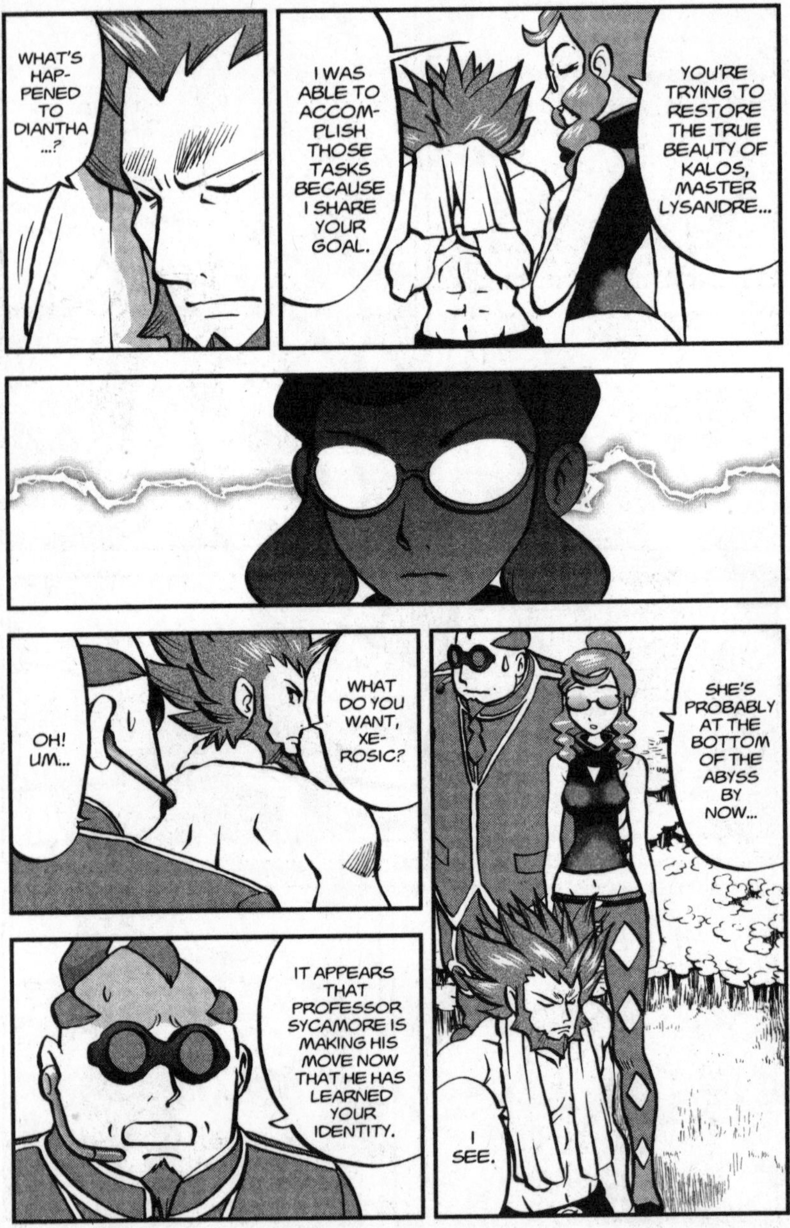
YOU'RE TRYING TO RESTORE THE TRUE BEAUTY OF KALOS, MASTER LYSANDRE...
I WAS ABLE TO ACCOMPLISH THOSE TASKS BECAUSE I SHARE YOUR GOAL.
WHAT'S HAPPENED TO DIANTHA...?
SHE'S PROBABLY AT THE BOTTOM OF THE ABYSS BY NOW...
I SEE.
WHAT DO YOU WANT, XEROSIC?
OH! UM...
IT APPEARS THAT PROFESSOR SYCAMORE IS MAKING HIS MOVE NOW THAT HE HAS LEARNED YOUR IDENTITY.

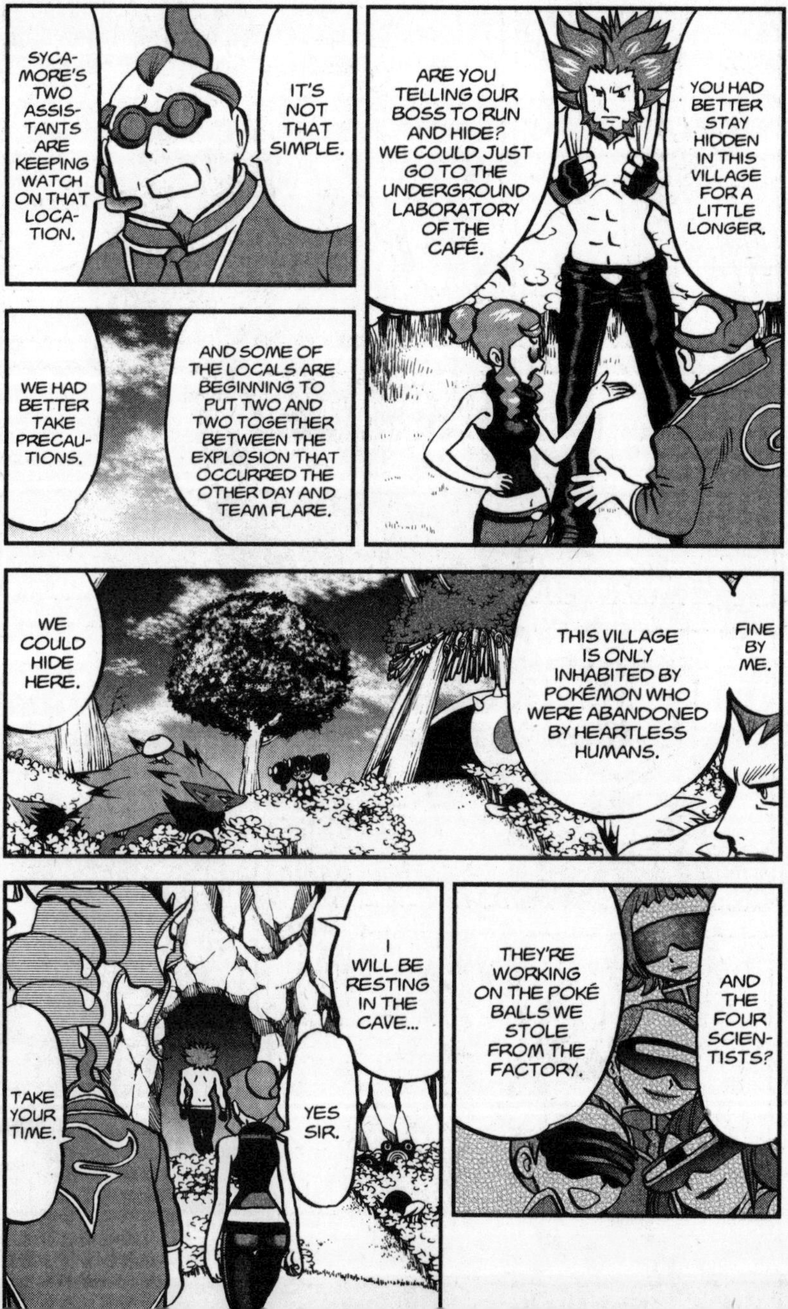
YOU HAD BETTER STAY HIDDEN IN THIS VILLAGE FOR A LITTLE LONGER.
ARE YOU TELLING OUR BOSS TO RUN AND HIDE? WE COULD JUST GO TO THE UNDERGROUND LABORATORY OF THE CAFÉ.
IT'S NOT THAT SIMPLE.
SYCAMORE'S TWO ASSISTANTS ARE KEEPING WATCH ON THAT LOCATION.
AND SOME OF THE LOCALS ARE BEGINNING TO PUT TWO AND TWO TOGETHER BETWEEN THE EXPLOSION THAT OCCURRED THE OTHER DAY AND TEAM FLARE.
WE HAD BETTER TAKE PRECAUTIONS.
FINE BY ME.
THIS VILLAGE IS ONLY INHABITED BY POKÉMON WHO WERE ABANDONED BY HEARTLESS HUMANS.
WE COULD HIDE HERE.
AND THE FOUR SCIENTISTS?
THEY'RE WORKING ON THE POKÉ BALLS WE STOLE FROM THE FACTORY.
I WILL BE RESTING IN THE CAVE...
YES SIR.
TAKE YOUR TIME.

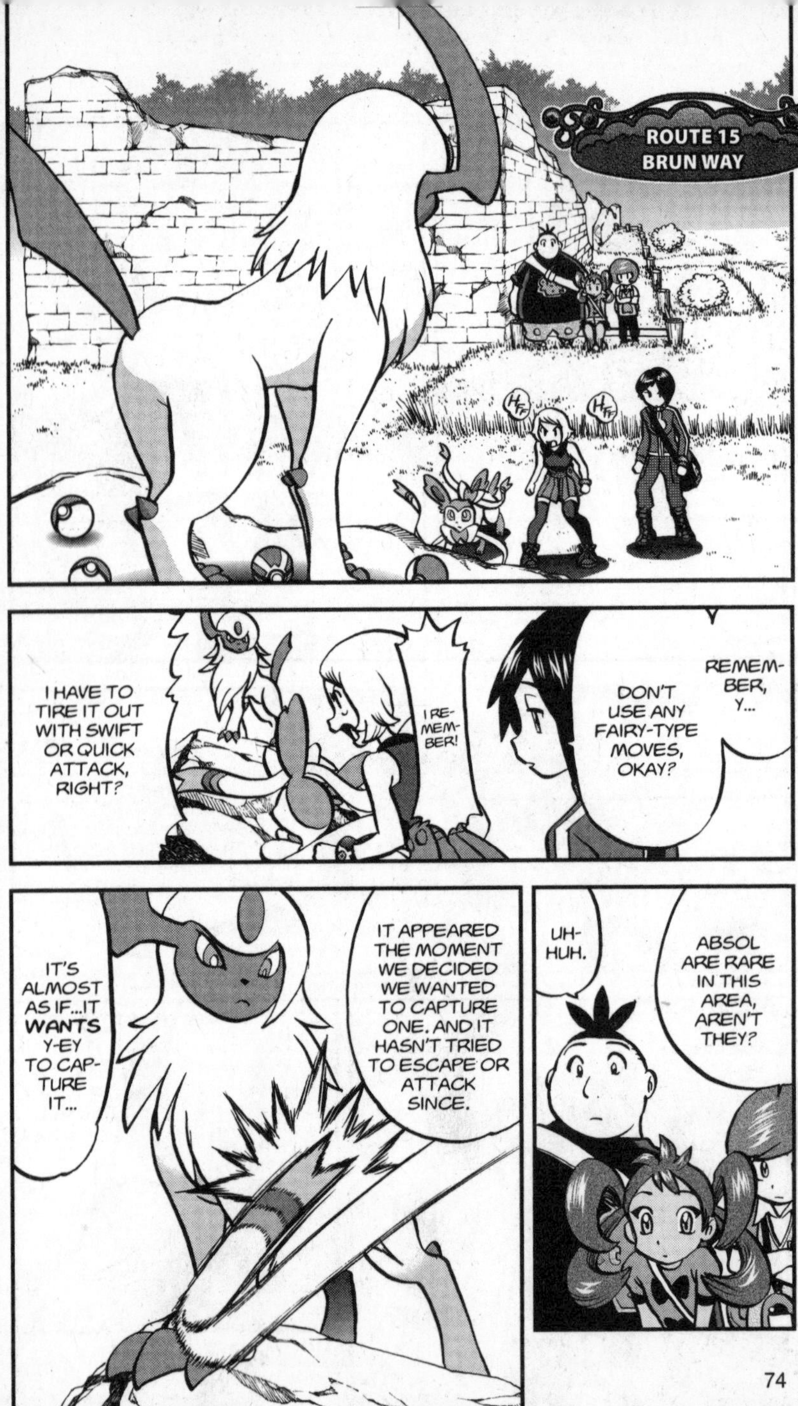
ROUTE 15
BRUN WAY
HFF
HFF
REMEMBER, Y...
DON'T USE ANY FAIRY-TYPE MOVES, OKAY?
I REMEMBER!
I HAVE TO TIRE IT OUT WITH SWIFT OR QUICK ATTACK, RIGHT?
ABSOL ARE RARE IN THIS AREA, AREN'T THEY?
UH-HUH.
IT APPEARED THE MOMENT WE DECIDED WE WANTED TO CAPTURE ONE. AND IT HASN'T TRIED TO ESCAPE OR ATTACK SINCE.
IT'S ALMOST AS IF...IT **WANTS** Y-EY TO CAPTURE IT...

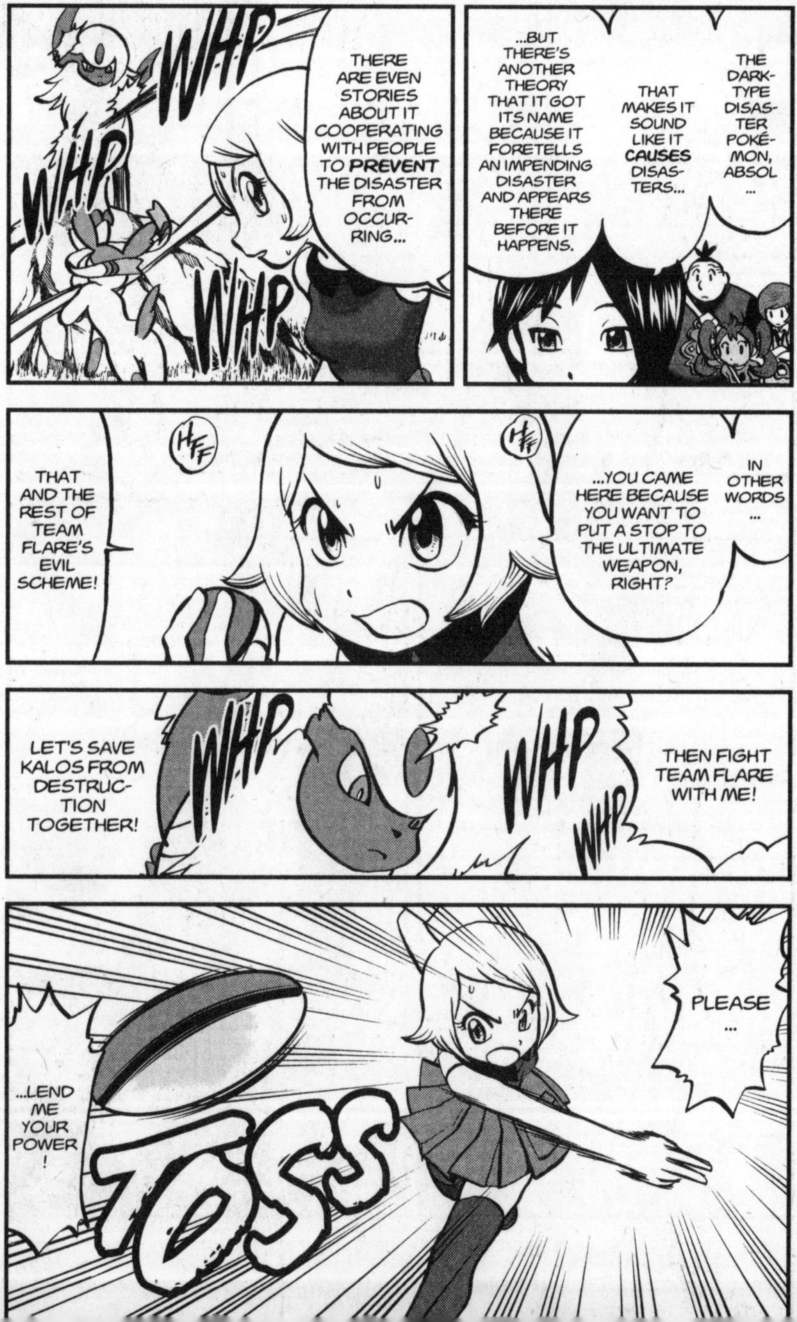
THE DARK-TYPE DISASTER POKÉMON, ABSOL...
THAT MAKES IT SOUND LIKE IT **CAUSES** DISASTERS...
...BUT THERE'S ANOTHER THEORY THAT IT GOT ITS NAME BECAUSE IT FORETELLS AN IMPENDING DISASTER AND APPEARS THERE BEFORE IT HAPPENS.
WHP
WHP
THERE ARE EVEN STORIES ABOUT IT COOPERATING WITH PEOPLE TO **PREVENT** THE DISASTER FROM OCCURRING...
WHP
IN OTHER WORDS...
HFF
...YOU CAME HERE BECAUSE YOU WANT TO PUT A STOP TO THE ULTIMATE WEAPON, RIGHT?
HFF
THAT AND THE REST OF TEAM FLARE'S EVIL SCHEME!
THEN FIGHT TEAM FLARE WITH ME!
WHP
WHP
WHP
LET'S SAVE KALOS FROM DESTRUCTION TOGETHER!
PLEASE...
TOSS
...LEND ME YOUR POWER!

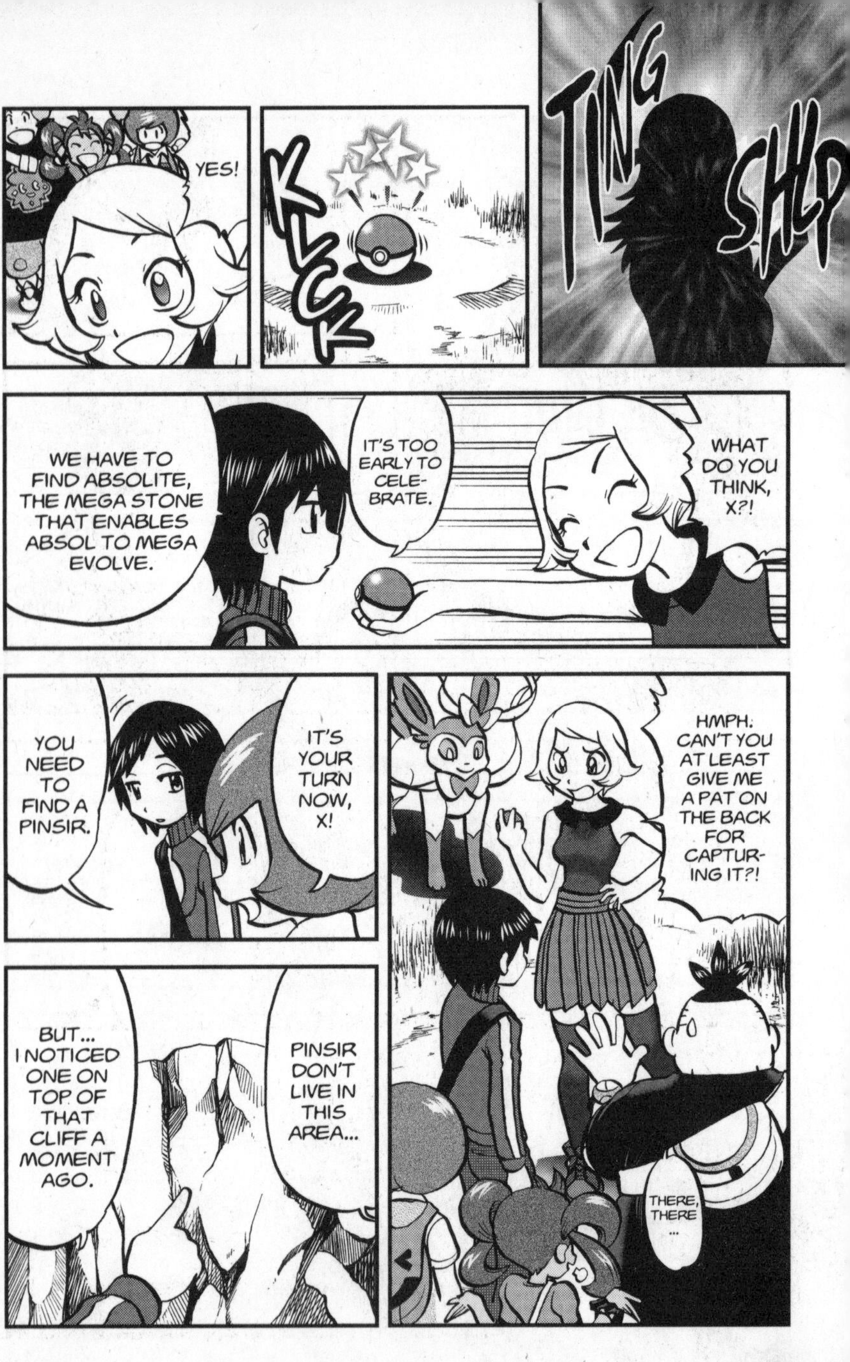
TING
SHLP
KLLCK
YES!
WHAT DO YOU THINK, X?!
IT'S TOO EARLY TO CELE-BRATE.
WE HAVE TO FIND ABSOLITE, THE MEGA STONE THAT ENABLES ABSOL TO MEGA EVOLVE.
HMPH: CAN'T YOU AT LEAST GIVE ME A PAT ON THE BACK FOR CAPTUR-ING IT?!
THERE, THERE ...
IT'S YOUR TURN NOW, X!
YOU NEED TO FIND A PINSIR.
PINSIR DON'T LIVE IN THIS AREA...
BUT... I NOTICED ONE ON TOP OF THAT CLIFF A MOMENT AGO.

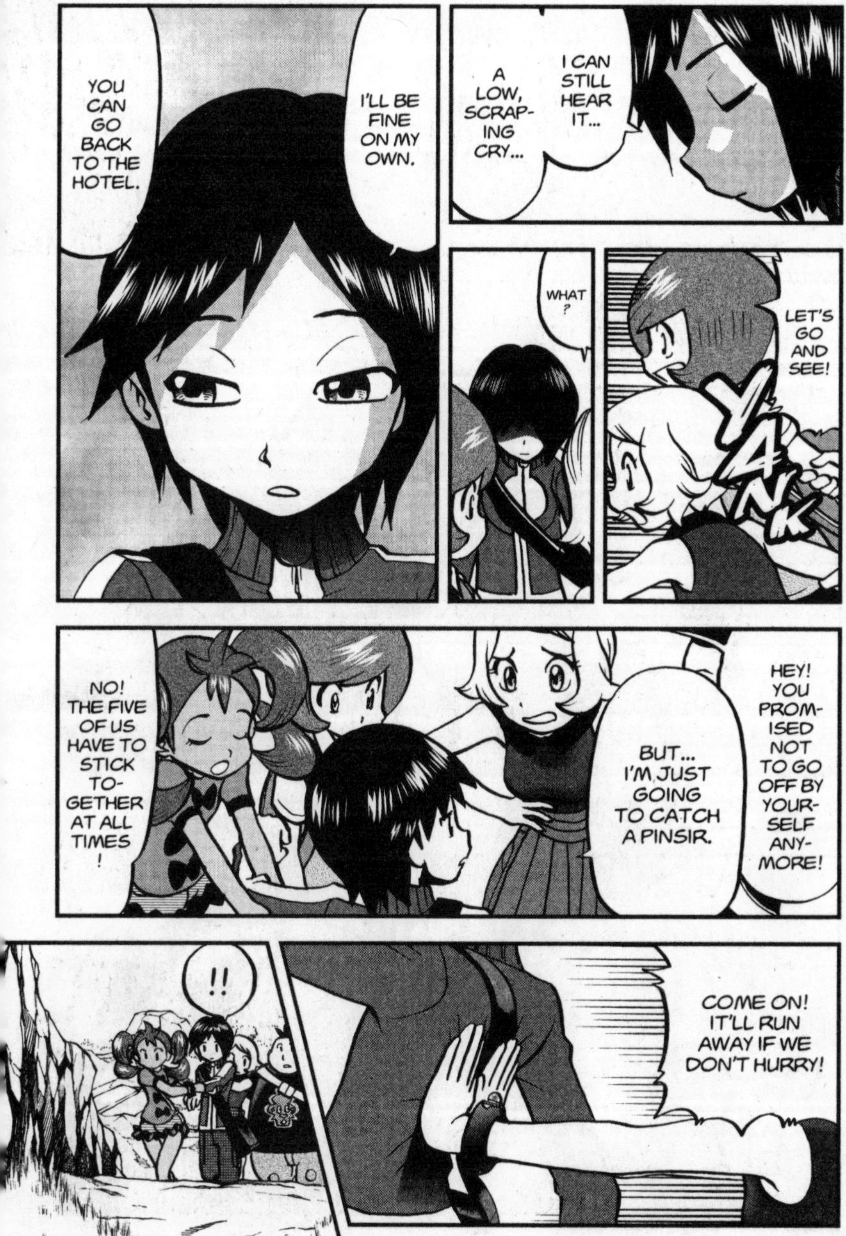

I CAN STILL HEAR IT...
A LOW, SCRAPING CRY...
LET'S GO AND SEE!
YANK
WHAT?
I'LL BE FINE ON MY OWN.
YOU CAN GO BACK TO THE HOTEL.
HEY! YOU PROMISED NOT TO GO OFF BY YOURSELF ANYMORE!
BUT... I'M JUST GOING TO CATCH A PINSIR.
NO! THE FIVE OF US HAVE TO STICK TOGETHER AT ALL TIMES!
COME ON! IT'LL RUN AWAY IF WE DON'T HURRY!
!!

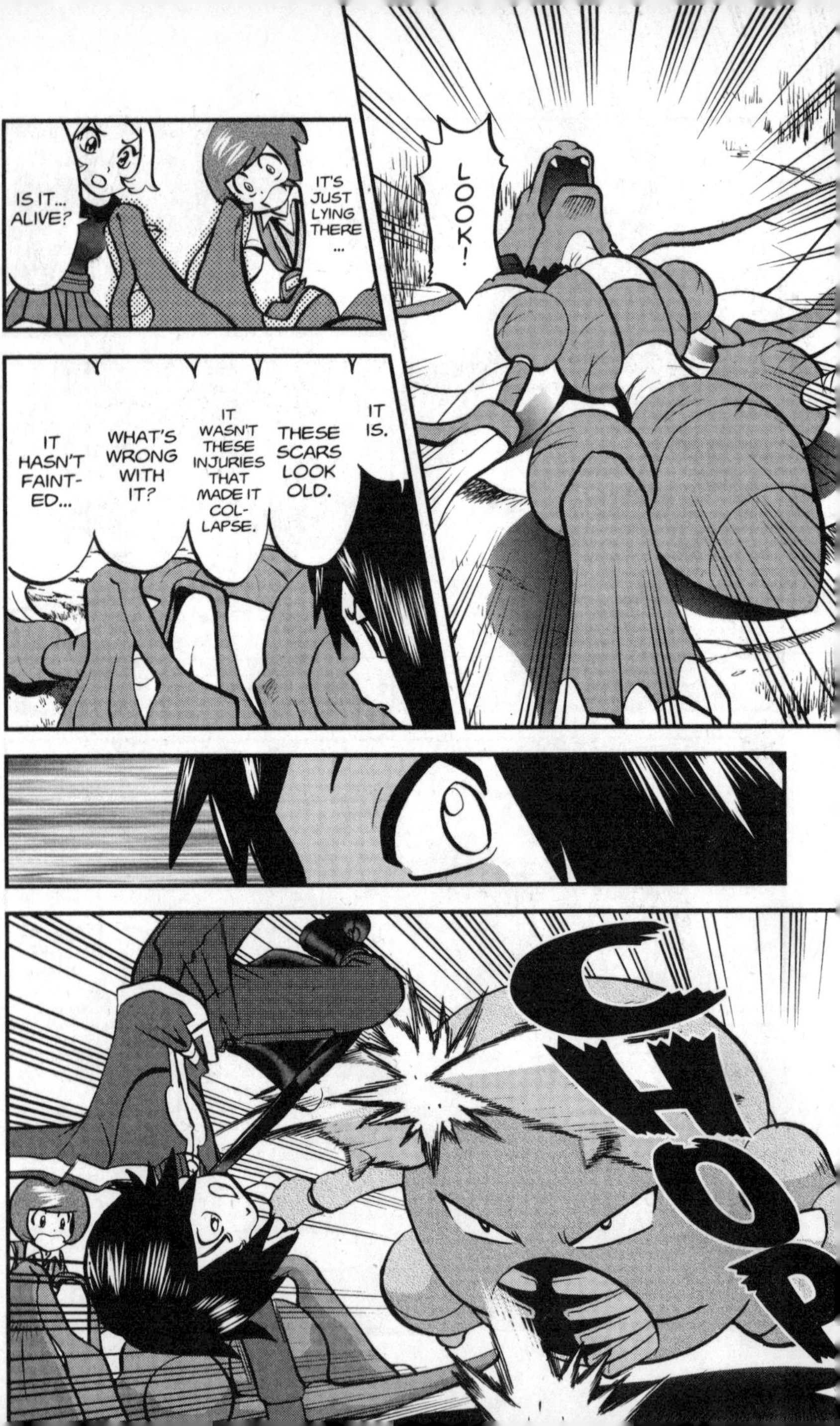
LOOK!
IT'S JUST LYING THERE ...
IS IT... ALIVE?
IT IS.
THESE SCARS LOOK OLD.
IT WASN'T THESE INJURIES THAT MADE IT COLLAPSE.
WHAT'S WRONG WITH IT?
IT HASN'T FAINTED...
CHOP

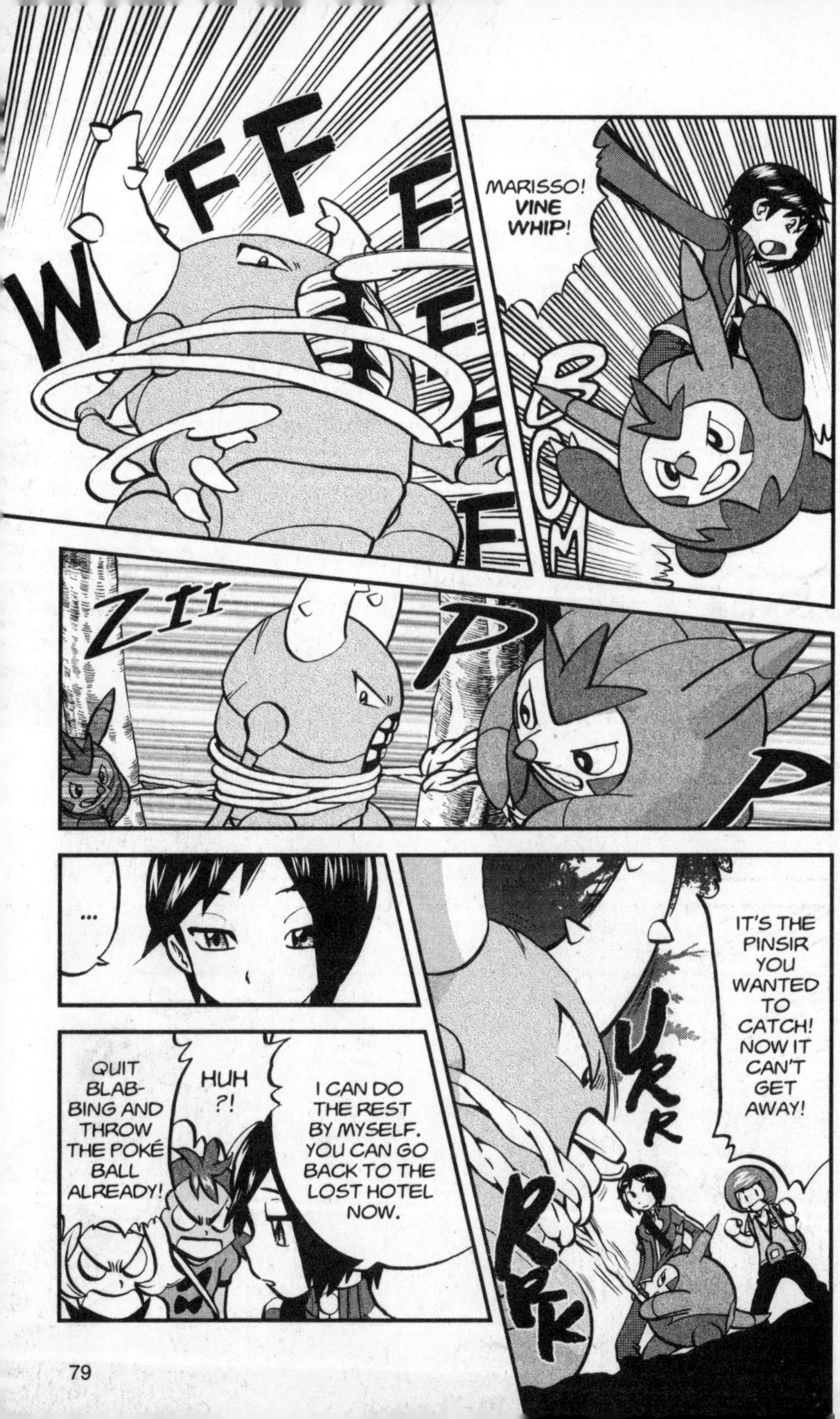
MARISSO! VINE WHIP!
BOOM
WFFF
ZIIPP
IT'S THE PINSIR YOU WANTED TO CATCH! NOW IT CAN'T GET AWAY!
URRKK
...
I CAN DO THE REST BY MYSELF. YOU CAN GO BACK TO THE LOST HOTEL NOW.
HUH?!
QUIT BLAB-BING AND THROW THE POKÉ BALL ALREADY!

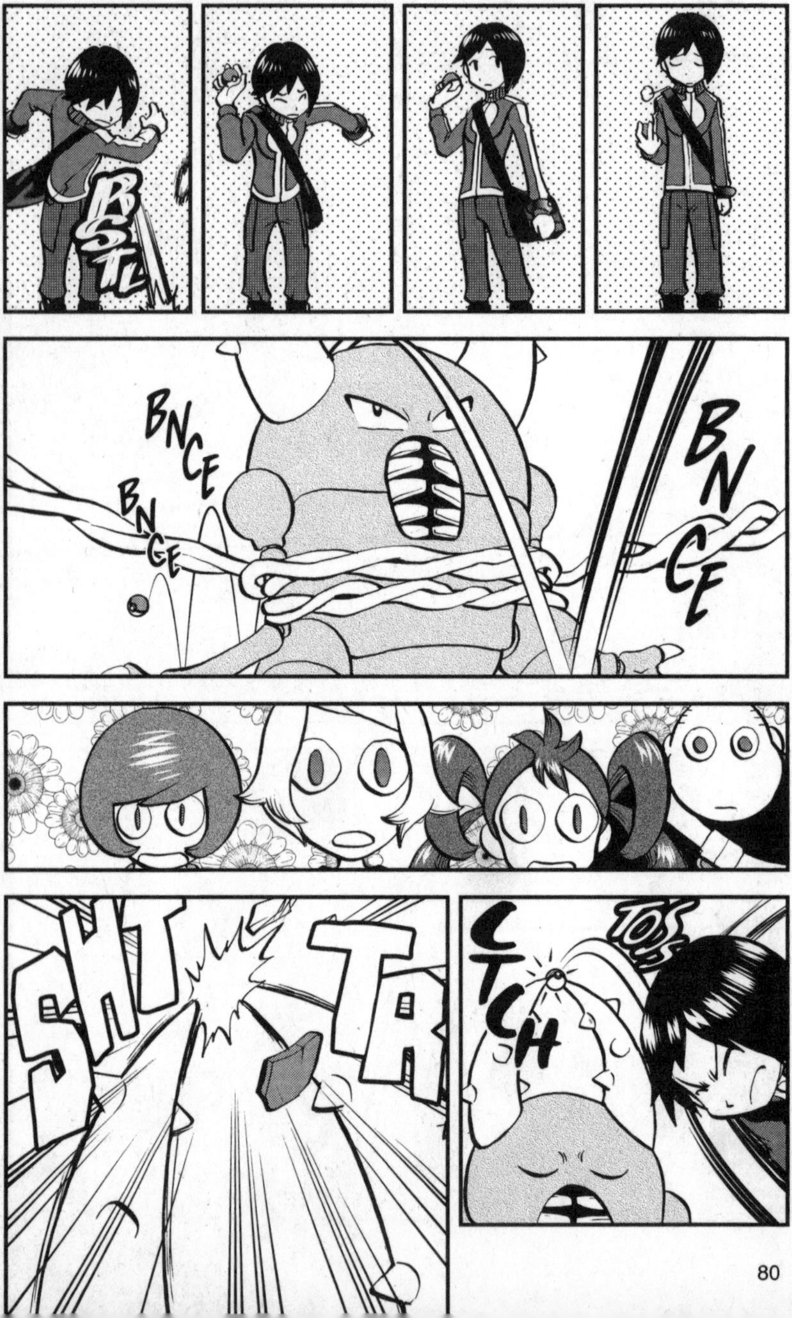
RSTL
BNCE
BNCE
BNCE
TOSS
CTCH
SHT
TA

?

THE WAY YOU THROW IT IS ONE THING, BUT YOU'RE NEVER GONNA HIT THAT POKÉMON IF YOU KEEP CLOSING YOUR EYES.

COME TO THINK OF IT... WE'VE NEVER SEEN X CATCH A POKÉMON, HAVE WE?

DON'T TELL ME HE SUCKS AT **CATCH-ING** POKÉ-MON!

WHY IS HE THROWING THE BALL SO WEIRDLY?

WHAT'S HE DOING?

FLAP

WHO'S THIS GUY?

I'M SORRY... NOT ONLY WAS I NO HELP TO YOU, BUT I CAUSED YOU WORRY TOO...

YOU'RE ALL RIGHT?!

DIAN-THA!

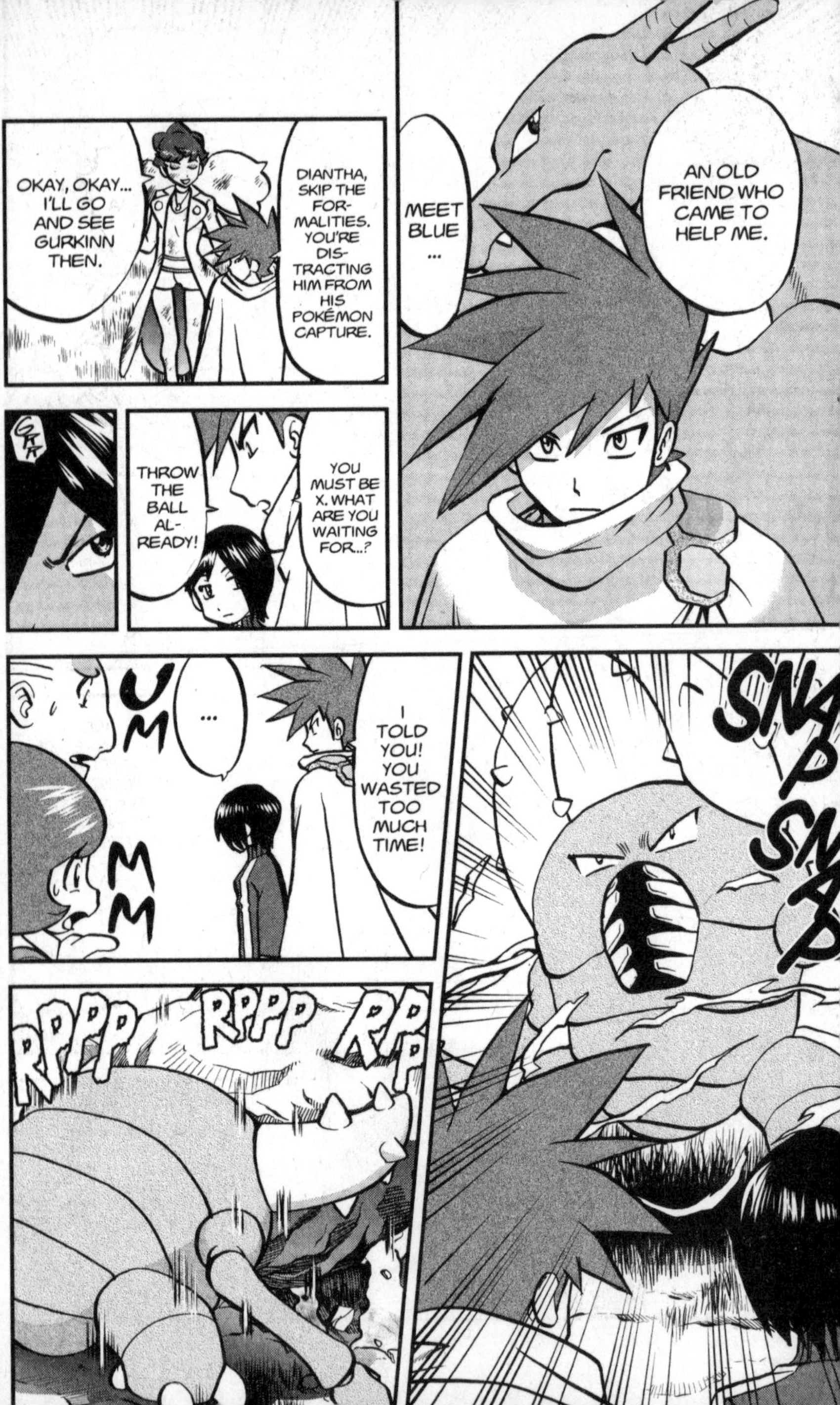
AN OLD FRIEND WHO CAME TO HELP ME.
MEET BLUE ...
DIANTHA, SKIP THE FORMALITIES. YOU'RE DISTRACTING HIM FROM HIS POKÉMON CAPTURE.
OKAY, OKAY... I'LL GO AND SEE GURKINN THEN.
YOU MUST BE X. WHAT ARE YOU WAITING FOR...?
THROW THE BALL ALREADY!
GRR
SNAP SNAP
I TOLD YOU! YOU WASTED TOO MUCH TIME!
...
UMMMM
RPPP RPPP RPP

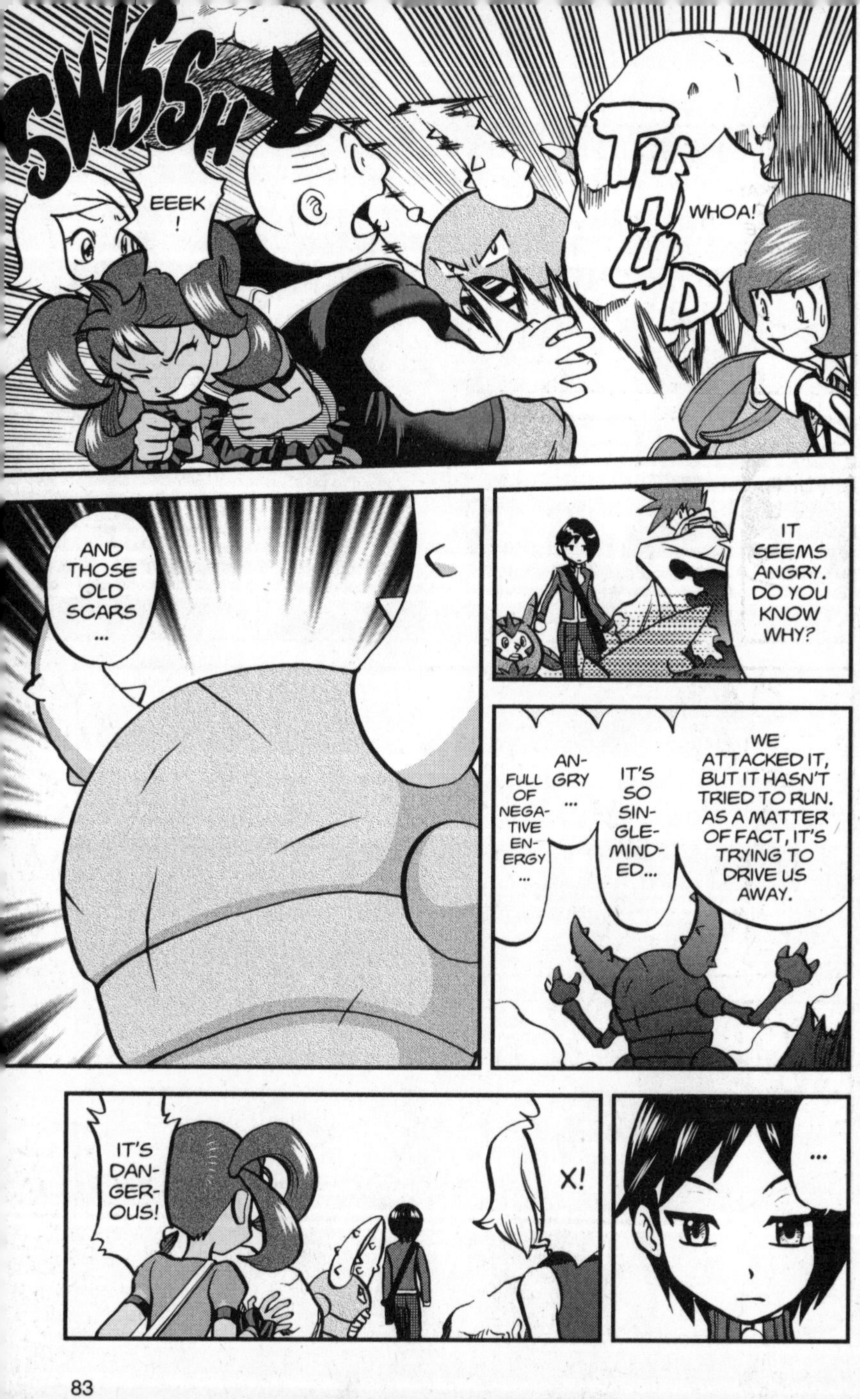
THUD
WHOA!
SWSSH
EEEK!
IT SEEMS ANGRY. DO YOU KNOW WHY?
WE ATTACKED IT, BUT IT HASN'T TRIED TO RUN. AS A MATTER OF FACT, IT'S TRYING TO DRIVE US AWAY.
IT'S SO SINGLE-MINDED...
ANGRY...
FULL OF NEGATIVE ENERGY...
AND THOSE OLD SCARS...
...
X!
IT'S DANGEROUS!

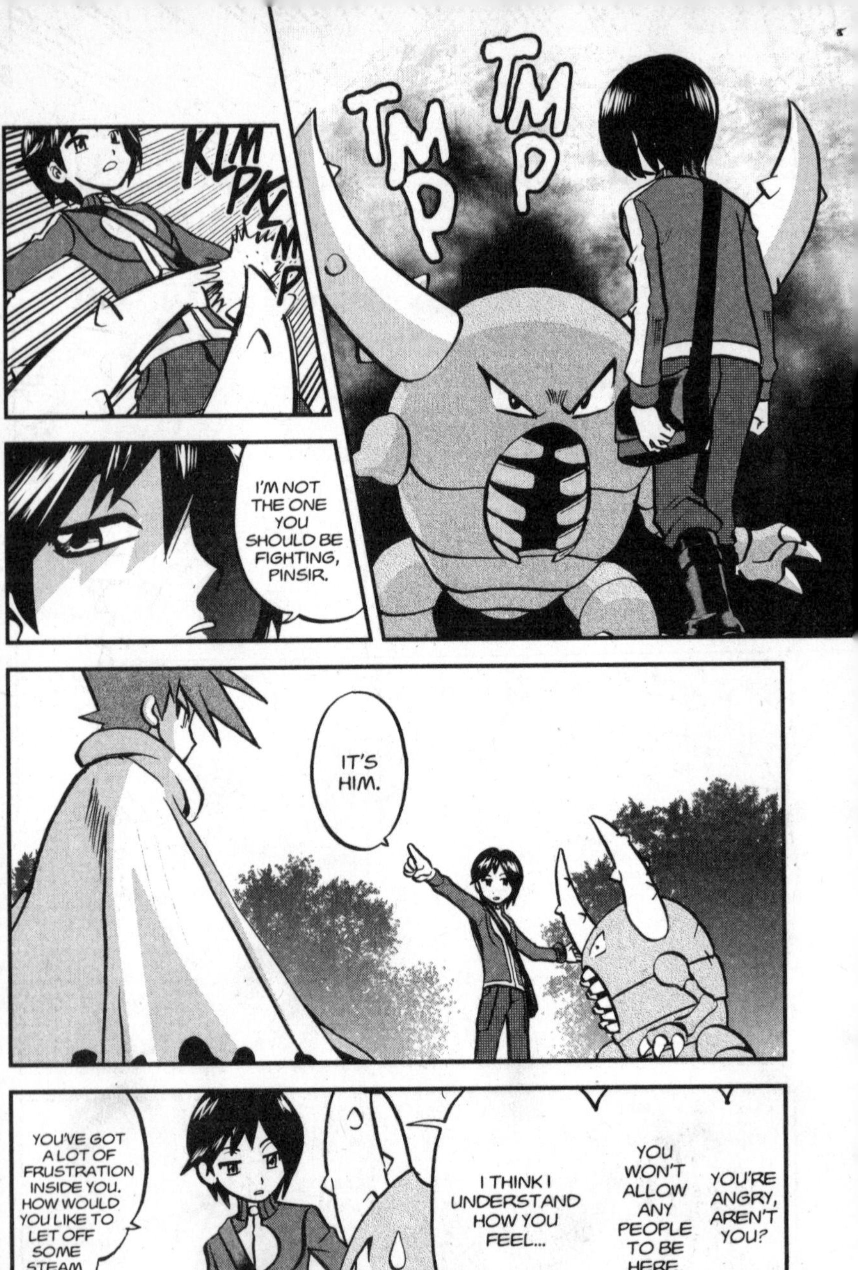
TMP
TMP
KLMP
KLMP
I'M NOT THE ONE YOU SHOULD BE FIGHTING, PINSIR.
IT'S HIM.
YOU'RE ANGRY, AREN'T YOU?
YOU WON'T ALLOW ANY PEOPLE TO BE HERE.
I THINK I UNDERSTAND HOW YOU FEEL...
YOU'VE GOT A LOT OF FRUSTRATION INSIDE YOU. HOW WOULD YOU LIKE TO LET OFF SOME STEAM?

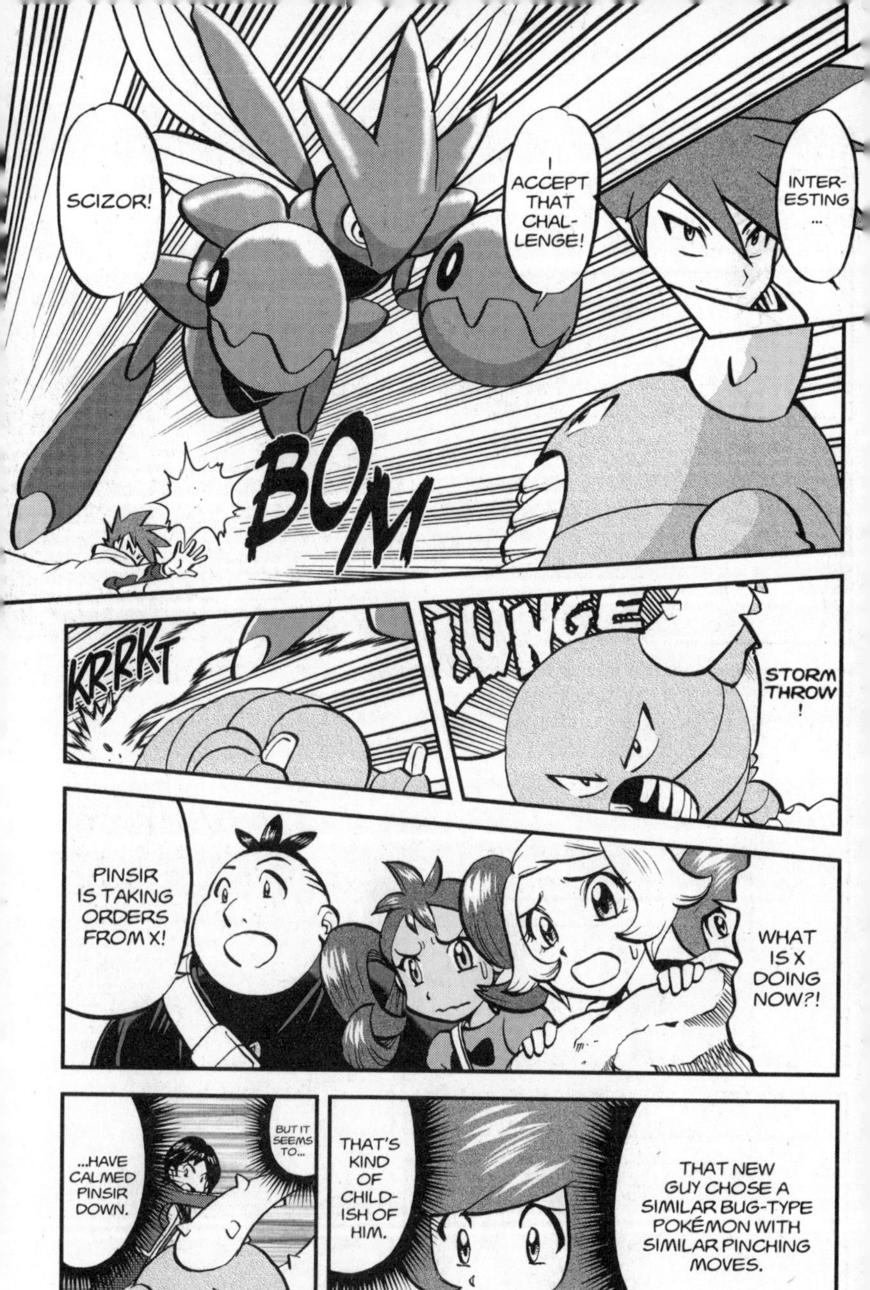
INTERESTING...
I ACCEPT THAT CHALLENGE!
SCIZOR!
BOM
LUNGE
STORM THROW!
KRRKT
WHAT IS X DOING NOW?!
PINSIR IS TAKING ORDERS FROM X!
THAT NEW GUY CHOSE A SIMILAR BUG-TYPE POKÉMON WITH SIMILAR PINCHING MOVES.
THAT'S KIND OF CHILDISH OF HIM.
BUT IT SEEMS TO...
...HAVE CALMED PINSIR DOWN.

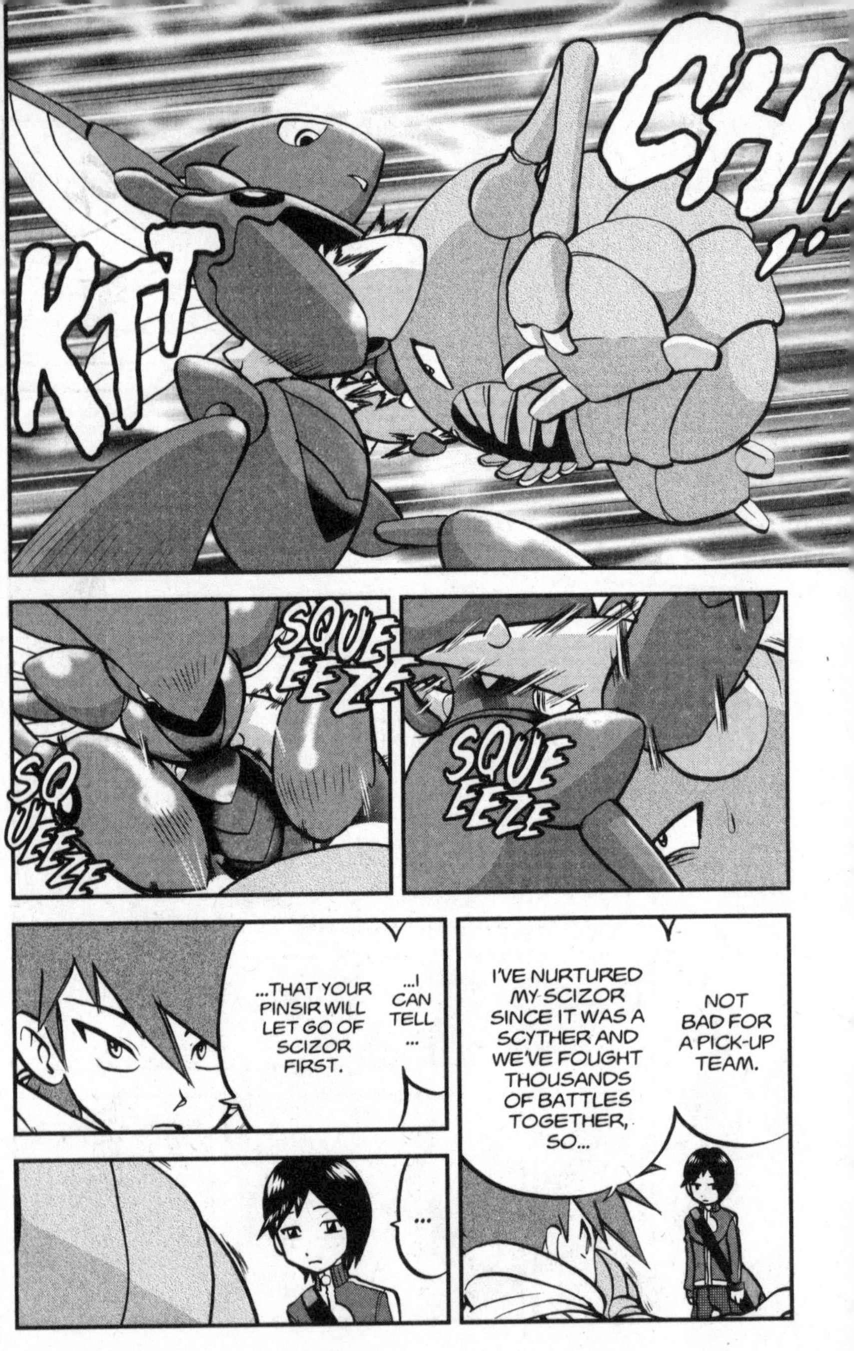
CH!!
KTT
SQUE EEZE
SQUE EEZE
SQ UEEZE
NOT BAD FOR A PICK-UP TEAM.
I'VE NURTURED MY SCIZOR SINCE IT WAS A SCYTHER AND WE'VE FOUGHT THOUSANDS OF BATTLES TOGETHER, SO...
...I CAN TELL...
...THAT YOUR PINSIR WILL LET GO OF SCIZOR FIRST.
...

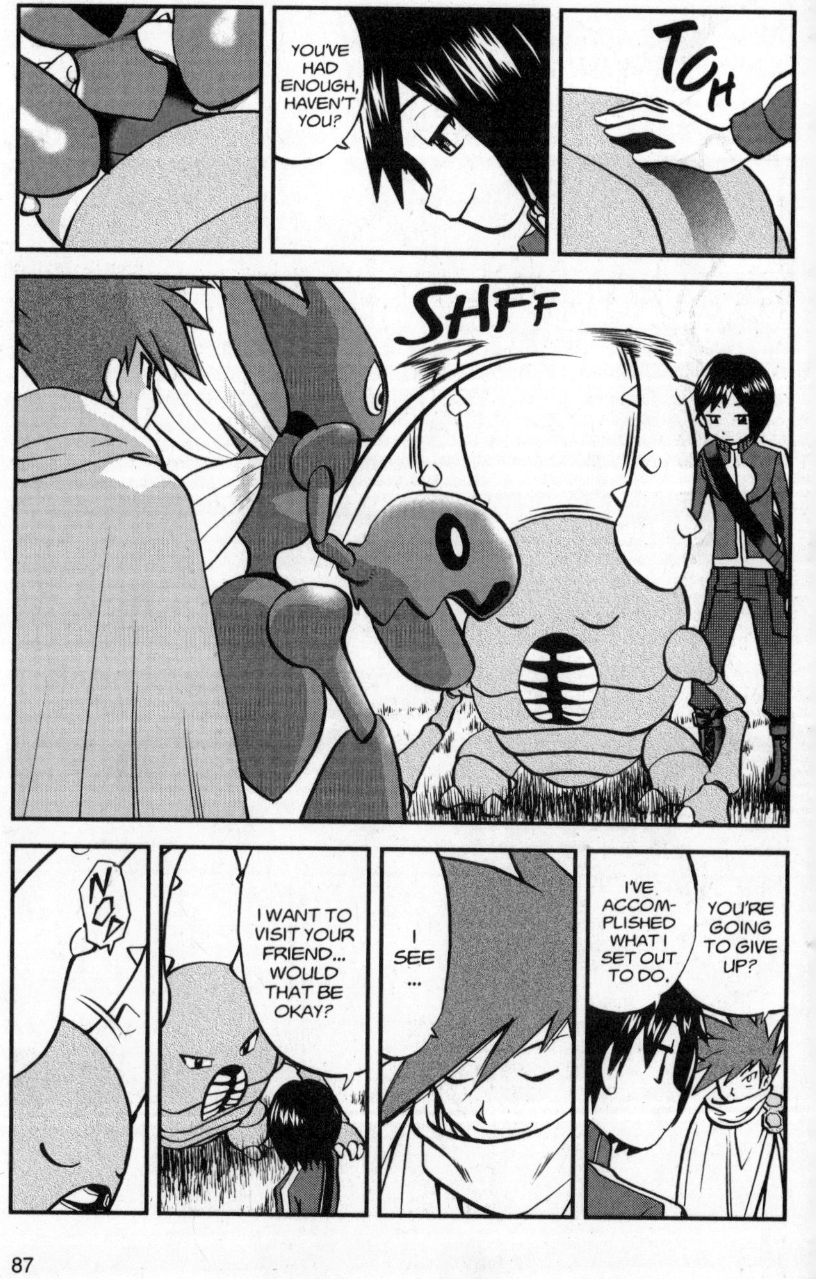
TOH
YOU'VE HAD ENOUGH, HAVEN'T YOU?
SHFF
YOU'RE GOING TO GIVE UP?
I'VE ACCOMPLISHED WHAT I SET OUT TO DO.
I SEE ...
I WANT TO VISIT YOUR FRIEND... WOULD THAT BE OKAY?
NOD

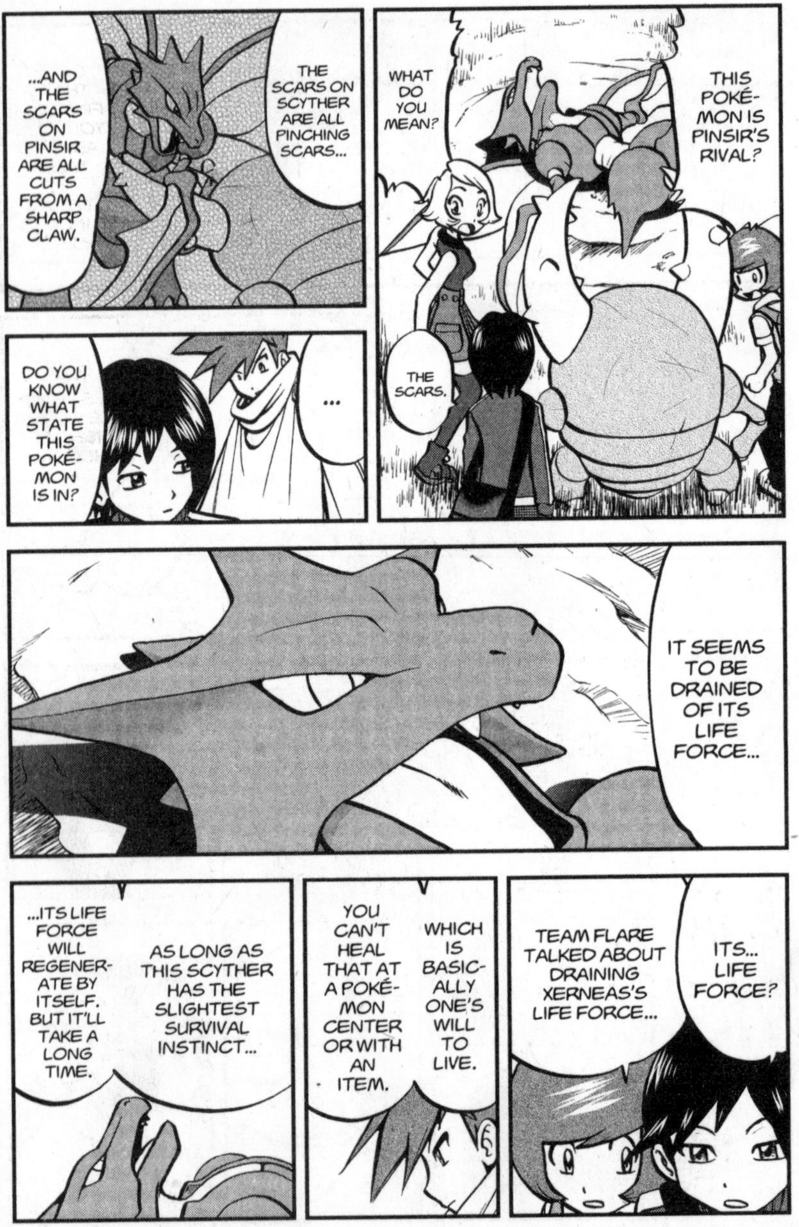
THIS POKÉMON IS PINSIR'S RIVAL?
WHAT DO YOU MEAN?
THE SCARS.
THE SCARS ON SCYTHER ARE ALL PINCHING SCARS...
...AND THE SCARS ON PINSIR ARE ALL CUTS FROM A SHARP CLAW.
...
DO YOU KNOW WHAT STATE THIS POKÉMON IS IN?
IT SEEMS TO BE DRAINED OF ITS LIFE FORCE...
ITS... LIFE FORCE?
TEAM FLARE TALKED ABOUT DRAINING XERNEAS'S LIFE FORCE...
WHICH IS BASICALLY ONE'S WILL TO LIVE.
YOU CAN'T HEAL THAT AT A POKÉMON CENTER OR WITH AN ITEM.
AS LONG AS THIS SCYTHER HAS THE SLIGHTEST SURVIVAL INSTINCT...
...ITS LIFE FORCE WILL REGENERATE BY ITSELF. BUT IT'LL TAKE A LONG TIME.

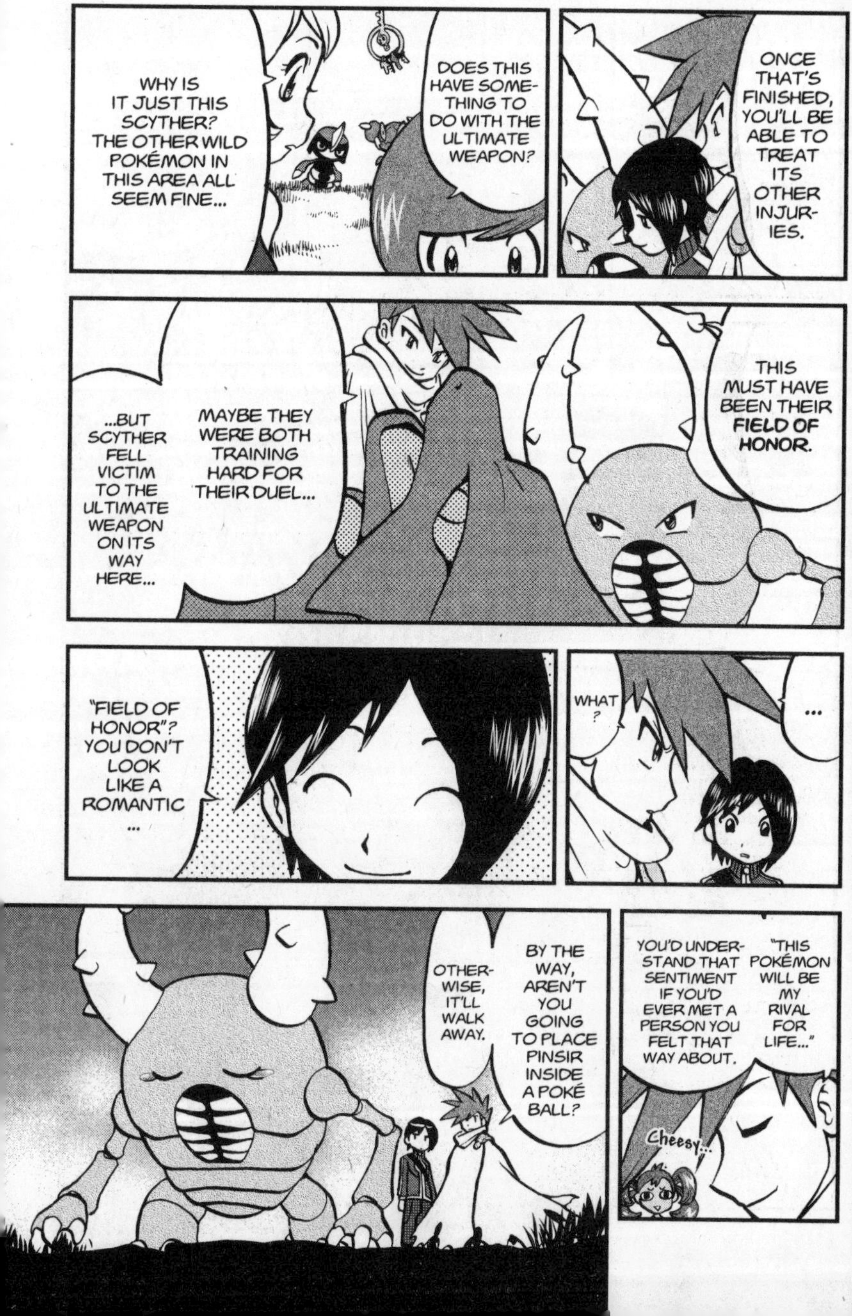
ONCE THAT'S FINISHED, YOU'LL BE ABLE TO TREAT ITS OTHER INJURIES.
DOES THIS HAVE SOMETHING TO DO WITH THE ULTIMATE WEAPON?
WHY IS IT JUST THIS SCYTHER? THE OTHER WILD POKéMON IN THIS AREA ALL SEEM FINE...
THIS MUST HAVE BEEN THEIR **FIELD OF HONOR.**
MAYBE THEY WERE BOTH TRAINING HARD FOR THEIR DUEL...
...BUT SCYTHER FELL VICTIM TO THE ULTIMATE WEAPON ON ITS WAY HERE...
...
WHAT?
"FIELD OF HONOR"? YOU DON'T LOOK LIKE A ROMANTIC...
"THIS POKéMON WILL BE MY RIVAL FOR LIFE..."
YOU'D UNDERSTAND THAT SENTIMENT IF YOU'D EVER MET A PERSON YOU FELT THAT WAY ABOUT.
Cheesy...
BY THE WAY, AREN'T YOU GOING TO PLACE PINSIR INSIDE A POKé BALL?
OTHERWISE, IT'LL WALK AWAY.

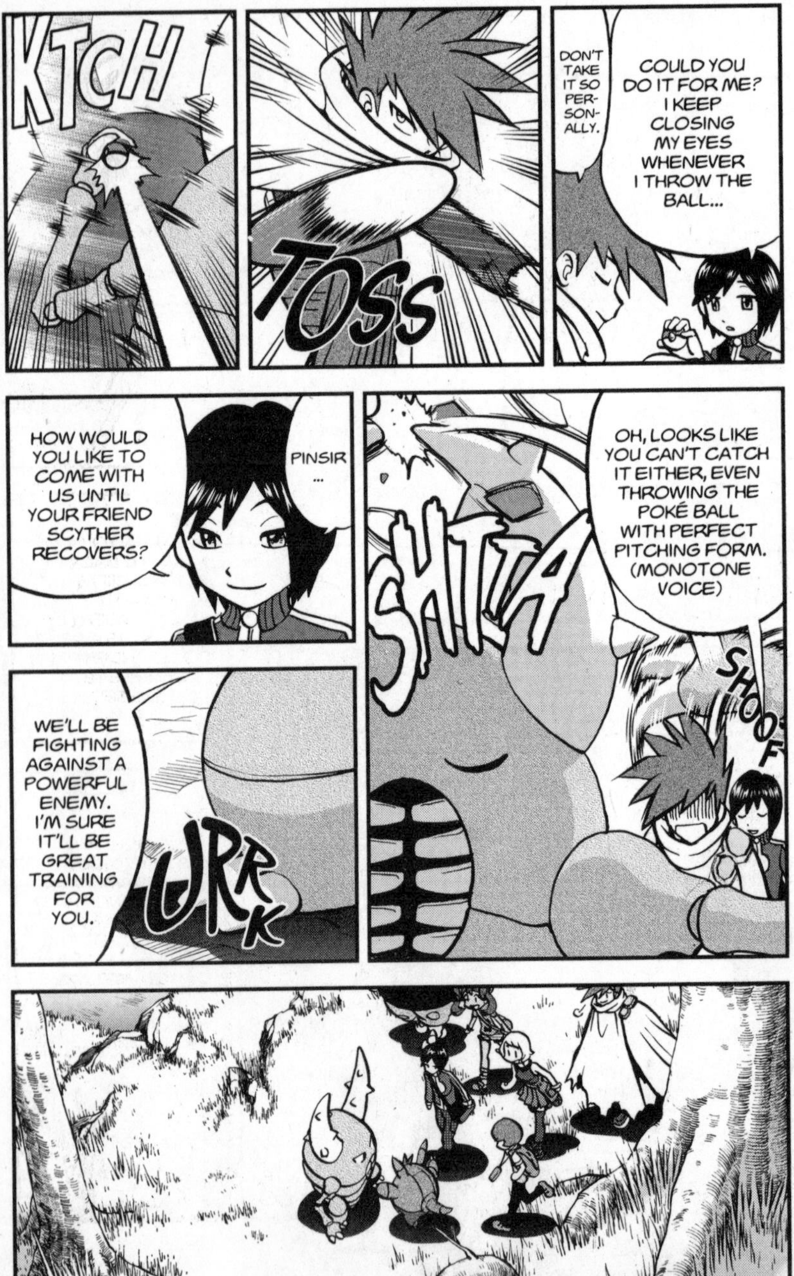
COULD YOU DO IT FOR ME? I KEEP CLOSING MY EYES WHENEVER I THROW THE BALL...
DON'T TAKE IT SO PER-SON-ALLY.
TOSS
KTCH
OH, LOOKS LIKE YOU CAN'T CATCH IT EITHER, EVEN THROWING THE POKÉ BALL WITH PERFECT PITCHING FORM. (MONOTONE VOICE)
SHTTA
SHOOF
PINSIR ...
HOW WOULD YOU LIKE TO COME WITH US UNTIL YOUR FRIEND SCYTHER RECOVERS?
WE'LL BE FIGHTING AGAINST A POWERFUL ENEMY. I'M SURE IT'LL BE GREAT TRAINING FOR YOU.
URRK

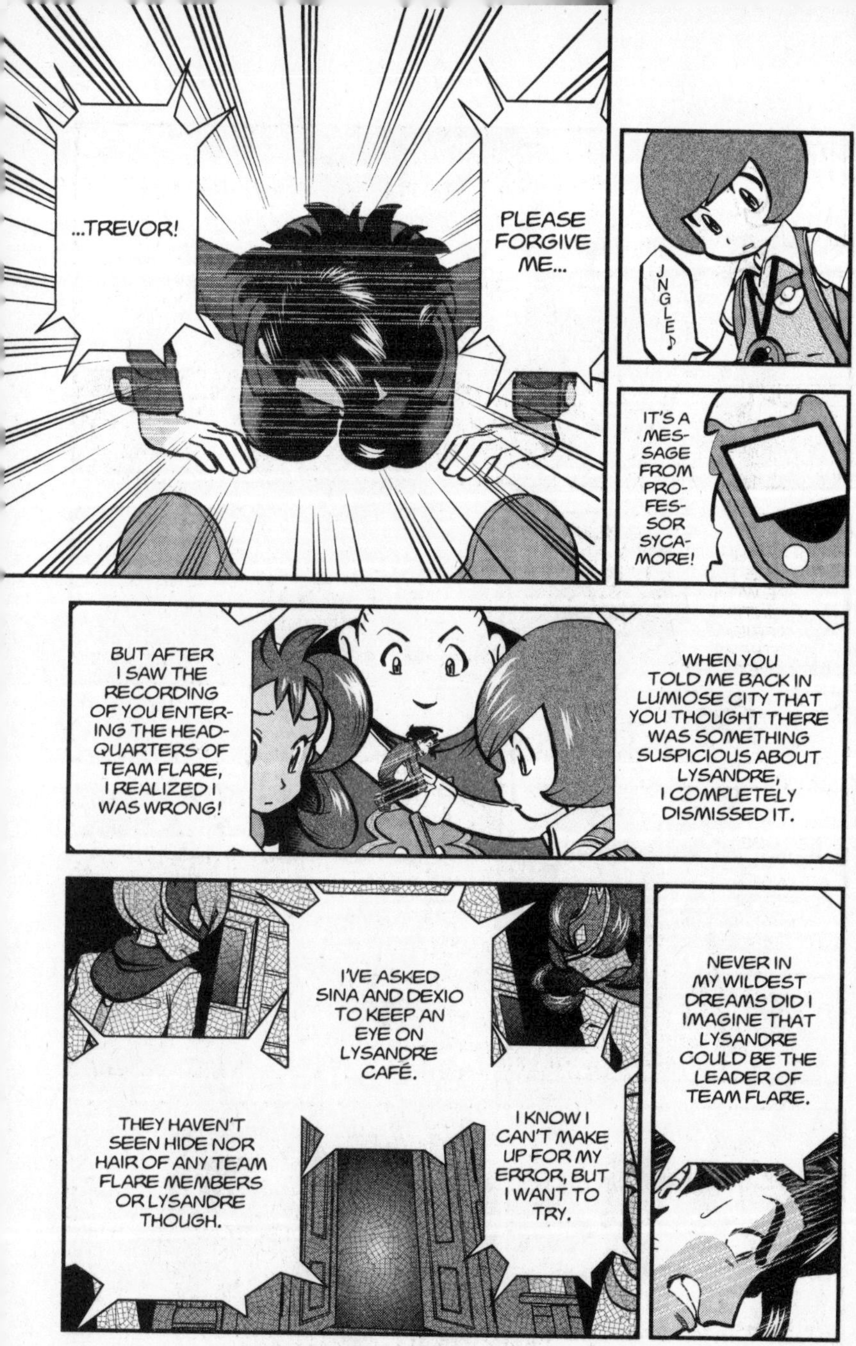
JNGLE♪
IT'S A MESSAGE FROM PROFESSOR SYCAMORE!
PLEASE FORGIVE ME...
...TREVOR!
WHEN YOU TOLD ME BACK IN LUMIOSE CITY THAT YOU THOUGHT THERE WAS SOMETHING SUSPICIOUS ABOUT LYSANDRE, I COMPLETELY DISMISSED IT.
BUT AFTER I SAW THE RECORDING OF YOU ENTERING THE HEADQUARTERS OF TEAM FLARE, I REALIZED I WAS WRONG!
NEVER IN MY WILDEST DREAMS DID I IMAGINE THAT LYSANDRE COULD BE THE LEADER OF TEAM FLARE.
I KNOW I CAN'T MAKE UP FOR MY ERROR, BUT I WANT TO TRY.
I'VE ASKED SINA AND DEXIO TO KEEP AN EYE ON LYSANDRE CAFÉ.
THEY HAVEN'T SEEN HIDE NOR HAIR OF ANY TEAM FLARE MEMBERS OR LYSANDRE THOUGH.

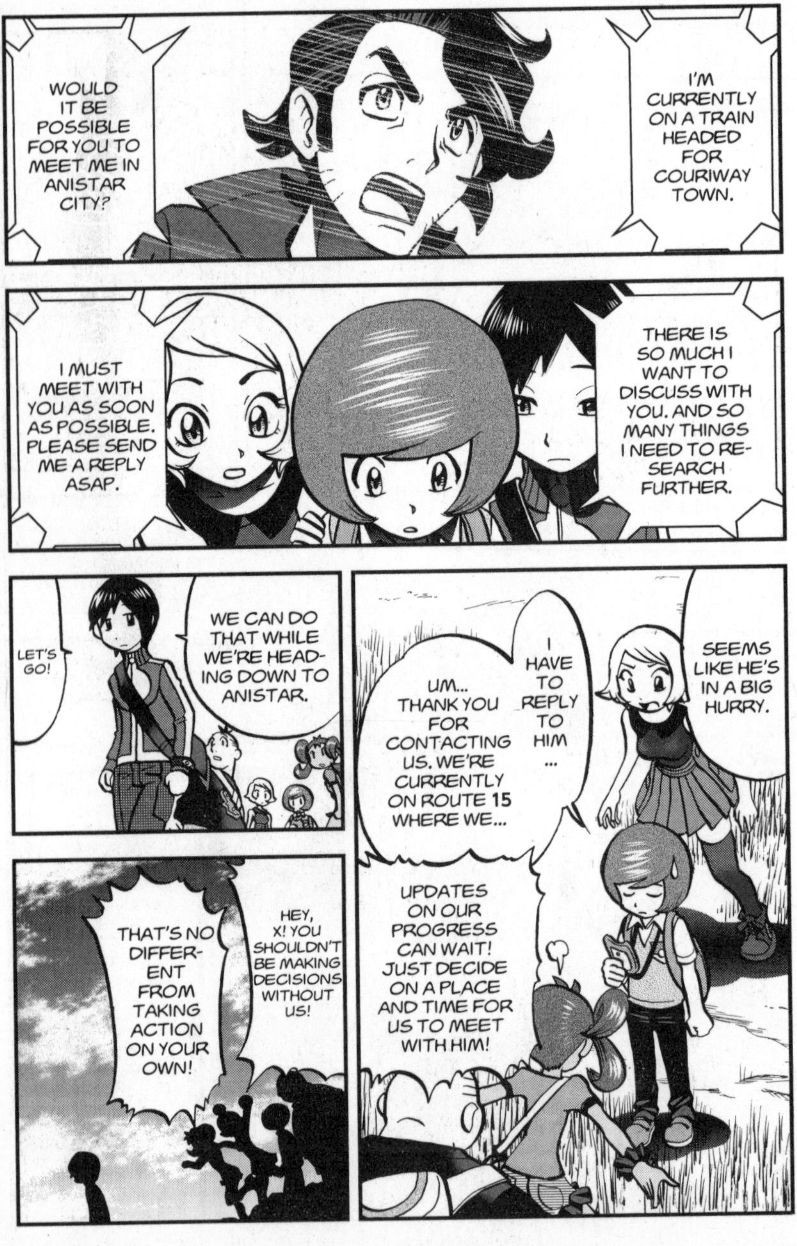
I'M CURRENTLY ON A TRAIN HEADED FOR COURIWAY TOWN.
WOULD IT BE POSSIBLE FOR YOU TO MEET ME IN ANISTAR CITY?
THERE IS SO MUCH I WANT TO DISCUSS WITH YOU. AND SO MANY THINGS I NEED TO RE-SEARCH FURTHER.
I MUST MEET WITH YOU AS SOON AS POSSIBLE. PLEASE SEND ME A REPLY ASAP.
SEEMS LIKE HE'S IN A BIG HURRY.
I HAVE TO REPLY TO HIM ...
UM... THANK YOU FOR CONTACTING US. WE'RE CURRENTLY ON ROUTE 15 WHERE WE...
UPDATES ON OUR PROGRESS CAN WAIT! JUST DECIDE ON A PLACE AND TIME FOR US TO MEET WITH HIM!
WE CAN DO THAT WHILE WE'RE HEAD-ING DOWN TO ANISTAR.
LET'S GO!
HEY, X! YOU SHOULDN'T BE MAKING DECISIONS WITHOUT US!
THAT'S NO DIFFER-ENT FROM TAKING ACTION ON YOUR OWN!

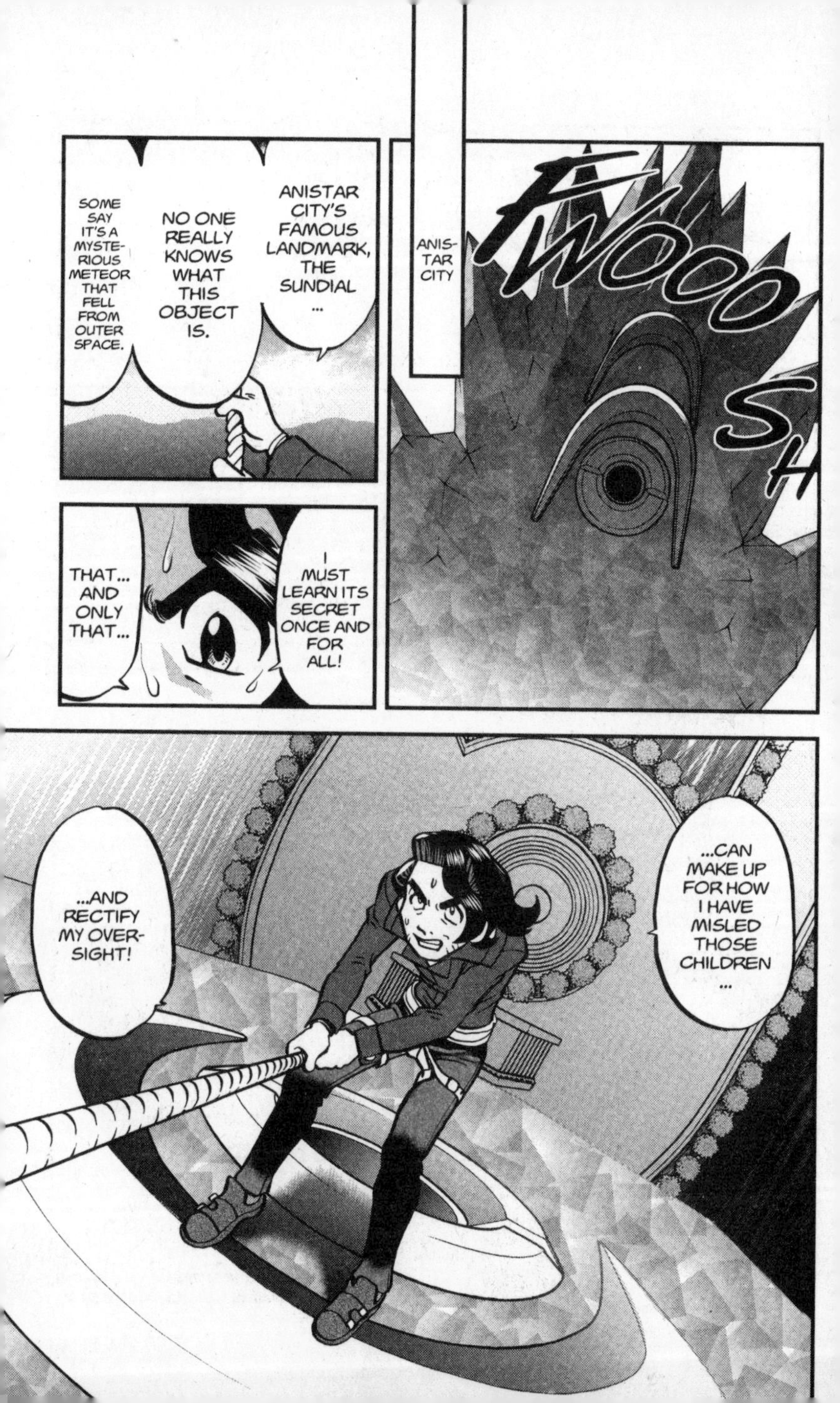
ANISTAR CITY
FWOOOSH
ANISTAR CITY'S FAMOUS LANDMARK, THE SUNDIAL...
NO ONE REALLY KNOWS WHAT THIS OBJECT IS.
SOME SAY IT'S A MYSTERIOUS METEOR THAT FELL FROM OUTER SPACE.
I MUST LEARN ITS SECRET ONCE AND FOR ALL!
THAT... AND ONLY THAT...
...CAN MAKE UP FOR HOW I HAVE MISLED THOSE CHILDREN...
...AND RECTIFY MY OVERSIGHT!

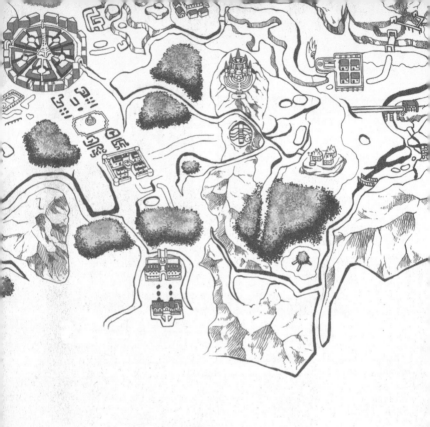

Current Location

Route 15
Brun Way

This path has become a popular hangout for the wild and directionless youths of Lumiose City.

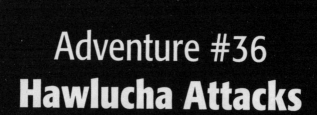

Adventure #36
Hawlucha Attacks

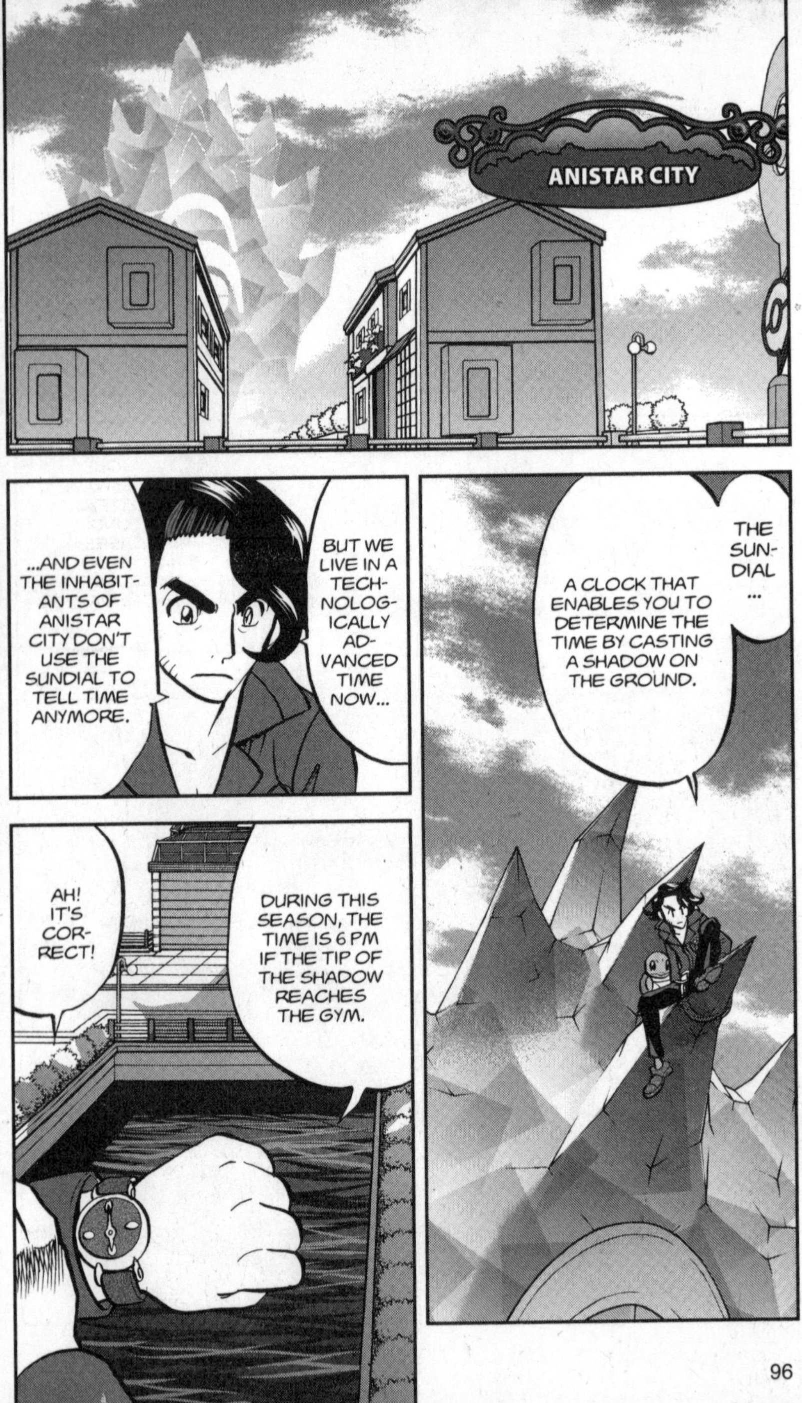
ANISTAR CITY
THE SUNDIAL...
A CLOCK THAT ENABLES YOU TO DETERMINE THE TIME BY CASTING A SHADOW ON THE GROUND.
BUT WE LIVE IN A TECHNOLOGICALLY ADVANCED TIME NOW...
...AND EVEN THE INHABITANTS OF ANISTAR CITY DON'T USE THE SUNDIAL TO TELL TIME ANYMORE.
DURING THIS SEASON, THE TIME IS 6 PM IF THE TIP OF THE SHADOW REACHES THE GYM.
AH! IT'S CORRECT!

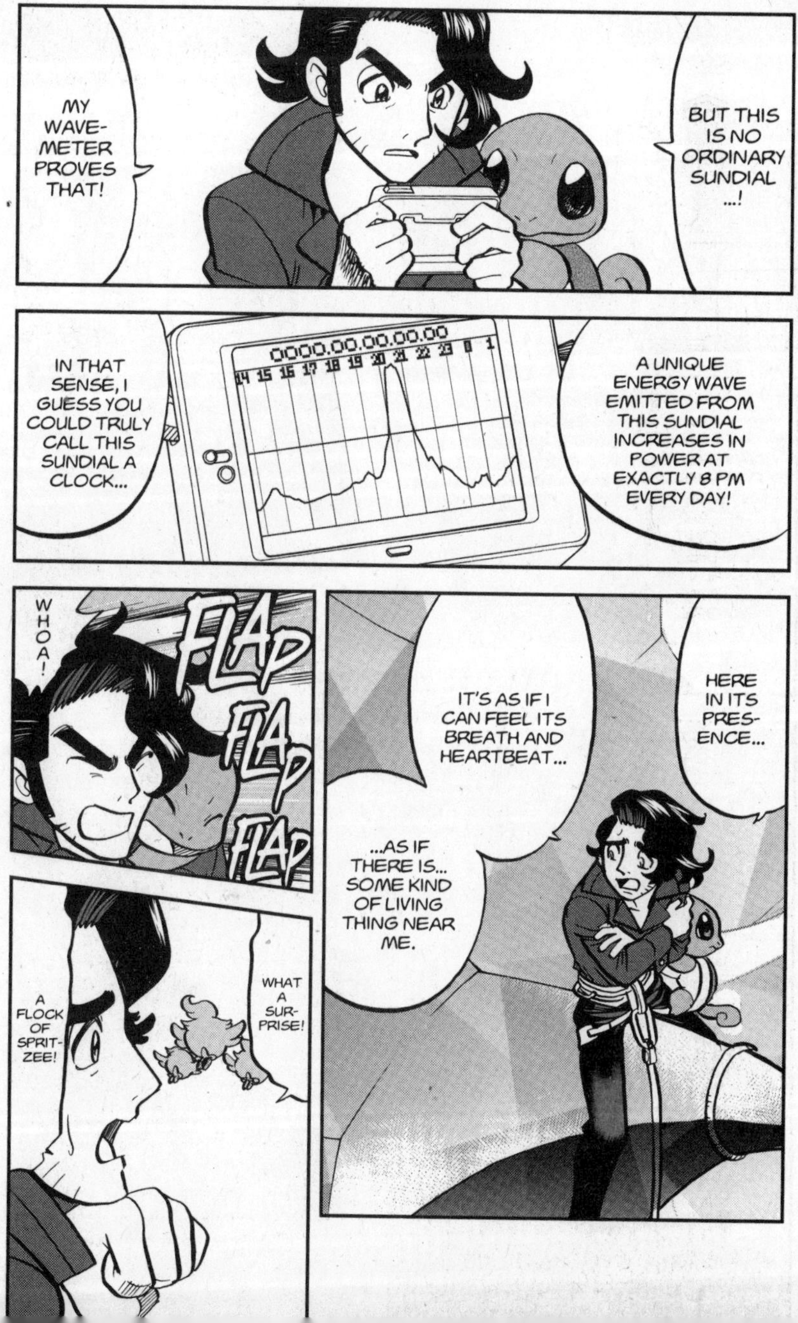
BUT THIS IS NO ORDINARY SUNDIAL ...!
MY WAVE-METER PROVES THAT!
A UNIQUE ENERGY WAVE EMITTED FROM THIS SUNDIAL INCREASES IN POWER AT EXACTLY 8 PM EVERY DAY!
0000.00.00.00.00
14 15 16 17 18 19 20 21 22 23 0 1
IN THAT SENSE, I GUESS YOU COULD TRULY CALL THIS SUNDIAL A CLOCK...
HERE IN ITS PRES-ENCE...
IT'S AS IF I CAN FEEL ITS BREATH AND HEARTBEAT...
...AS IF THERE IS... SOME KIND OF LIVING THING NEAR ME.
FLAP FLAP FLAP
WHOA!
WHAT A SUR-PRISE!
A FLOCK OF SPRIT-ZEE!

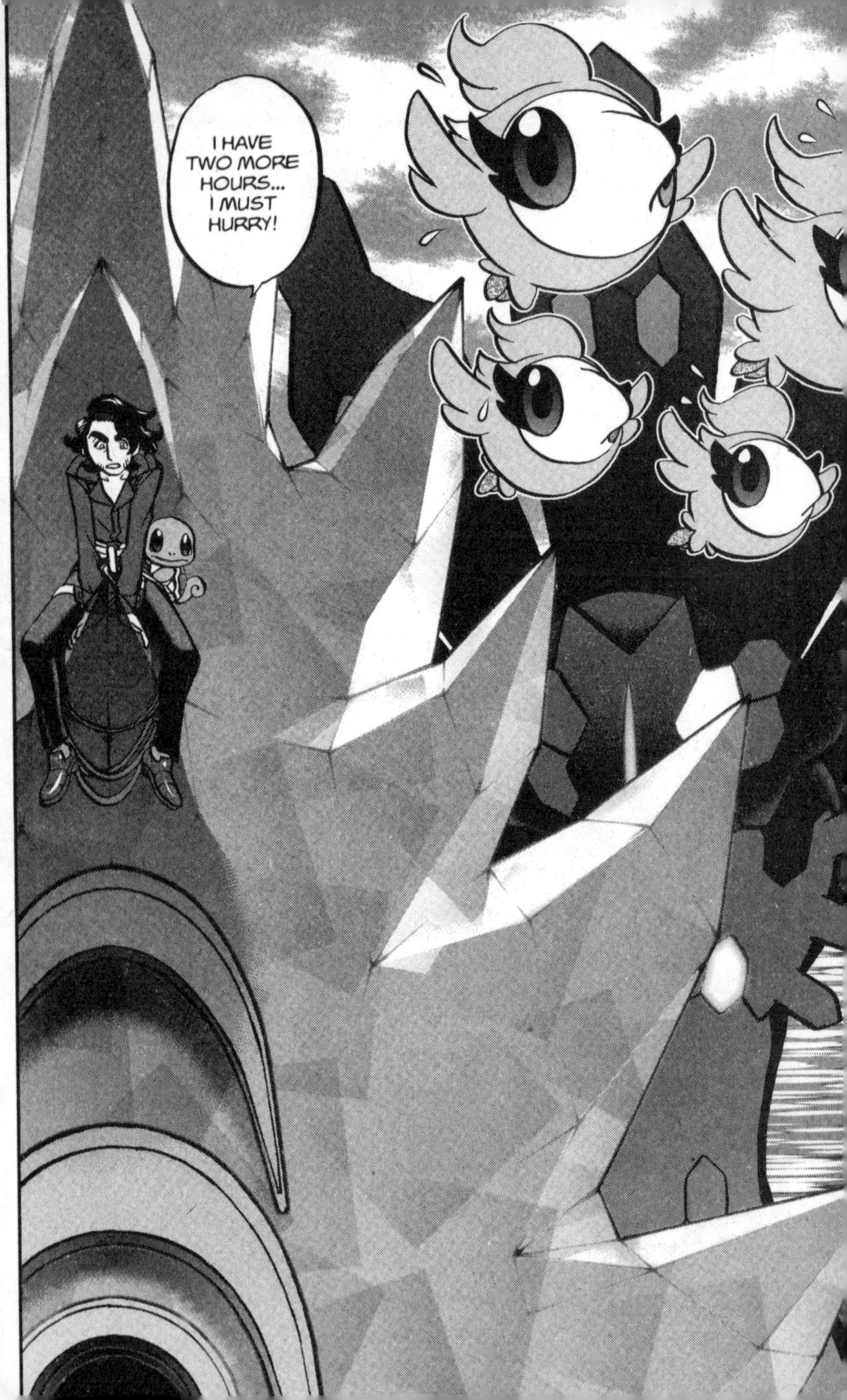
I HAVE TWO MORE HOURS... I MUST HURRY!

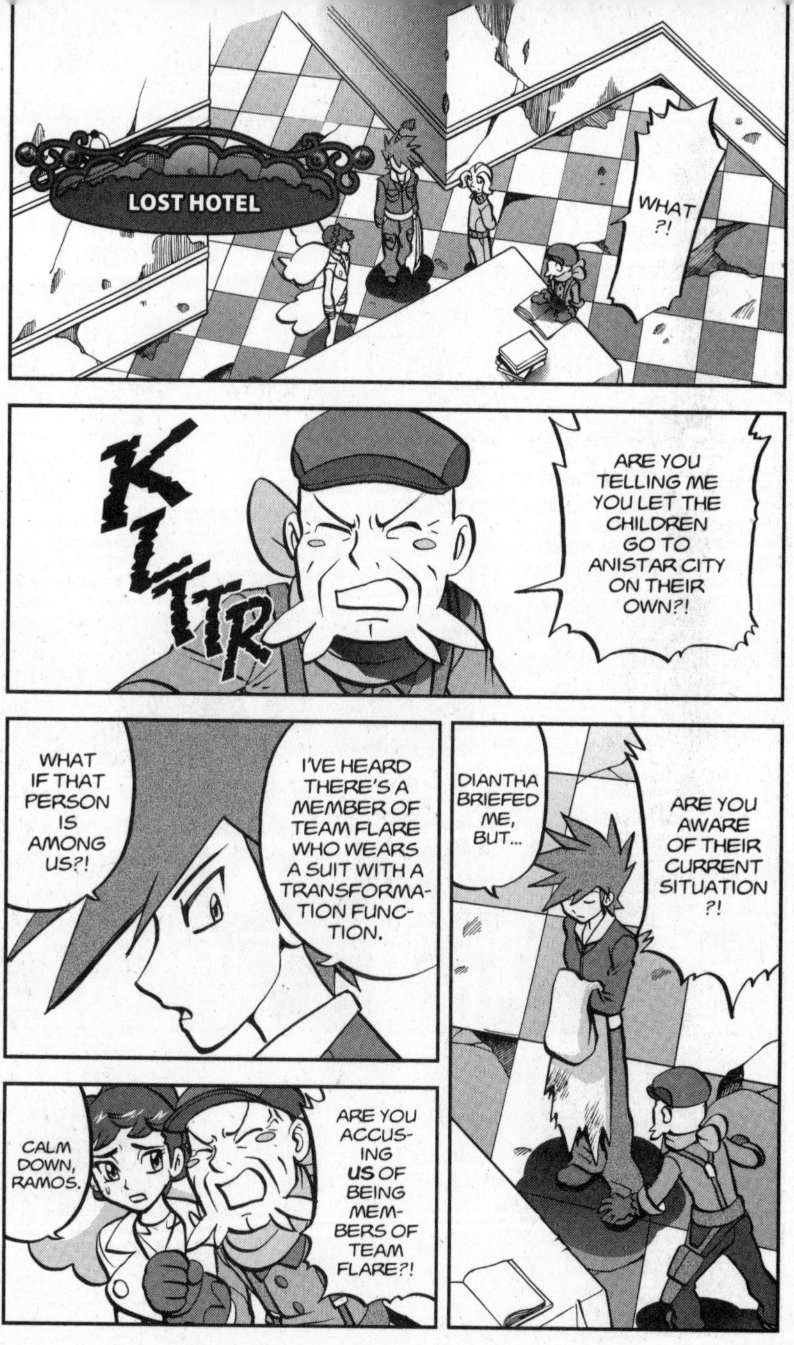
LOST HOTEL
WHAT?!
KLTTR
ARE YOU TELLING ME YOU LET THE CHILDREN GO TO ANISTAR CITY ON THEIR OWN?!
DIANTHA BRIEFED ME, BUT...
ARE YOU AWARE OF THEIR CURRENT SITUATION?!
I'VE HEARD THERE'S A MEMBER OF TEAM FLARE WHO WEARS A SUIT WITH A TRANSFORMATION FUNCTION.
WHAT IF THAT PERSON IS AMONG US?!
ARE YOU ACCUSING US OF BEING MEMBERS OF TEAM FLARE?!
CALM DOWN, RAMOS.

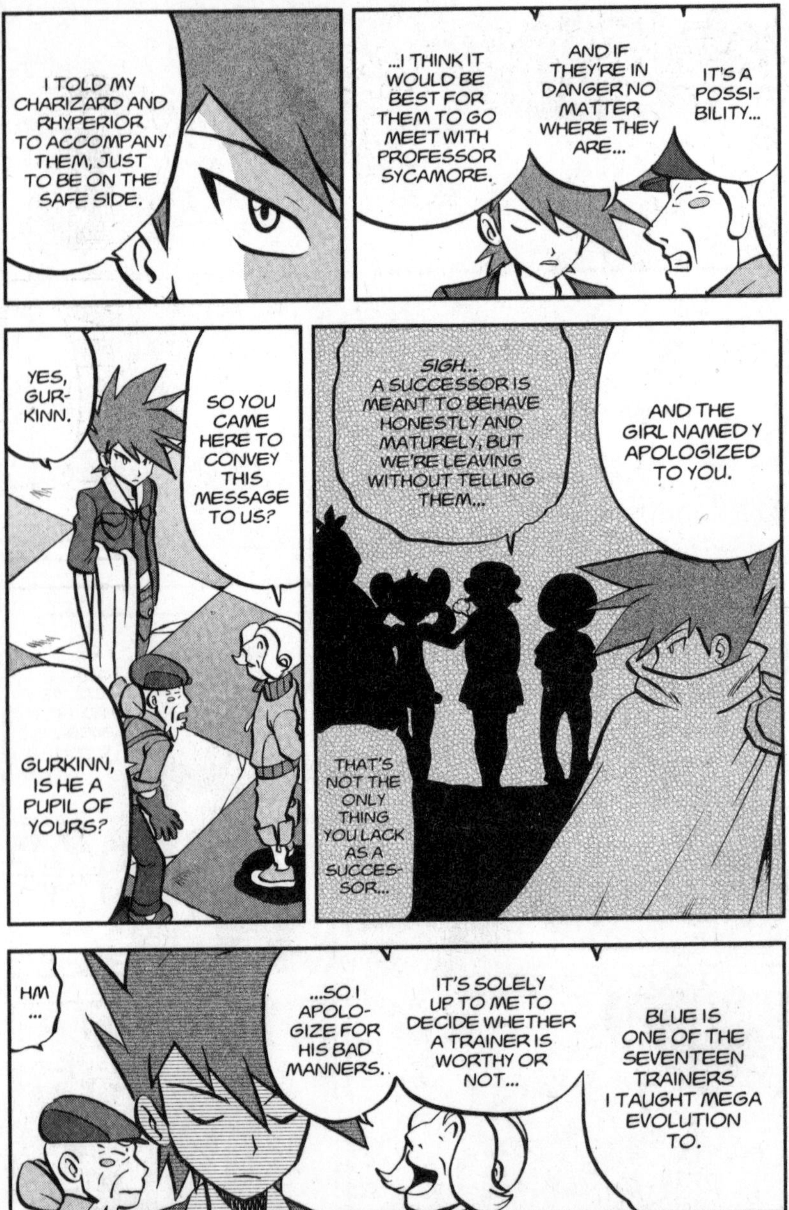
IT'S A POSSI-BILITY...
AND IF THEY'RE IN DANGER NO MATTER WHERE THEY ARE...
...I THINK IT WOULD BE BEST FOR THEM TO GO MEET WITH PROFESSOR SYCAMORE.
I TOLD MY CHARIZARD AND RHYPERIOR TO ACCOMPANY THEM, JUST TO BE ON THE SAFE SIDE.
AND THE GIRL NAMED Y APOLOGIZED TO YOU.
SIGH... A SUCCESSOR IS MEANT TO BEHAVE HONESTLY AND MATURELY, BUT WE'RE LEAVING WITHOUT TELLING THEM...
THAT'S NOT THE ONLY THING YOU LACK AS A SUCCES-SOR...
SO YOU CAME HERE TO CONVEY THIS MESSAGE TO US?
YES, GUR-KINN.
GURKINN, IS HE A PUPIL OF YOURS?
BLUE IS ONE OF THE SEVENTEEN TRAINERS I TAUGHT MEGA EVOLUTION TO.
IT'S SOLELY UP TO ME TO DECIDE WHETHER A TRAINER IS WORTHY OR NOT...
...SO I APOLO-GIZE FOR HIS BAD MANNERS.
HM ...

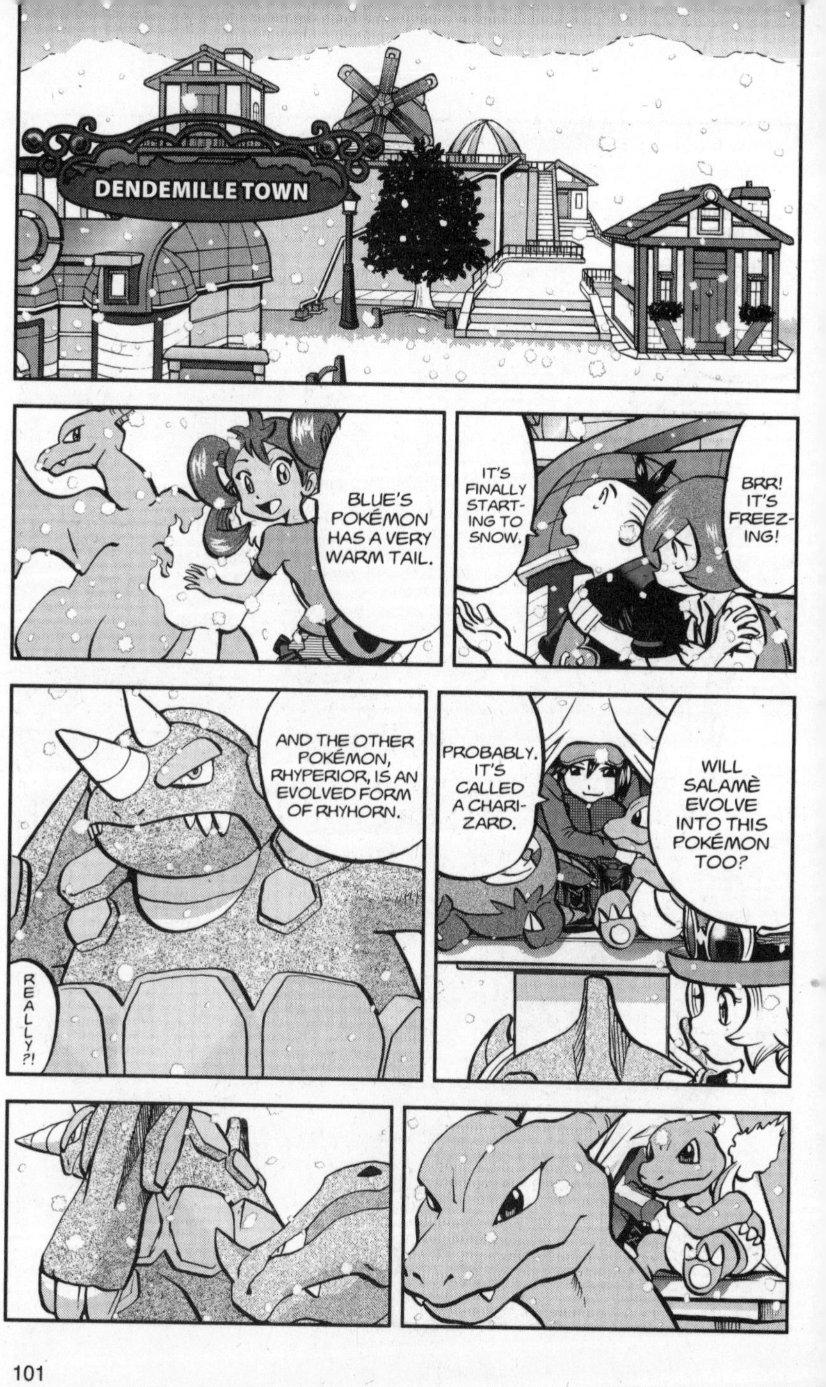
DENDEMILLE TOWN
BRR! IT'S FREEZING!
IT'S FINALLY STARTING TO SNOW.
BLUE'S POKÉMON HAS A VERY WARM TAIL.
WILL SALAMÈ EVOLVE INTO THIS POKÉMON TOO?
PROBABLY. IT'S CALLED A CHARIZARD.
AND THE OTHER POKÉMON, RHYPERIOR, IS AN EVOLVED FORM OF RHYHORN.
REALLY?!

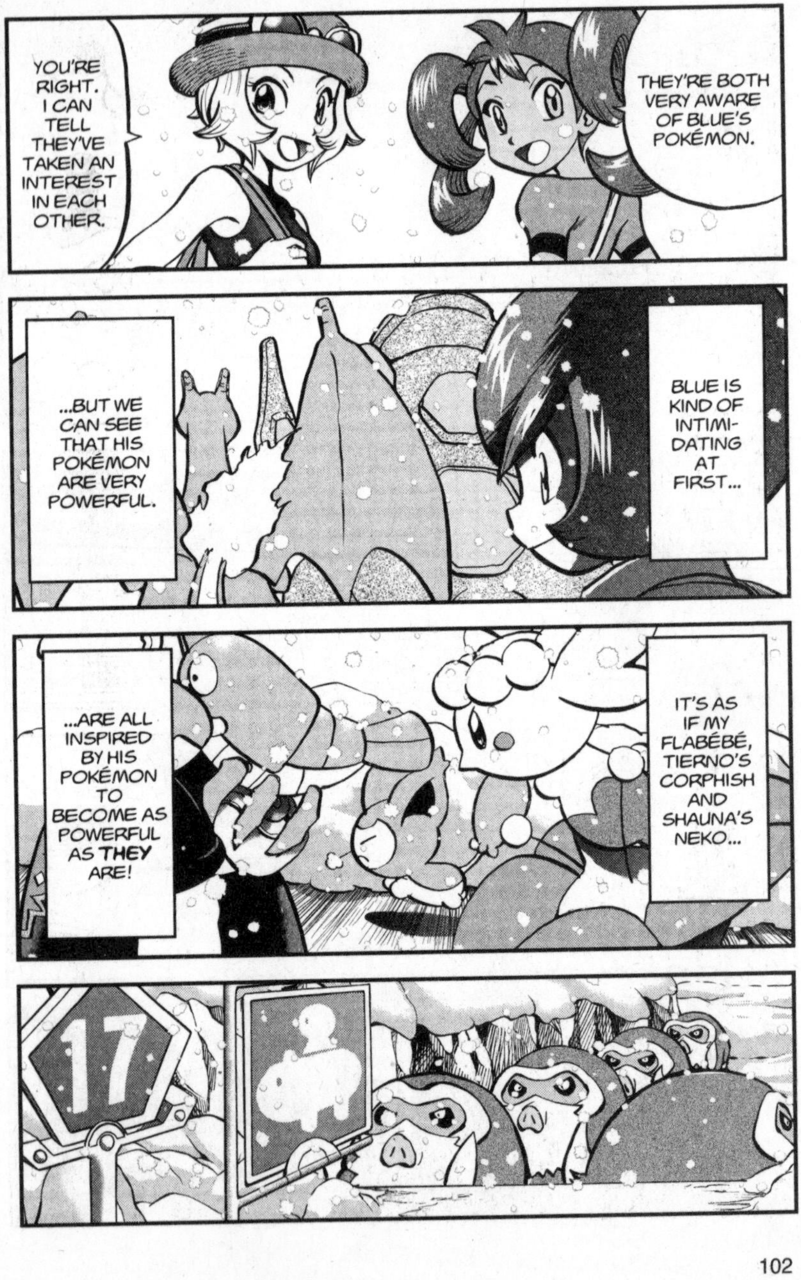
THEY'RE BOTH VERY AWARE OF BLUE'S POKéMON.
YOU'RE RIGHT. I CAN TELL THEY'VE TAKEN AN INTEREST IN EACH OTHER.
BLUE IS KIND OF INTIMI-DATING AT FIRST...
...BUT WE CAN SEE THAT HIS POKéMON ARE VERY POWERFUL.
IT'S AS IF MY FLABéBé, TIERNO'S CORPHISH AND SHAUNA'S NEKO...
...ARE ALL INSPIRED BY HIS POKéMON TO BECOME AS POWERFUL AS **THEY** ARE!
17

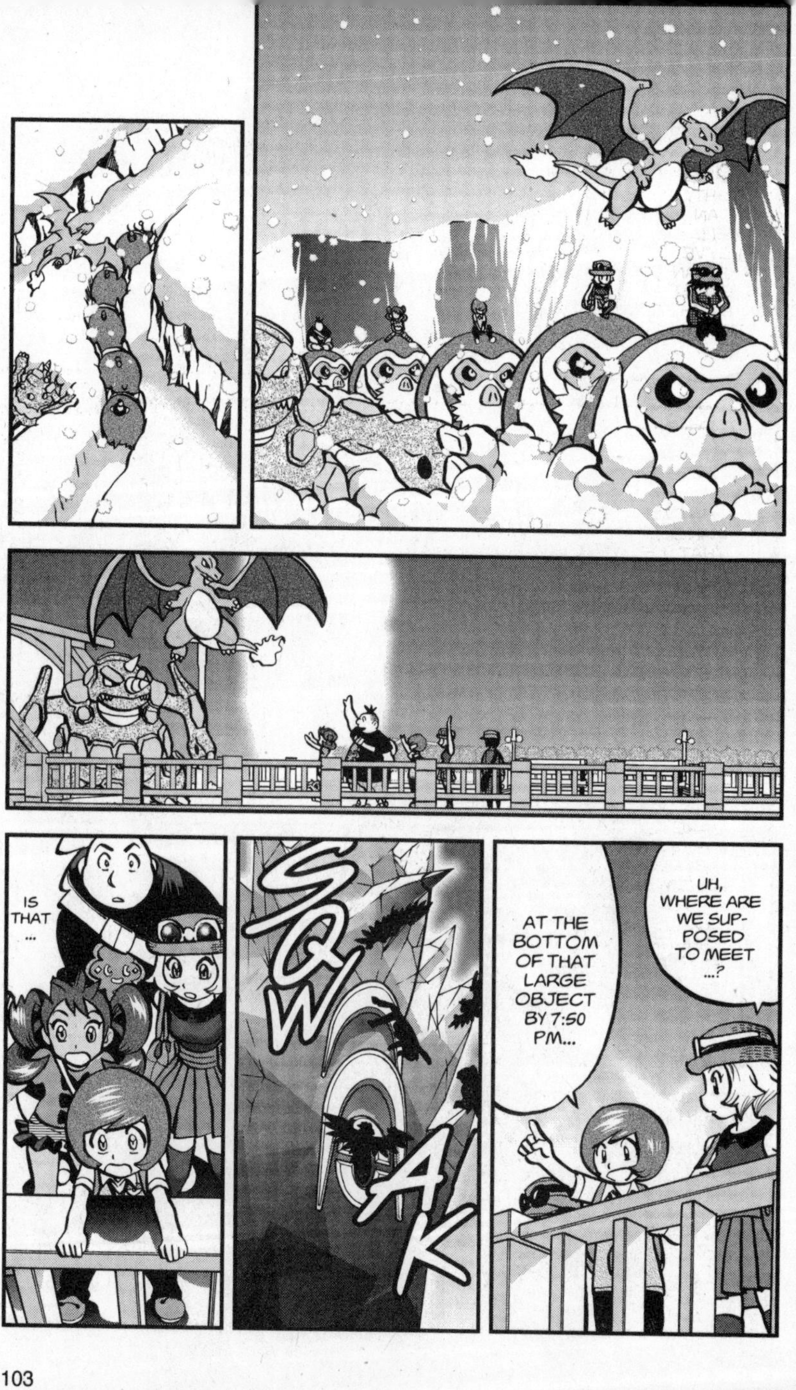
UH, WHERE ARE WE SUP-POSED TO MEET ...?
AT THE BOTTOM OF THAT LARGE OBJECT BY 7:50 PM...
SQWAK
IS THAT ...

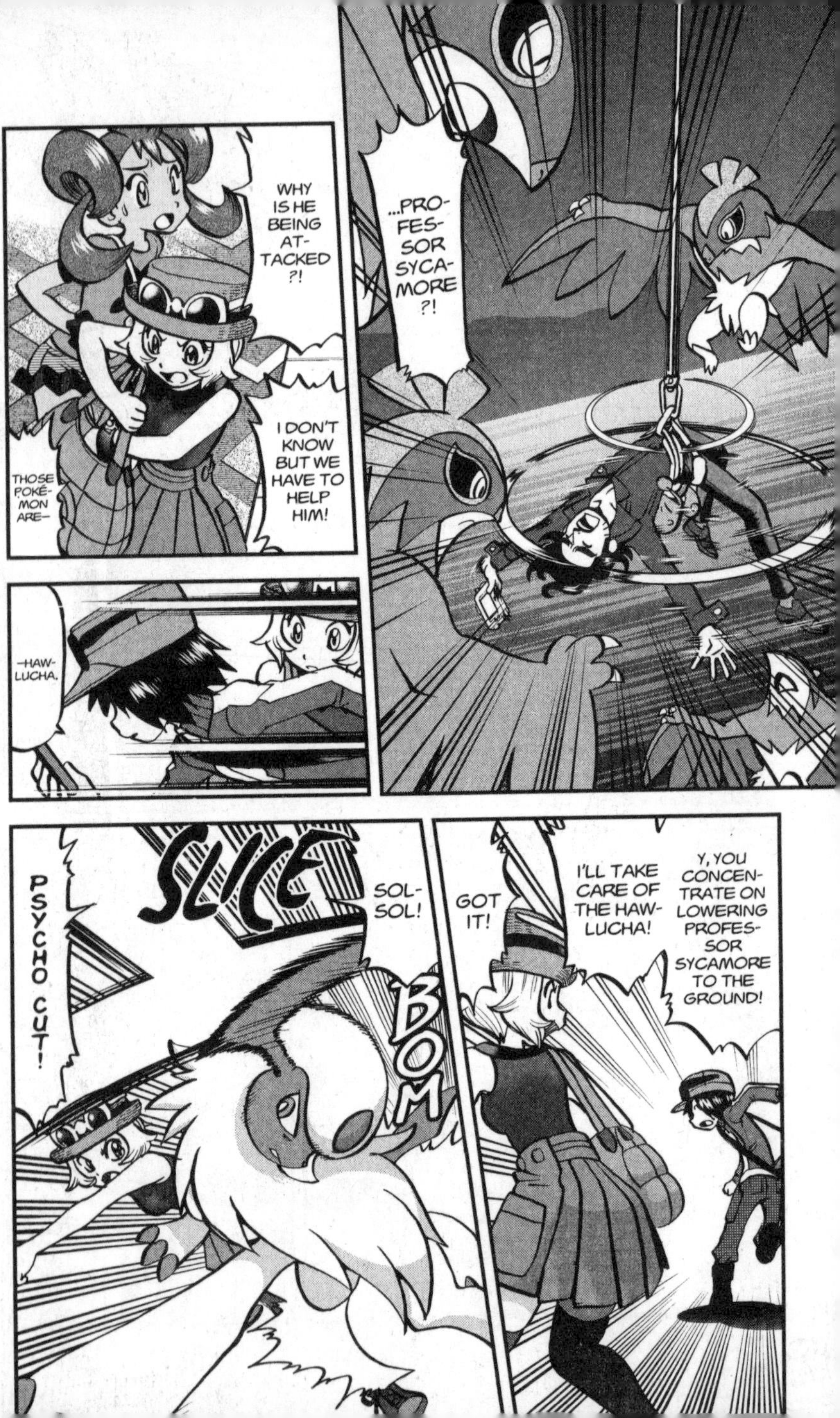
...PROFESSOR SYCAMORE?!
WHY IS HE BEING ATTACKED?!
I DON'T KNOW BUT WE HAVE TO HELP HIM!
THOSE POKÉMON ARE—
—HAWLUCHA.
Y, YOU CONCENTRATE ON LOWERING PROFESSOR SYCAMORE TO THE GROUND!
I'LL TAKE CARE OF THE HAWLUCHA!
GOT IT!
BOM
SOL-SOL!
SLICE
PSYCHO CUT!

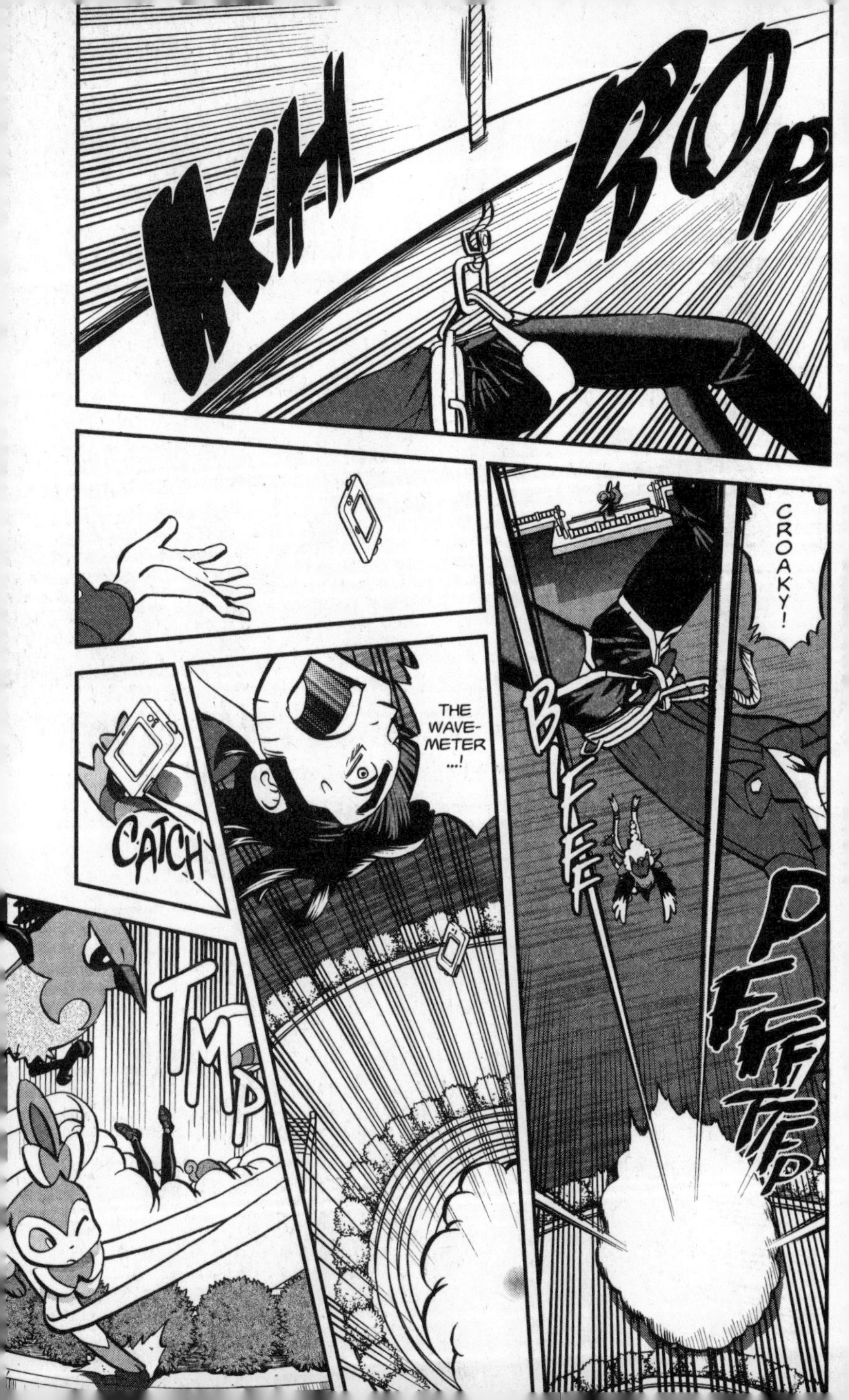
KH ROP
CROAKY!
BIFFFF
PFFFTFP
THE WAVE-METER...!
CATCH
TMP

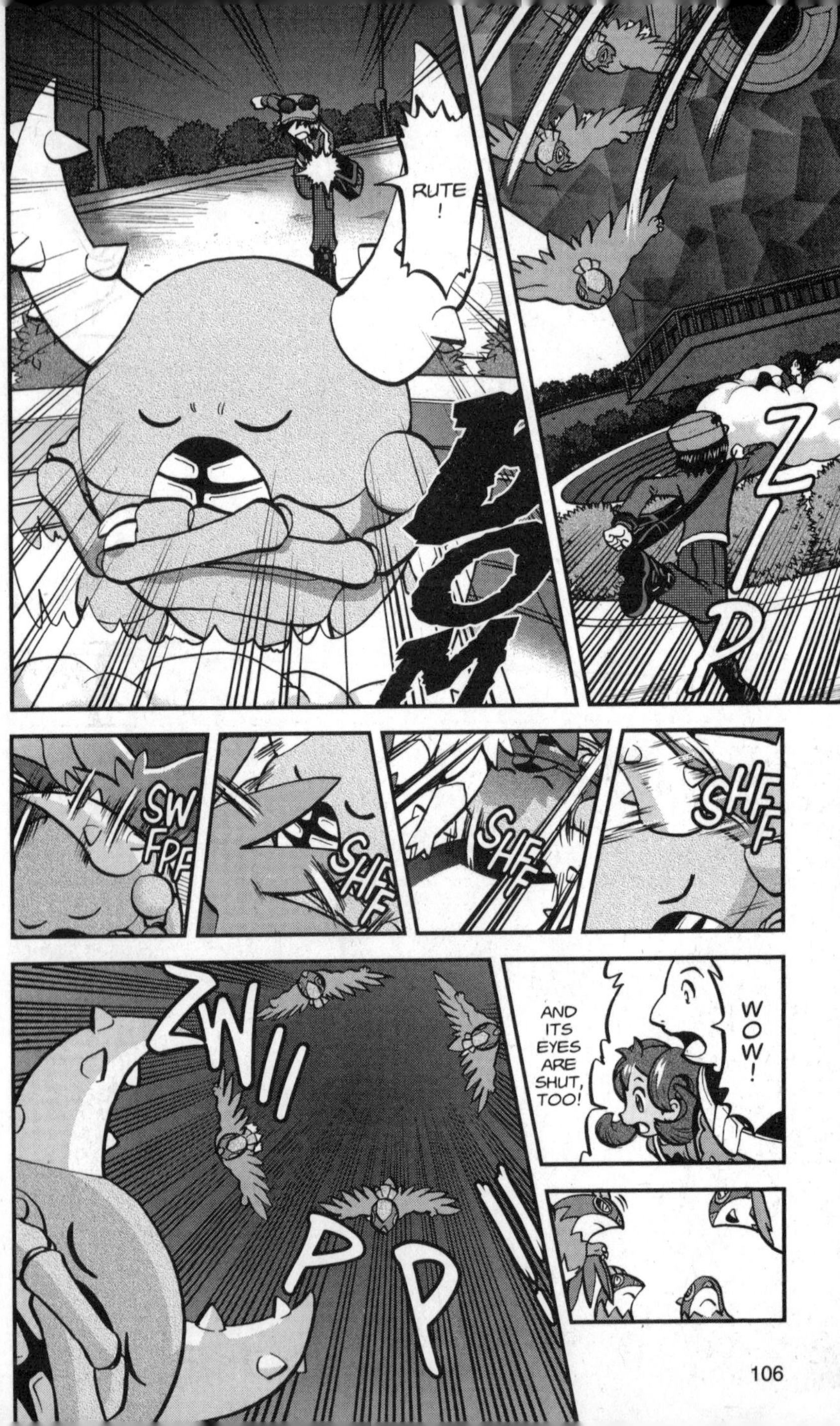
ZIP
RUTE!
BOM
SHFF
SHF
SHFF
SWFFF
WOW!
AND ITS EYES ARE SHUT, TOO!
ZWIIPP

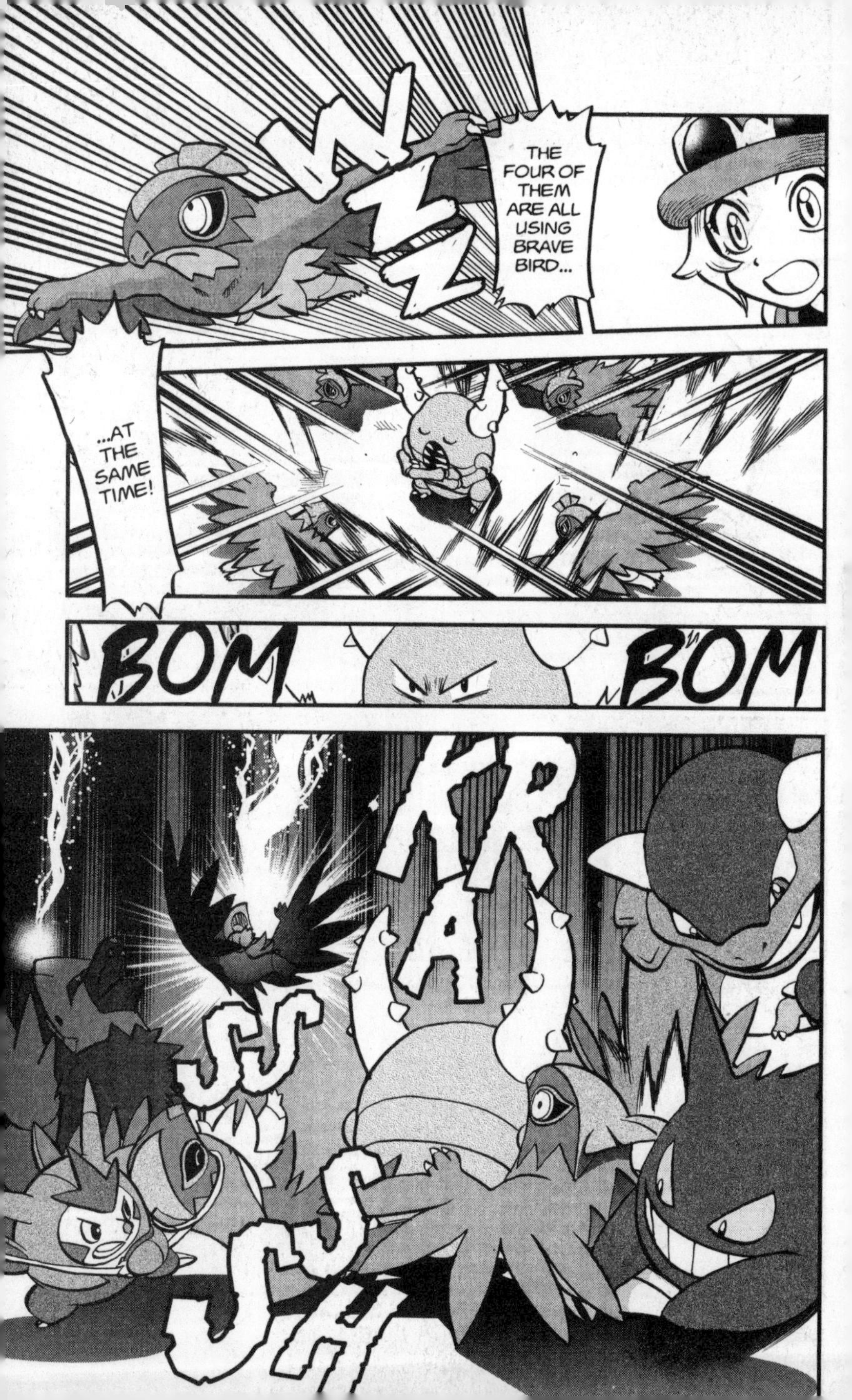
THE FOUR OF THEM ARE ALL USING BRAVE BIRD...
...AT THE SAME TIME!
BOM
BOM
KRA

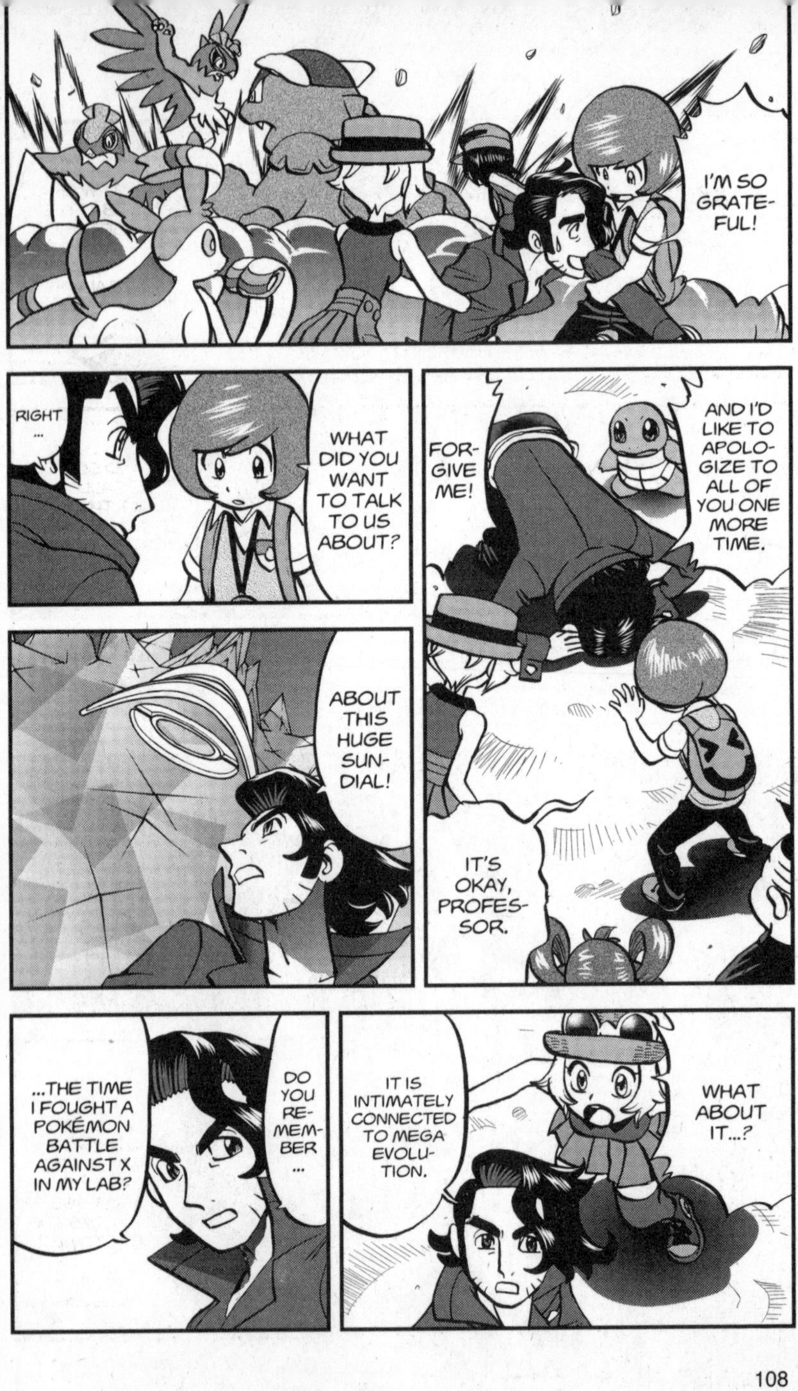
I'M SO GRATEFUL!
AND I'D LIKE TO APOLOGIZE TO ALL OF YOU ONE MORE TIME.
FORGIVE ME!
IT'S OKAY, PROFESSOR.
WHAT DID YOU WANT TO TALK TO US ABOUT?
RIGHT...
ABOUT THIS HUGE SUNDIAL!
WHAT ABOUT IT...?
IT IS INTIMATELY CONNECTED TO MEGA EVOLUTION.
DO YOU REMEMBER...
...THE TIME I FOUGHT A POKÉMON BATTLE AGAINST X IN MY LAB?

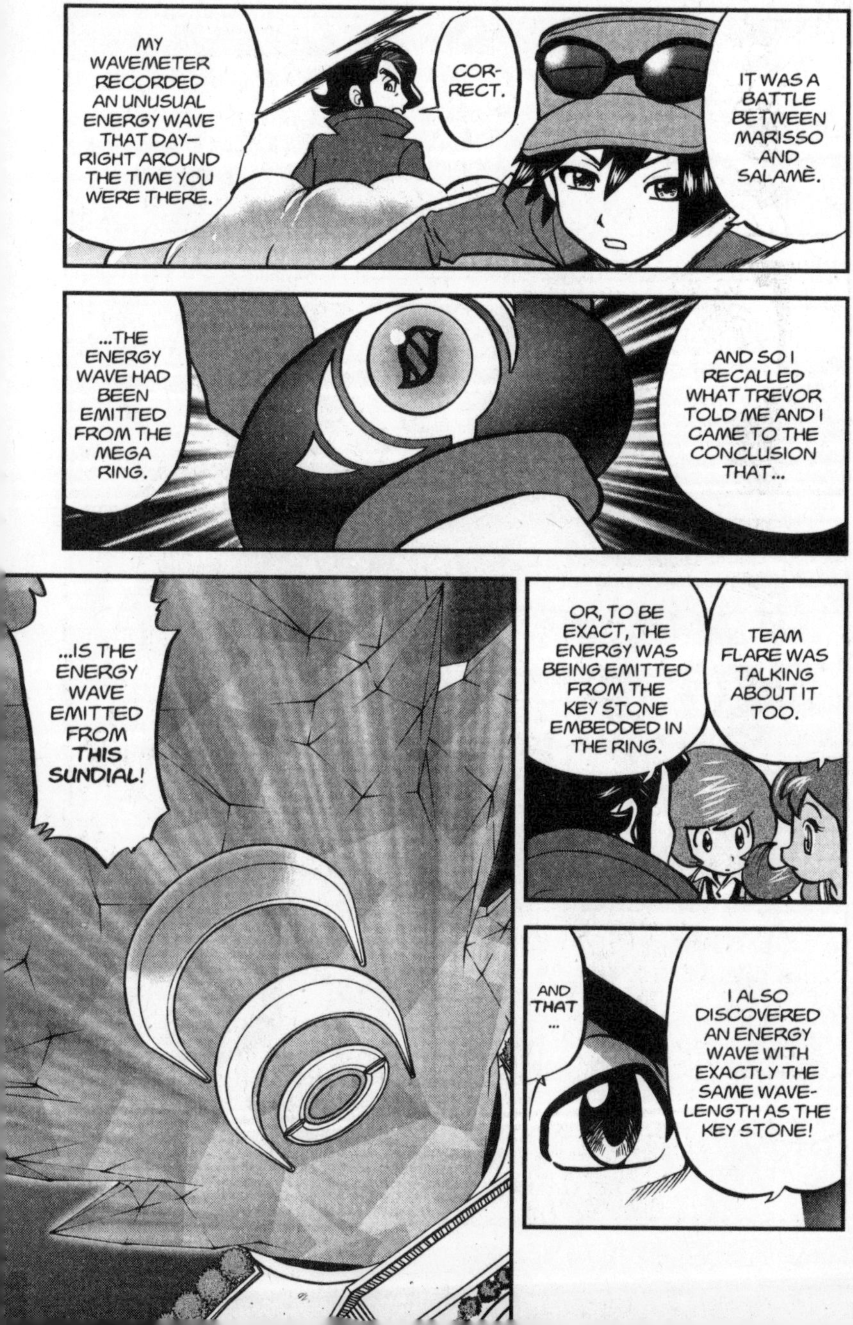
IT WAS A BATTLE BETWEEN MARISSO AND SALAMÈ.
COR-RECT.
MY WAVEMETER RECORDED AN UNUSUAL ENERGY WAVE THAT DAY—RIGHT AROUND THE TIME YOU WERE THERE.
AND SO I RECALLED WHAT TREVOR TOLD ME AND I CAME TO THE CONCLUSION THAT...
...THE ENERGY WAVE HAD BEEN EMITTED FROM THE MEGA RING.
TEAM FLARE WAS TALKING ABOUT IT TOO.
OR, TO BE EXACT, THE ENERGY WAS BEING EMITTED FROM THE KEY STONE EMBEDDED IN THE RING.
I ALSO DISCOVERED AN ENERGY WAVE WITH EXACTLY THE SAME WAVE-LENGTH AS THE KEY STONE!
AND **THAT** ...
...IS THE ENERGY WAVE EMITTED FROM **THIS SUNDIAL**!

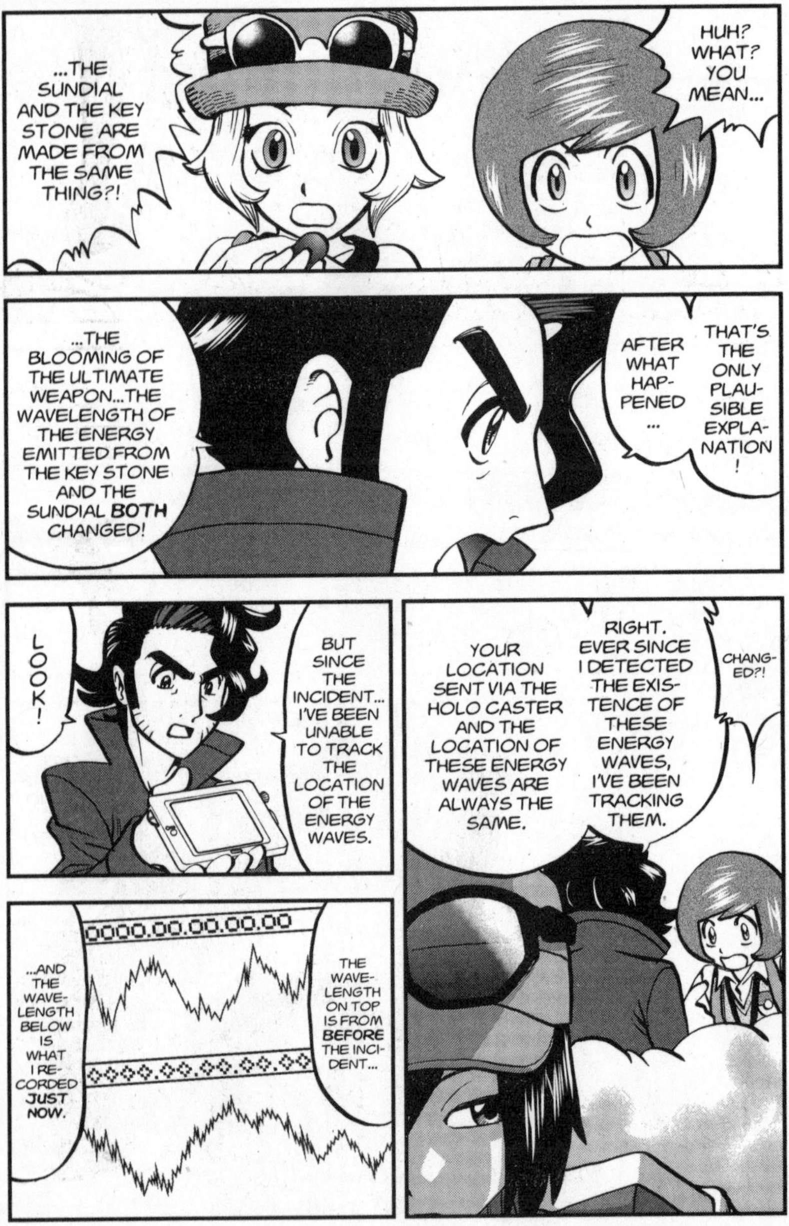
HUH? WHAT? YOU MEAN...
...THE SUNDIAL AND THE KEY STONE ARE MADE FROM THE SAME THING?!
THAT'S THE ONLY PLAUSIBLE EXPLANATION!
AFTER WHAT HAPPENED...
...THE BLOOMING OF THE ULTIMATE WEAPON...THE WAVELENGTH OF THE ENERGY EMITTED FROM THE KEY STONE AND THE SUNDIAL **BOTH** CHANGED!
CHANGED?!
RIGHT. EVER SINCE I DETECTED THE EXISTENCE OF THESE ENERGY WAVES, I'VE BEEN TRACKING THEM.
YOUR LOCATION SENT VIA THE HOLO CASTER AND THE LOCATION OF THESE ENERGY WAVES ARE ALWAYS THE SAME.
BUT SINCE THE INCIDENT... I'VE BEEN UNABLE TO TRACK THE LOCATION OF THE ENERGY WAVES.
LOOK!
THE WAVELENGTH ON TOP IS FROM **BEFORE** THE INCIDENT...
0000.00.00.00.00
...AND THE WAVELENGTH BELOW IS WHAT I RECORDED **JUST NOW.**

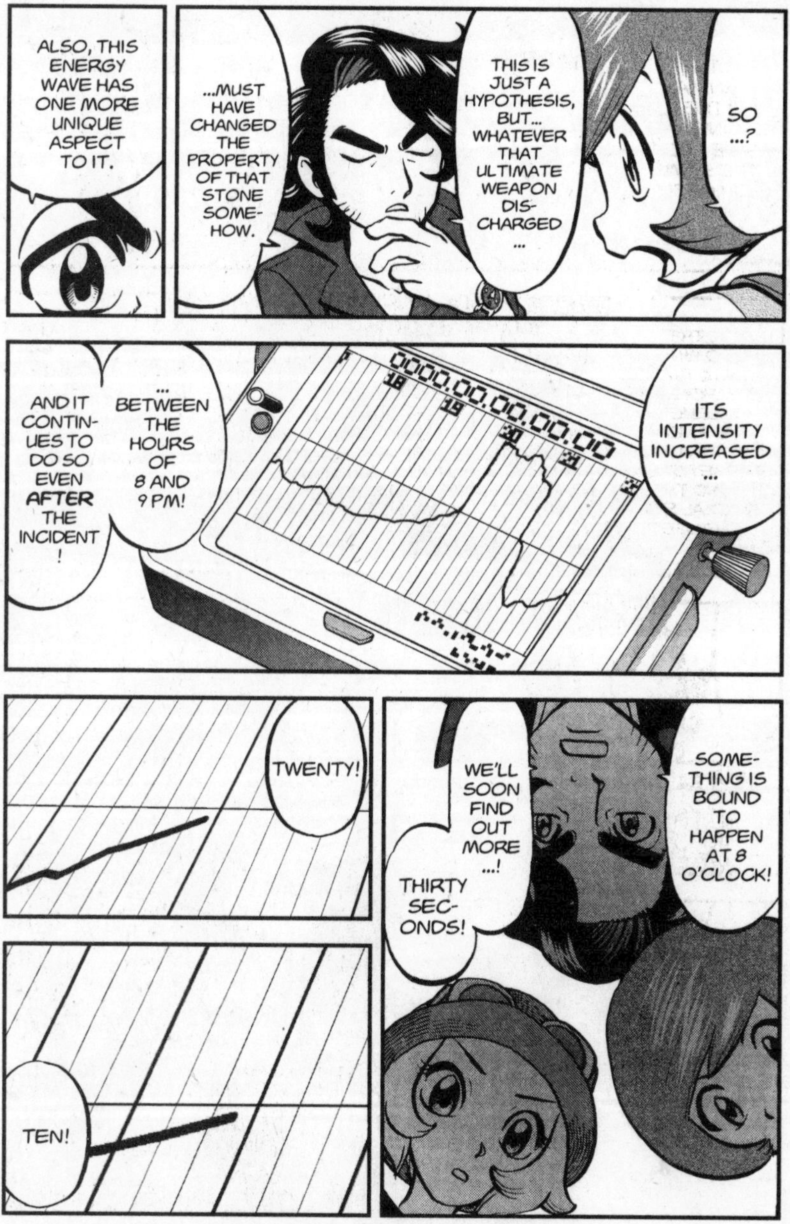
SO ...?
THIS IS JUST A HYPOTHESIS, BUT... WHATEVER THAT ULTIMATE WEAPON DIS-CHARGED ...
...MUST HAVE CHANGED THE PROPERTY OF THAT STONE SOME-HOW.
ALSO, THIS ENERGY WAVE HAS ONE MORE UNIQUE ASPECT TO IT.
ITS INTENSITY INCREASED ...
... BETWEEN THE HOURS OF 8 AND 9 PM!
AND IT CONTIN-UES TO DO SO EVEN **AFTER** THE INCIDENT !
SOME-THING IS BOUND TO HAPPEN AT 8 O'CLOCK!
WE'LL SOON FIND OUT MORE ...!
THIRTY SEC-ONDS!
TWENTY!
TEN!

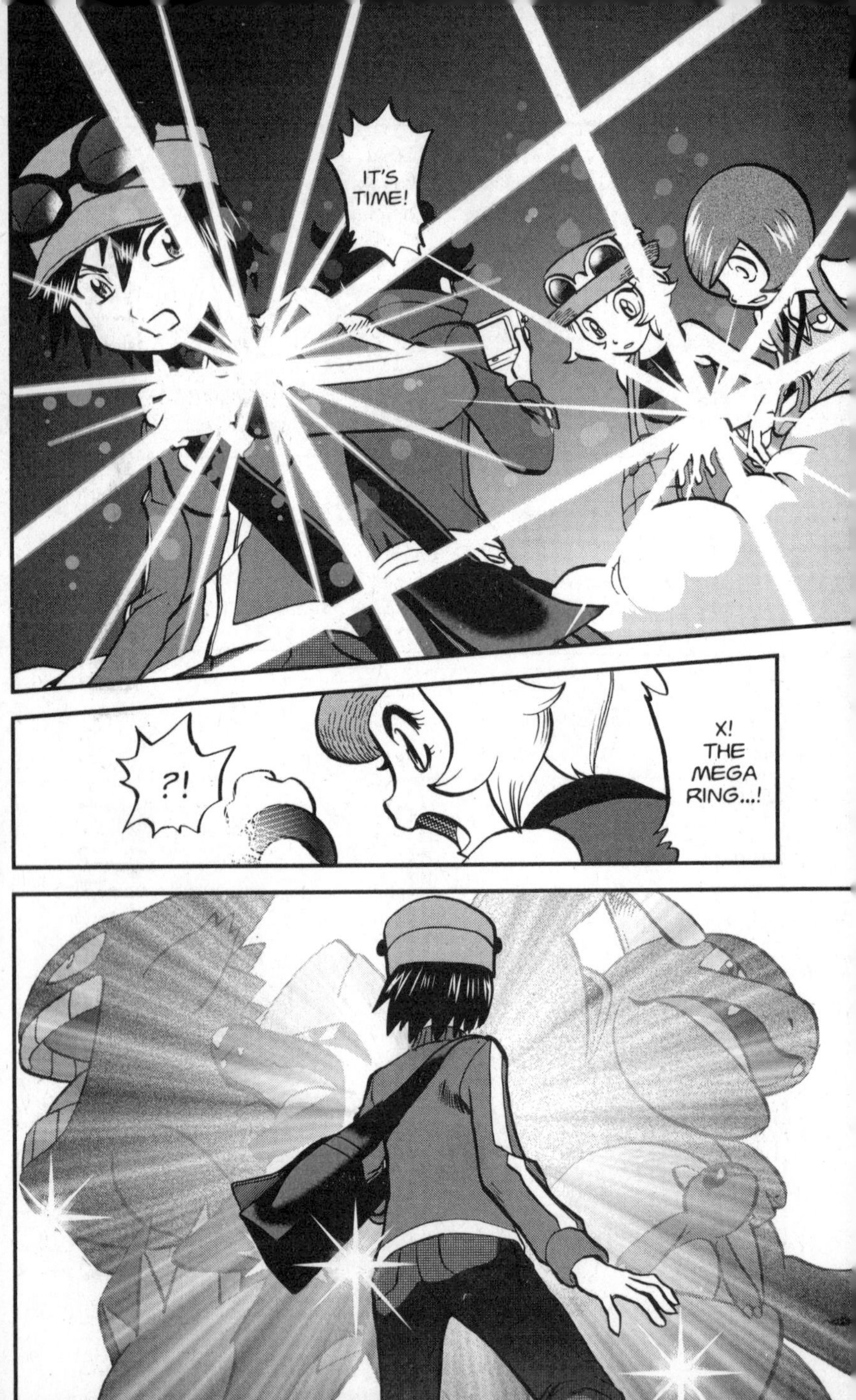
IT'S TIME!
X! THE MEGA RING...!
?!

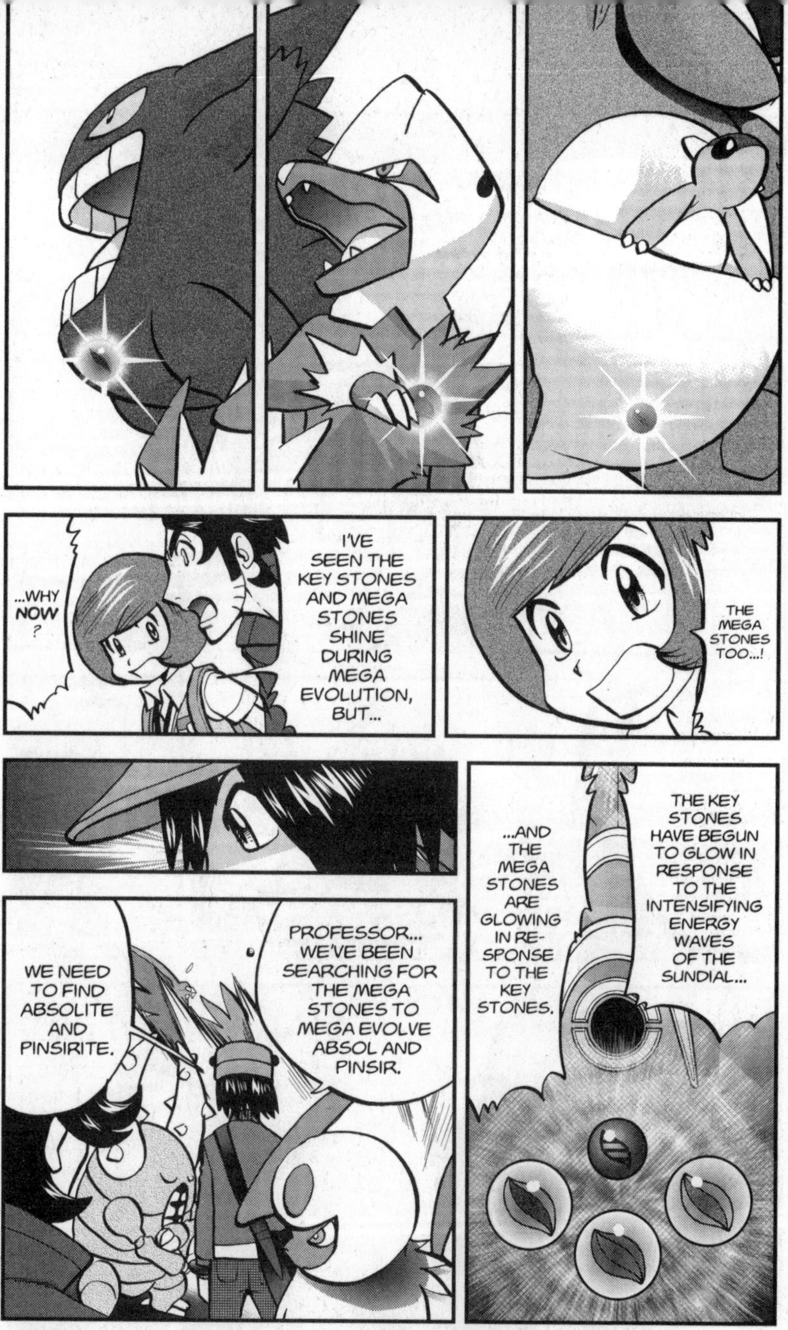
THE MEGA STONES TOO...!
I'VE SEEN THE KEY STONES AND MEGA STONES SHINE DURING MEGA EVOLUTION, BUT...
...WHY NOW?
THE KEY STONES HAVE BEGUN TO GLOW IN RESPONSE TO THE INTENSIFYING ENERGY WAVES OF THE SUNDIAL...
...AND THE MEGA STONES ARE GLOWING IN RE-SPONSE TO THE KEY STONES.
PROFESSOR... WE'VE BEEN SEARCHING FOR THE MEGA STONES TO MEGA EVOLVE ABSOL AND PINSIR.
WE NEED TO FIND ABSOLITE AND PINSIRITE.

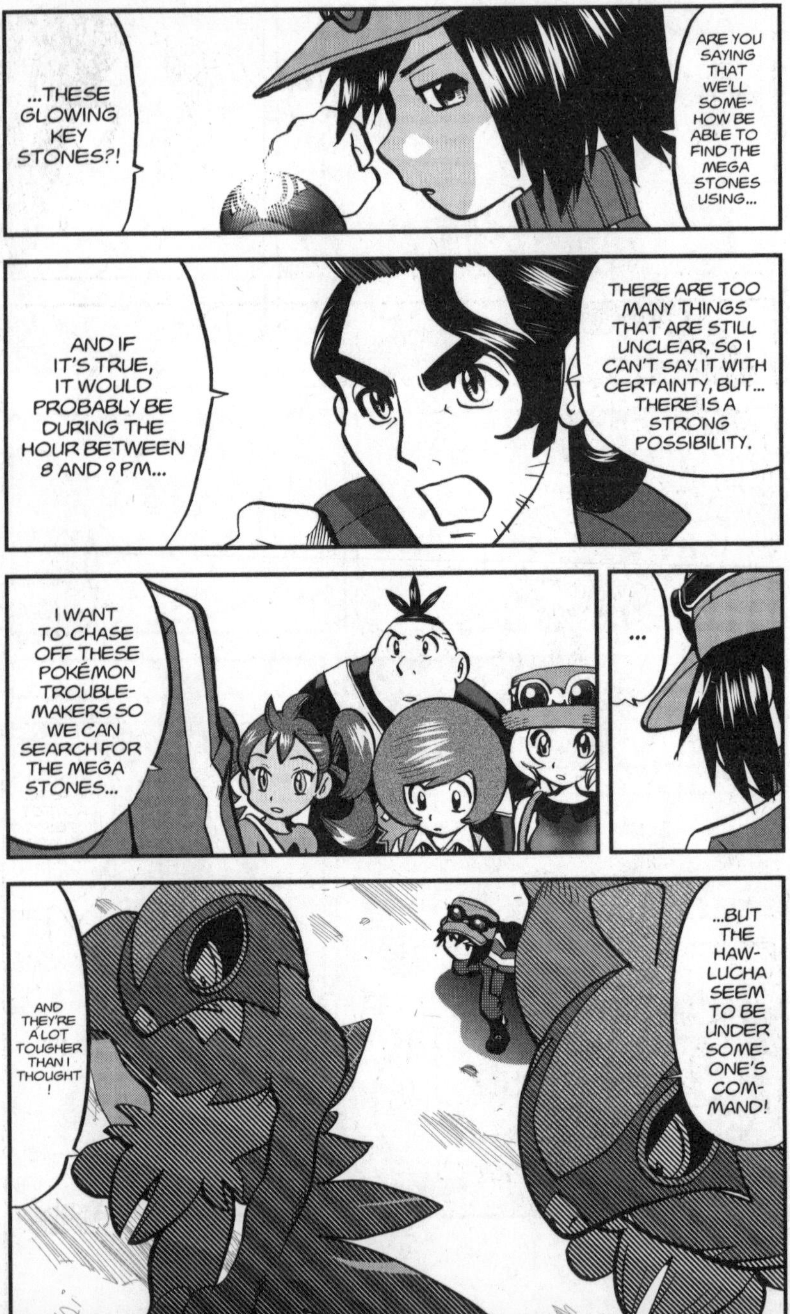
ARE YOU SAYING THAT WE'LL SOME-HOW BE ABLE TO FIND THE MEGA STONES USING...
...THESE GLOWING KEY STONES?!
THERE ARE TOO MANY THINGS THAT ARE STILL UNCLEAR, SO I CAN'T SAY IT WITH CERTAINTY, BUT... THERE IS A STRONG POSSIBILITY.
AND IF IT'S TRUE, IT WOULD PROBABLY BE DURING THE HOUR BETWEEN 8 AND 9 PM...
...
I WANT TO CHASE OFF THESE POKÉMON TROUBLE-MAKERS SO WE CAN SEARCH FOR THE MEGA STONES...
...BUT THE HAW-LUCHA SEEM TO BE UNDER SOME-ONE'S COM-MAND!
AND THEY'RE A LOT TOUGHER THAN I THOUGHT!

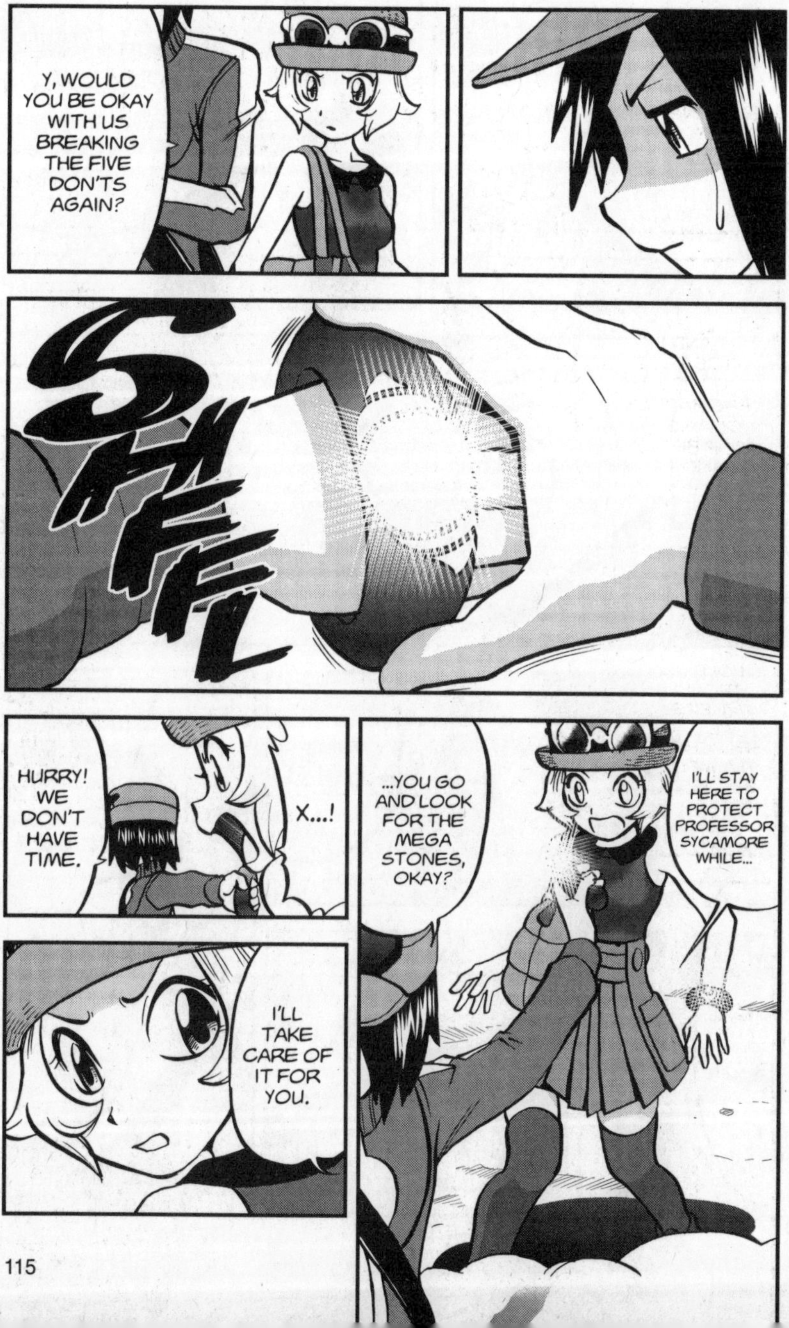
Y, WOULD YOU BE OKAY WITH US BREAKING THE FIVE DON'TS AGAIN?
SHFFL
I'LL STAY HERE TO PROTECT PROFESSOR SYCAMORE WHILE...
...YOU GO AND LOOK FOR THE MEGA STONES, OKAY?
X...!
HURRY! WE DON'T HAVE TIME.
I'LL TAKE CARE OF IT FOR YOU.

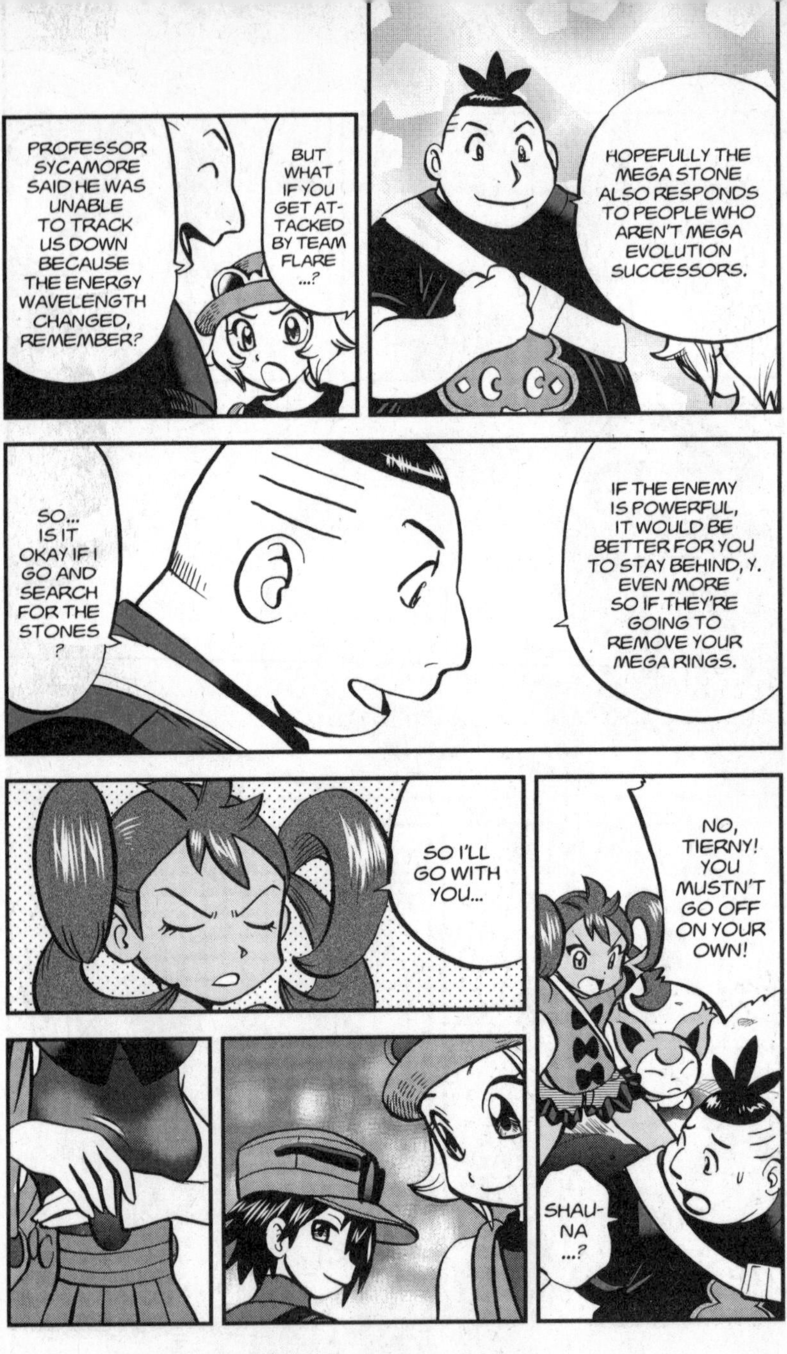
HOPEFULLY THE MEGA STONE ALSO RESPONDS TO PEOPLE WHO AREN'T MEGA EVOLUTION SUCCESSORS.
BUT WHAT IF YOU GET ATTACKED BY TEAM FLARE ...?
PROFESSOR SYCAMORE SAID HE WAS UNABLE TO TRACK US DOWN BECAUSE THE ENERGY WAVELENGTH CHANGED, REMEMBER?
IF THE ENEMY IS POWERFUL, IT WOULD BE BETTER FOR YOU TO STAY BEHIND, Y. EVEN MORE SO IF THEY'RE GOING TO REMOVE YOUR MEGA RINGS.
SO... IS IT OKAY IF I GO AND SEARCH FOR THE STONES ?
NO, TIERNY! YOU MUSTN'T GO OFF ON YOUR OWN!
SHAU-NA ...?
SO I'LL GO WITH YOU...

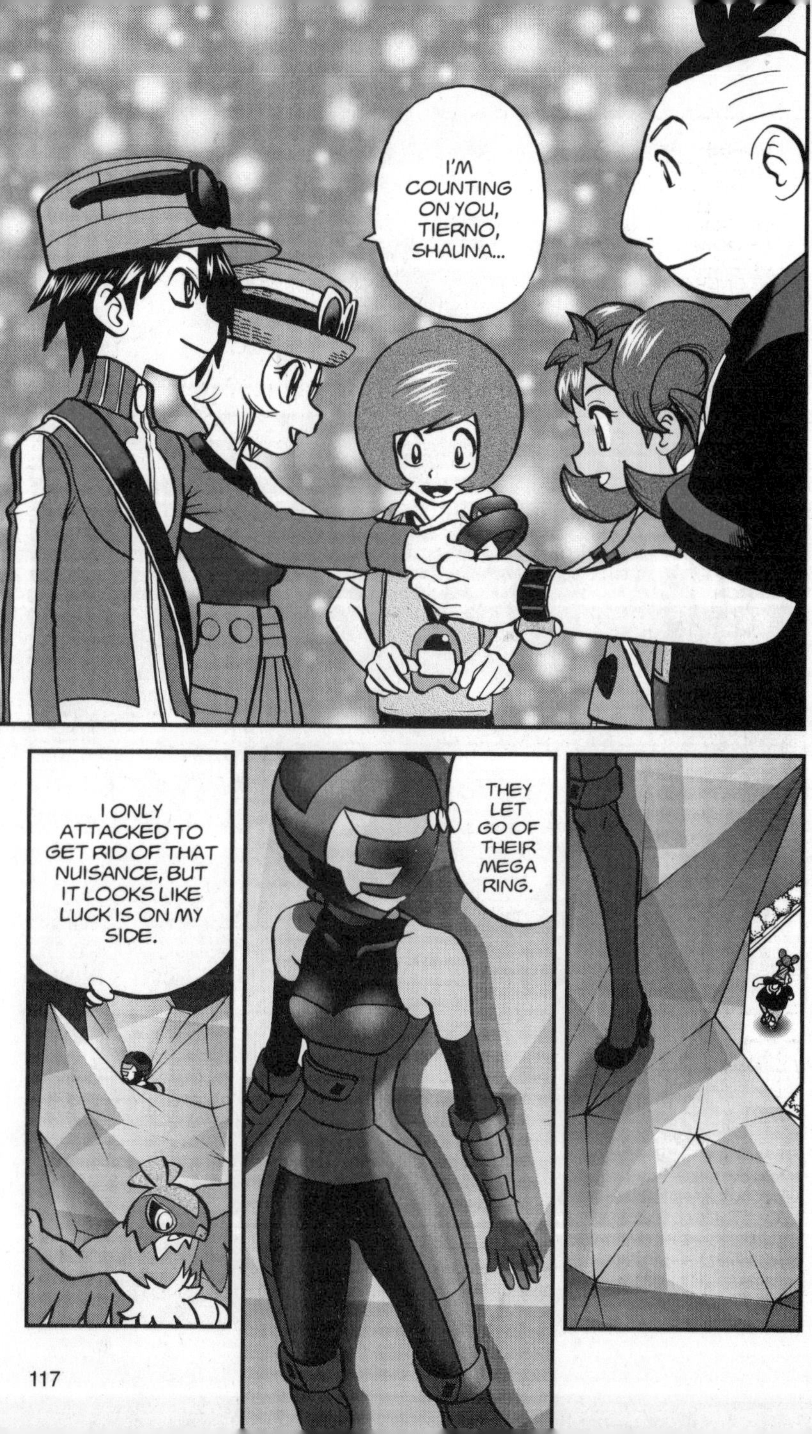
I'M COUNTING ON YOU, TIERNO, SHAUNA...
THEY LET GO OF THEIR MEGA RING.
I ONLY ATTACKED TO GET RID OF THAT NUISANCE, BUT IT LOOKS LIKE LUCK IS ON MY SIDE.

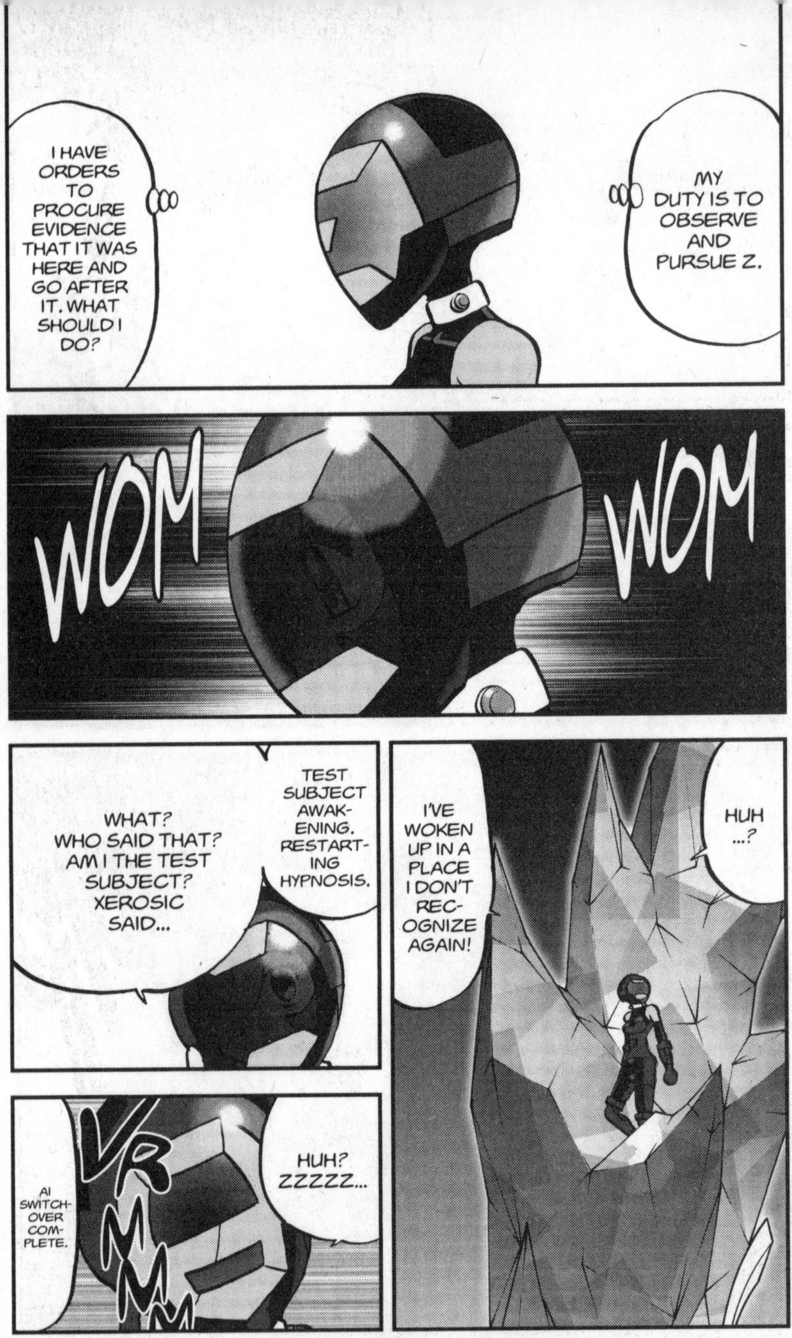
MY DUTY IS TO OBSERVE AND PURSUE Z.
I HAVE ORDERS TO PROCURE EVIDENCE THAT IT WAS HERE AND GO AFTER IT. WHAT SHOULD I DO?
WOM
WOM
HUH ...?
I'VE WOKEN UP IN A PLACE I DON'T REC-OGNIZE AGAIN!
TEST SUBJECT AWAK-ENING. RESTART-ING HYPNOSIS.
WHAT? WHO SAID THAT? AM I THE TEST SUBJECT? XEROSIC SAID...
HUH? ZZZZZ...
VRMMM
AI SWITCH-OVER COM-PLETE.

YOU MUST BE, UM... ESSEN-TIA!

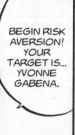

BEGIN RISK AVERSION! YOUR TARGET IS... YVONNE GABENA.

I FOUND YOU!

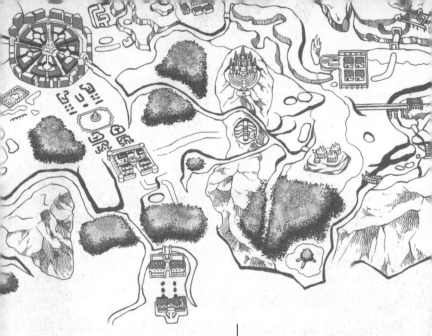

Current Location

Route 15
Brun Way

This path has become a popular hangout for the wild and directionless youths of Lumiose City.

▼

Dendemille Town

A rural town where Pokémon and windmills work together to farm the land in a chilly latitude.

▼

Route 17
Mamoswine Road

Due to constant snowstorms and heavy snowfall, humans have no hope of traversing this road on foot.

▼

Anistar City

Some say the enigmatic device used as a sundial came from outer space.

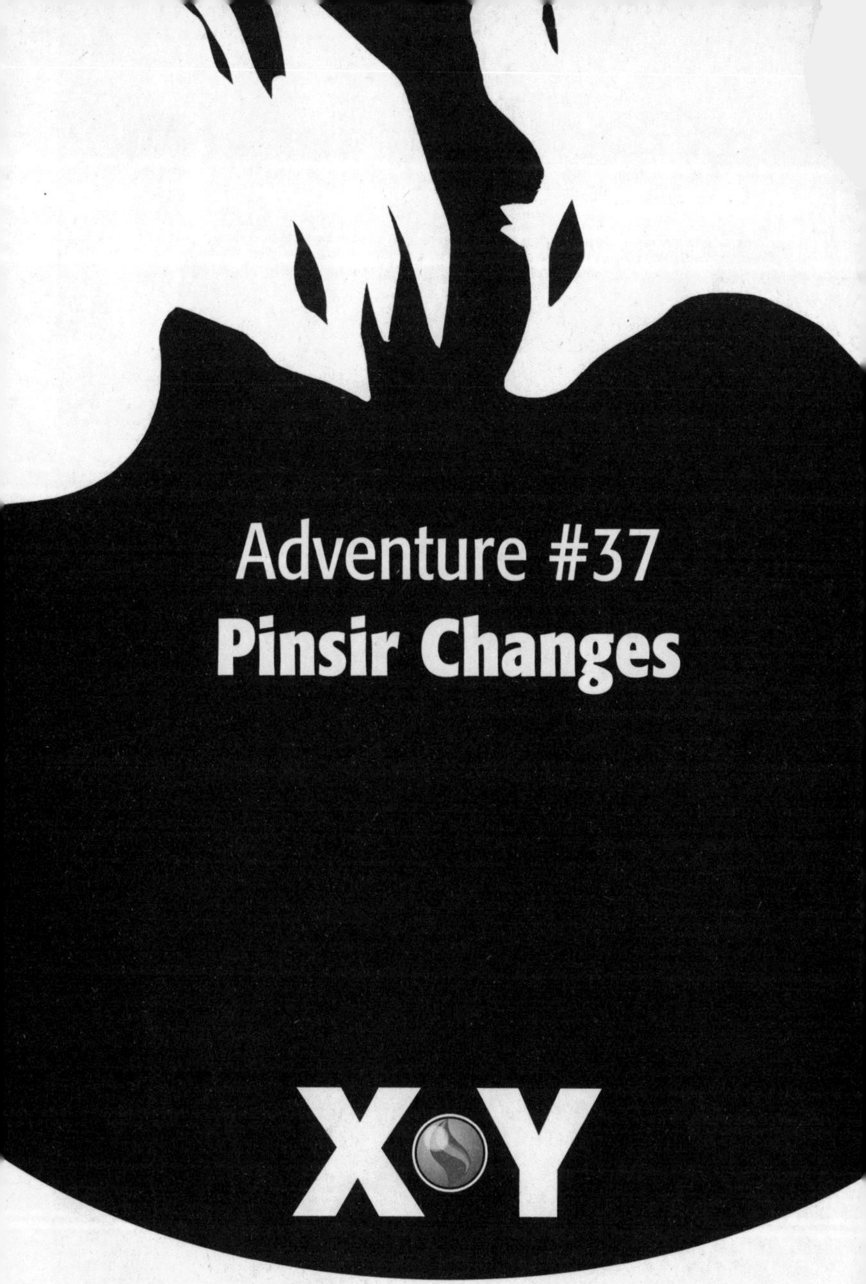

Adventure #37
Pinsir Changes

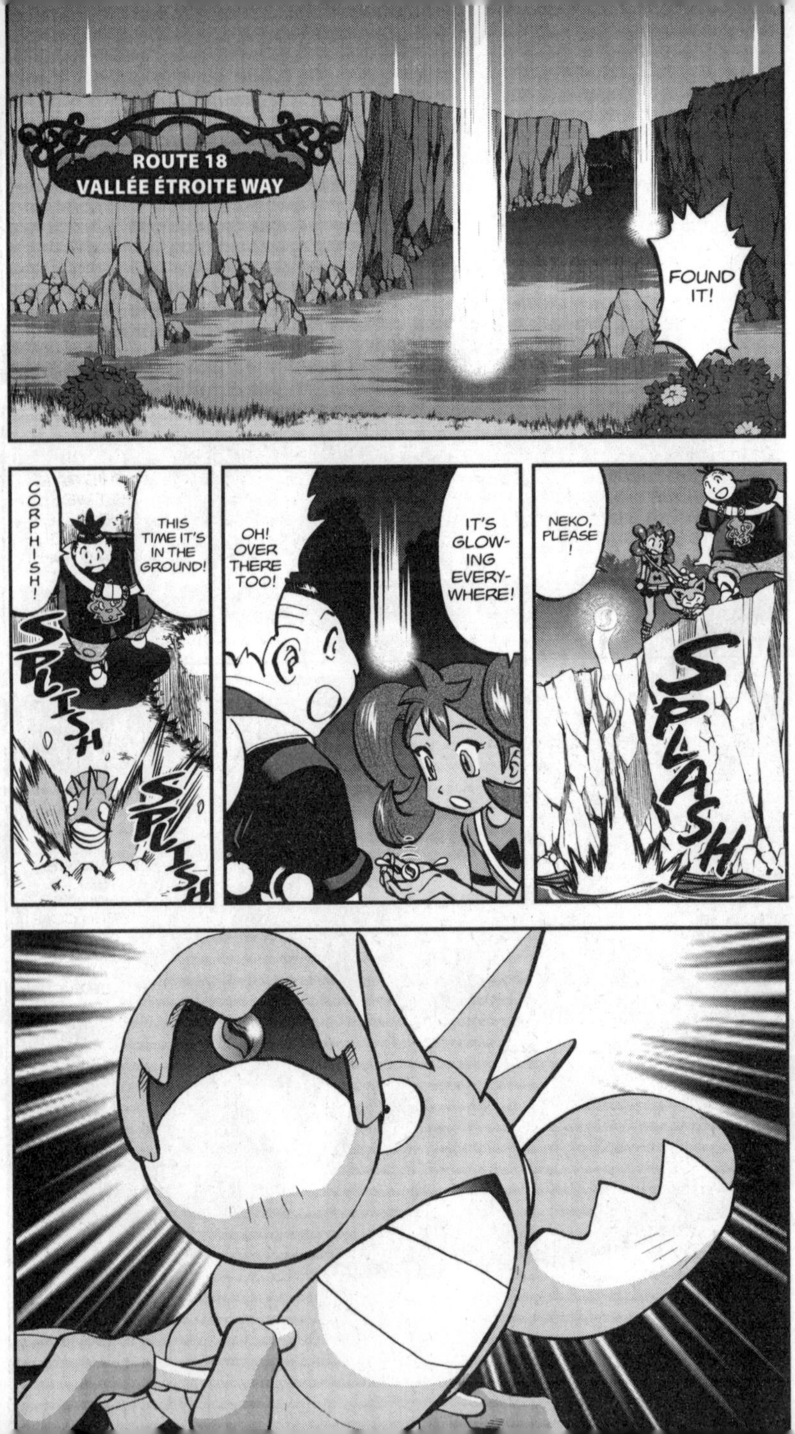
ROUTE 18
VALLÉE ÉTROITE WAY
FOUND IT!
NEKO, PLEASE!
SPLASH
IT'S GLOWING EVERYWHERE!
OH! OVER THERE TOO!
THIS TIME IT'S IN THE GROUND!
CORPHISH!
SPLISH
SPLISH

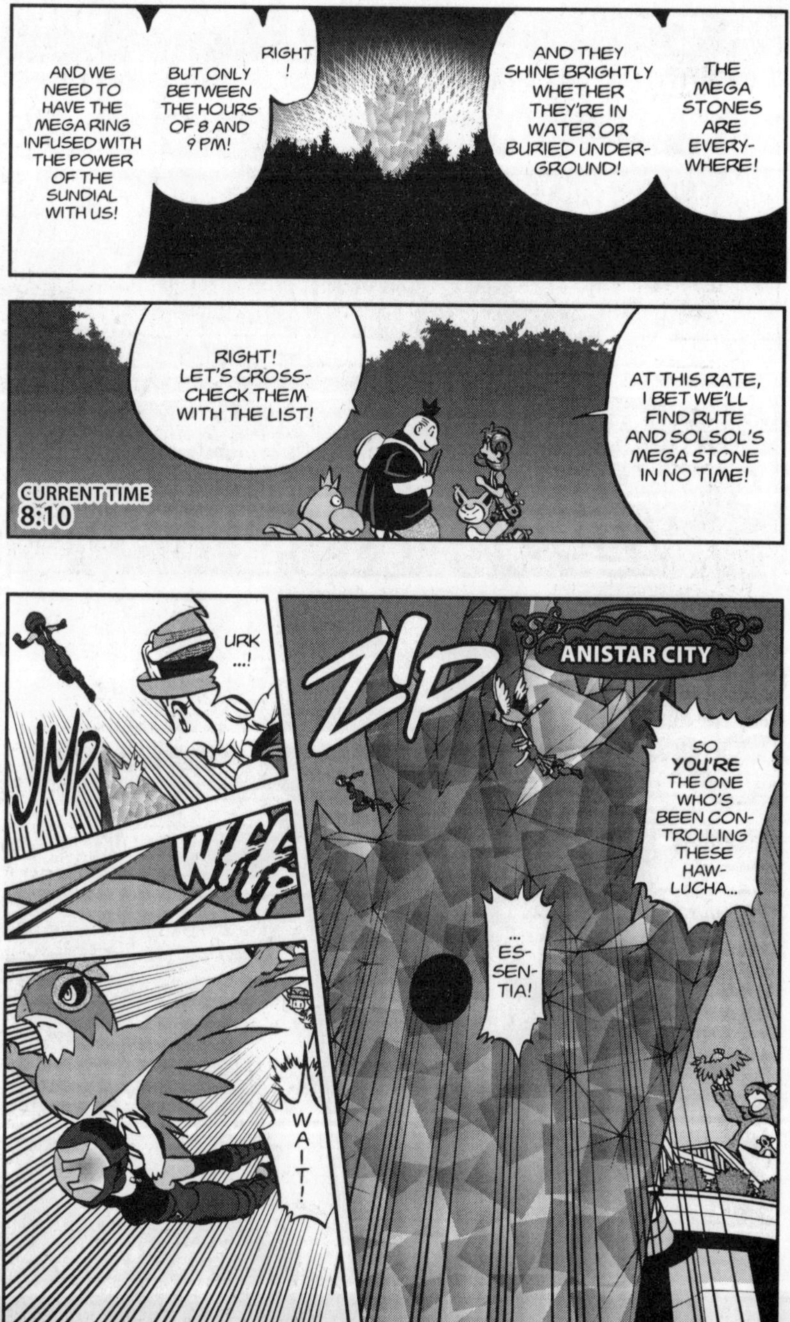
THE MEGA STONES ARE EVERYWHERE!
AND THEY SHINE BRIGHTLY WHETHER THEY'RE IN WATER OR BURIED UNDERGROUND!
RIGHT!
BUT ONLY BETWEEN THE HOURS OF 8 AND 9 PM!
AND WE NEED TO HAVE THE MEGA RING INFUSED WITH THE POWER OF THE SUNDIAL WITH US!
AT THIS RATE, I BET WE'LL FIND RUTE AND SOLSOL'S MEGA STONE IN NO TIME!
RIGHT! LET'S CROSS-CHECK THEM WITH THE LIST!
CURRENT TIME 8:10
ANISTAR CITY
ZIP
SO YOU'RE THE ONE WHO'S BEEN CONTROLLING THESE HAWLUCHA...
...ESSENTIA!
URK...!
JMP
WAIT!

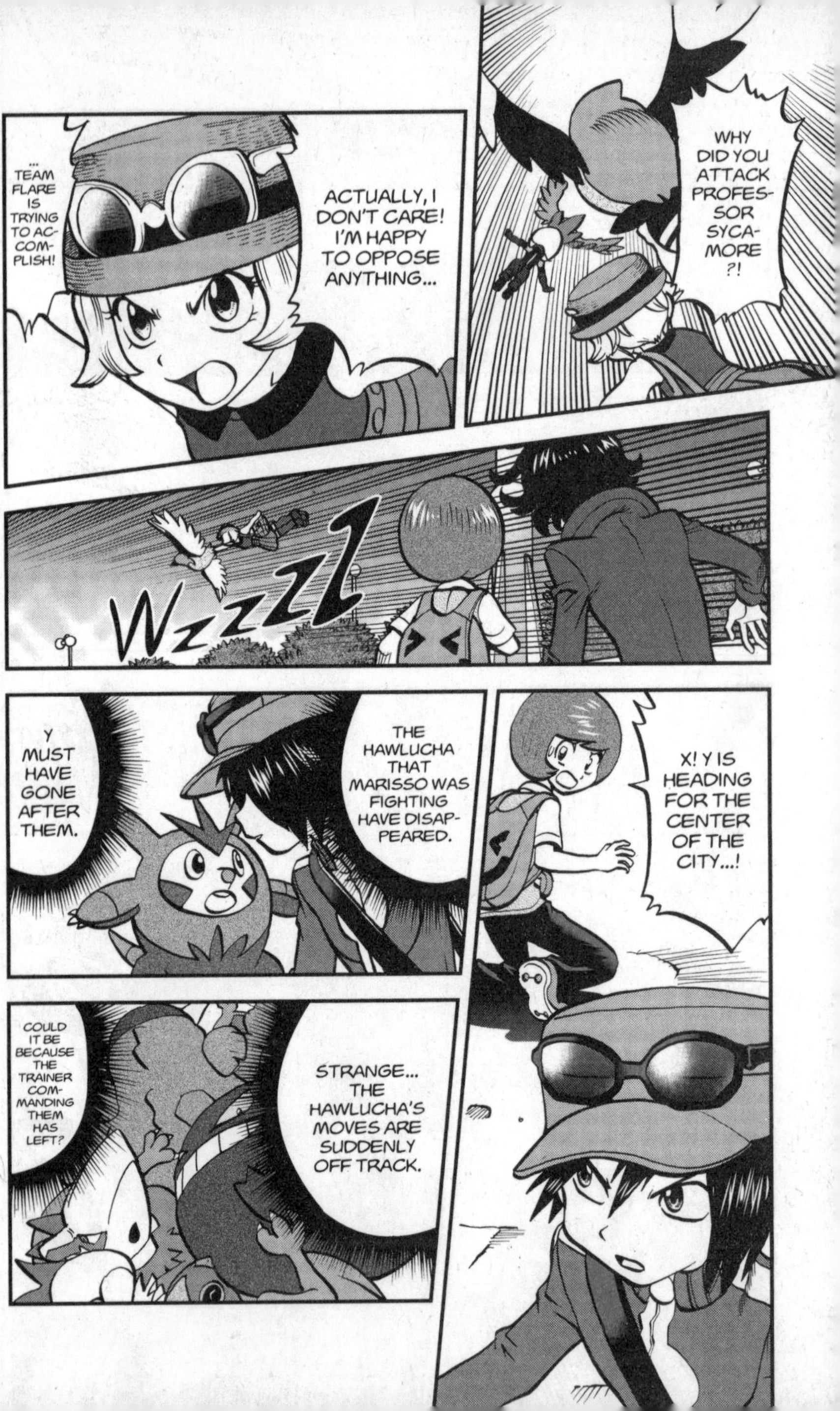
WHY DID YOU ATTACK PROFESSOR SYCAMORE?!
ACTUALLY, I DON'T CARE! I'M HAPPY TO OPPOSE ANYTHING...
...TEAM FLARE IS TRYING TO ACCOMPLISH!
WZZZZ
X! Y IS HEADING FOR THE CENTER OF THE CITY...!
THE HAWLUCHA THAT MARISSO WAS FIGHTING HAVE DISAPPEARED.
Y MUST HAVE GONE AFTER THEM.
STRANGE... THE HAWLUCHA'S MOVES ARE SUDDENLY OFF TRACK.
COULD IT BE BECAUSE THE TRAINER COMMANDING THEM HAS LEFT?

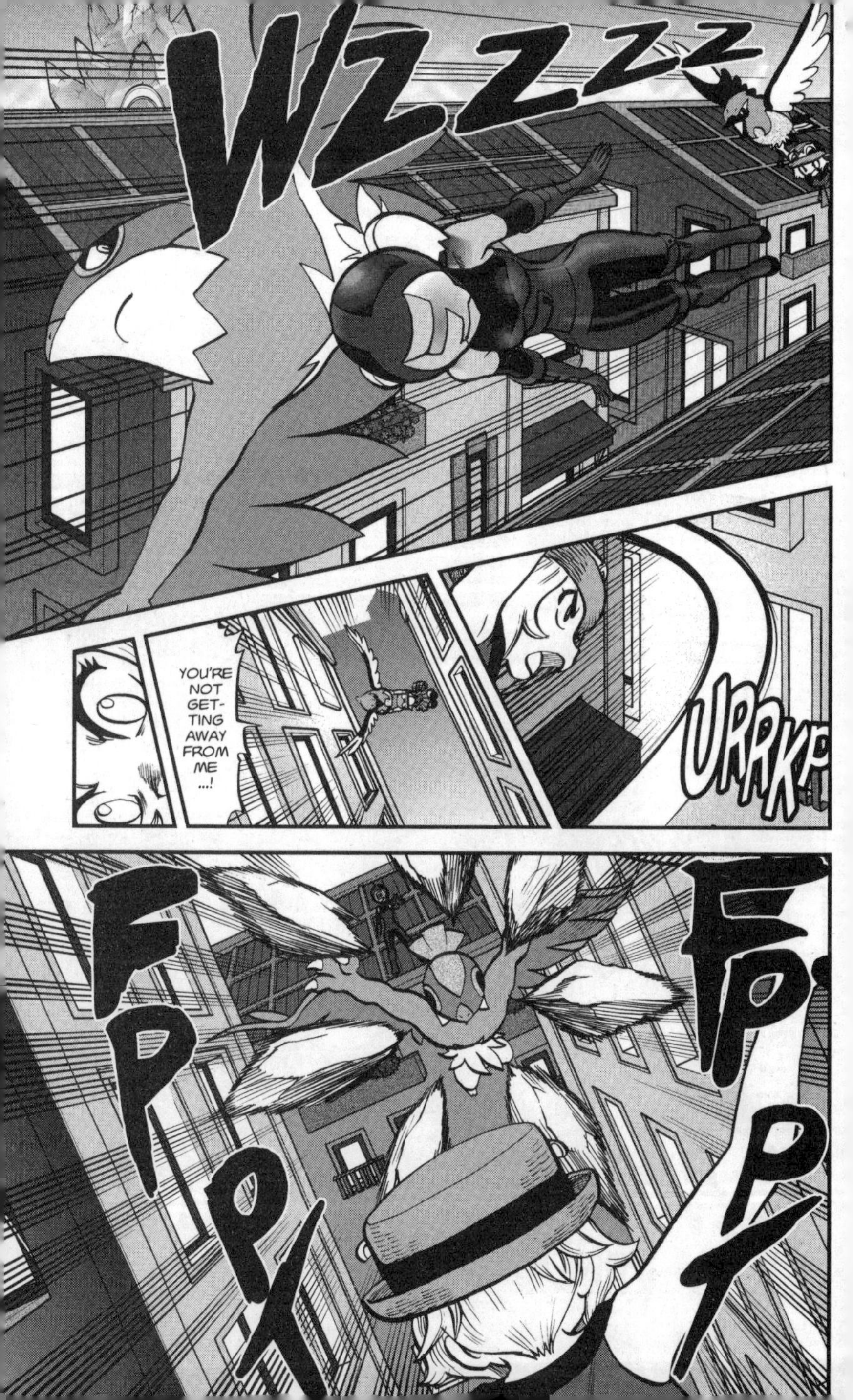
WZZZZZ
URRKP
YOU'RE NOT GETTING AWAY FROM ME ...!

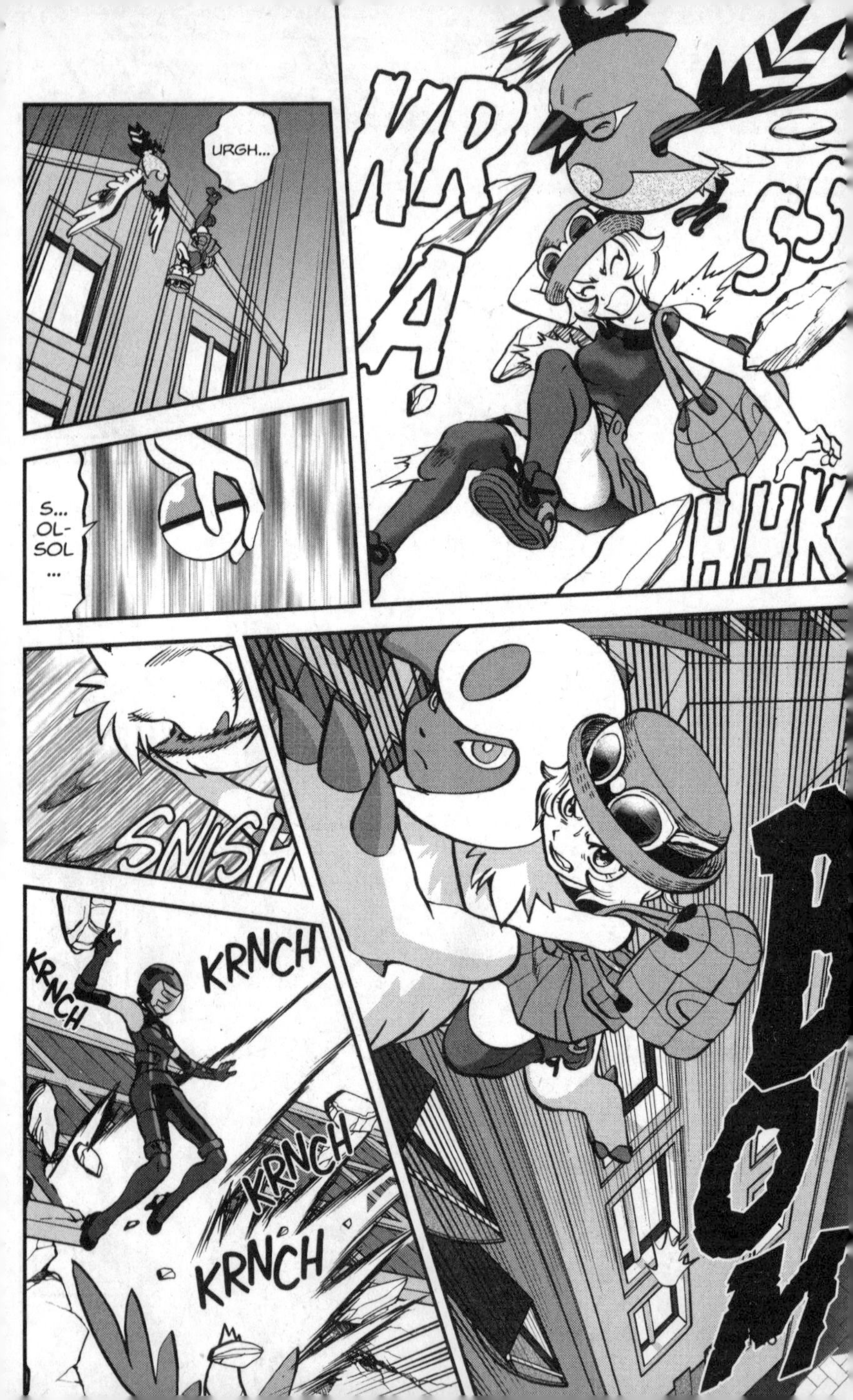
KRASSHHK
URGH...
S... OL-SOL ...
BOM
SNISH
KRNCH
KRNCH
KRNCH
KRNCH

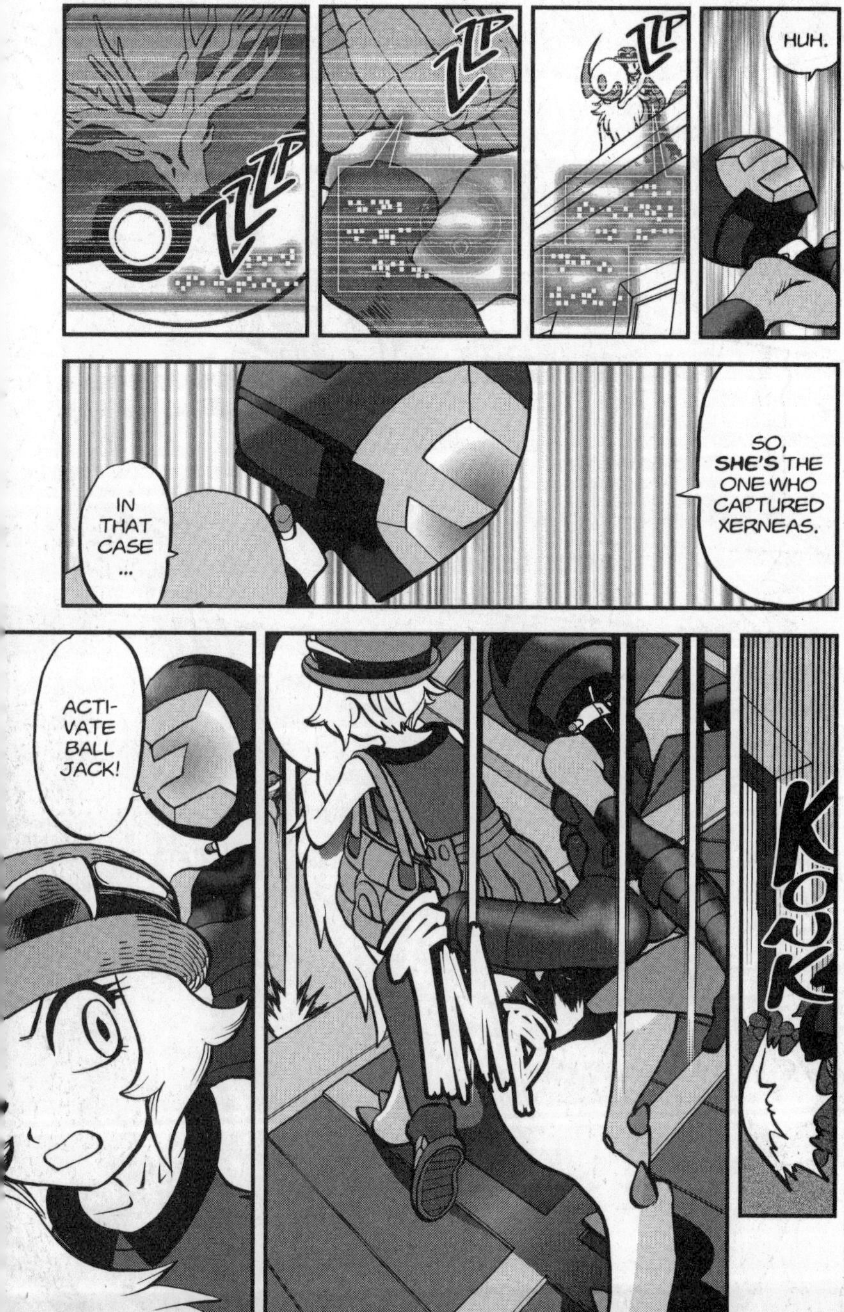
HUH.
ZZZP
ZZZP
ZZZP
SO, SHE'S THE ONE WHO CAPTURED XERNEAS.
IN THAT CASE ...
TMP
ACTI-VATE BALL JACK!

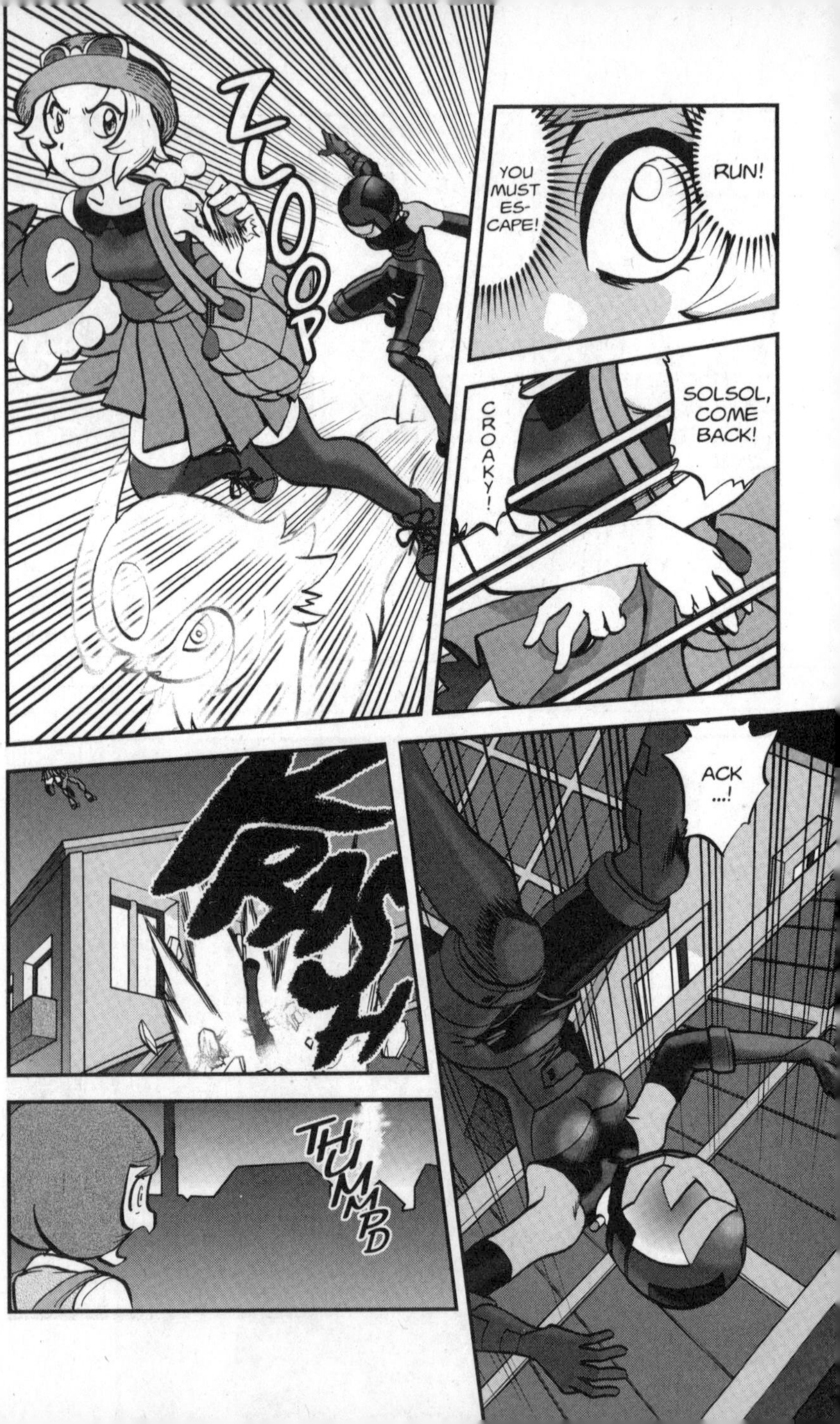
RUN!
YOU MUST ES-CAPE!
SOLSOL, COME BACK!
CROAKY!
ZZOOP
ACK ...!
KRASH
THUMMPD

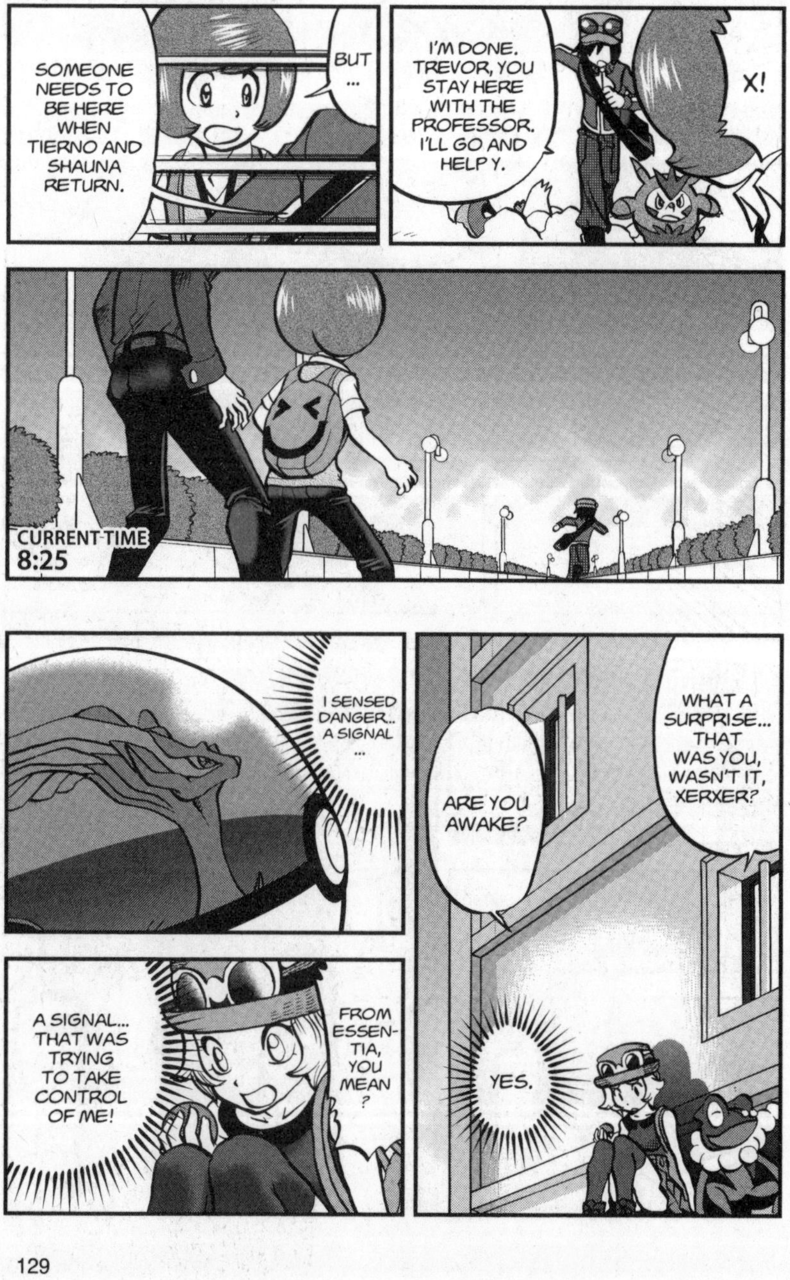
X!
I'M DONE. TREVOR, YOU STAY HERE WITH THE PROFESSOR. I'LL GO AND HELP Y.
BUT ...
SOMEONE NEEDS TO BE HERE WHEN TIERNO AND SHAUNA RETURN.
CURRENT TIME 8:25
WHAT A SURPRISE... THAT WAS YOU, WASN'T IT, XERXER?
ARE YOU AWAKE?
YES.
I SENSED DANGER... A SIGNAL ...
FROM ESSENTIA, YOU MEAN?
A SIGNAL... THAT WAS TRYING TO TAKE CONTROL OF ME!

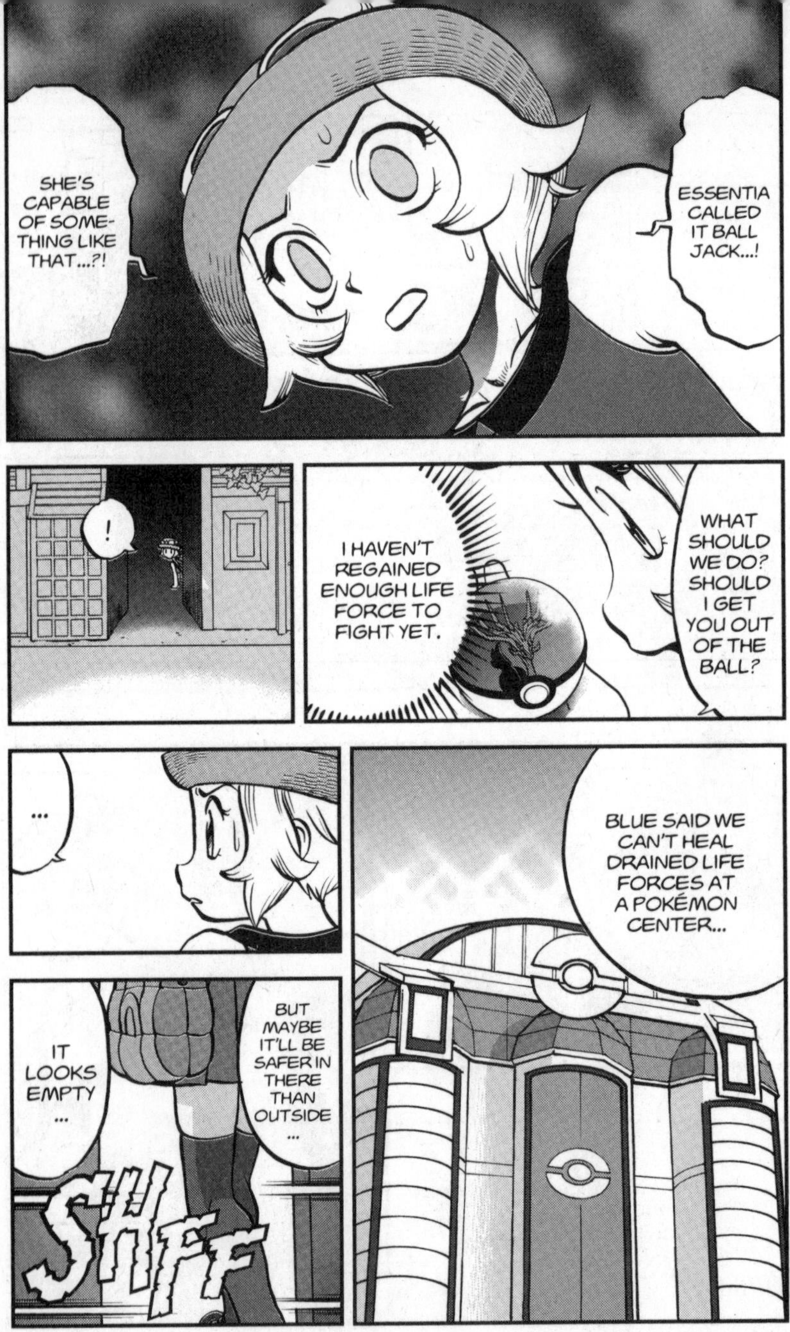
ESSENTIA CALLED IT BALL JACK...!
SHE'S CAPABLE OF SOMETHING LIKE THAT...?!
WHAT SHOULD WE DO? SHOULD I GET YOU OUT OF THE BALL?
I HAVEN'T REGAINED ENOUGH LIFE FORCE TO FIGHT YET.
!
BLUE SAID WE CAN'T HEAL DRAINED LIFE FORCES AT A POKÉMON CENTER...
...
BUT MAYBE IT'LL BE SAFER IN THERE THAN OUTSIDE...
IT LOOKS EMPTY...
SHFF

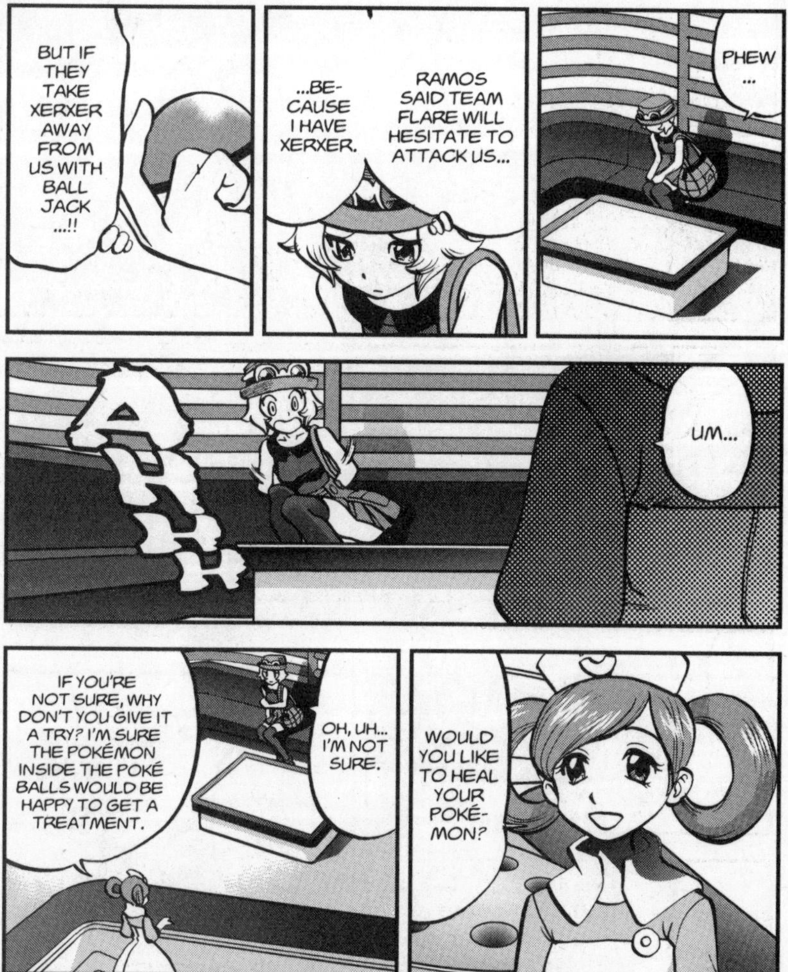
PHEW ...
RAMOS SAID TEAM FLARE WILL HESITATE TO ATTACK US...
...BE-CAUSE I HAVE XERXER.
BUT IF THEY TAKE XERXER AWAY FROM US WITH BALL JACK ...!!
UM...
AHH
WOULD YOU LIKE TO HEAL YOUR POKÉ-MON?
OH, UH... I'M NOT SURE.
IF YOU'RE NOT SURE, WHY DON'T YOU GIVE IT A TRY? I'M SURE THE POKÉMON INSIDE THE POKÉ BALLS WOULD BE HAPPY TO GET A TREATMENT.
RIGHT. FLETCHY IS HURT, SO MAYBE I'LL DO THAT.

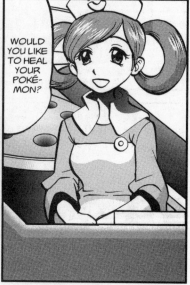

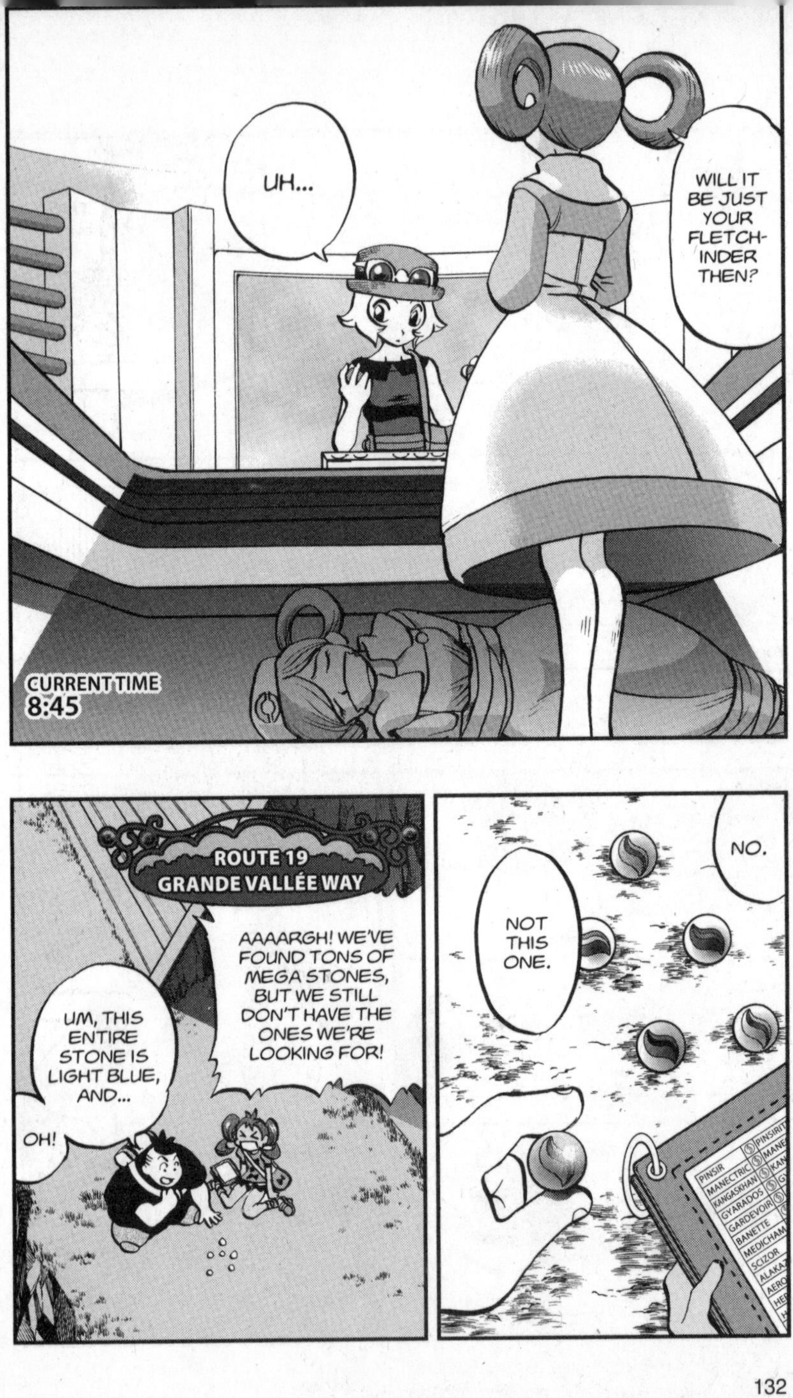
WILL IT BE JUST YOUR FLETCH-INDER THEN?
UH...
CURRENT TIME 8:45
NO.
NOT THIS ONE.
PINSIR
MANECTRIC
KANGASKHAN
GYARADOS
GARDEVOIR
BANETTE
MEDICHAM
SCIZOR
ROUTE 19 GRANDE VALLÉE WAY
AAAARGH! WE'VE FOUND TONS OF MEGA STONES, BUT WE STILL DON'T HAVE THE ONES WE'RE LOOKING FOR!
UM, THIS ENTIRE STONE IS LIGHT BLUE, AND...
OH!

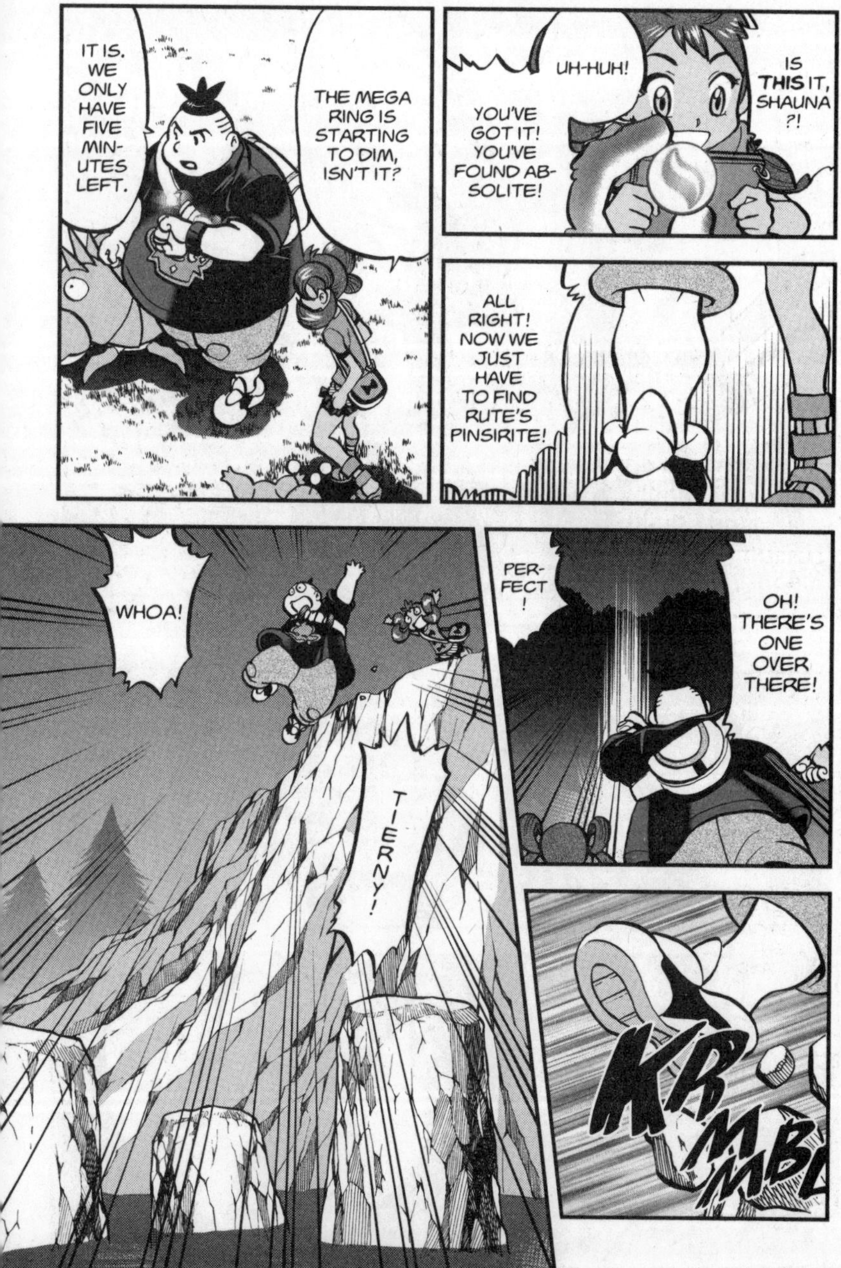
IS THIS IT, SHAUNA?!
UH-HUH!
YOU'VE GOT IT! YOU'VE FOUND ABSOLITE!
ALL RIGHT! NOW WE JUST HAVE TO FIND RUTE'S PINSIRITE!
THE MEGA RING IS STARTING TO DIM, ISN'T IT?
IT IS. WE ONLY HAVE FIVE MINUTES LEFT.
OH! THERE'S ONE OVER THERE!
PERFECT!
KRMMBL
WHOA!
TIERNY!

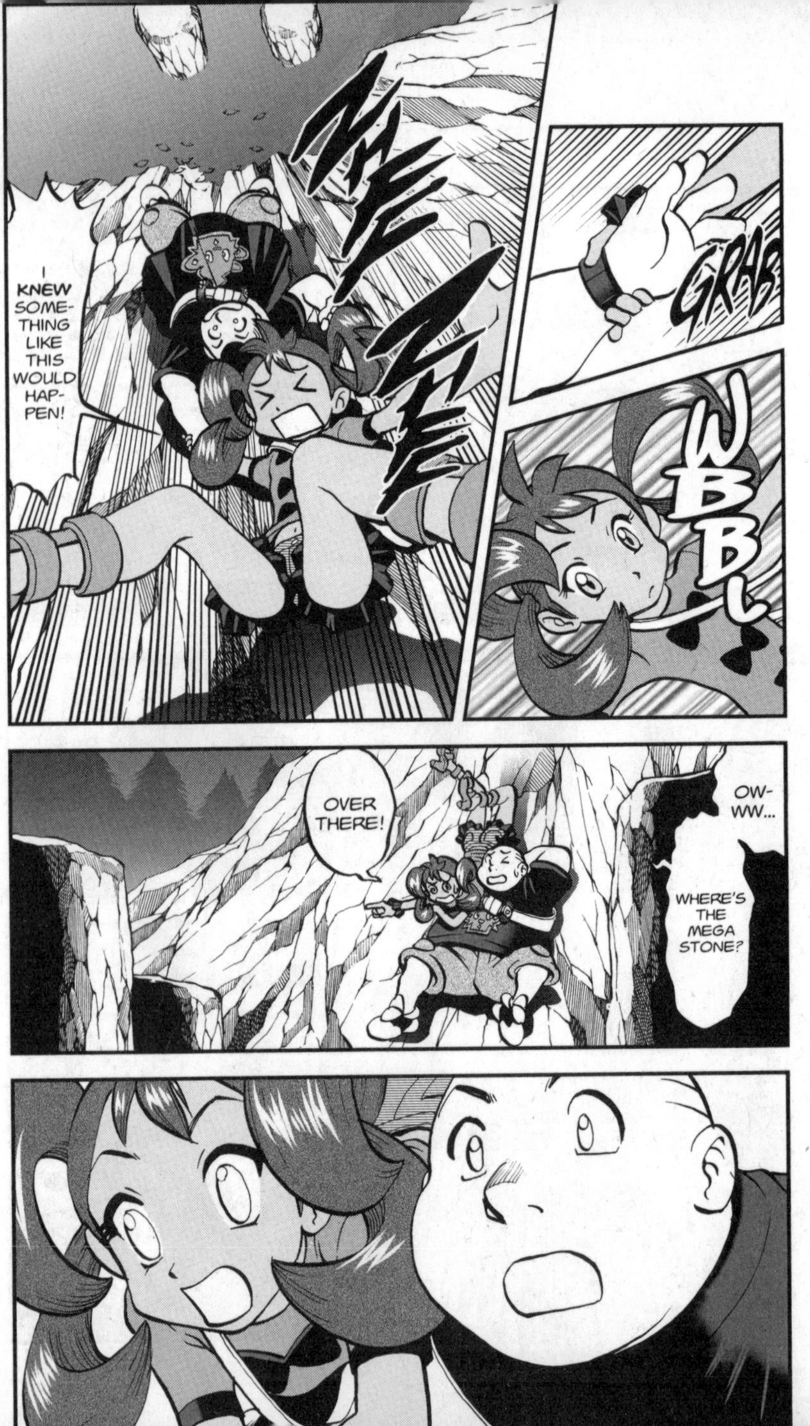
GRAB
WBBL
WHEEEEE
I KNEW SOMETHING LIKE THIS WOULD HAPPEN!
OW-WW...
WHERE'S THE MEGA STONE?
OVER THERE!

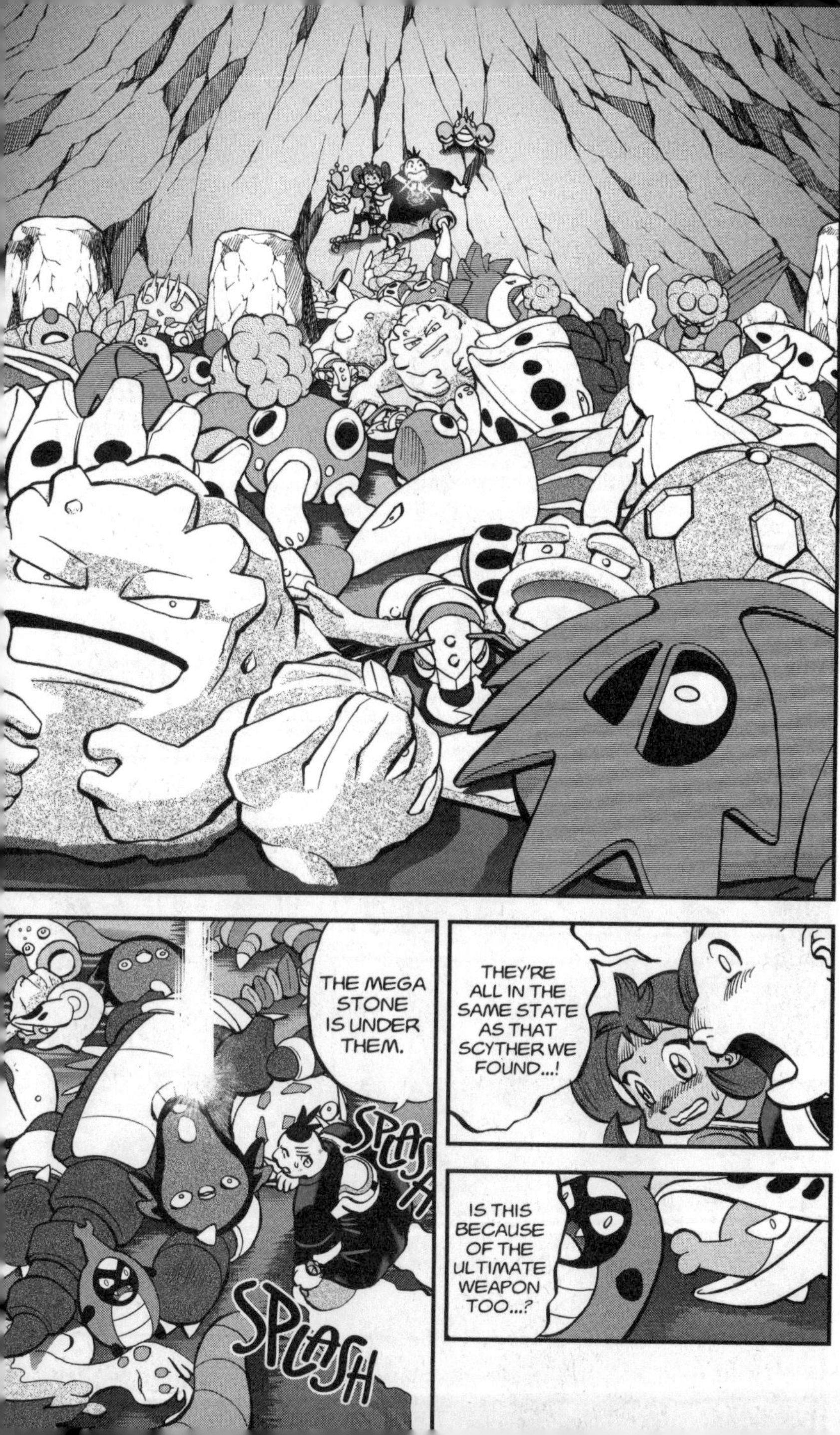
THEY'RE ALL IN THE SAME STATE AS THAT SCYTHER WE FOUND...!
IS THIS BECAUSE OF THE ULTIMATE WEAPON TOO...?
THE MEGA STONE IS UNDER THEM.
SPLASH
SPLASH

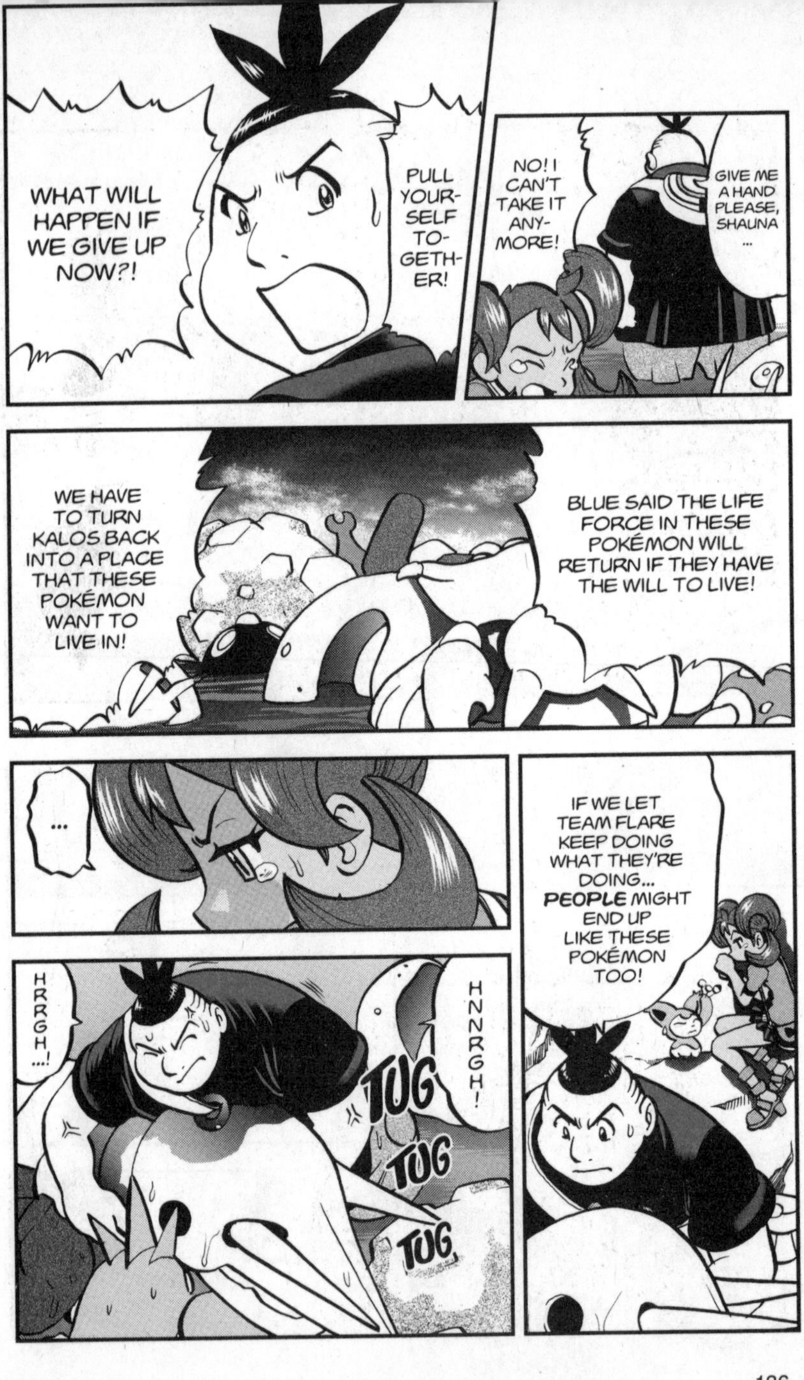
GIVE ME A HAND PLEASE, SHAUNA ...
NO! I CAN'T TAKE IT ANY-MORE!
PULL YOUR-SELF TO-GETH-ER!
WHAT WILL HAPPEN IF WE GIVE UP NOW?!
BLUE SAID THE LIFE FORCE IN THESE POKÉMON WILL RETURN IF THEY HAVE THE WILL TO LIVE!
WE HAVE TO TURN KALOS BACK INTO A PLACE THAT THESE POKÉMON WANT TO LIVE IN!
IF WE LET TEAM FLARE KEEP DOING WHAT THEY'RE DOING... **PEOPLE** MIGHT END UP LIKE THESE POKÉMON TOO!
...
HNNRGH!
TUG
TUG
TUG
HRRGH...!

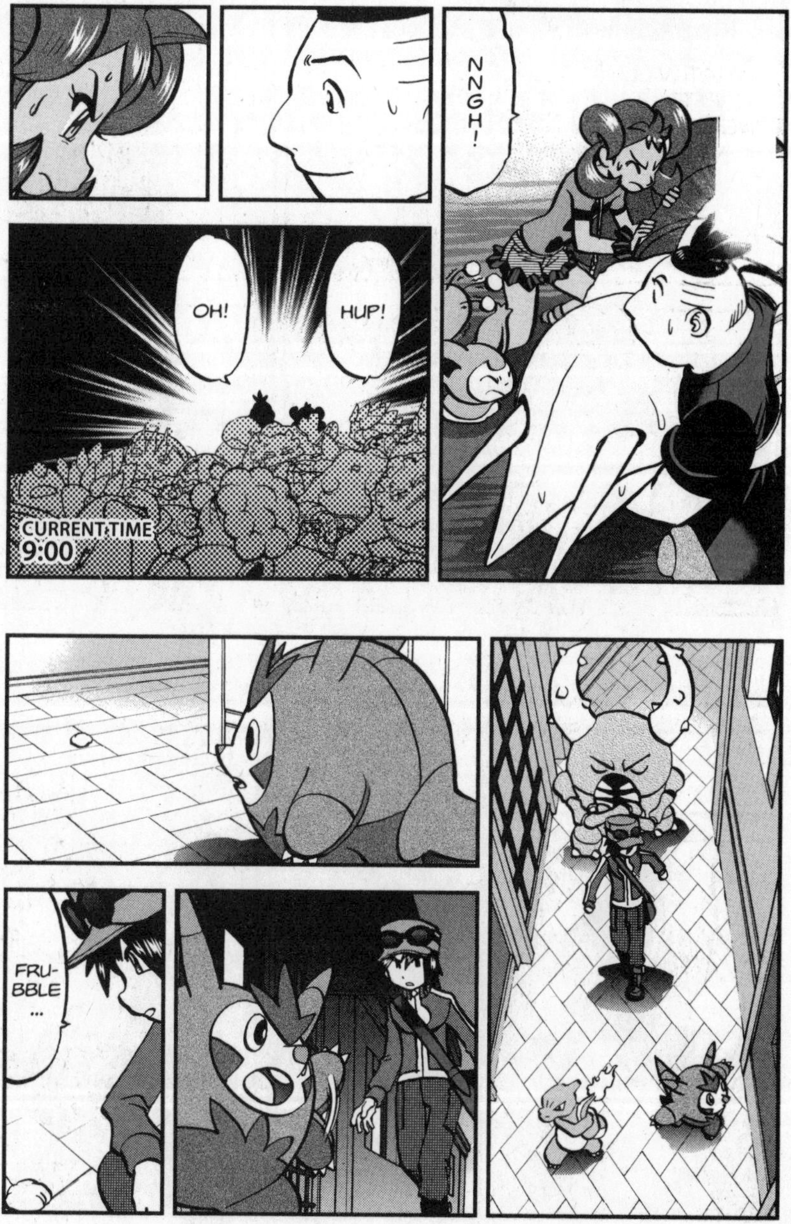
NNGH!
HUP!
OH!
CURRENT TIME
9:00
FRUBBLE...

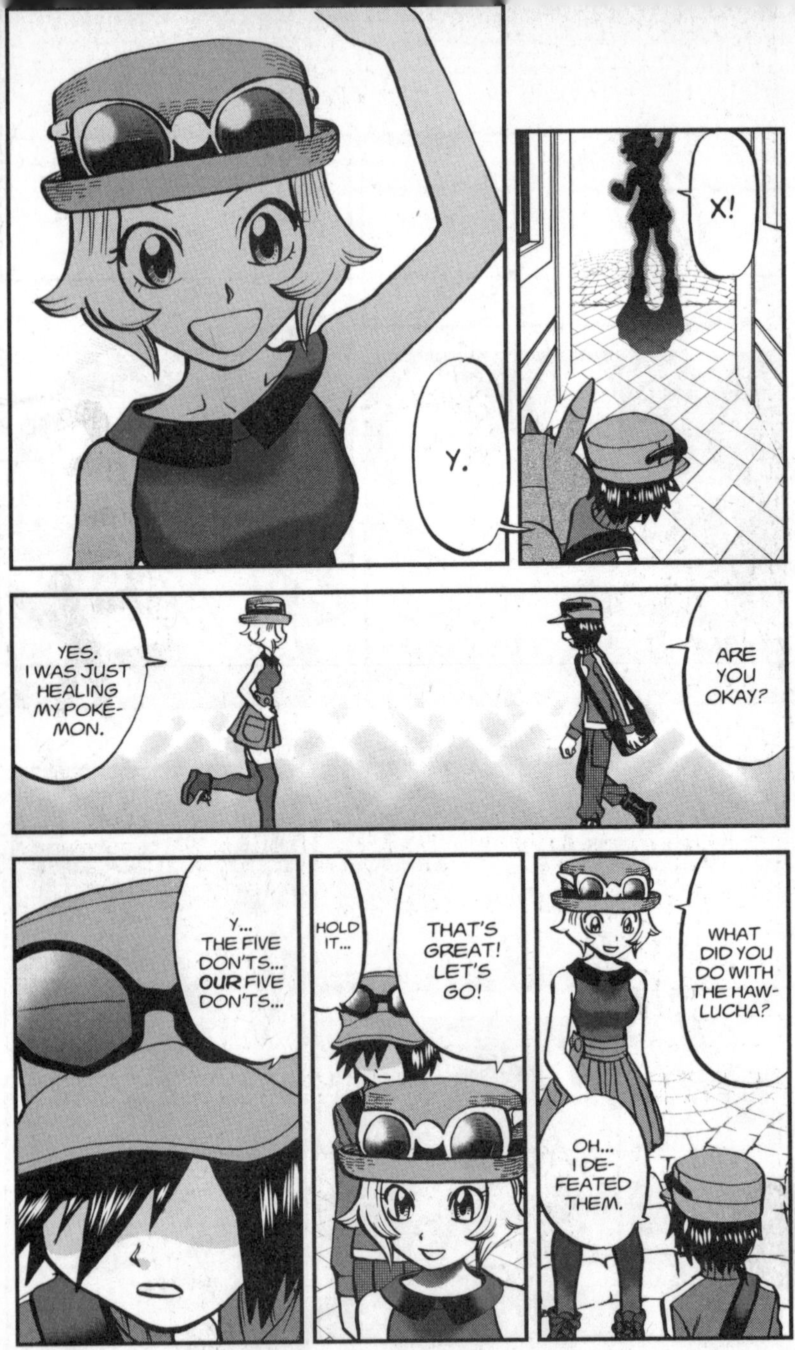
X!
Y.
ARE YOU OKAY?
YES. I WAS JUST HEALING MY POKÉ-MON.
WHAT DID YOU DO WITH THE HAW-LUCHA?
OH... I DE-FEATED THEM.
THAT'S GREAT! LET'S GO!
HOLD IT...
Y... THE FIVE DON'TS... **OUR** FIVE DON'TS...

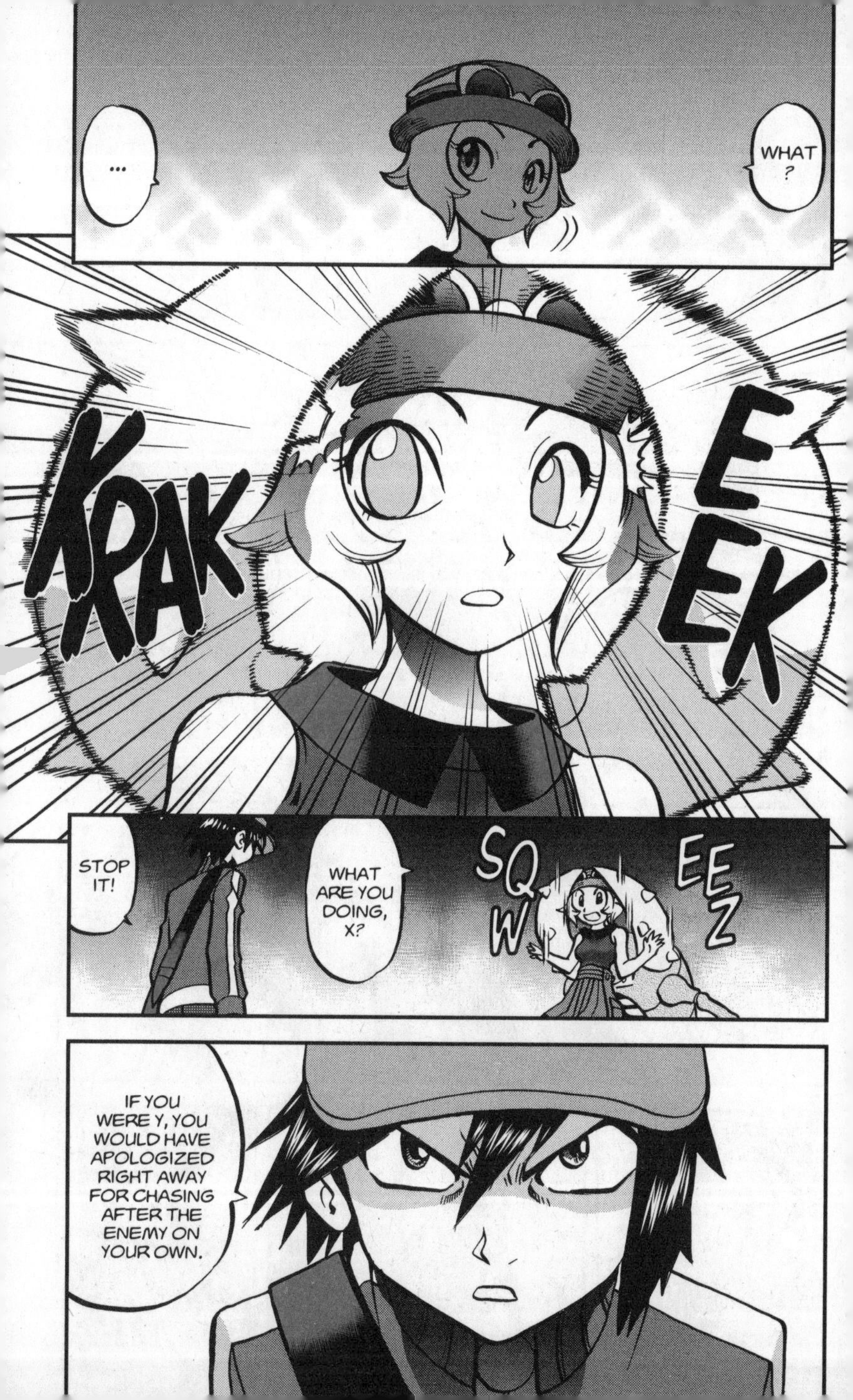
WHAT ?
...
EEK
KRAK
SQWEEZ
WHAT ARE YOU DOING, X?
STOP IT!
IF YOU WERE Y, YOU WOULD HAVE APOLOGIZED RIGHT AWAY FOR CHASING AFTER THE ENEMY ON YOUR OWN.

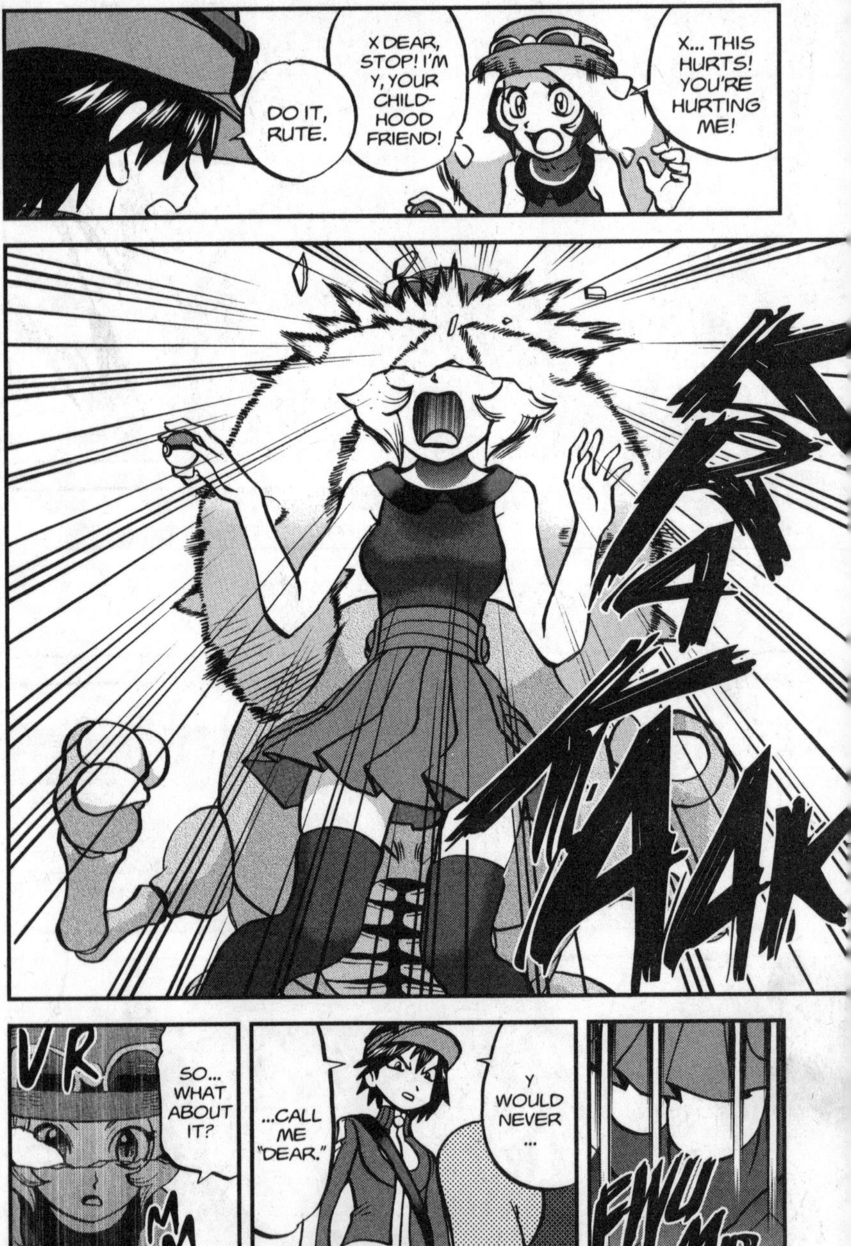
X... THIS HURTS! YOU'RE HURTING ME!
X DEAR, STOP! I'M Y, YOUR CHILD-HOOD FRIEND!
DO IT, RUTE.
Y WOULD NEVER ...
...CALL ME "DEAR."
SO... WHAT ABOUT IT?

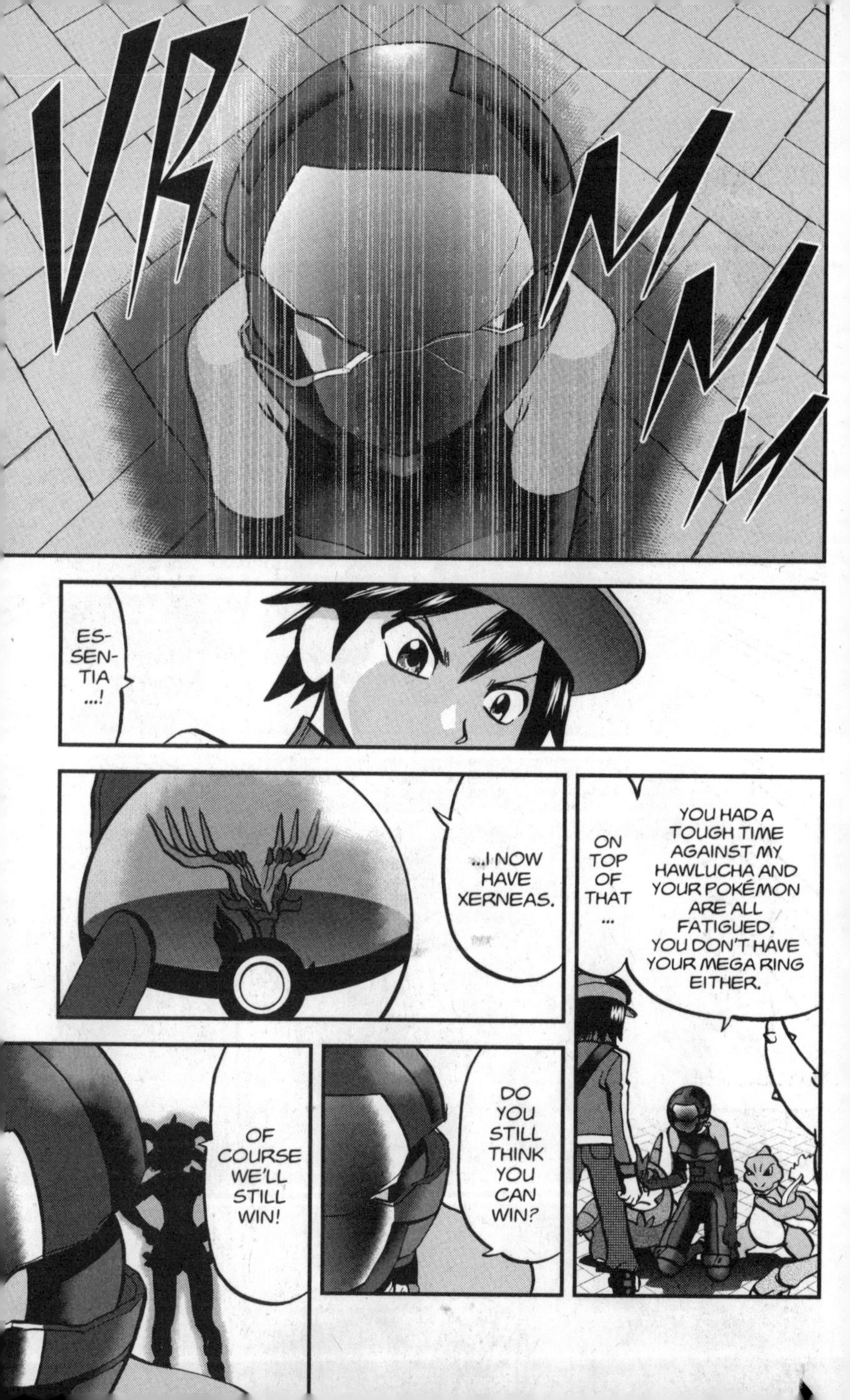
VRMMMM
ES-SEN-TIA ...!
YOU HAD A TOUGH TIME AGAINST MY HAWLUCHA AND YOUR POKÉMON ARE ALL FATIGUED. YOU DON'T HAVE YOUR MEGA RING EITHER.
ON TOP OF THAT ...
...I NOW HAVE XERNEAS.
DO YOU STILL THINK YOU CAN WIN?
OF COURSE WE'LL STILL WIN!

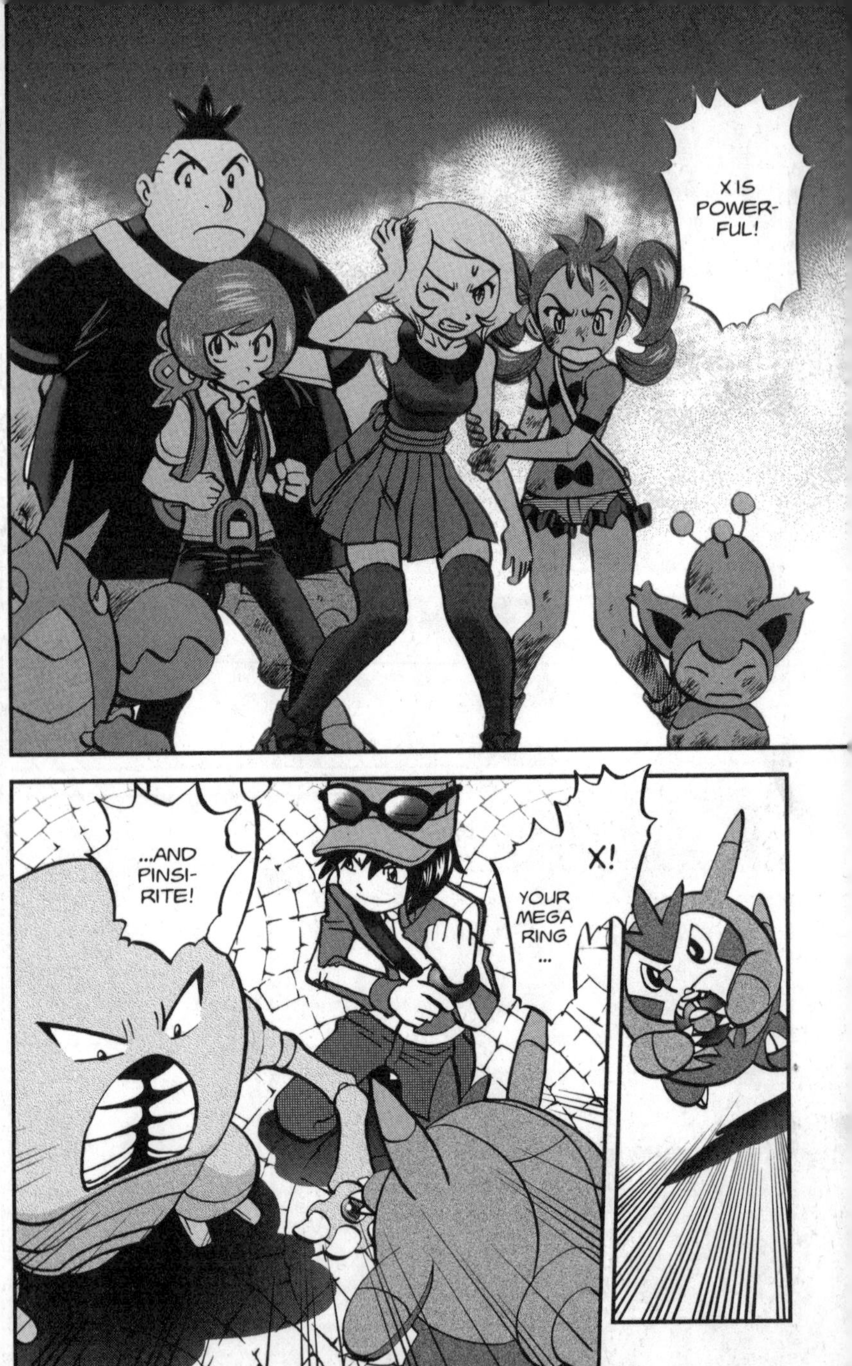
X IS POWER-FUL!
X!
YOUR MEGA RING ...
...AND PINSI-RITE!

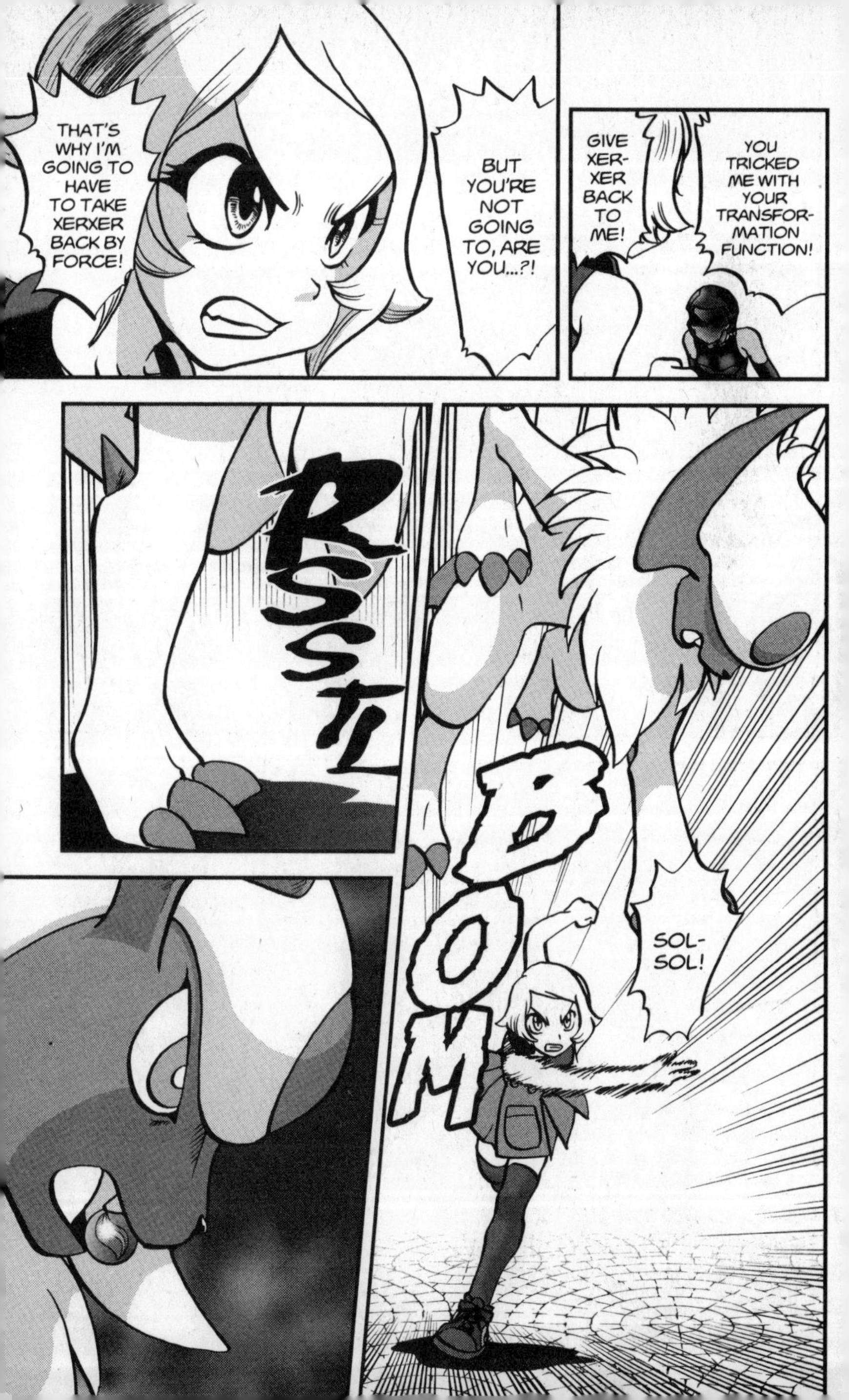
YOU TRICKED ME WITH YOUR TRANSFORMATION FUNCTION!
GIVE XERXER BACK TO ME!
BUT YOU'RE NOT GOING TO, ARE YOU...?!
THAT'S WHY I'M GOING TO HAVE TO TAKE XERXER BACK BY FORCE!
BOOM
SOL-SOL!
BSSTL

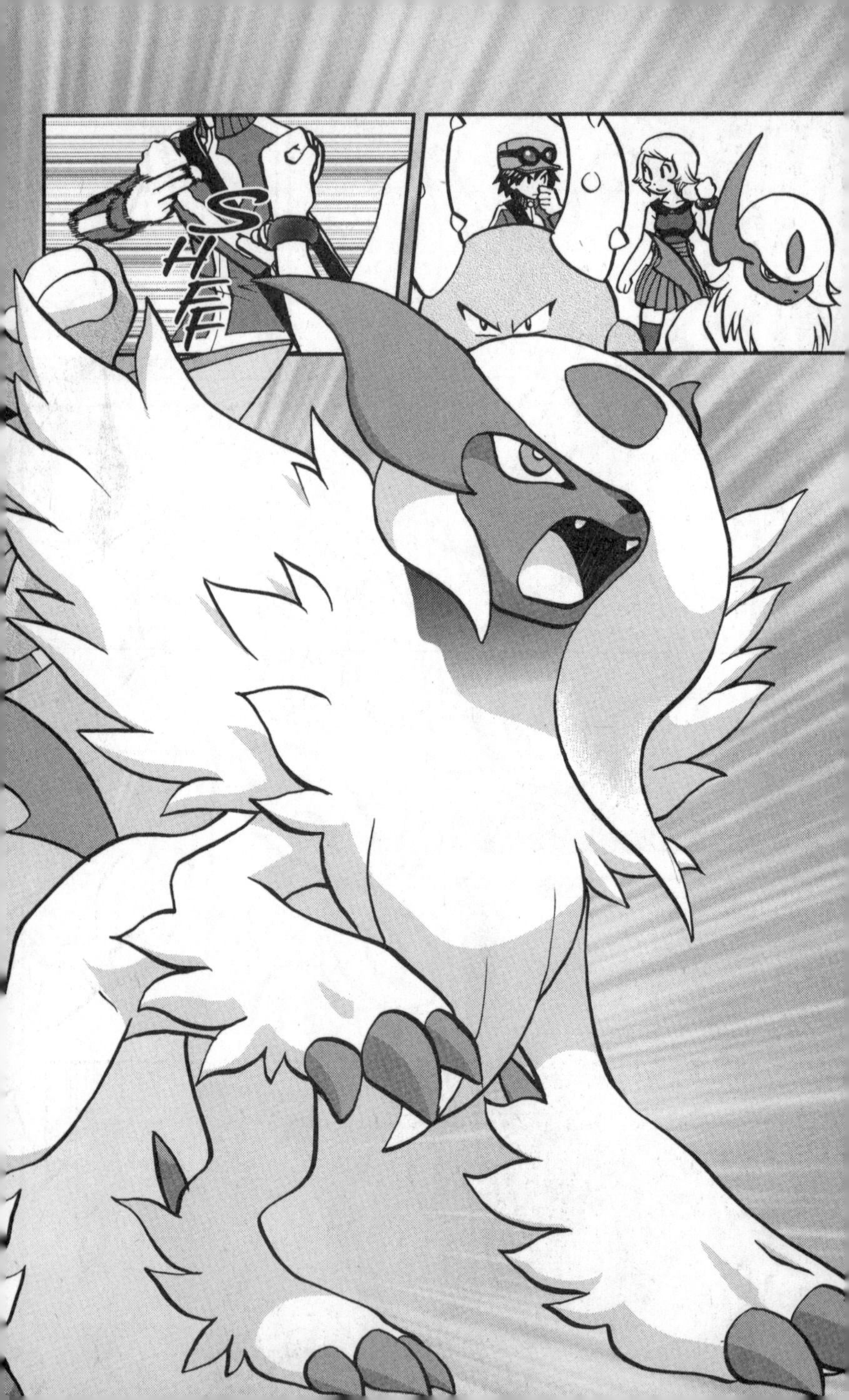
SHFF

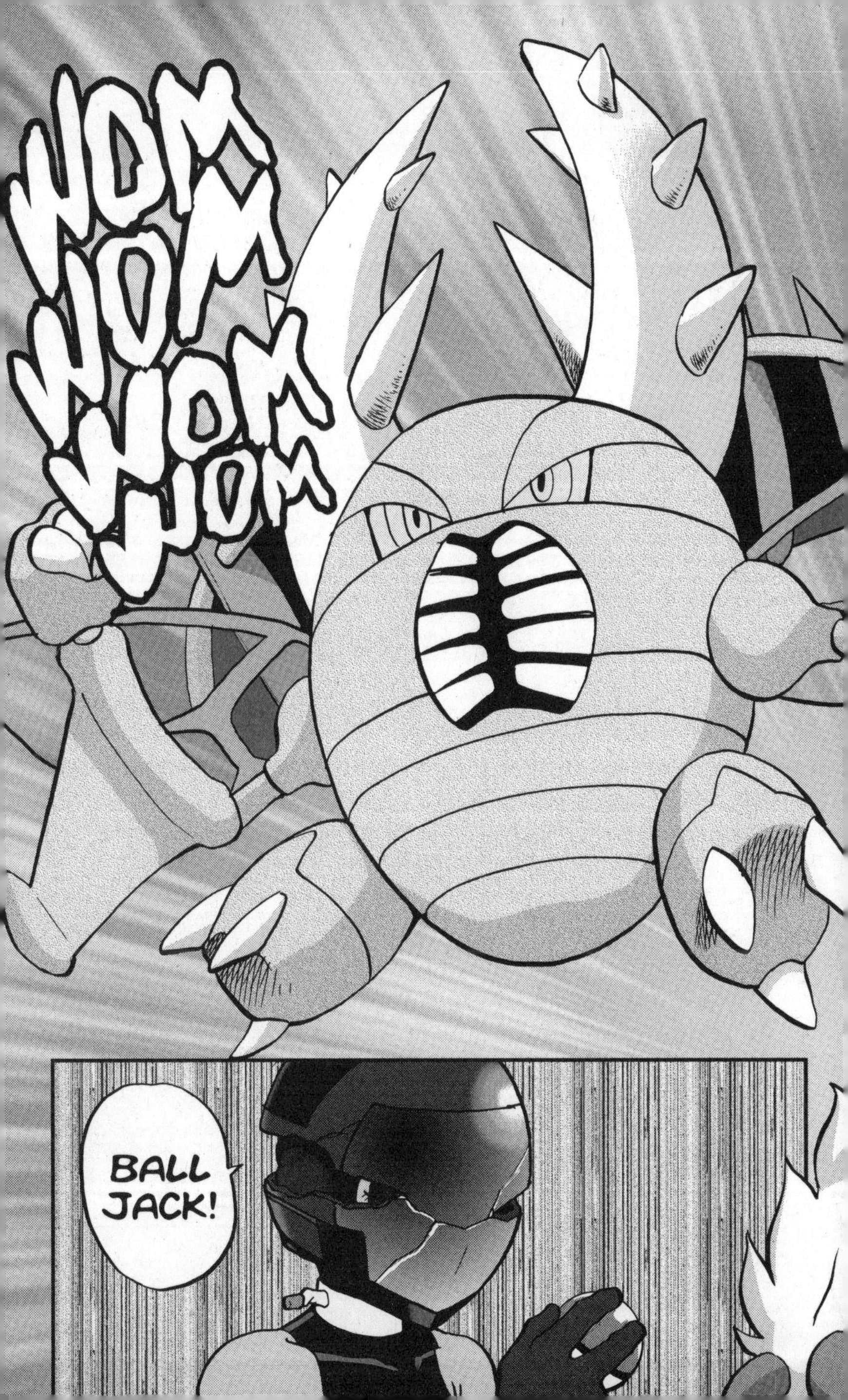
WOM WOM WOM WOM
BALL JACK!

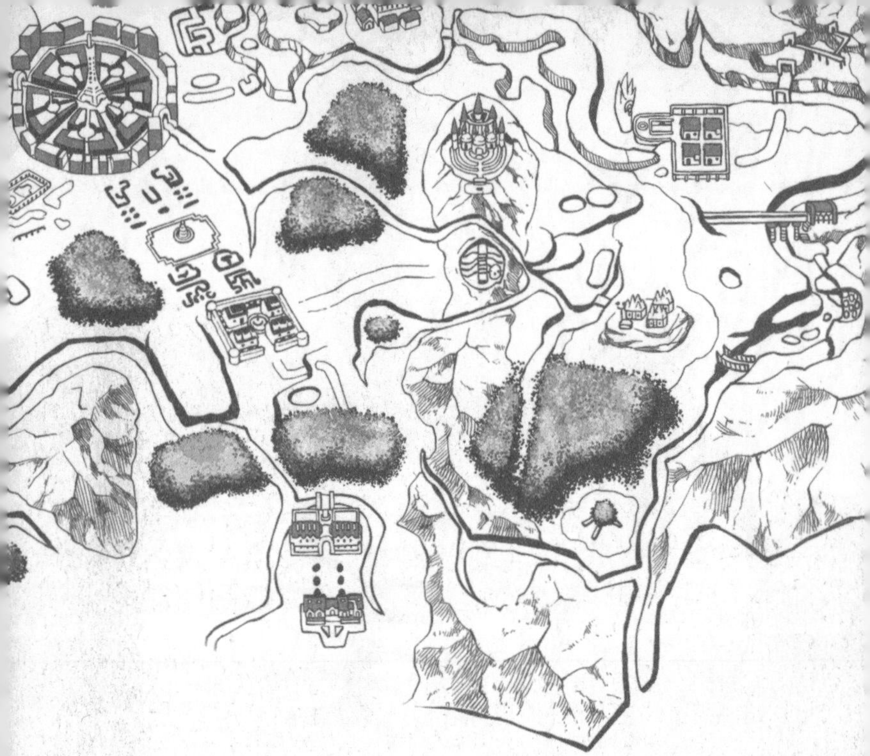

Current Location

Anistar City

Some say the enigmatic device used as a sundial came from outer space.

Adventure #38
Zygarde Appears

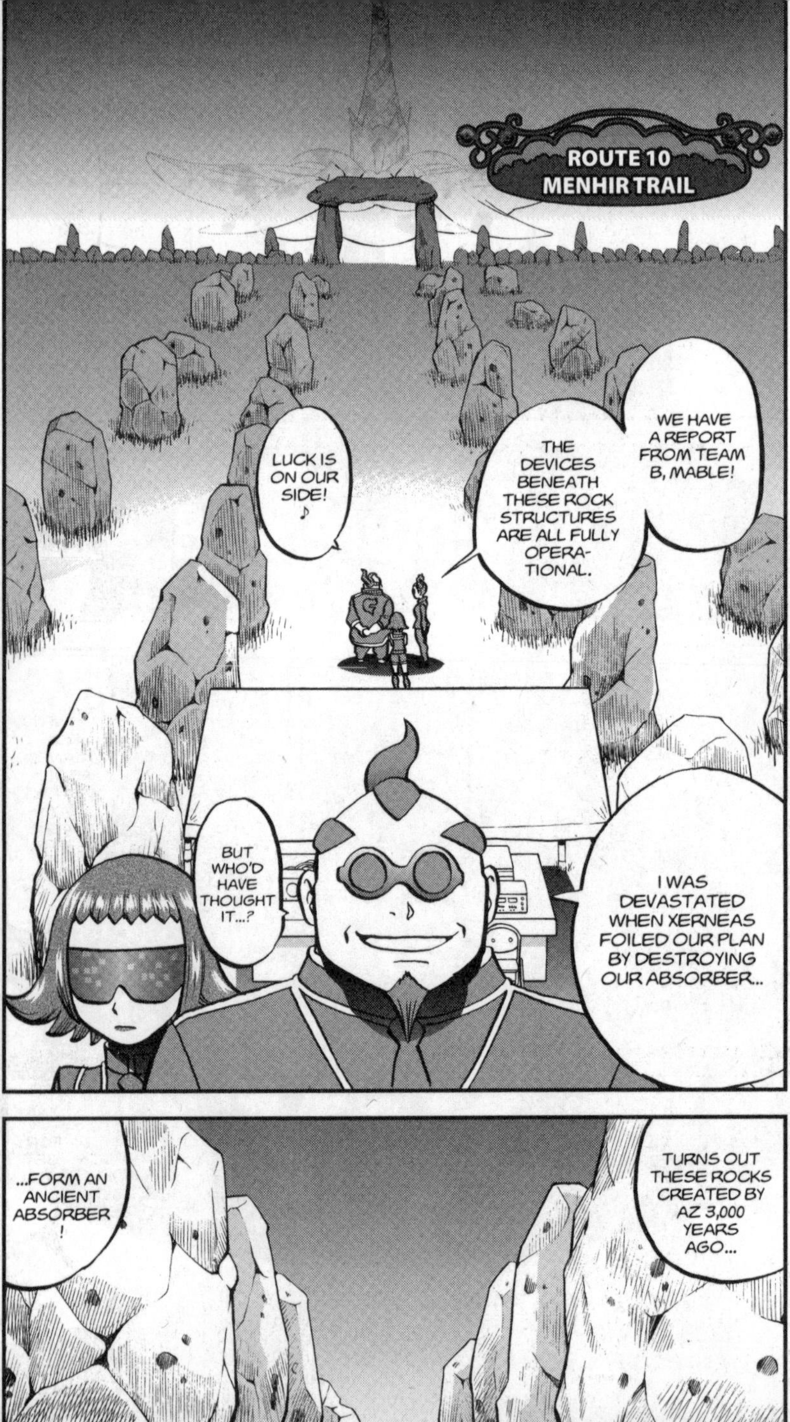
ROUTE 10
MENHIR TRAIL
WE HAVE A REPORT FROM TEAM B, MABLE!
THE DEVICES BENEATH THESE ROCK STRUCTURES ARE ALL FULLY OPERA-TIONAL.
LUCK IS ON OUR SIDE! ♪
I WAS DEVASTATED WHEN XERNEAS FOILED OUR PLAN BY DESTROYING OUR ABSORBER...
BUT WHO'D HAVE THOUGHT IT...?
TURNS OUT THESE ROCKS CREATED BY AZ 3,000 YEARS AGO...
...FORM AN ANCIENT ABSORBER!

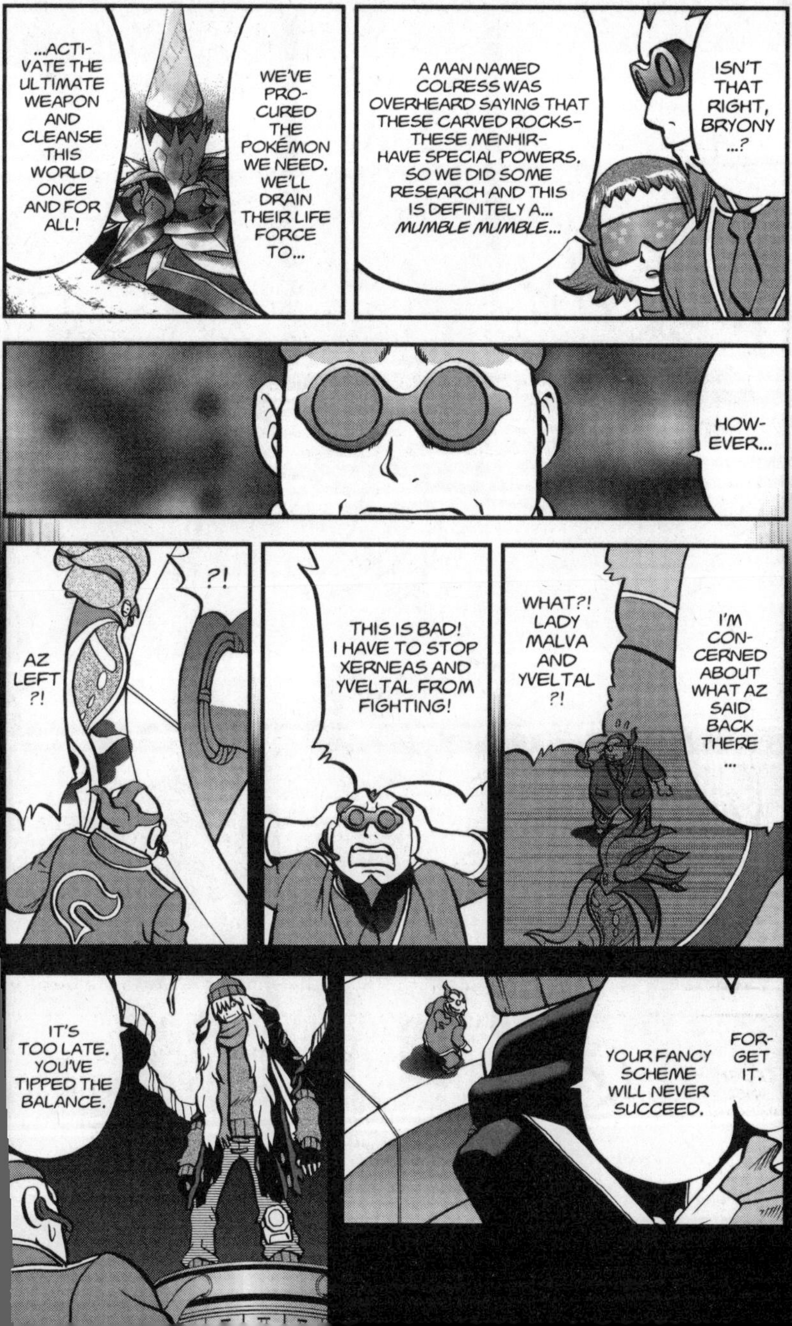
ISN'T THAT RIGHT, BRYONY ...?
A MAN NAMED COLRESS WAS OVERHEARD SAYING THAT THESE CARVED ROCKS—THESE MENHIR—HAVE SPECIAL POWERS. SO WE DID SOME RESEARCH AND THIS IS DEFINITELY A... *MUMBLE MUMBLE*...
WE'VE PROCURED THE POKÉMON WE NEED. WE'LL DRAIN THEIR LIFE FORCE TO...
...ACTIVATE THE ULTIMATE WEAPON AND CLEANSE THIS WORLD ONCE AND FOR ALL!
HOWEVER...
I'M CONCERNED ABOUT WHAT AZ SAID BACK THERE...
WHAT?! LADY MALVA AND YVELTAL ?!
THIS IS BAD! I HAVE TO STOP XERNEAS AND YVELTAL FROM FIGHTING!
?!
AZ LEFT ?!
FORGET IT.
YOUR FANCY SCHEME WILL NEVER SUCCEED.
IT'S TOO LATE. YOU'VE TIPPED THE BALANCE.

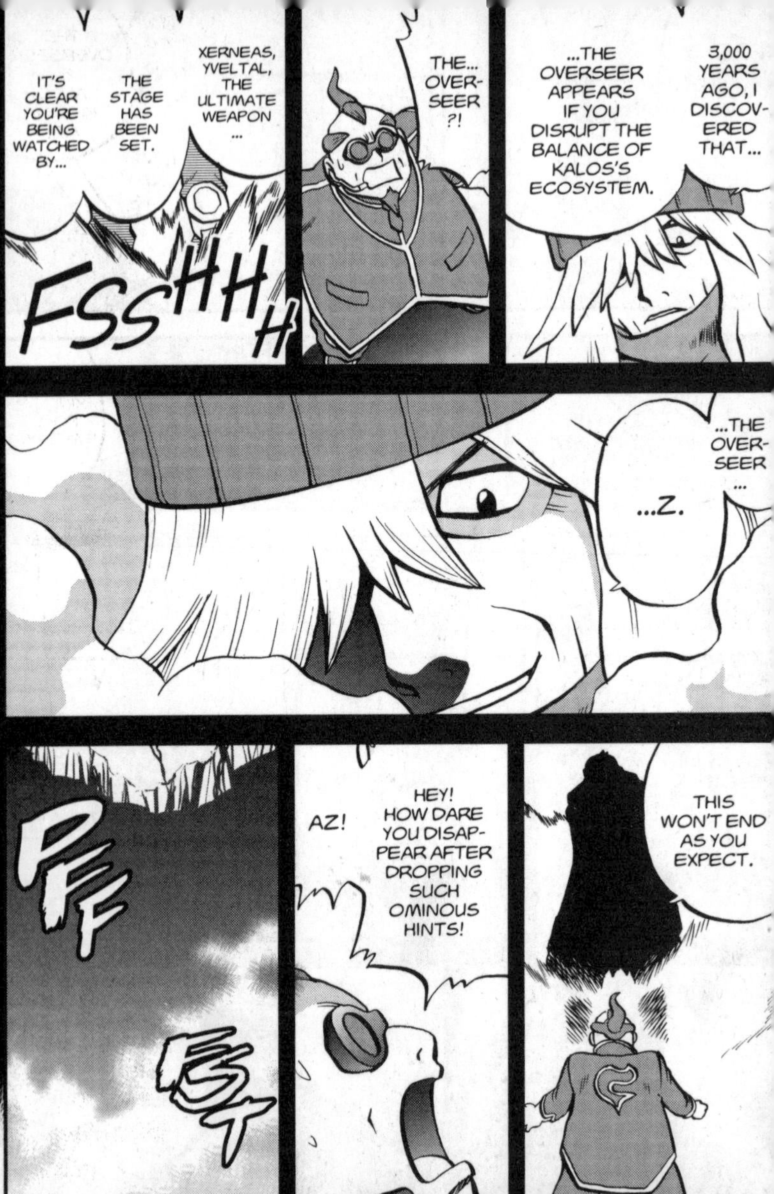
3,000 YEARS AGO, I DISCOVERED THAT...
...THE OVERSEER APPEARS IF YOU DISRUPT THE BALANCE OF KALOS'S ECOSYSTEM.
THE... OVERSEER?!
XERNEAS, YVELTAL, THE ULTIMATE WEAPON...
THE STAGE HAS BEEN SET.
IT'S CLEAR YOU'RE BEING WATCHED BY...
FSSHHHH
...THE OVERSEER...
...Z.
THIS WON'T END AS YOU EXPECT.
HEY! HOW DARE YOU DISAPPEAR AFTER DROPPING SUCH OMINOUS HINTS!
AZ!
PFF
FST

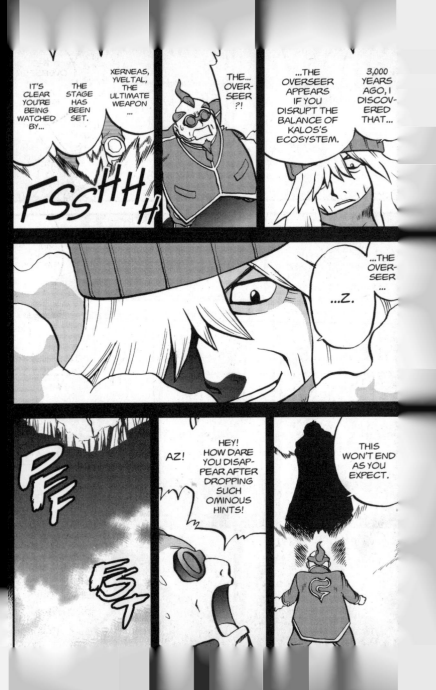

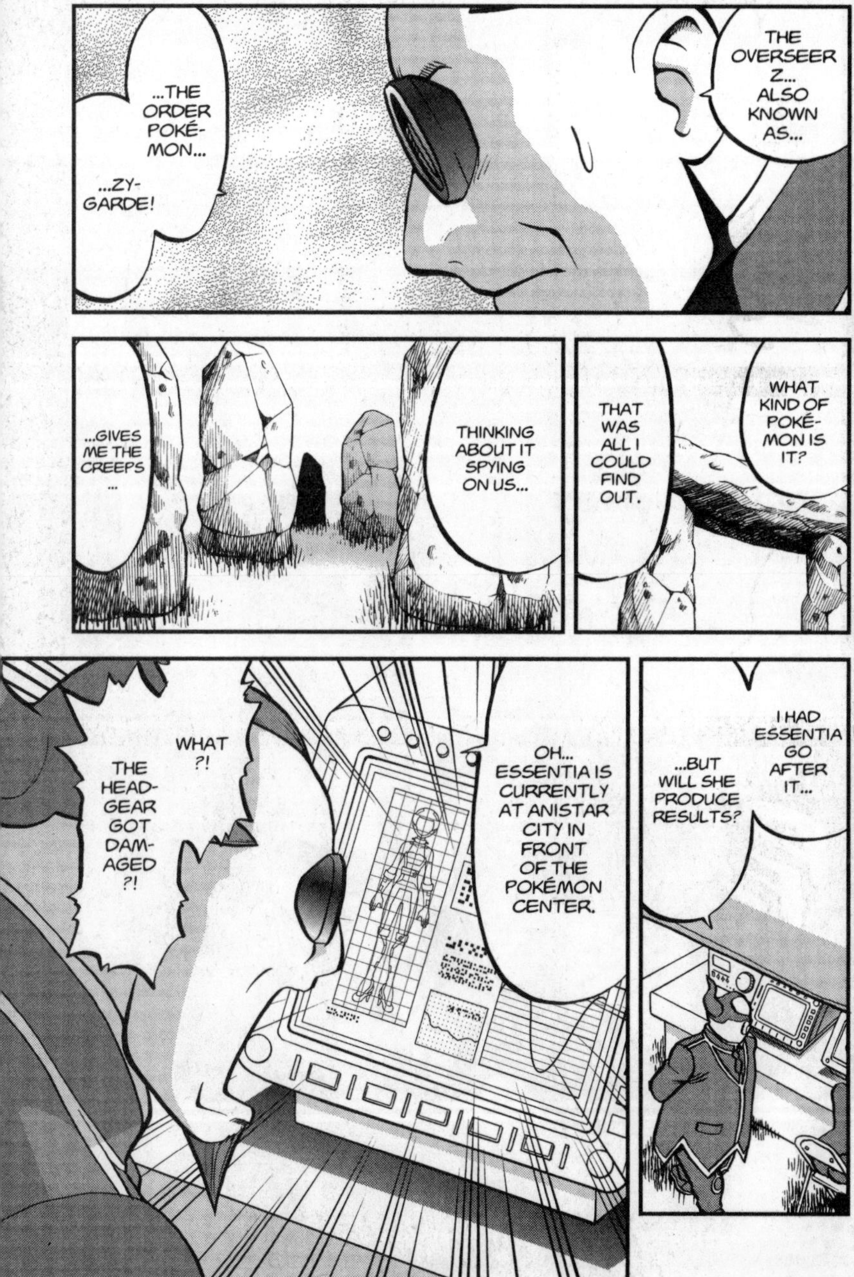
THE OVERSEER Z... ALSO KNOWN AS...
...THE ORDER POKÉMON...
...ZYGARDE!
WHAT KIND OF POKÉMON IS IT?
THAT WAS ALL I COULD FIND OUT.
THINKING ABOUT IT SPYING ON US...
...GIVES ME THE CREEPS...
I HAD ESSENTIA GO AFTER IT...
...BUT WILL SHE PRODUCE RESULTS?
OH... ESSENTIA IS CURRENTLY AT ANISTAR CITY IN FRONT OF THE POKÉMON CENTER.
WHAT?!
THE HEADGEAR GOT DAMAGED?!

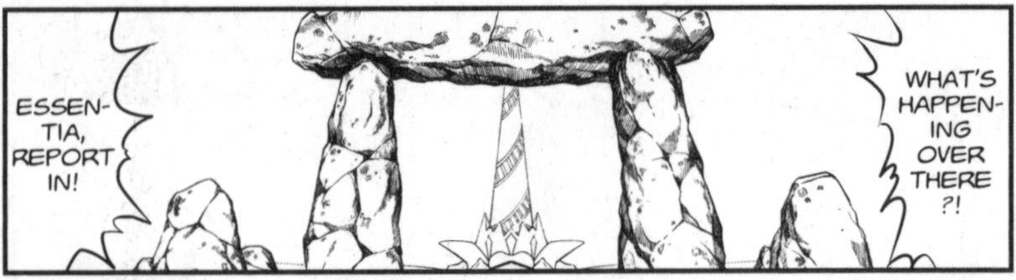
WHAT'S HAPPENING OVER THERE?!
ESSENTIA, REPORT IN!

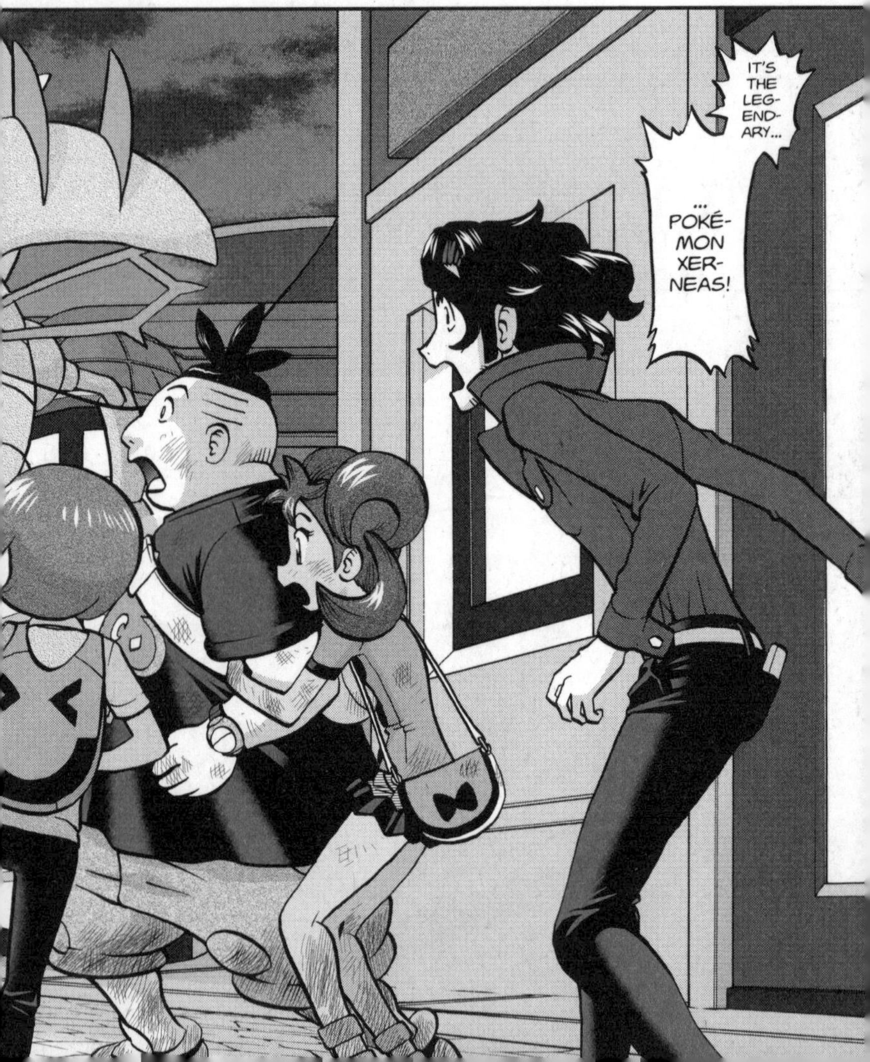
IT'S THE LEGENDARY...
...POKÉMON XERNEAS!

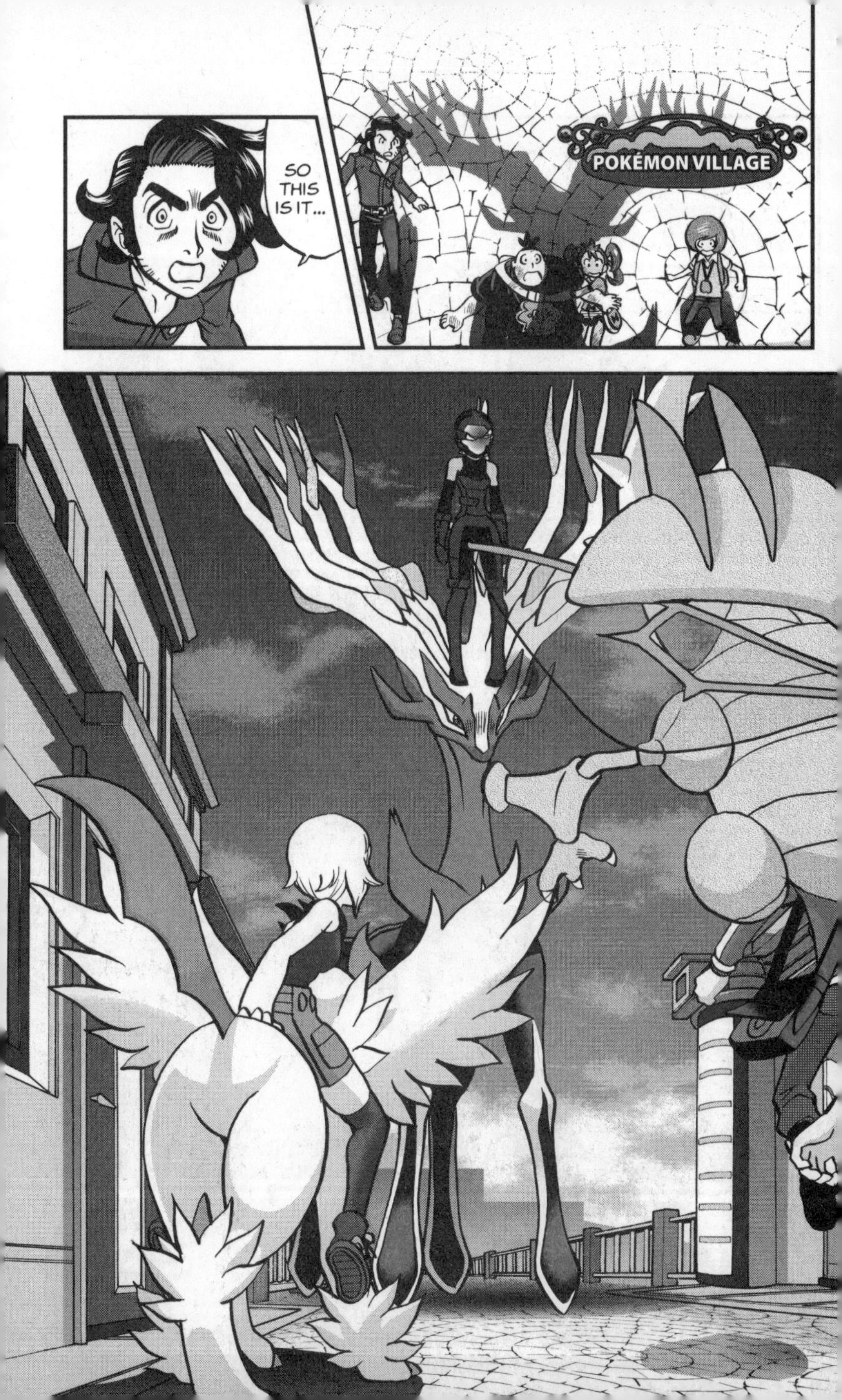
POKÉMON VILLAGE
SO THIS IS IT...

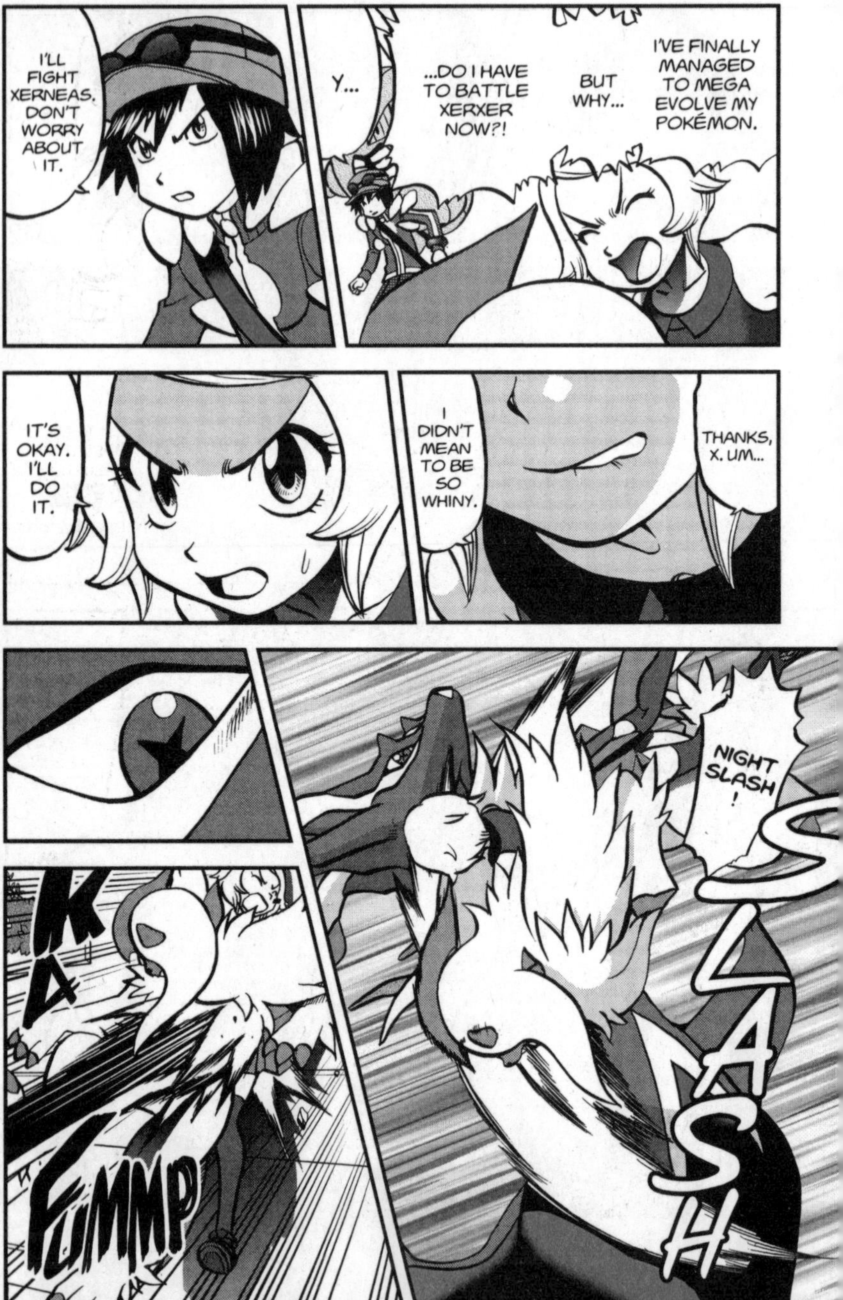
I'VE FINALLY MANAGED TO MEGA EVOLVE MY POKÉMON.
BUT WHY...
...DO I HAVE TO BATTLE XERXER NOW?!
Y...
I'LL FIGHT XERNEAS. DON'T WORRY ABOUT IT.
THANKS, X. UM...
I DIDN'T MEAN TO BE SO WHINY.
IT'S OKAY. I'LL DO IT.
NIGHT SLASH!
SLASH
KA
FUMMP

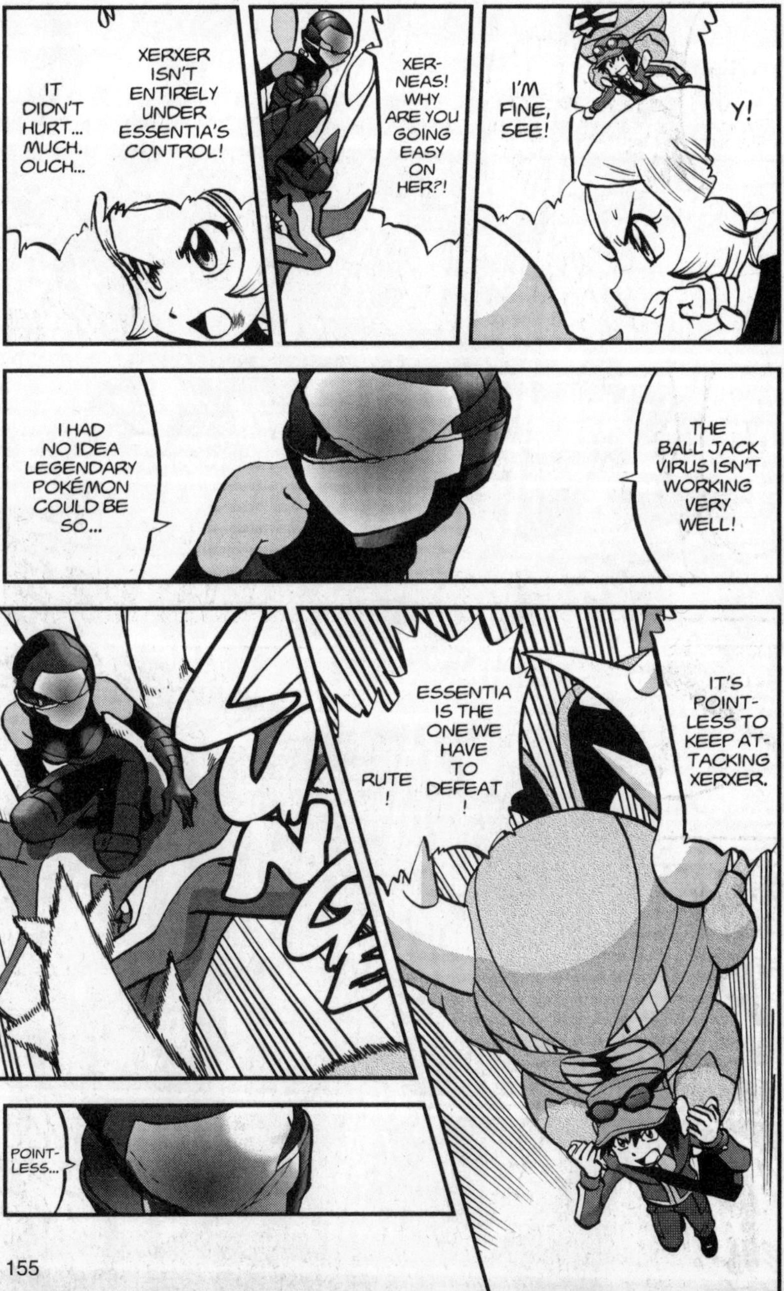
Y!
I'M FINE, SEE!
XERNEAS! WHY ARE YOU GOING EASY ON HER?!
XERXER ISN'T ENTIRELY UNDER ESSENTIA'S CONTROL!
IT DIDN'T HURT... MUCH. OUCH...
THE BALL JACK VIRUS ISN'T WORKING VERY WELL!
I HAD NO IDEA LEGENDARY POKÉMON COULD BE SO...
IT'S POINTLESS TO KEEP ATTACKING XERXER.
ESSENTIA IS THE ONE WE HAVE TO DEFEAT!
RUTE!
POINTLESS...

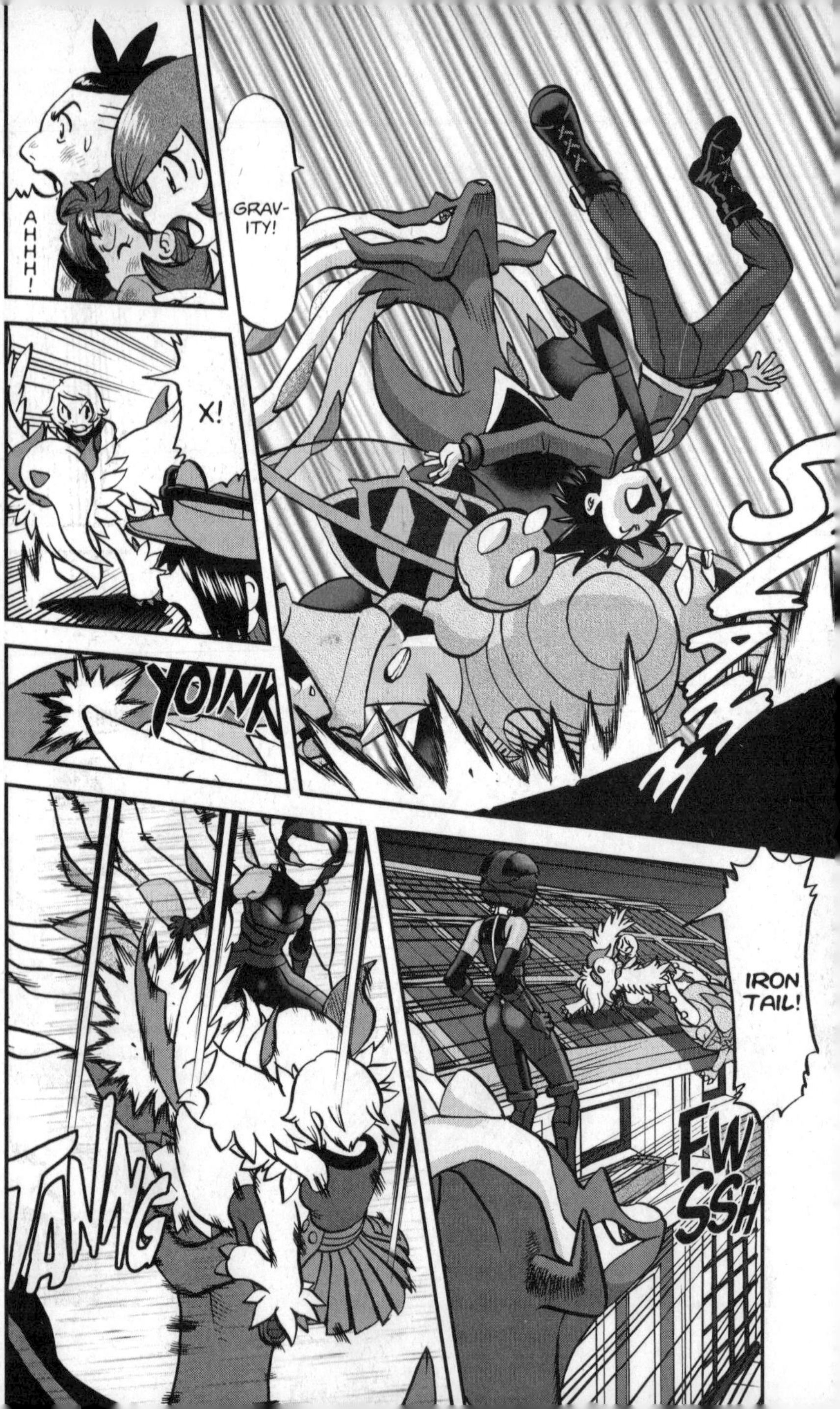
GRAV-
ITY!
AHHHH!
X!
YOINK
IRON
TAIL!
FW
SSH

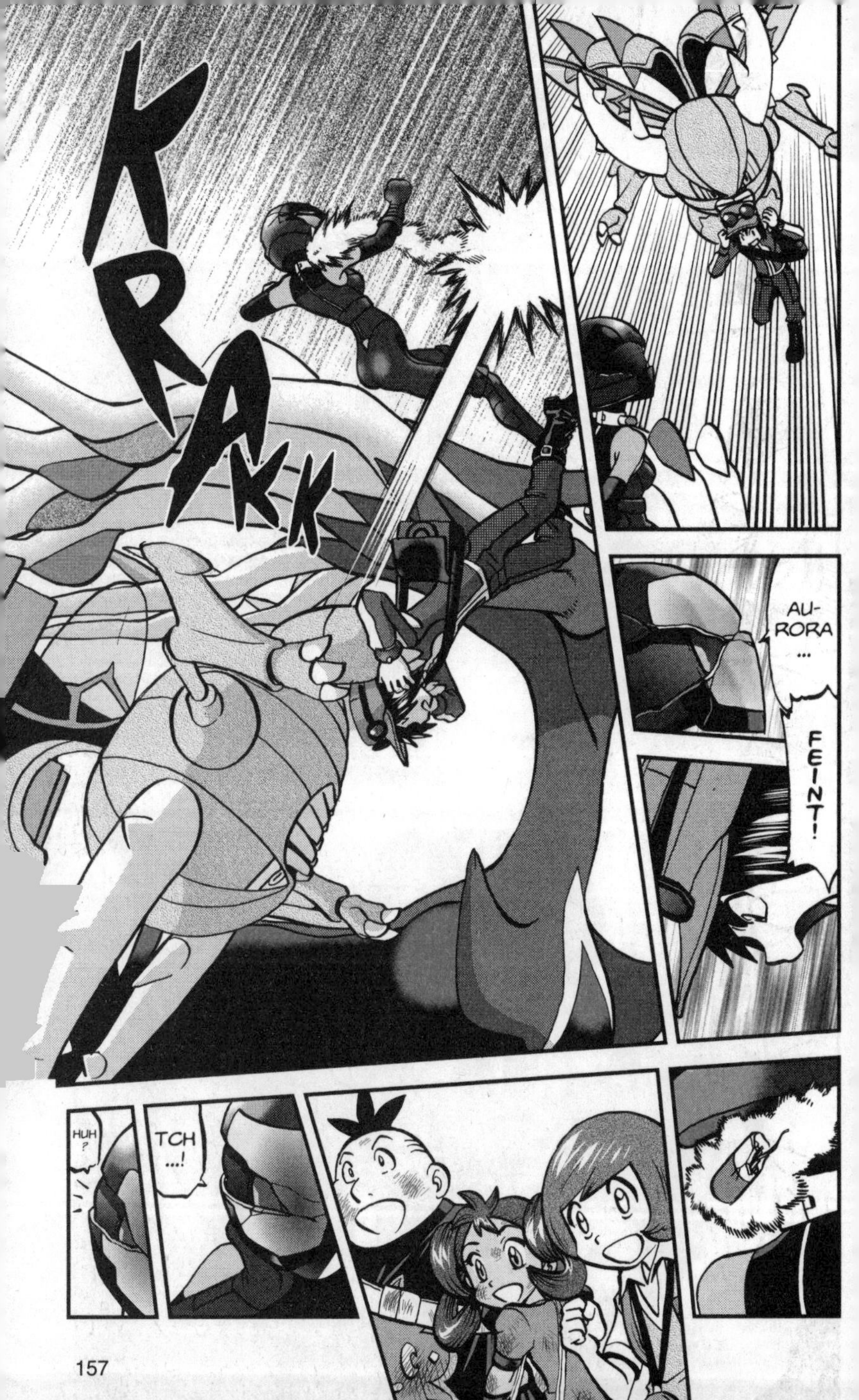

KRAKK
AU-RORA...
FEINT!
TCH...!
HUH?

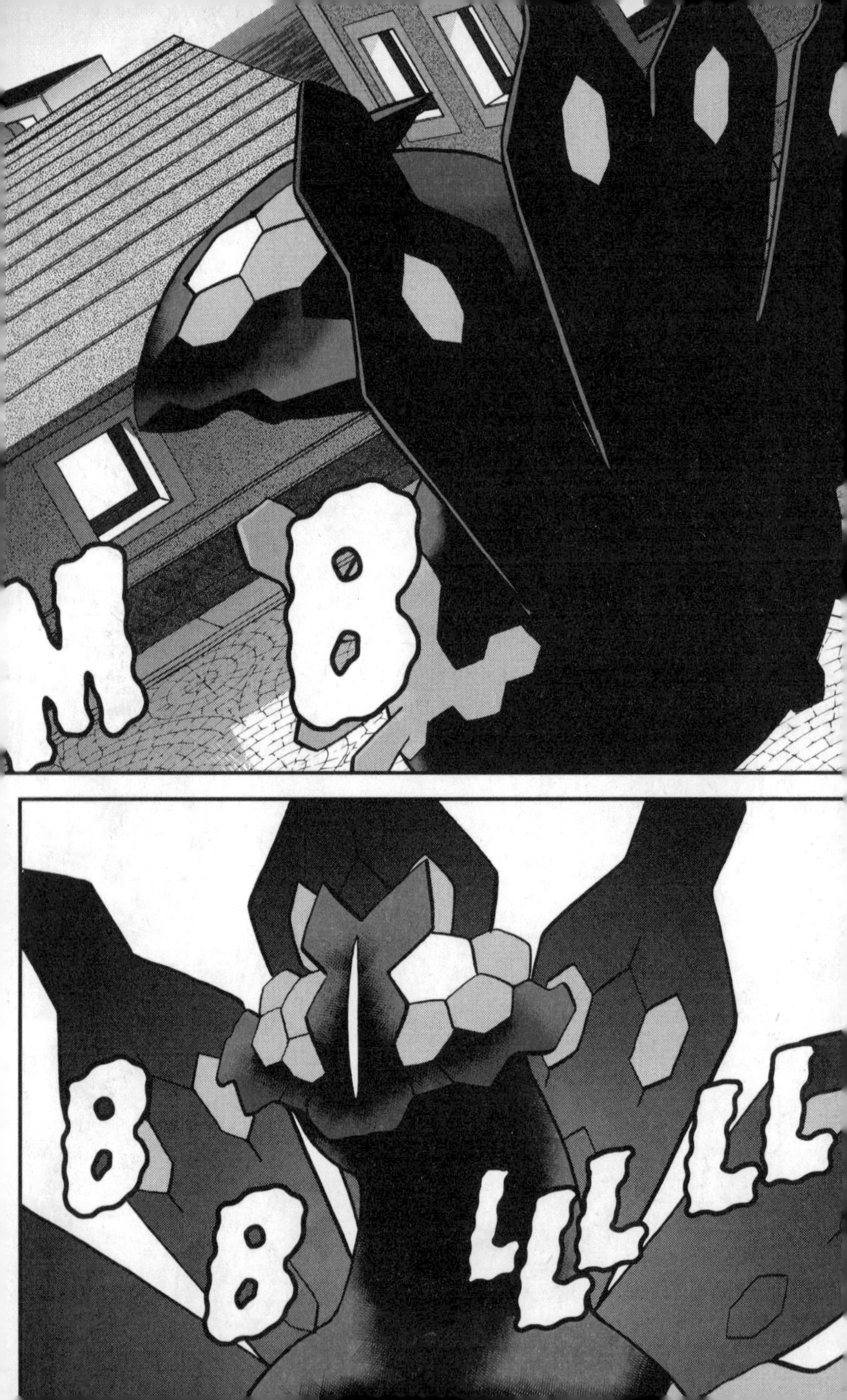

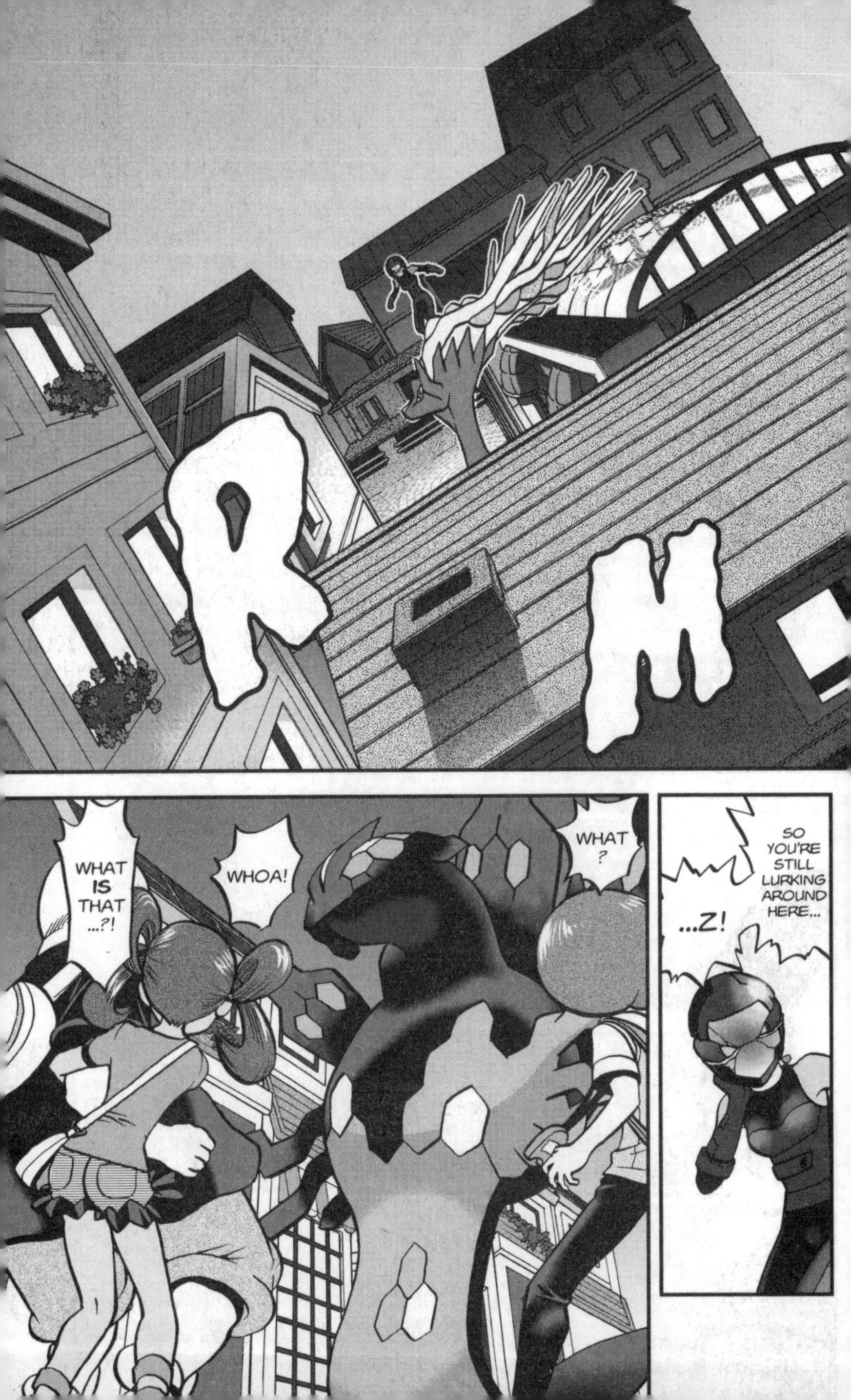
RM
SO YOU'RE STILL LURKING AROUND HERE...
...Z!
WHAT?
WHOA!
WHAT **IS** THAT...?!

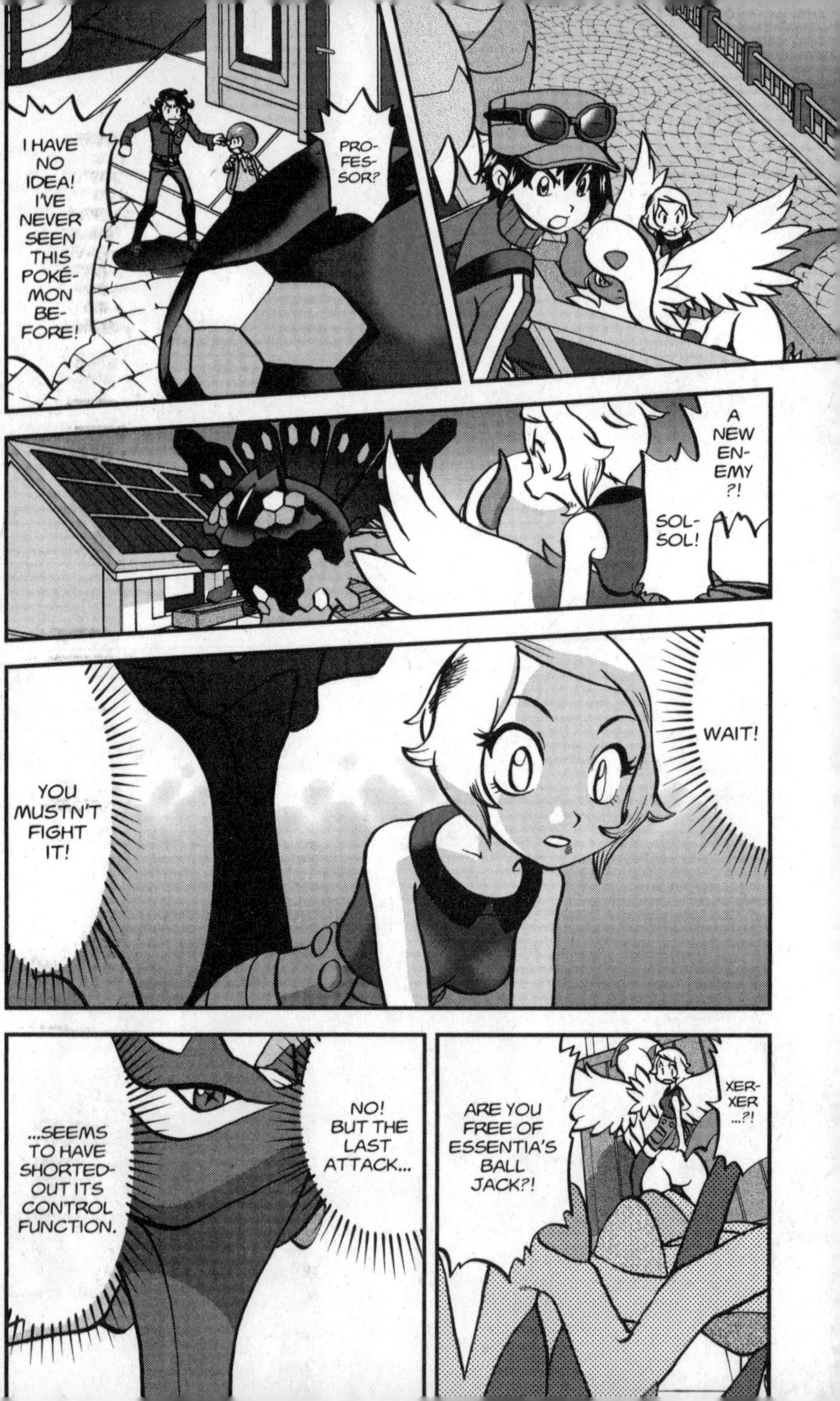
PRO-FES-SOR?
I HAVE NO IDEA! I'VE NEVER SEEN THIS POKÉ-MON BE-FORE!
A NEW EN-EMY?!
SOL-SOL!
WAIT!
YOU MUSTN'T FIGHT IT!
XER-XER...?!
ARE YOU FREE OF ESSENTIA'S BALL JACK?!
NO! BUT THE LAST ATTACK...
...SEEMS TO HAVE SHORTED-OUT ITS CONTROL FUNCTION.

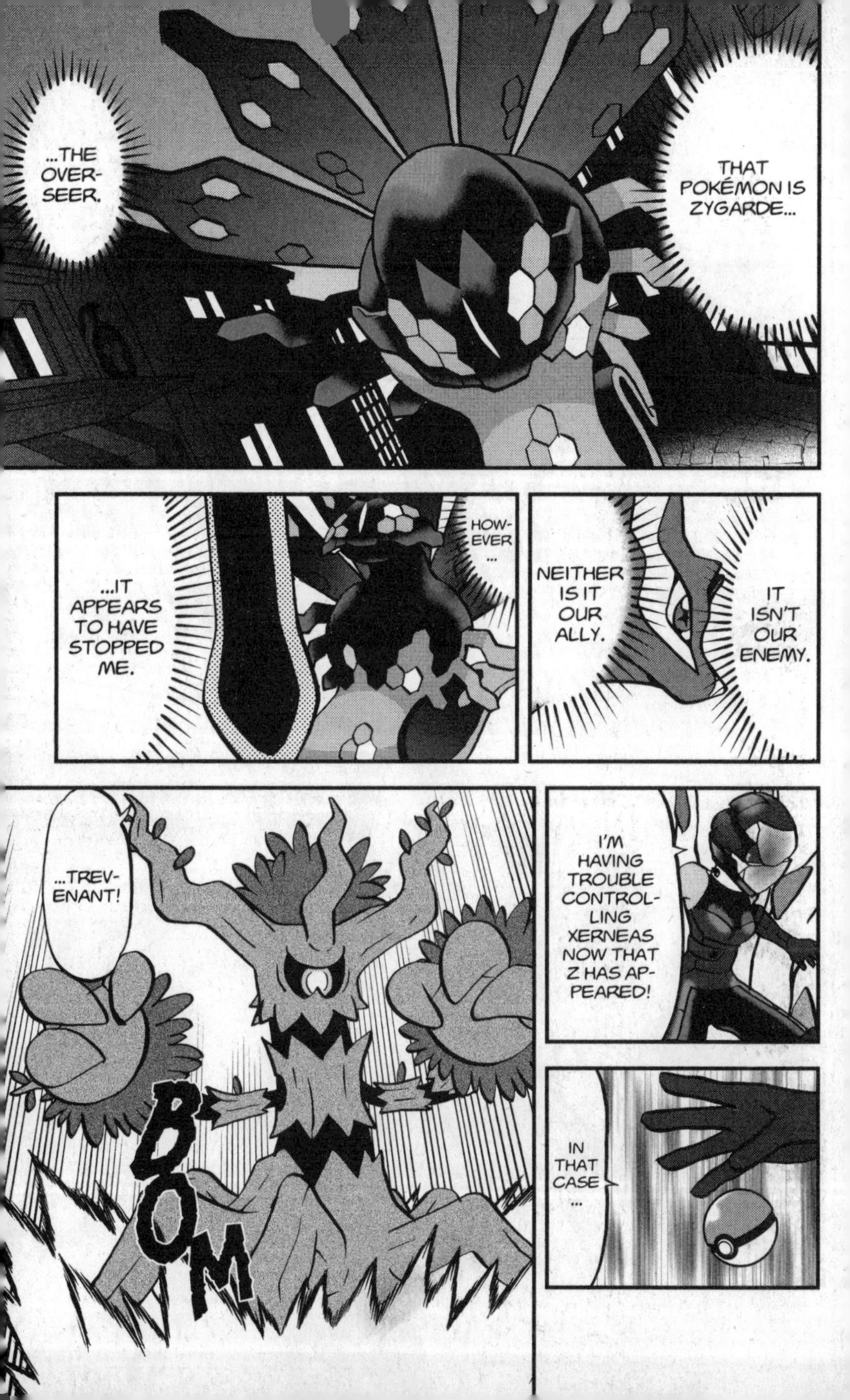
THAT POKÉMON IS ZYGARDE...
...THE OVER-SEER.
IT ISN'T OUR ENEMY.
NEITHER IS IT OUR ALLY.
HOW-EVER...
...IT APPEARS TO HAVE STOPPED ME.
I'M HAVING TROUBLE CONTROL-LING XERNEAS NOW THAT Z HAS AP-PEARED!
IN THAT CASE...
...TREV-ENANT!
BOM

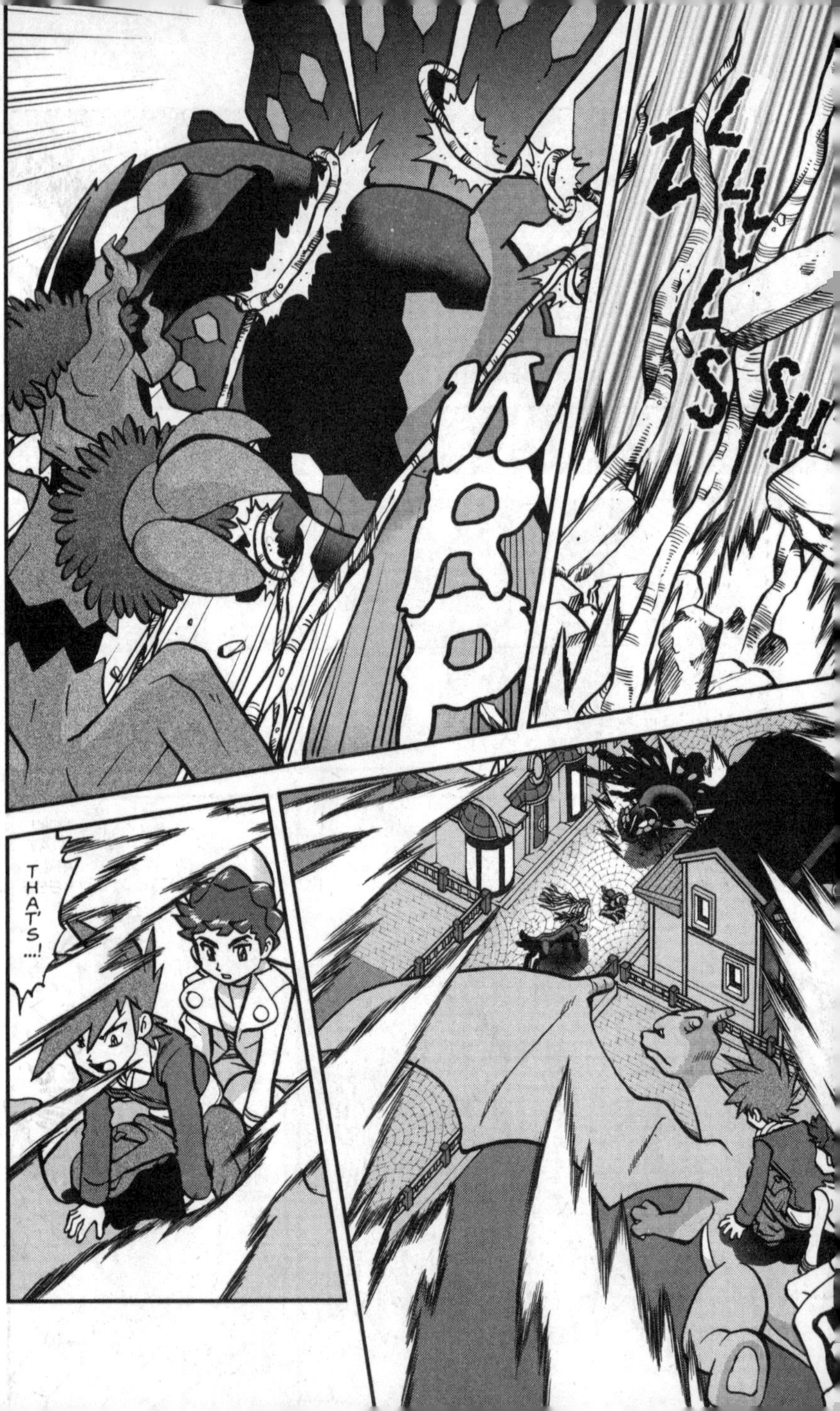
ZLLLLSSH
WRP
THAT'S...!

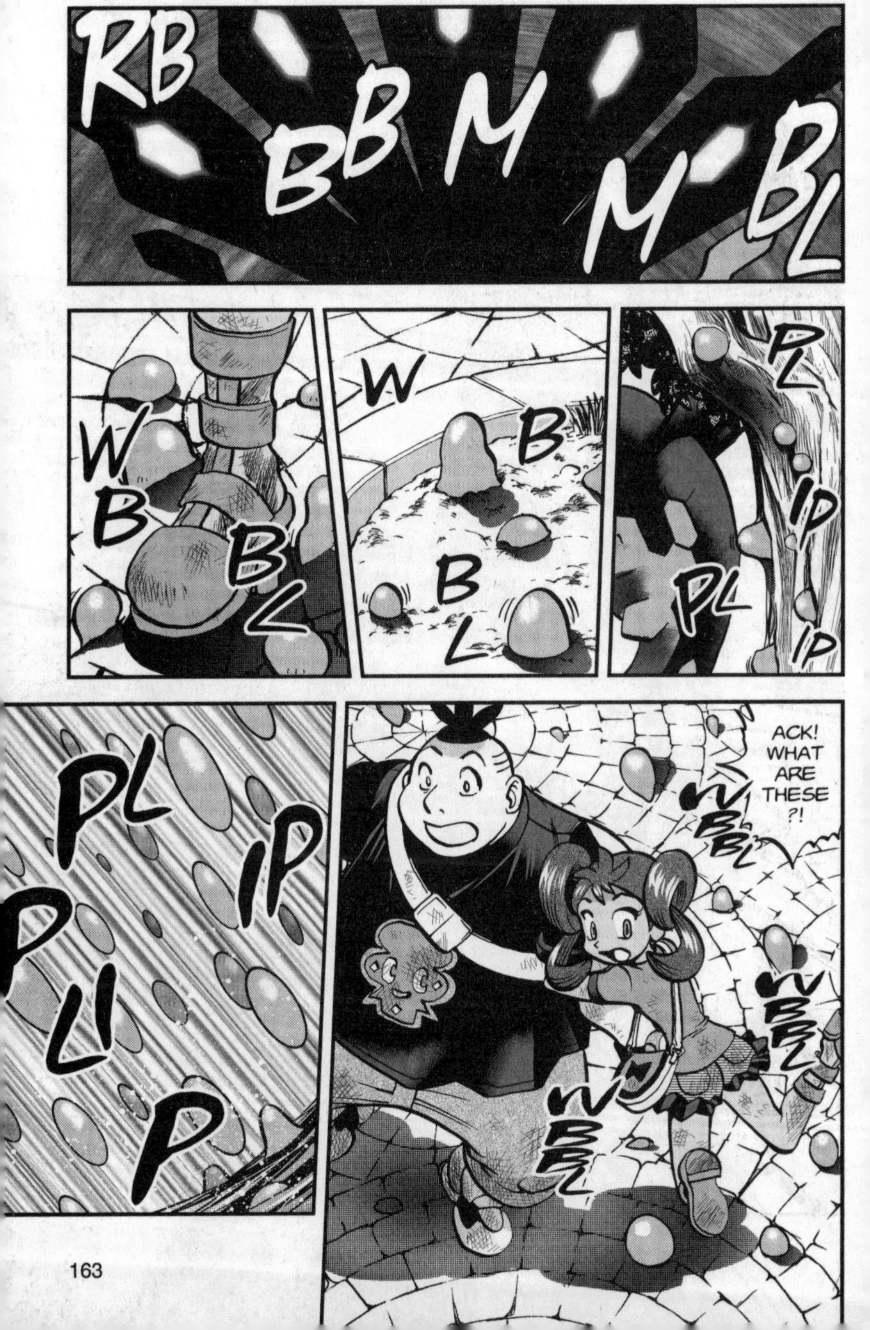
RBBBMMMBL
PLIP PLIP
WBBL
WBBL
ACK! WHAT ARE THESE?!
WBBL
WBBL
WBBL
PLIP PLIP

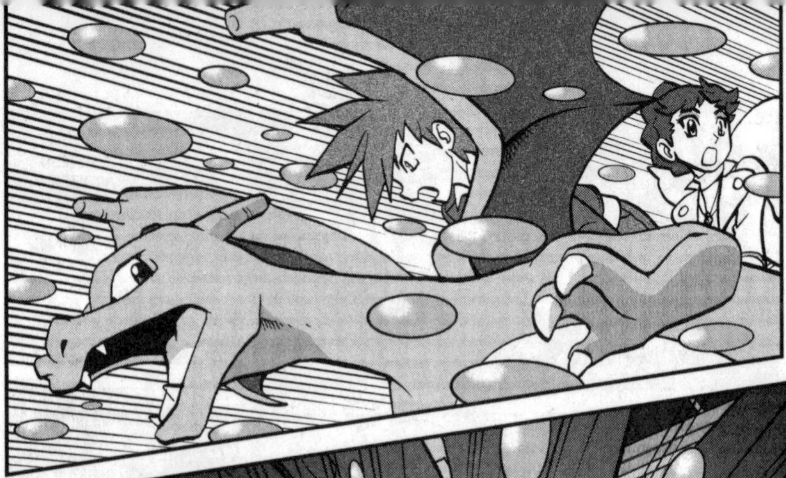
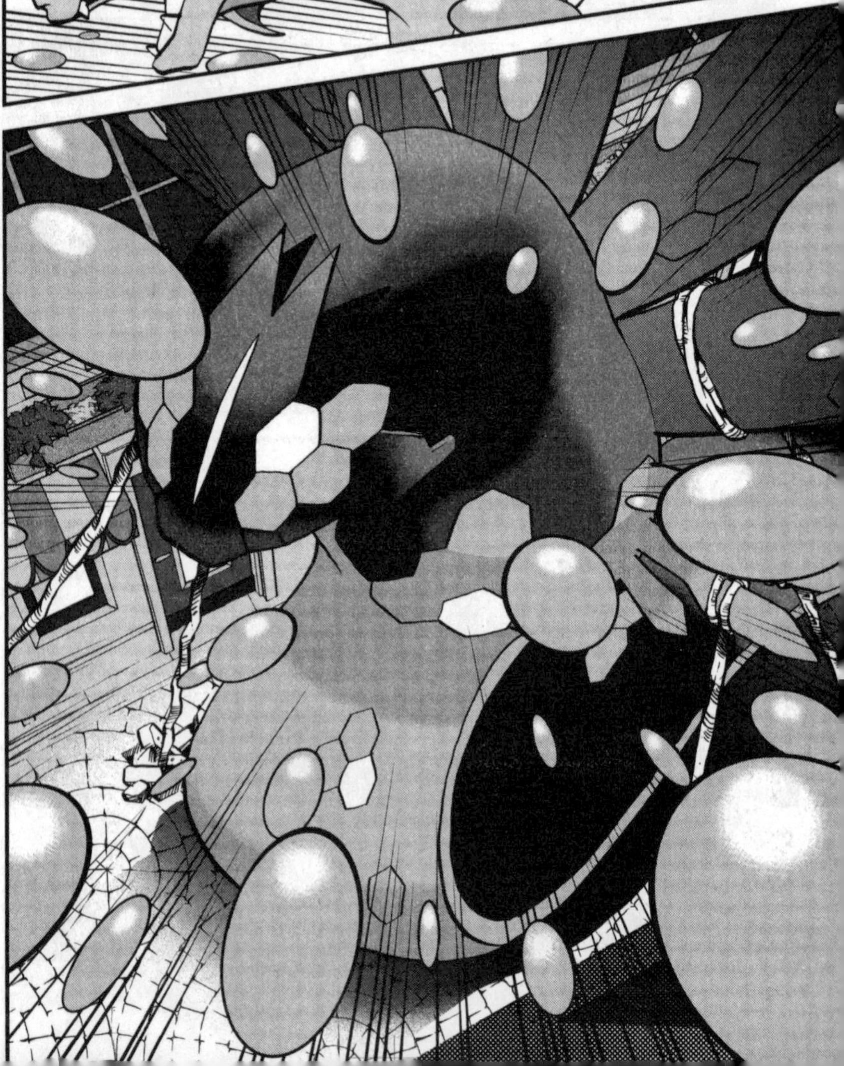

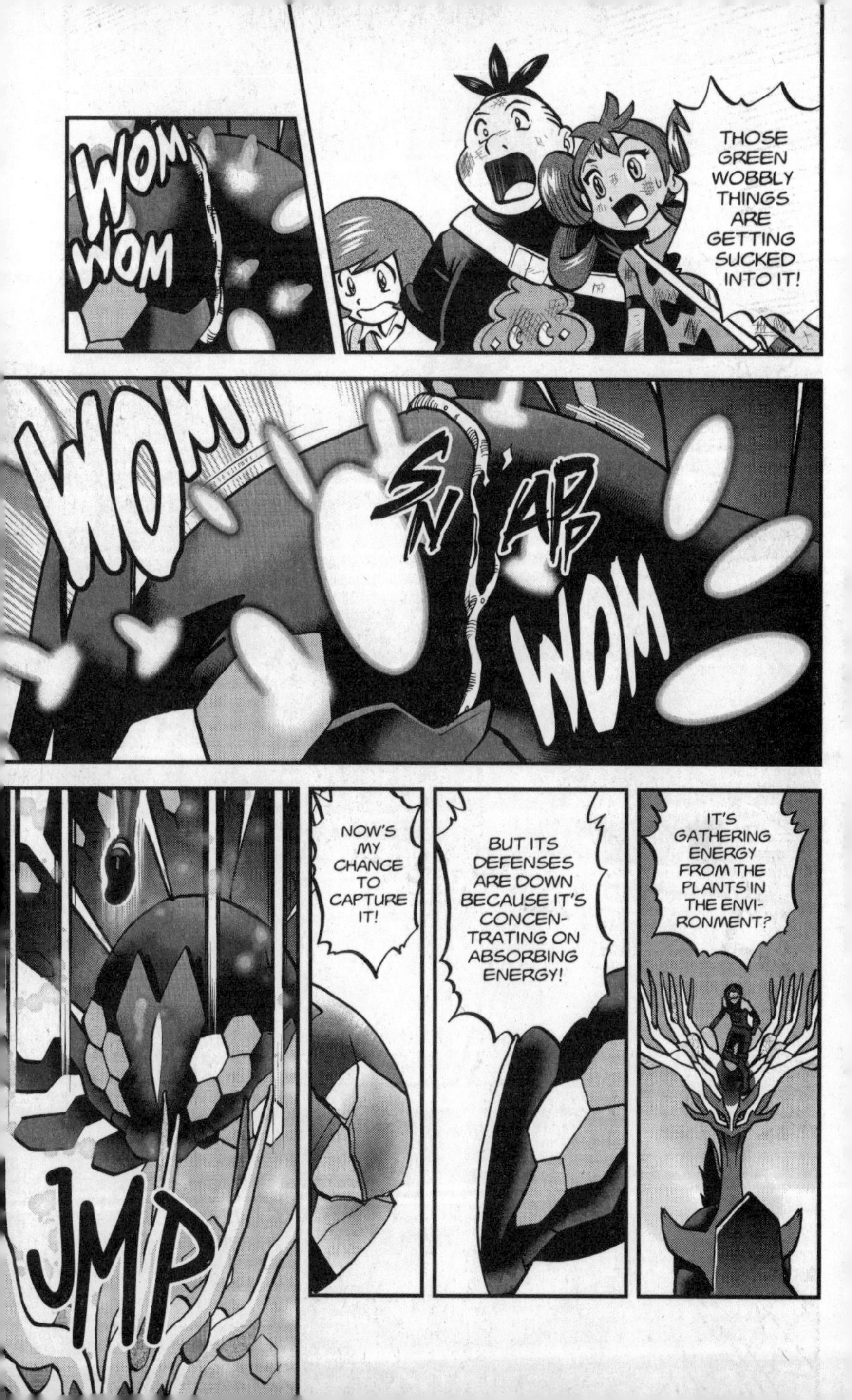
THOSE GREEN WOBBLY THINGS ARE GETTING SUCKED INTO IT!
WOM WOM
WOM
SNAB
WOM
IT'S GATHERING ENERGY FROM THE PLANTS IN THE ENVIRONMENT?
BUT ITS DEFENSES ARE DOWN BECAUSE IT'S CONCENTRATING ON ABSORBING ENERGY!
NOW'S MY CHANCE TO CAPTURE IT!
JMP

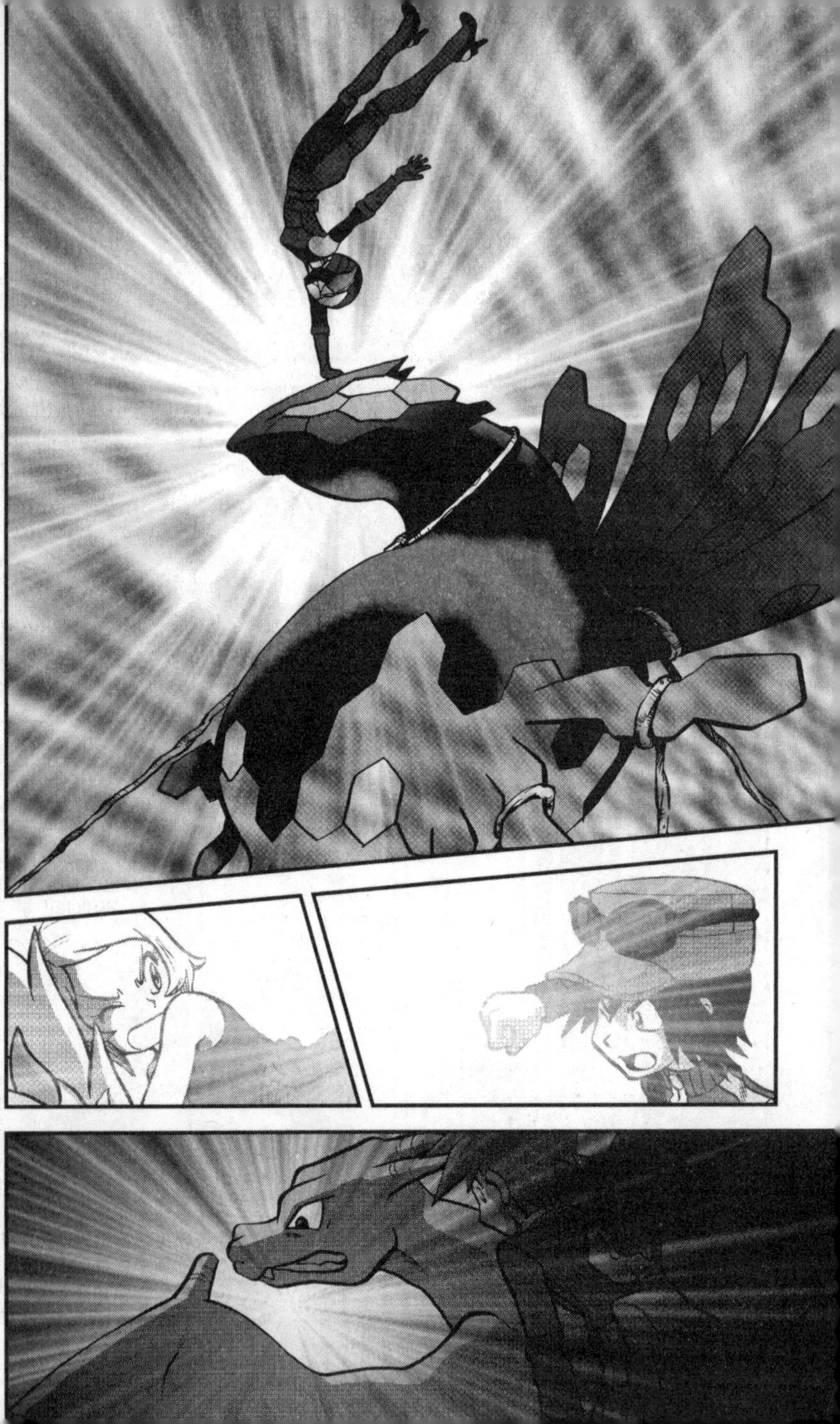

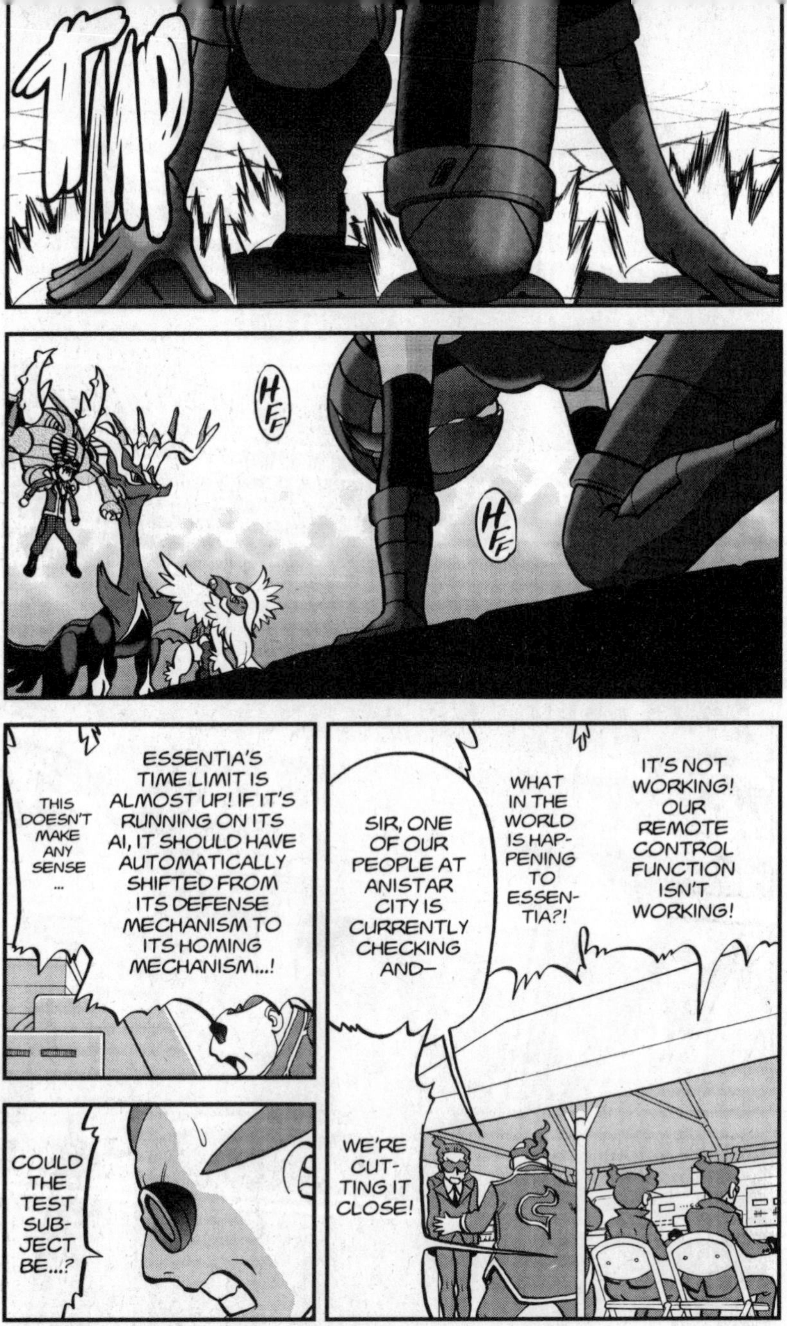
TMP
HFF
HFF
IT'S NOT WORKING! OUR REMOTE CONTROL FUNCTION ISN'T WORKING!
WHAT IN THE WORLD IS HAPPENING TO ESSENTIA?!
SIR, ONE OF OUR PEOPLE AT ANISTAR CITY IS CURRENTLY CHECKING AND—
WE'RE CUTTING IT CLOSE!
ESSENTIA'S TIME LIMIT IS ALMOST UP! IF IT'S RUNNING ON ITS AI, IT SHOULD HAVE AUTOMATICALLY SHIFTED FROM ITS DEFENSE MECHANISM TO ITS HOMING MECHANISM...!
THIS DOESN'T MAKE ANY SENSE...
COULD THE TEST SUBJECT BE...?

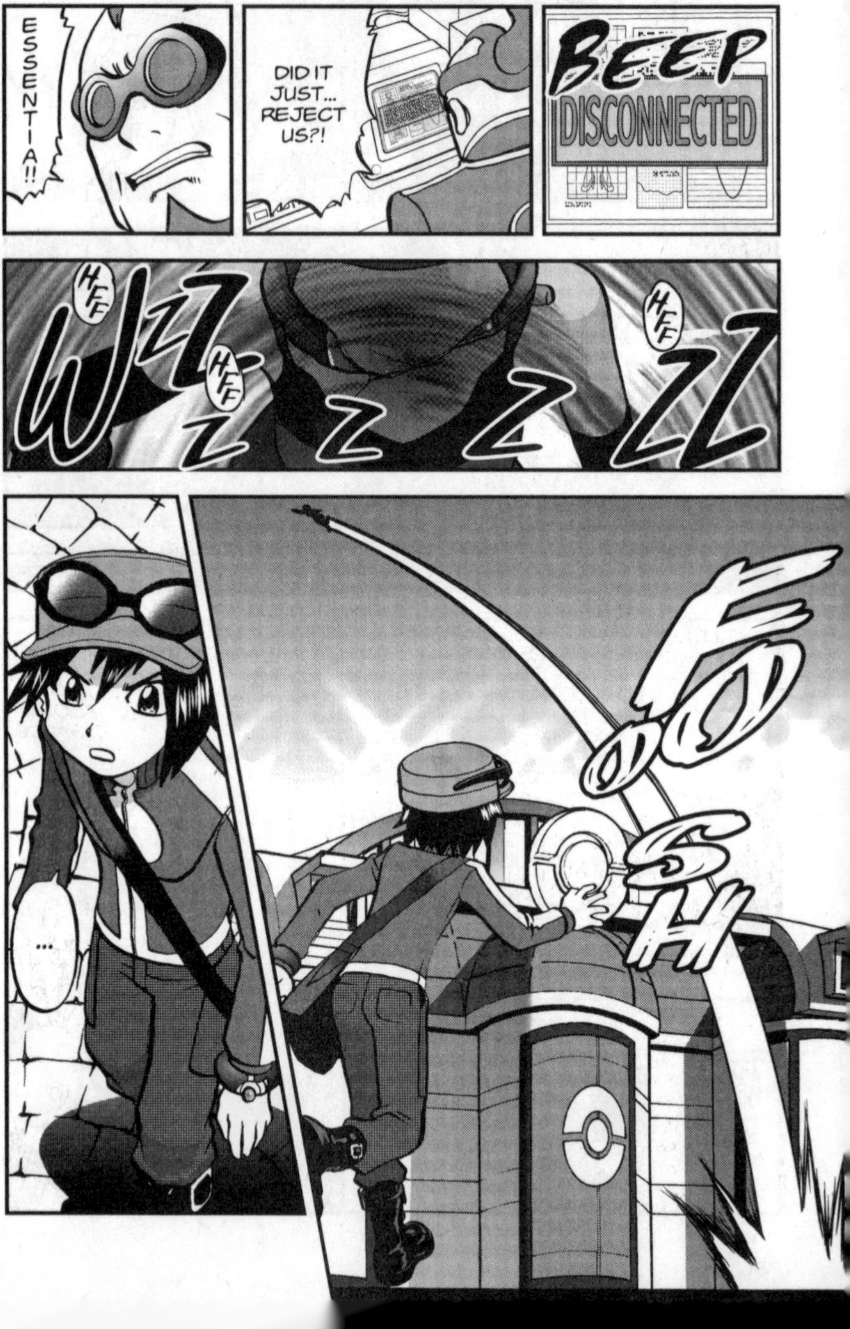
BEEP
DISCONNECTED
DID IT JUST... REJECT US?!
ESSENTIA!!
HEFF
WZZZZZ
HEFF
HEFF
FOOSH
...

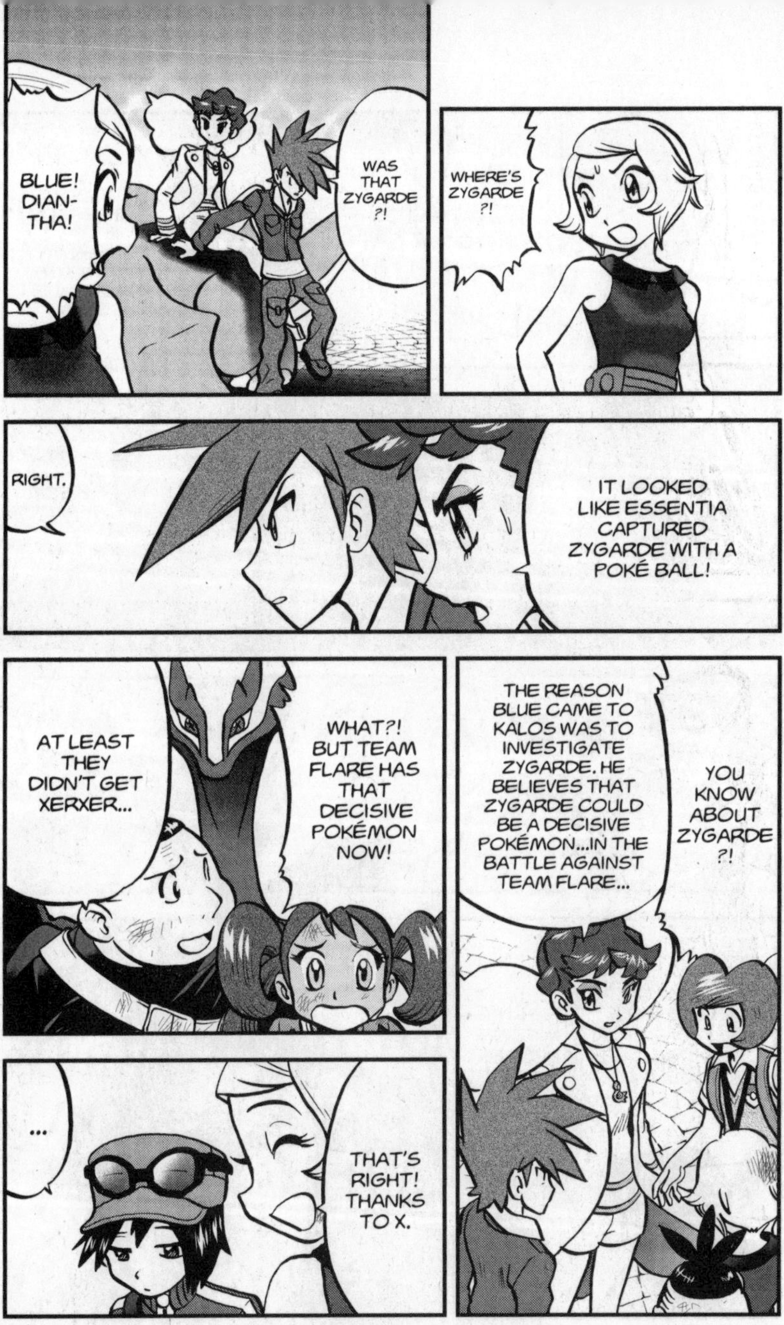
WHERE'S ZYGARDE ?!
WAS THAT ZYGARDE ?!
BLUE! DIAN-THA!
IT LOOKED LIKE ESSENTIA CAPTURED ZYGARDE WITH A POKÉ BALL!
RIGHT.
YOU KNOW ABOUT ZYGARDE ?!
THE REASON BLUE CAME TO KALOS WAS TO INVESTIGATE ZYGARDE. HE BELIEVES THAT ZYGARDE COULD BE A DECISIVE POKÉMON...IN THE BATTLE AGAINST TEAM FLARE...
WHAT?! BUT TEAM FLARE HAS THAT DECISIVE POKÉMON NOW!
AT LEAST THEY DIDN'T GET XERXER...
THAT'S RIGHT! THANKS TO X.
...

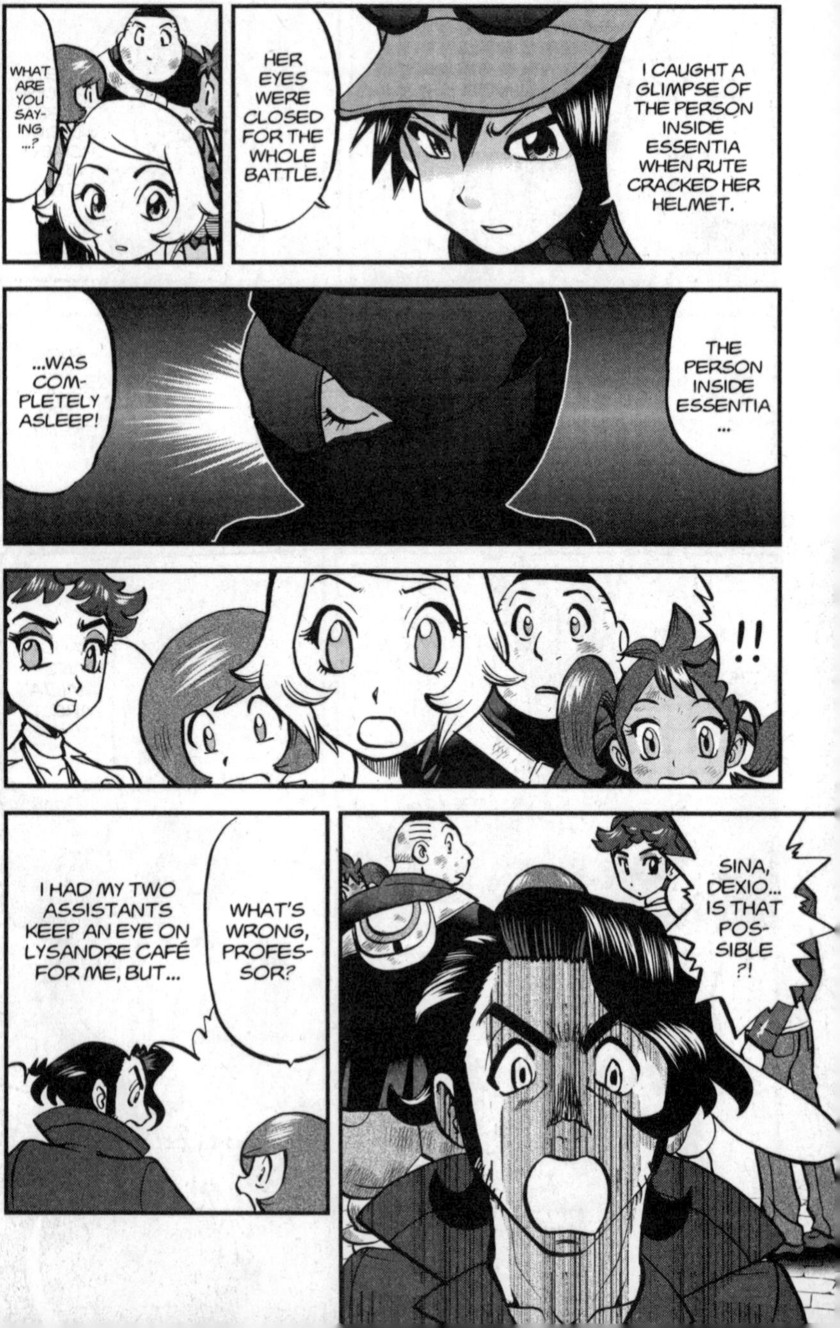
I CAUGHT A GLIMPSE OF THE PERSON INSIDE ESSENTIA WHEN RUTE CRACKED HER HELMET.
HER EYES WERE CLOSED FOR THE WHOLE BATTLE.
WHAT ARE YOU SAY-ING ...?
THE PERSON INSIDE ESSENTIA ...
...WAS COM-PLETELY ASLEEP!
!!
SINA, DEXIO... IS THAT POS-SIBLE ?!
WHAT'S WRONG, PROFES-SOR?
I HAD MY TWO ASSISTANTS KEEP AN EYE ON LYSANDRE CAFÉ FOR ME, BUT...

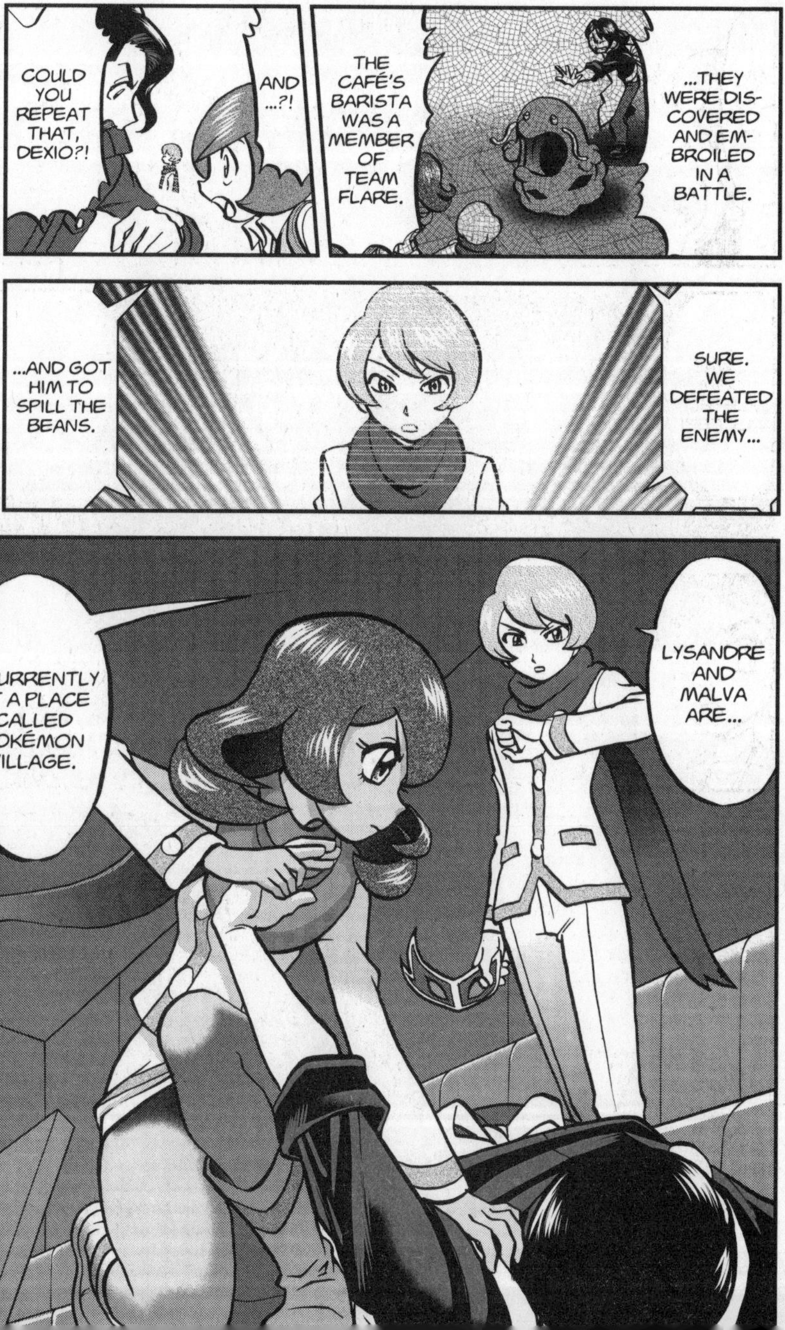
...THEY WERE DIS-COVERED AND EM-BROILED IN A BATTLE.
THE CAFÉ'S BARISTA WAS A MEMBER OF TEAM FLARE.
AND ...?!
COULD YOU REPEAT THAT, DEXIO?!
SURE. WE DEFEATED THE ENEMY...
...AND GOT HIM TO SPILL THE BEANS.
LYSANDRE AND MALVA ARE...
...CURRENTLY AT A PLACE CALLED POKÉMON VILLAGE.

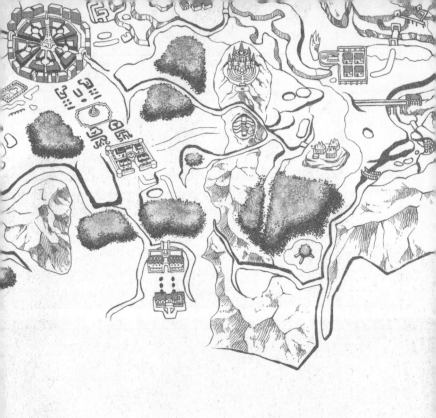

Current Location

Anistar City

Some say the enigmatic device used as a sundial came from outer space.

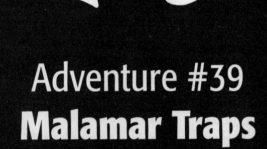

Adventure #39
Malamar Traps

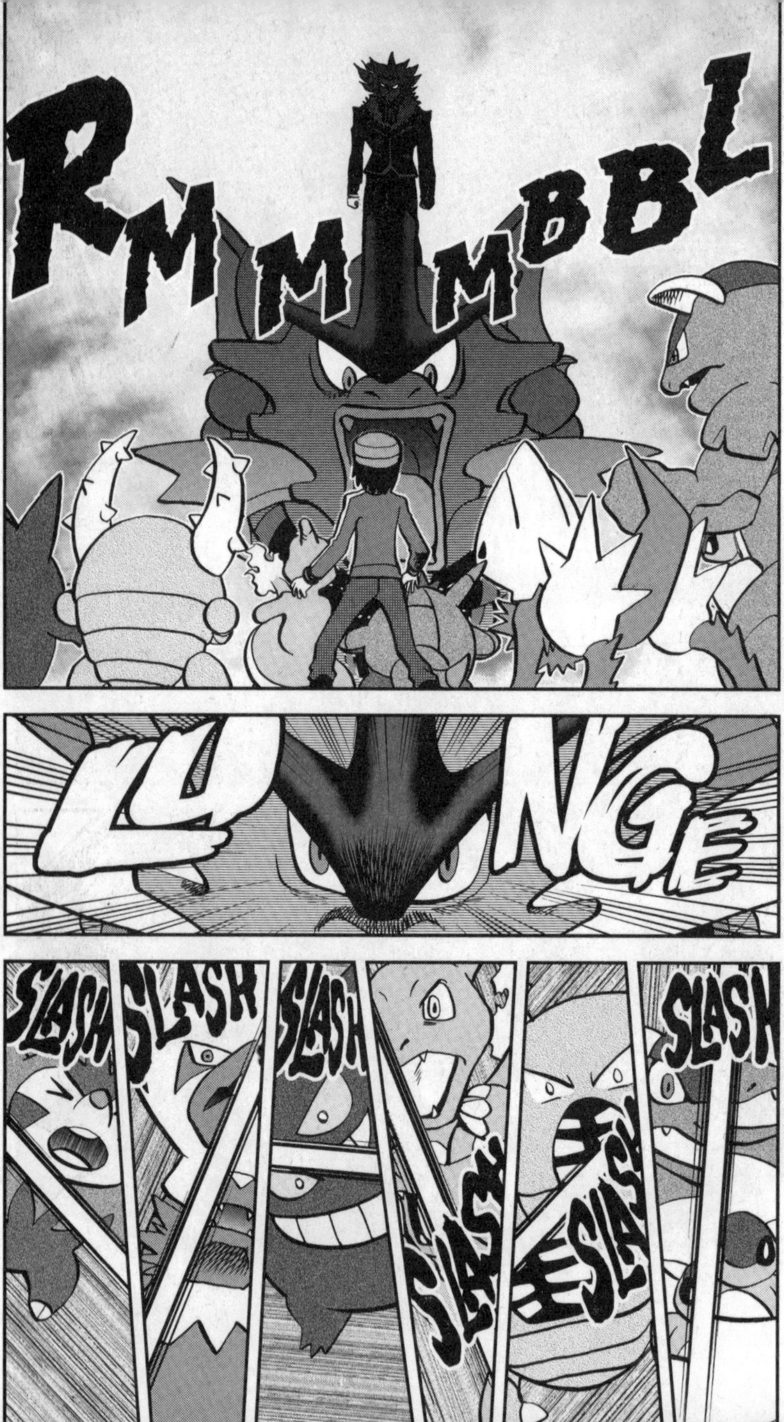
RMMMBBL
LUNGE
SLASH
SLASH
SLASH
SLASH
SLASH
SLASH
SLASH

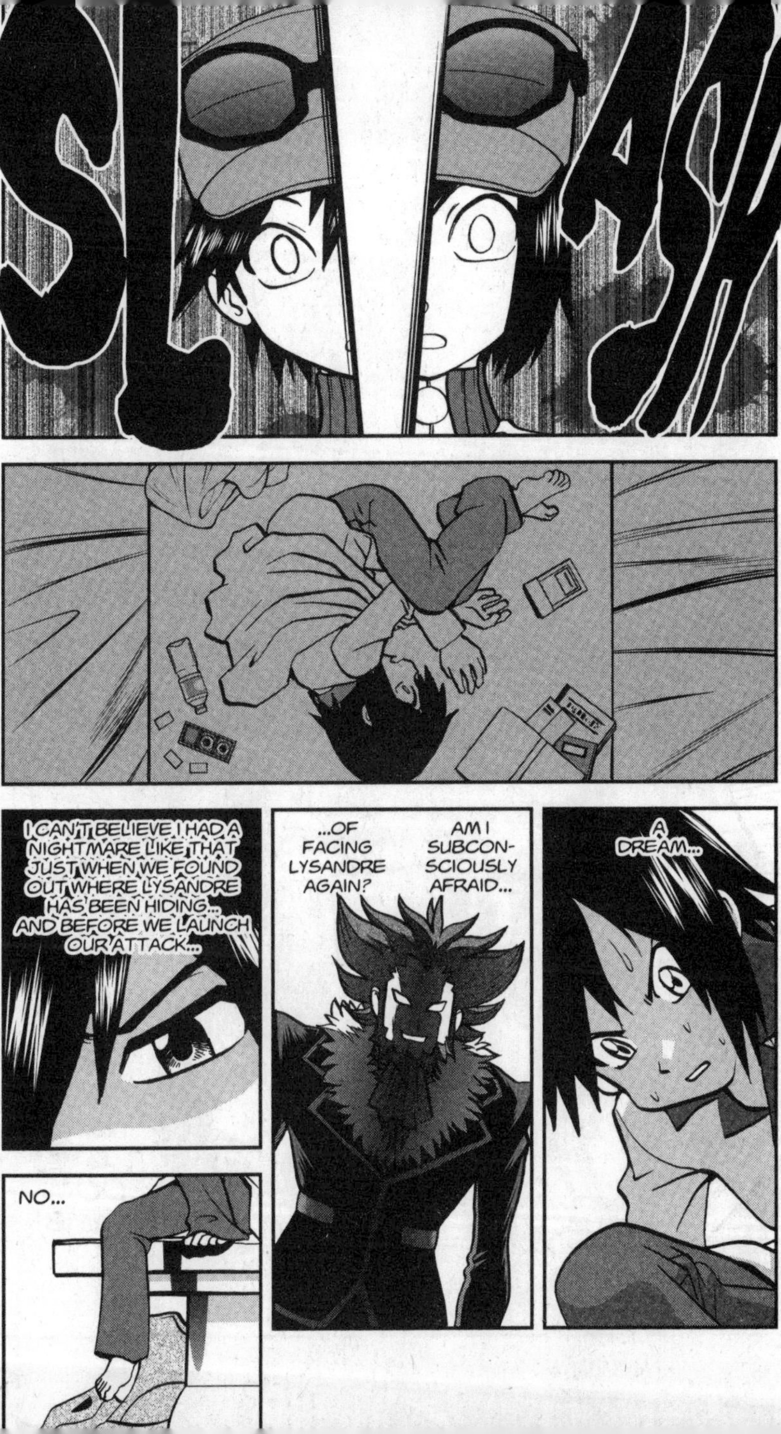
SLASH
A DREAM...
AM I SUBCONSCIOUSLY AFRAID...
...OF FACING LYSANDRE AGAIN?
I CAN'T BELIEVE I HAD A NIGHTMARE LIKE THAT JUST WHEN WE FOUND OUT WHERE LYSANDRE HAS BEEN HIDING... AND BEFORE WE LAUNCH OUR ATTACK...
NO...

ROUTE 18
FOREST ON THE OUTSKIRTS OF ANISTAR CITY
MY TEAM IS COMPLETE NOW THAT RUTE HAS JOINED US.
WE HAVE GOOD TEAM-WORK TOO.
THIS WON'T BE...
...LIKE THE LAST TIME!
NYYUU-URGH! MAAAG-NEEE-ETT BOOMM-MMB!
THNK THNK

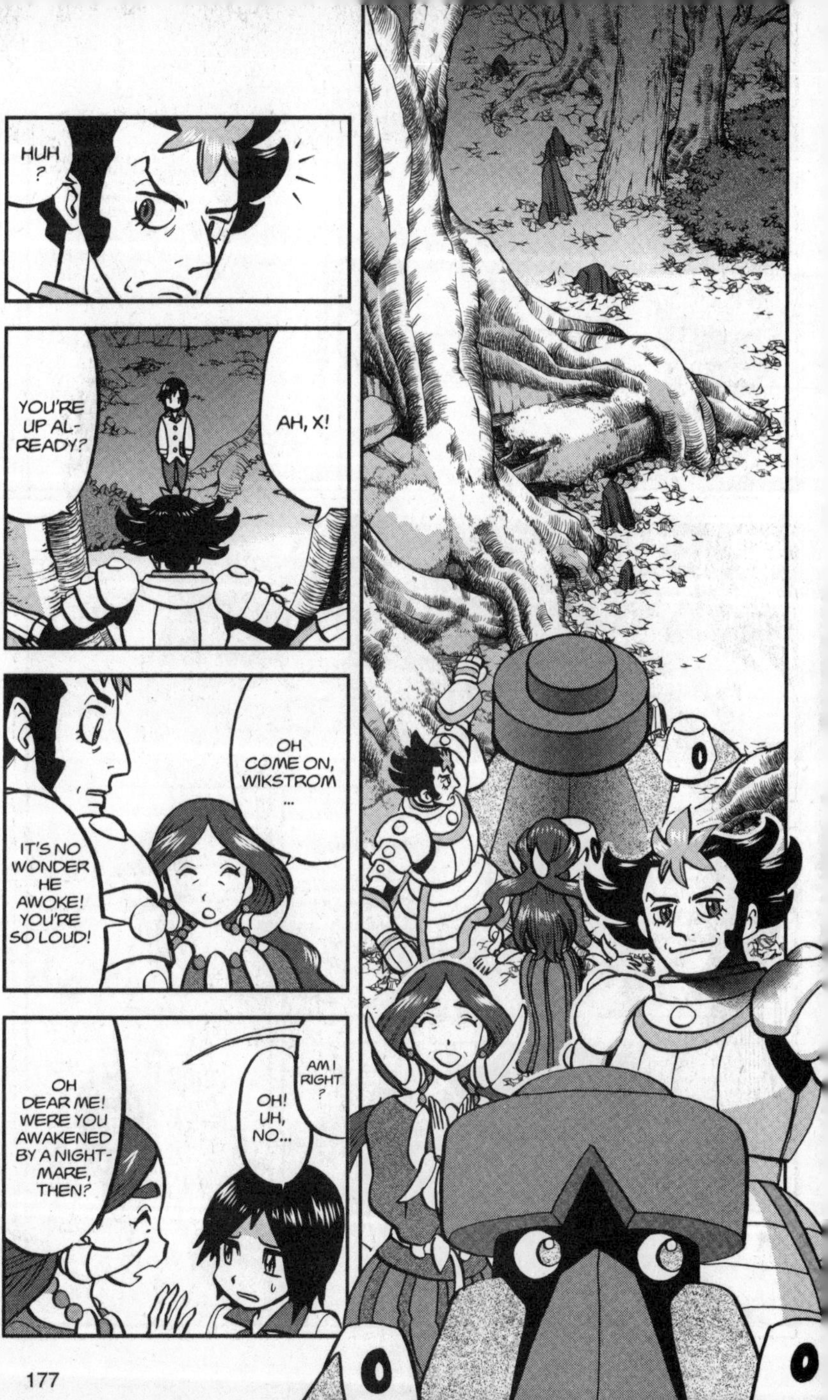
HUH?
AH, X!
YOU'RE UP AL-READY?
OH COME ON, WIKSTROM ...
IT'S NO WONDER HE AWOKE! YOU'RE SO LOUD!
OH DEAR ME! WERE YOU AWAKENED BY A NIGHT-MARE, THEN?
AM I RIGHT?
OH! UH, NO...

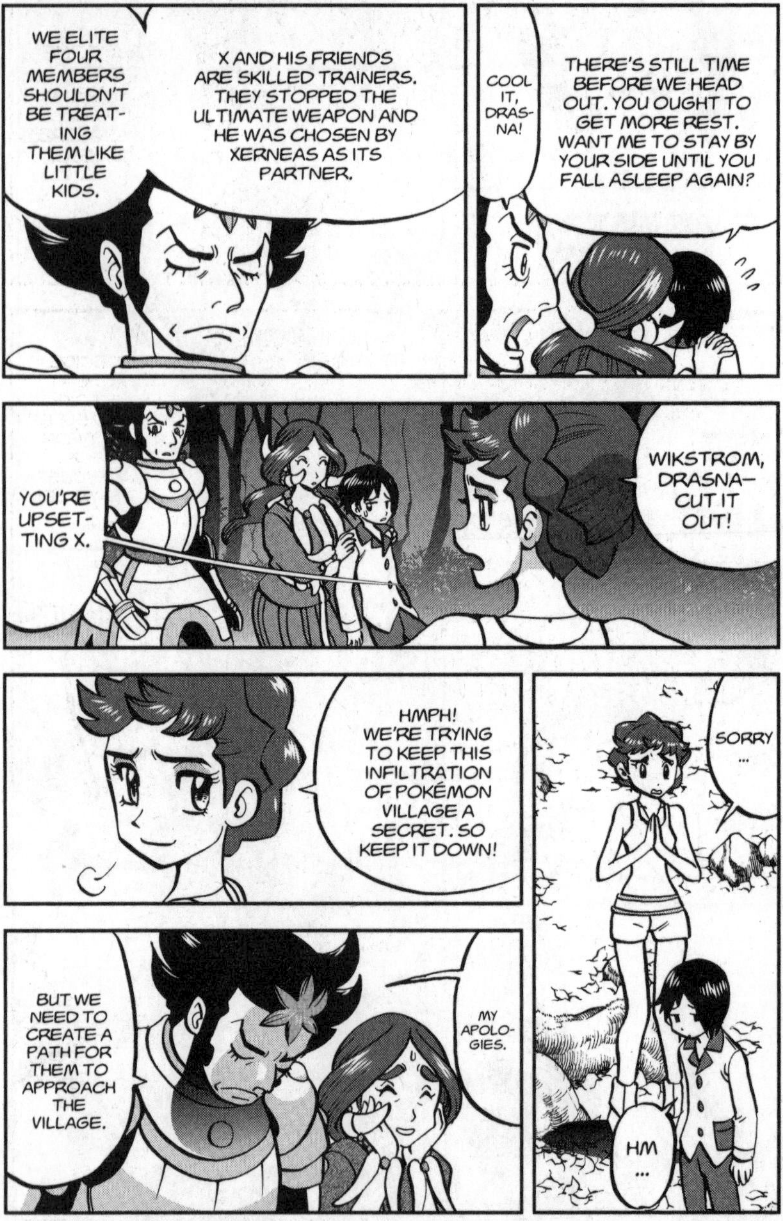
THERE'S STILL TIME BEFORE WE HEAD OUT. YOU OUGHT TO GET MORE REST. WANT ME TO STAY BY YOUR SIDE UNTIL YOU FALL ASLEEP AGAIN?
COOL IT, DRASNA!
WE ELITE FOUR MEMBERS SHOULDN'T BE TREATING THEM LIKE LITTLE KIDS. X AND HIS FRIENDS ARE SKILLED TRAINERS. THEY STOPPED THE ULTIMATE WEAPON AND HE WAS CHOSEN BY XERNEAS AS ITS PARTNER.
WIKSTROM, DRASNA— CUT IT OUT!
YOU'RE UPSETTING X.
SORRY...
HM...
HMPH! WE'RE TRYING TO KEEP THIS INFILTRATION OF POKÉMON VILLAGE A SECRET. SO KEEP IT DOWN!
MY APOLOGIES.
BUT WE NEED TO CREATE A PATH FOR THEM TO APPROACH THE VILLAGE.

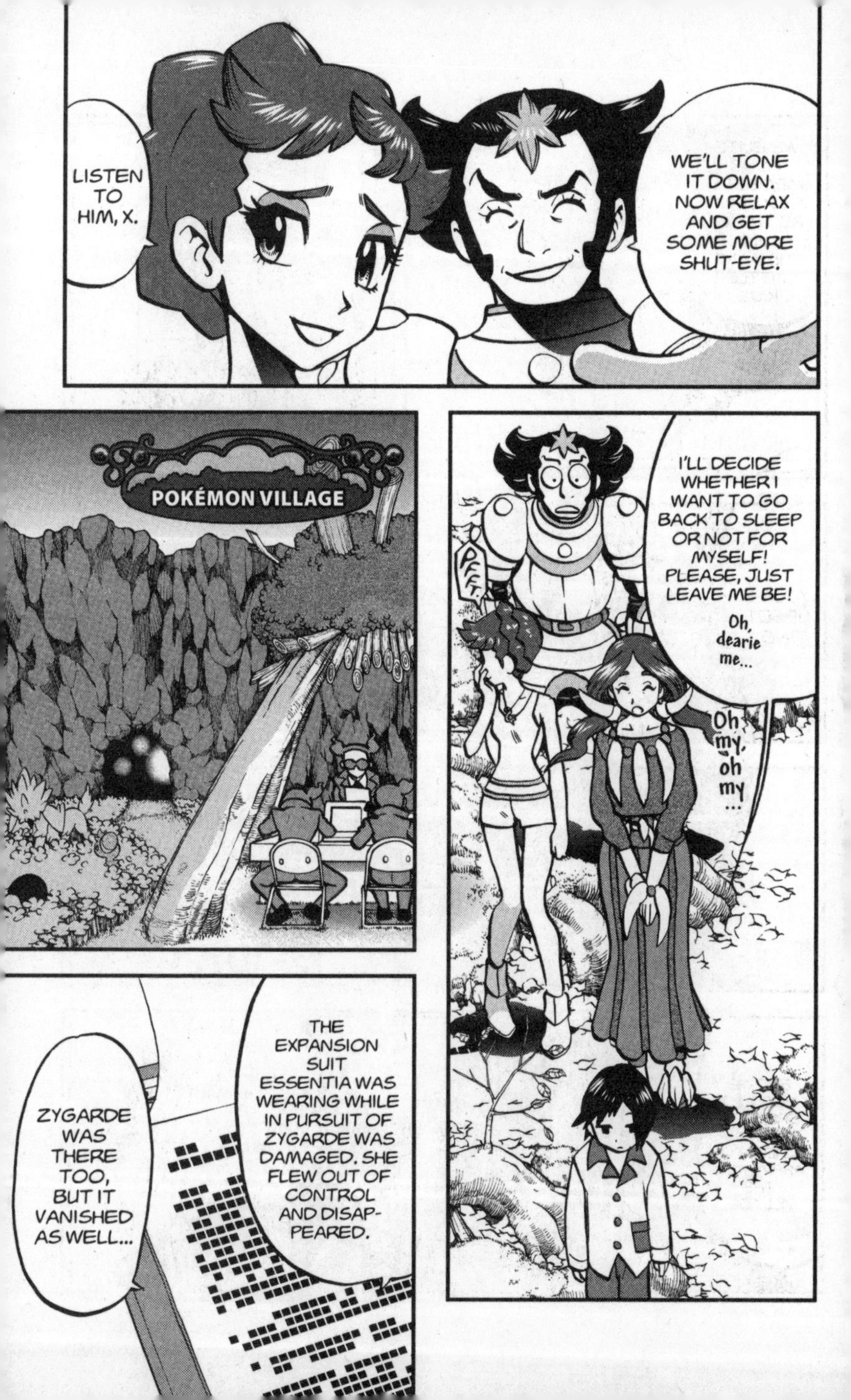
WE'LL TONE IT DOWN. NOW RELAX AND GET SOME MORE SHUT-EYE.
LISTEN TO HIM, X.
I'LL DECIDE WHETHER I WANT TO GO BACK TO SLEEP OR NOT FOR MYSELF! PLEASE, JUST LEAVE ME BE!
PFFT
Oh, dearie me...
Oh my, oh my...
POKÉMON VILLAGE
THE EXPANSION SUIT ESSENTIA WAS WEARING WHILE IN PURSUIT OF ZYGARDE WAS DAMAGED. SHE FLEW OUT OF CONTROL AND DISAP-PEARED.
ZYGARDE WAS THERE TOO, BUT IT VANISHED AS WELL...

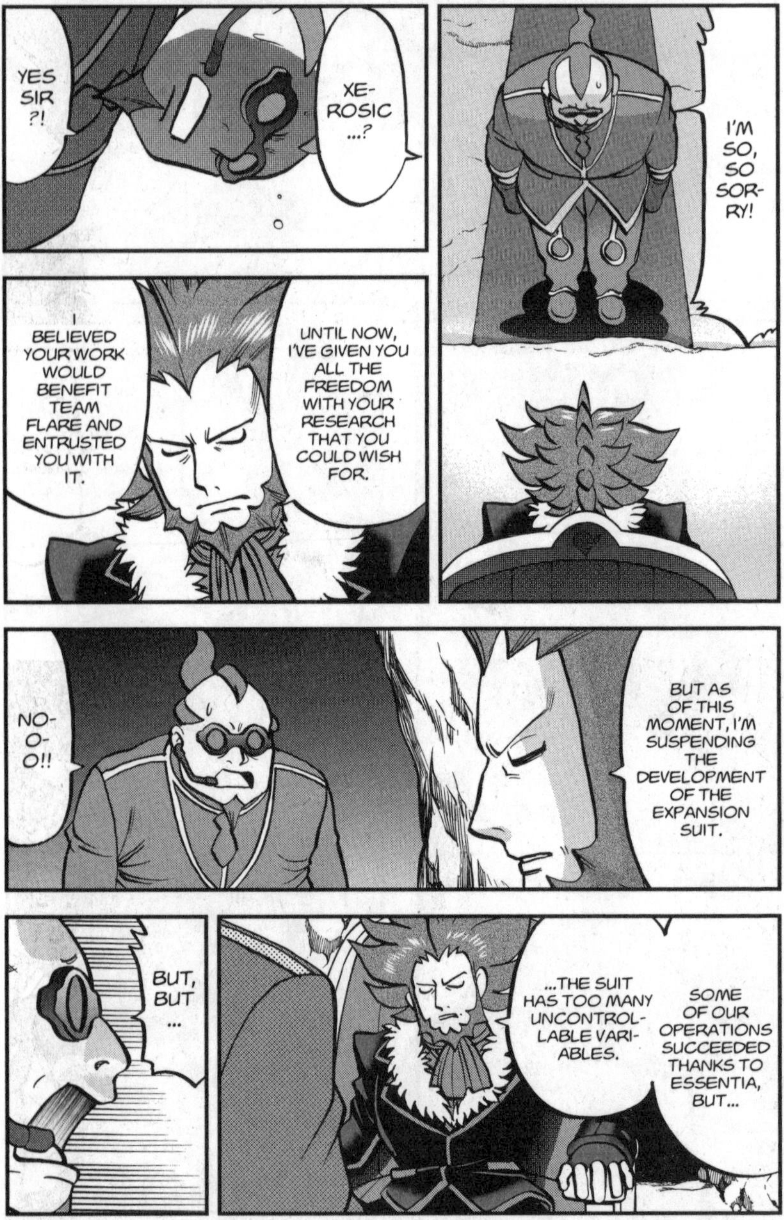

I'M SO, SO SORRY!
XEROSIC ...?
YES SIR ?!
UNTIL NOW, I'VE GIVEN YOU ALL THE FREEDOM WITH YOUR RESEARCH THAT YOU COULD WISH FOR.
I BELIEVED YOUR WORK WOULD BENEFIT TEAM FLARE AND ENTRUSTED YOU WITH IT.
BUT AS OF THIS MOMENT, I'M SUSPENDING THE DEVELOPMENT OF THE EXPANSION SUIT.
NO-O-O!!
SOME OF OUR OPERATIONS SUCCEEDED THANKS TO ESSENTIA, BUT...
...THE SUIT HAS TOO MANY UNCONTROLLABLE VARIABLES.
BUT, BUT ...

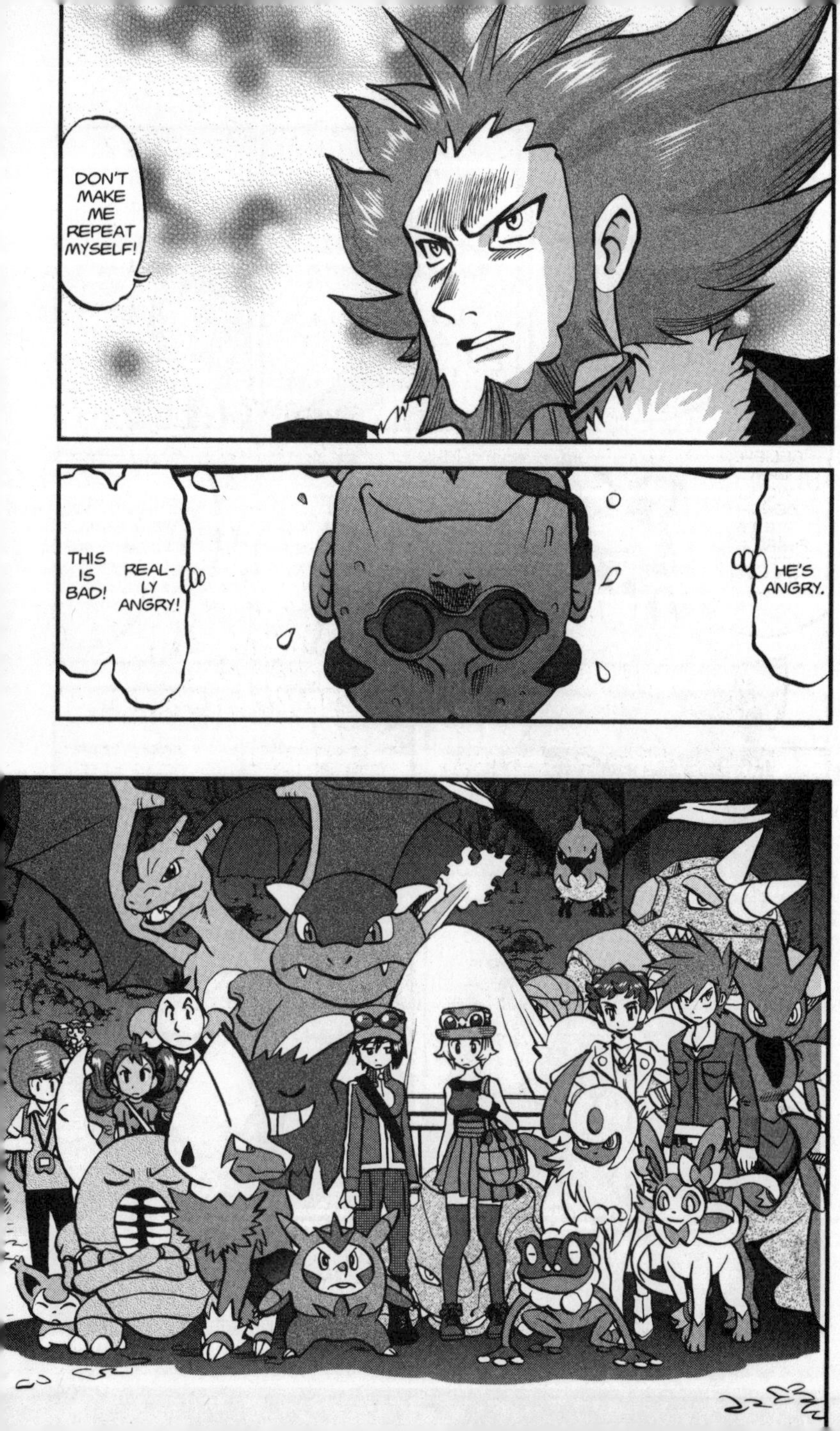
DON'T MAKE ME REPEAT MYSELF!
HE'S ANGRY.
REAL-LY ANGRY!
THIS IS BAD!

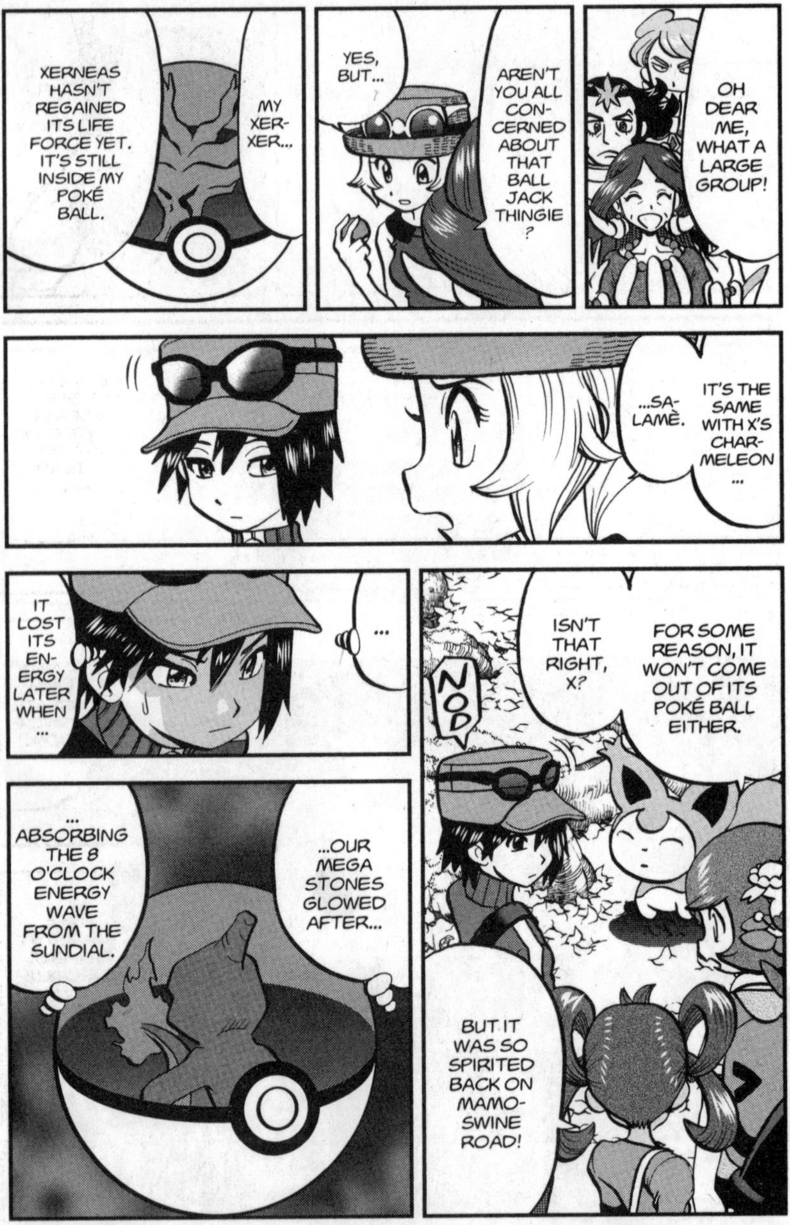
OH DEAR ME, WHAT A LARGE GROUP!
AREN'T YOU ALL CONCERNED ABOUT THAT BALL JACK THINGIE?
YES, BUT...
MY XERXER...
XERNEAS HASN'T REGAINED ITS LIFE FORCE YET. IT'S STILL INSIDE MY POKÉ BALL.
IT'S THE SAME WITH X'S CHARMELEON...
...SALAMÈ.
FOR SOME REASON, IT WON'T COME OUT OF ITS POKÉ BALL EITHER.
ISN'T THAT RIGHT, X?
NOD
BUT IT WAS SO SPIRITED BACK ON MAMOSWINE ROAD!
...
IT LOST ITS ENERGY LATER WHEN...
...OUR MEGA STONES GLOWED AFTER...
...ABSORBING THE 8 O'CLOCK ENERGY WAVE FROM THE SUNDIAL.

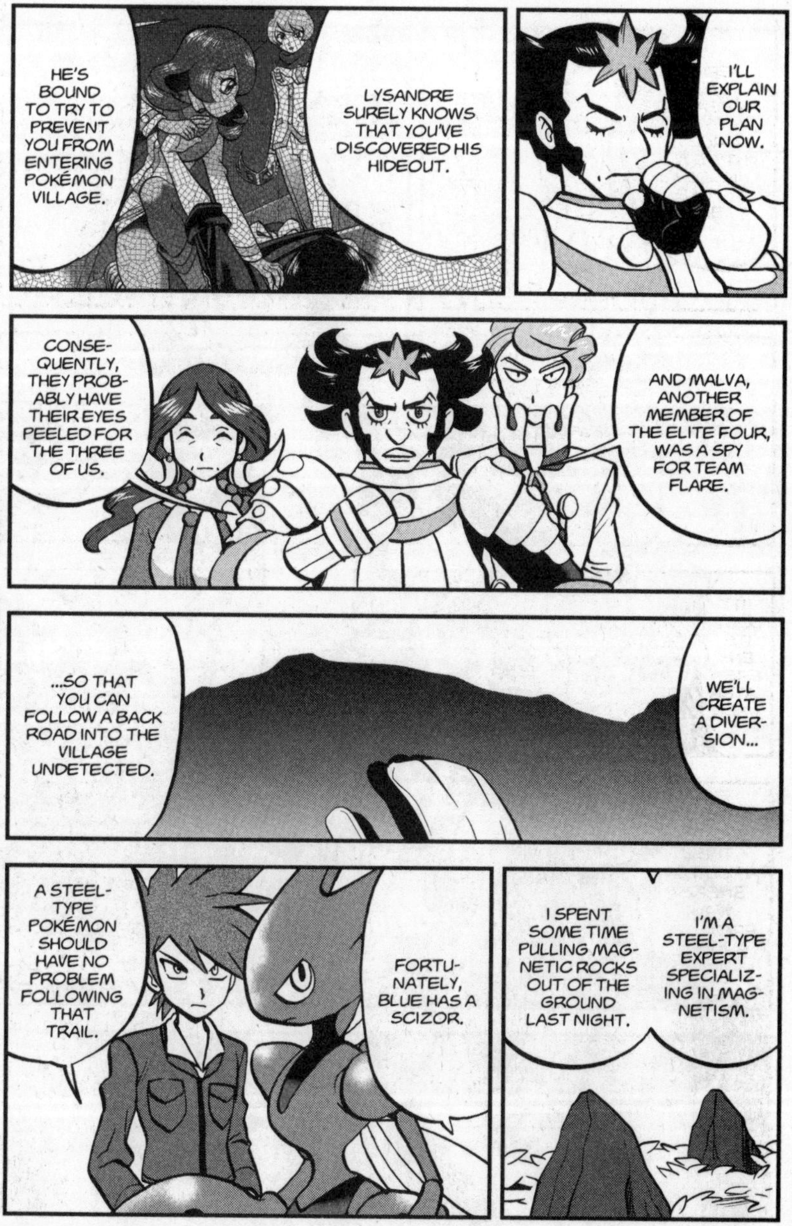
I'LL EXPLAIN OUR PLAN NOW.
LYSANDRE SURELY KNOWS THAT YOU'VE DISCOVERED HIS HIDEOUT.
HE'S BOUND TO TRY TO PREVENT YOU FROM ENTERING POKÉMON VILLAGE.
AND MALVA, ANOTHER MEMBER OF THE ELITE FOUR, WAS A SPY FOR TEAM FLARE.
CONSE-QUENTLY, THEY PROB-ABLY HAVE THEIR EYES PEELED FOR THE THREE OF US.
WE'LL CREATE A DIVER-SION...
...SO THAT YOU CAN FOLLOW A BACK ROAD INTO THE VILLAGE UNDETECTED.
I'M A STEEL-TYPE EXPERT SPECIALIZ-ING IN MAG-NETISM.
I SPENT SOME TIME PULLING MAG-NETIC ROCKS OUT OF THE GROUND LAST NIGHT.
FORTU-NATELY, BLUE HAS A SCIZOR.
A STEEL-TYPE POKÉMON SHOULD HAVE NO PROBLEM FOLLOWING THAT TRAIL.

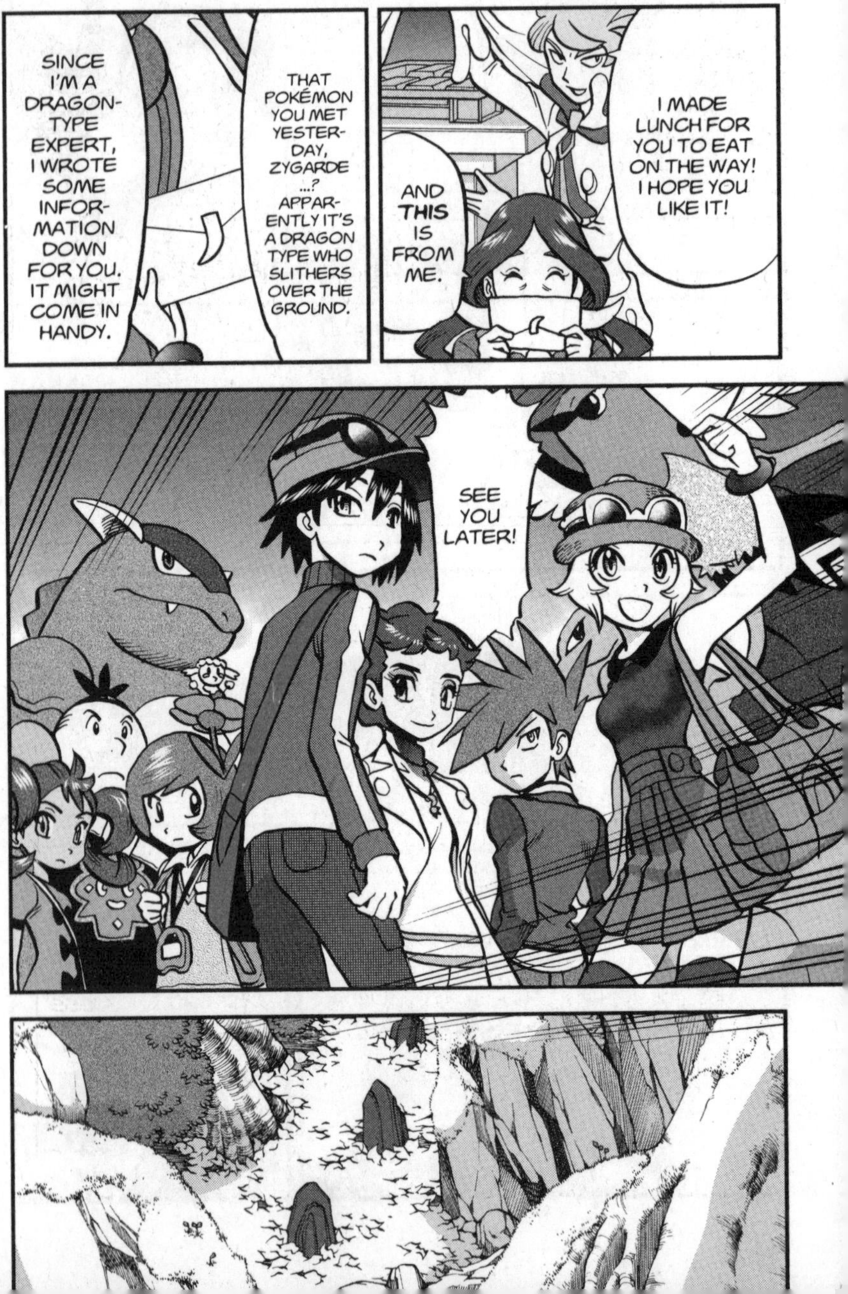
I MADE LUNCH FOR YOU TO EAT ON THE WAY! I HOPE YOU LIKE IT!
AND THIS IS FROM ME.
THAT POKÉMON YOU MET YESTER-DAY, ZYGARDE...? APPAR-ENTLY IT'S A DRAGON TYPE WHO SLITHERS OVER THE GROUND.
SINCE I'M A DRAGON-TYPE EXPERT, I WROTE SOME INFOR-MATION DOWN FOR YOU. IT MIGHT COME IN HANDY.
SEE YOU LATER!

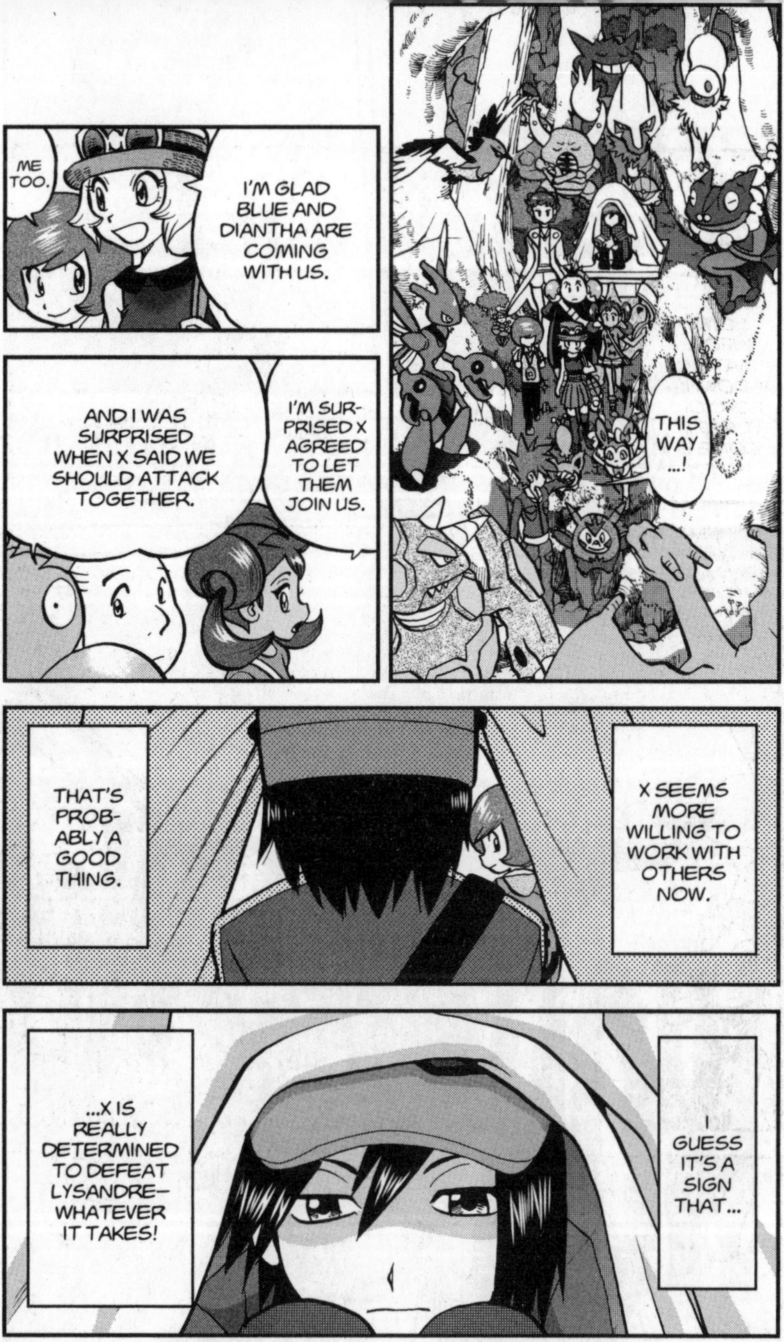
THIS WAY ...!
I'M GLAD BLUE AND DIANTHA ARE COMING WITH US.
ME TOO.
I'M SURPRISED X AGREED TO LET THEM JOIN US.
AND I WAS SURPRISED WHEN X SAID WE SHOULD ATTACK TOGETHER.
X SEEMS MORE WILLING TO WORK WITH OTHERS NOW.
THAT'S PROBABLY A GOOD THING.
I GUESS IT'S A SIGN THAT...
...X IS REALLY DETERMINED TO DEFEAT LYSANDRE—WHATEVER IT TAKES!

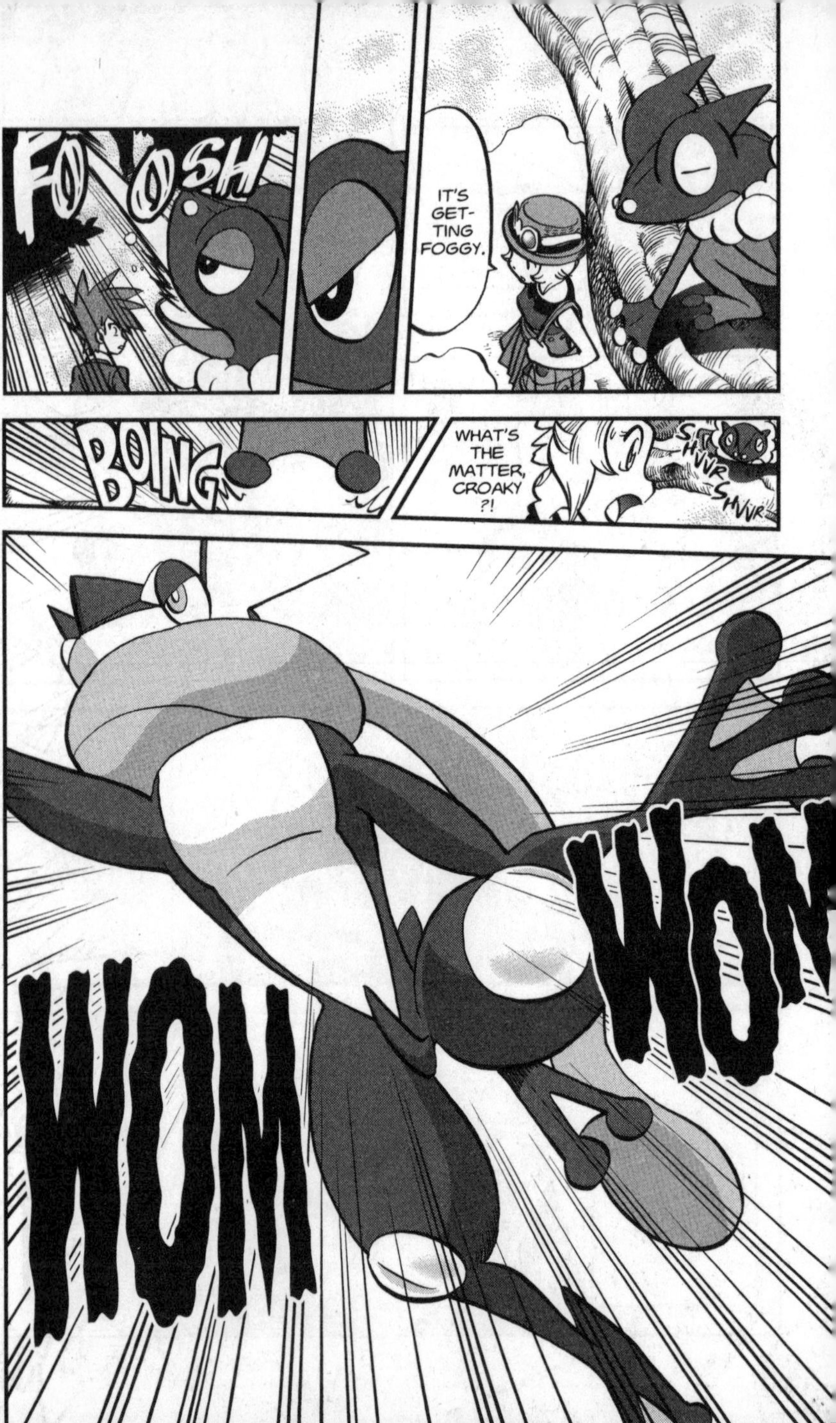
IT'S GETTING FOGGY.
FOOSH
SHVVR
SHVVR
WHAT'S THE MATTER, CROAKY?!
BOING
WOM
WOM

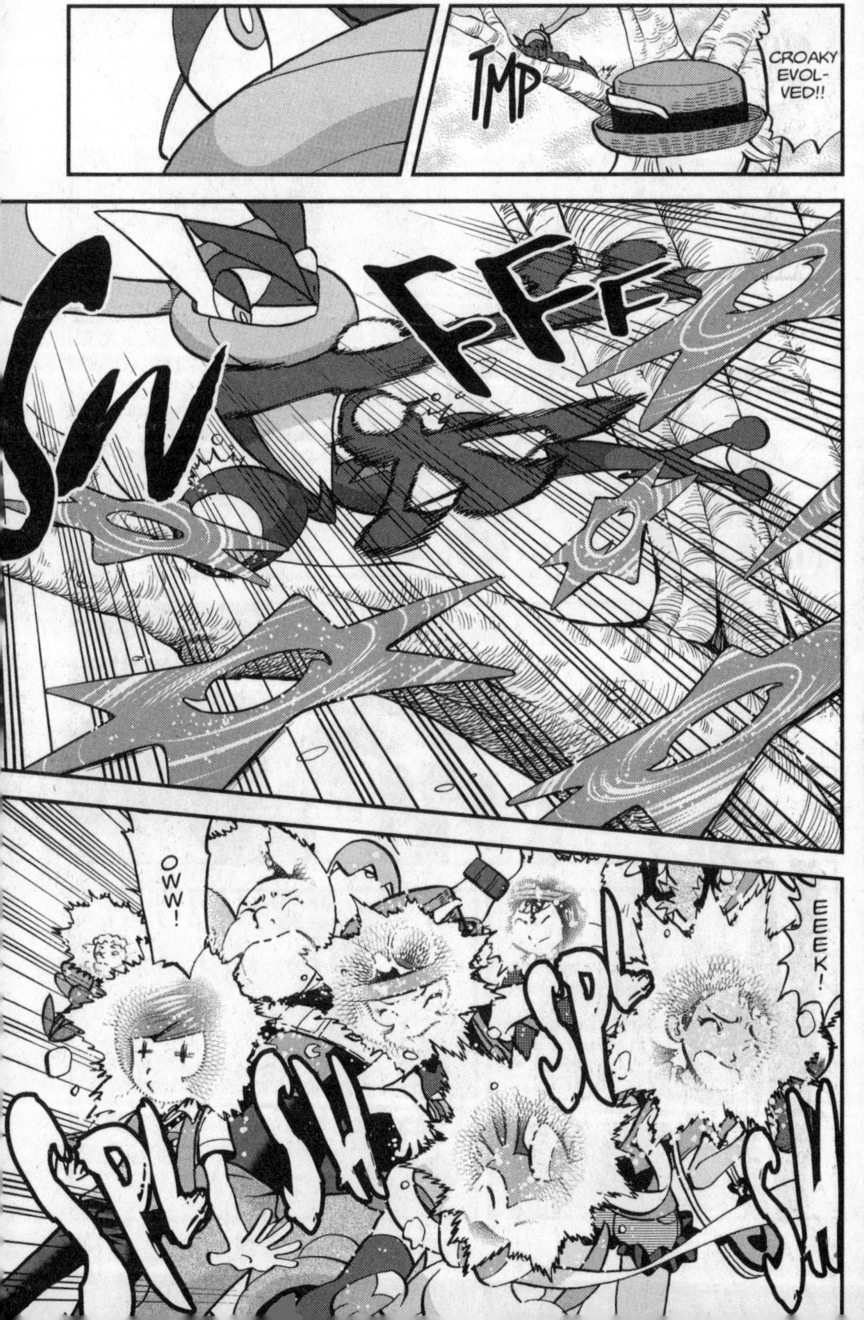
TMP
CROAKY EVOLVED!!
SWFFF
EEEEK!
SPL
SH
OWW!
SPLSH

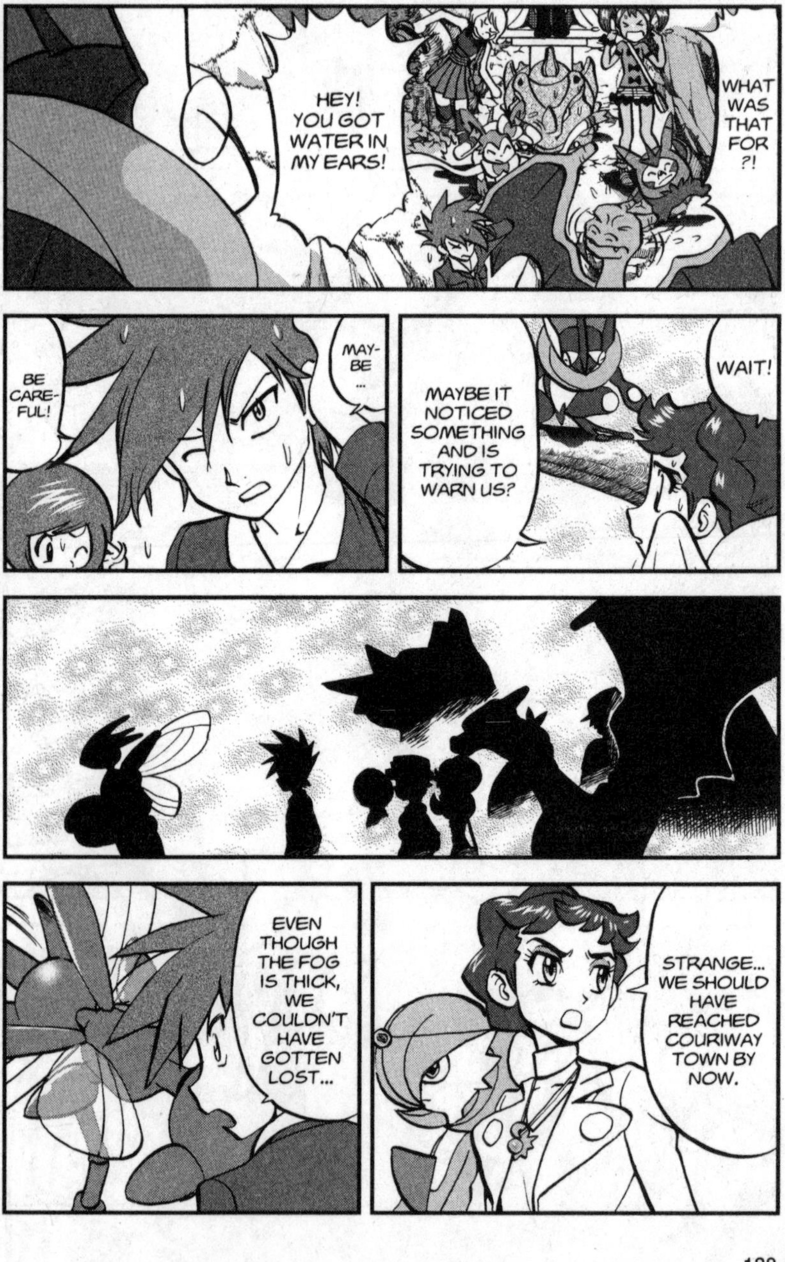
WHAT WAS THAT FOR?!
HEY! YOU GOT WATER IN MY EARS!
WAIT!
MAYBE IT NOTICED SOMETHING AND IS TRYING TO WARN US?
MAY-BE ...
BE CARE-FUL!
STRANGE... WE SHOULD HAVE REACHED COURIWAY TOWN BY NOW.
EVEN THOUGH THE FOG IS THICK, WE COULDN'T HAVE GOTTEN LOST...

ARGH...

SCIZOR...

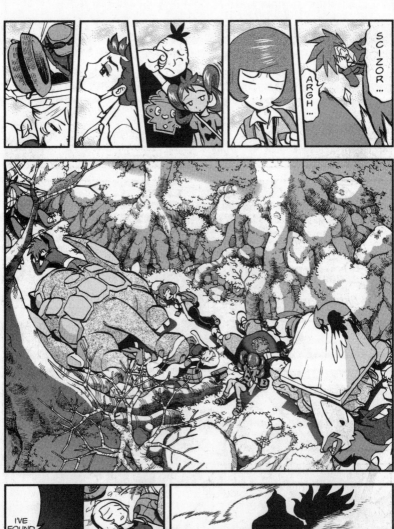

I'VE
FOUND
...

189

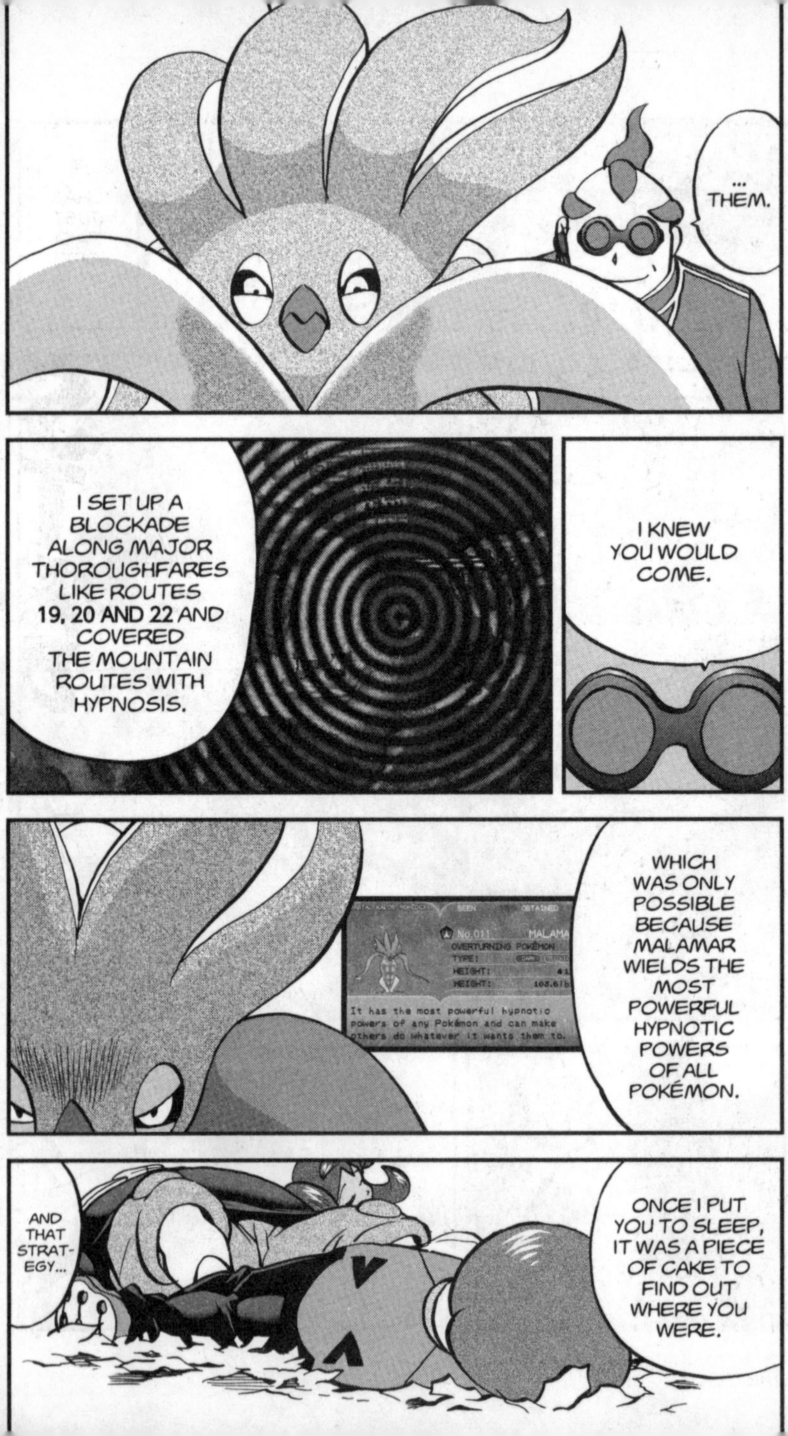
... THEM.
I KNEW YOU WOULD COME.
I SET UP A BLOCKADE ALONG MAJOR THOROUGHFARES LIKE ROUTES 19, 20 AND 22 AND COVERED THE MOUNTAIN ROUTES WITH HYPNOSIS.
WHICH WAS ONLY POSSIBLE BECAUSE MALAMAR WIELDS THE MOST POWERFUL HYPNOTIC POWERS OF ALL POKÉMON.
SEEN
OBTAINED
No.011
OVERTURNING POKÉMON
TYPE:
HEIGHT:
WEIGHT:
It has the most powerful hypnotic powers of any Pokémon and can make others do whatever it wants them to.
ONCE I PUT YOU TO SLEEP, IT WAS A PIECE OF CAKE TO FIND OUT WHERE YOU WERE.
AND THAT STRATEGY...

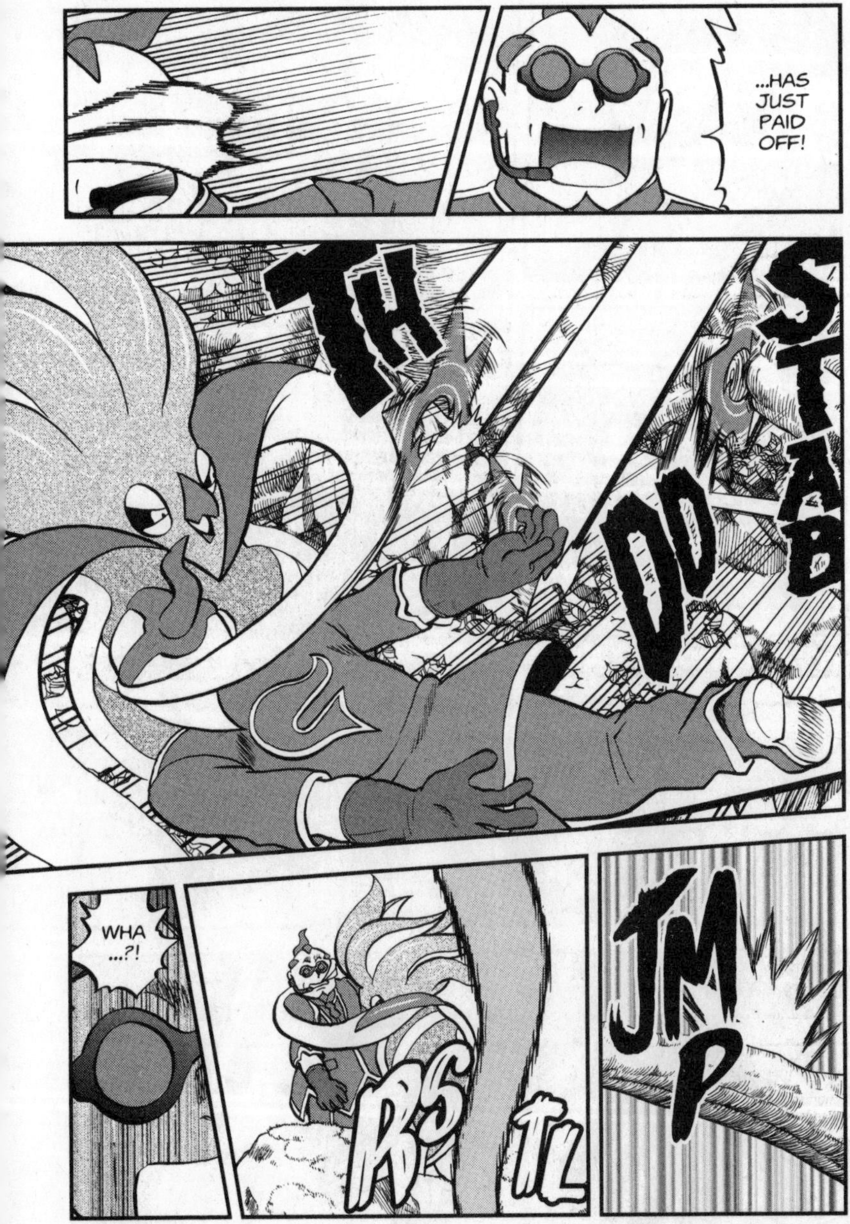
...HAS JUST PAID OFF!
STAB
THUD
JMP
RSTL
WHA ...?!

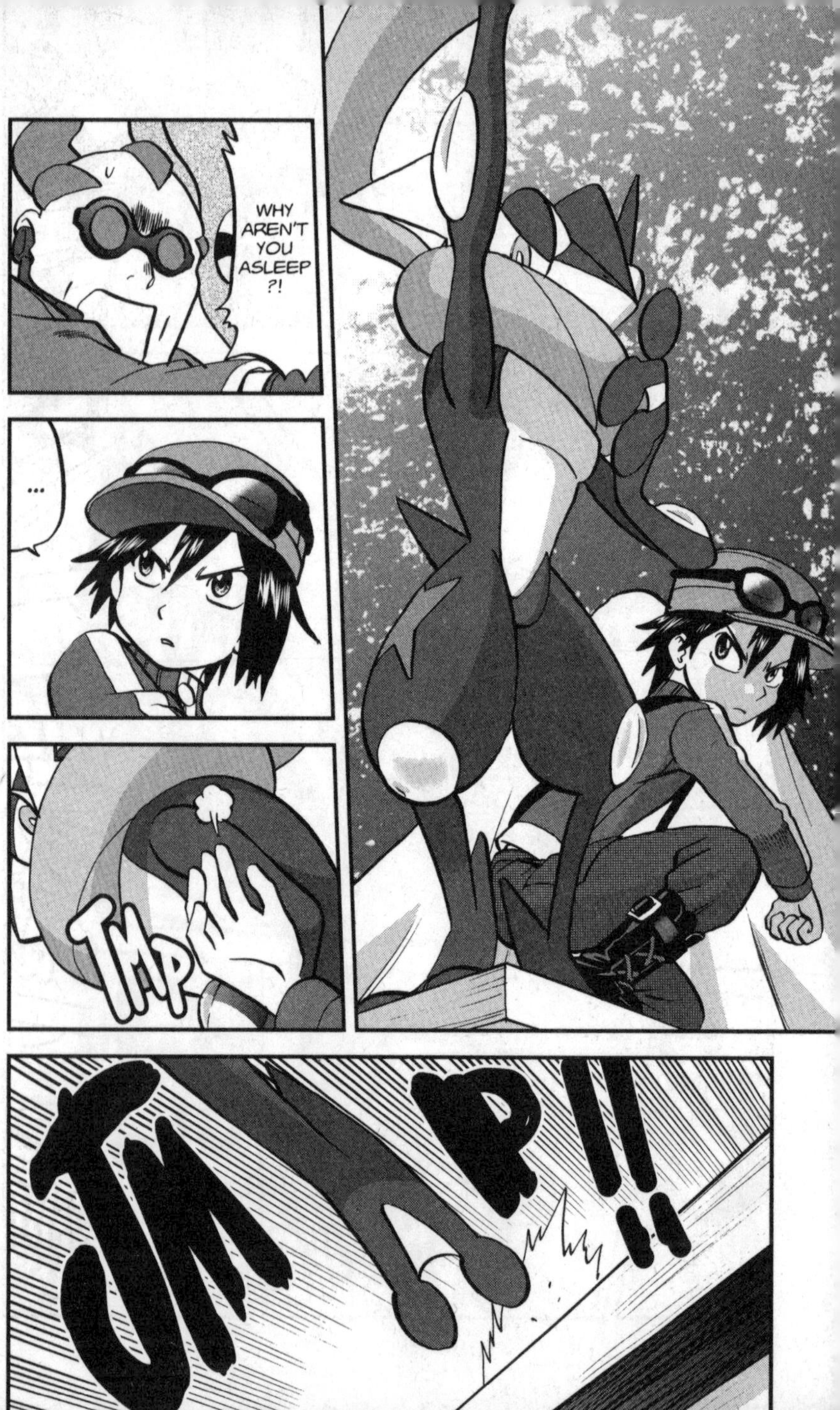
WHY AREN'T YOU ASLEEP?!
...
TMP
JMP!!

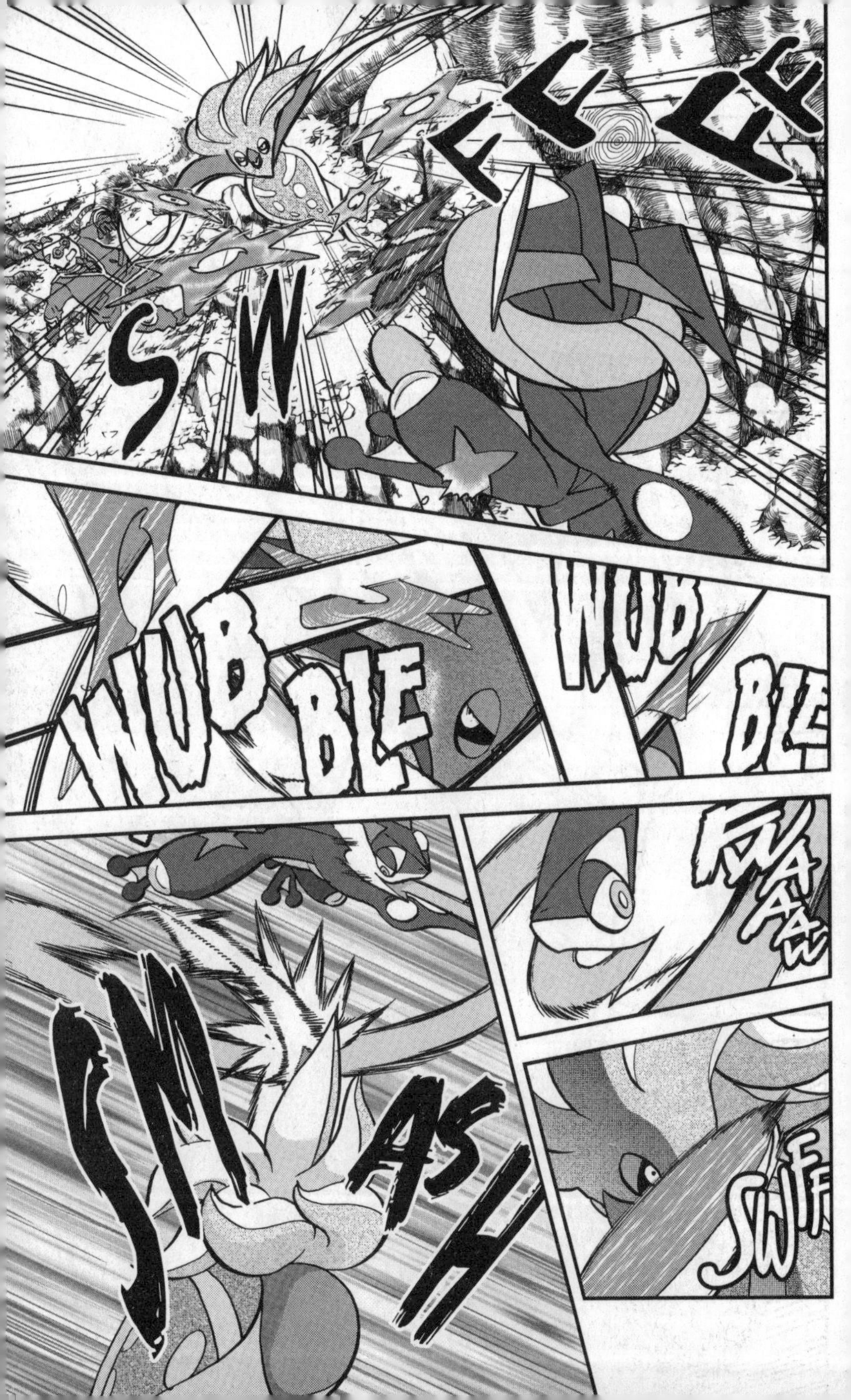
SW
WOB BLE
WOB BLE
SWFF
SMASH

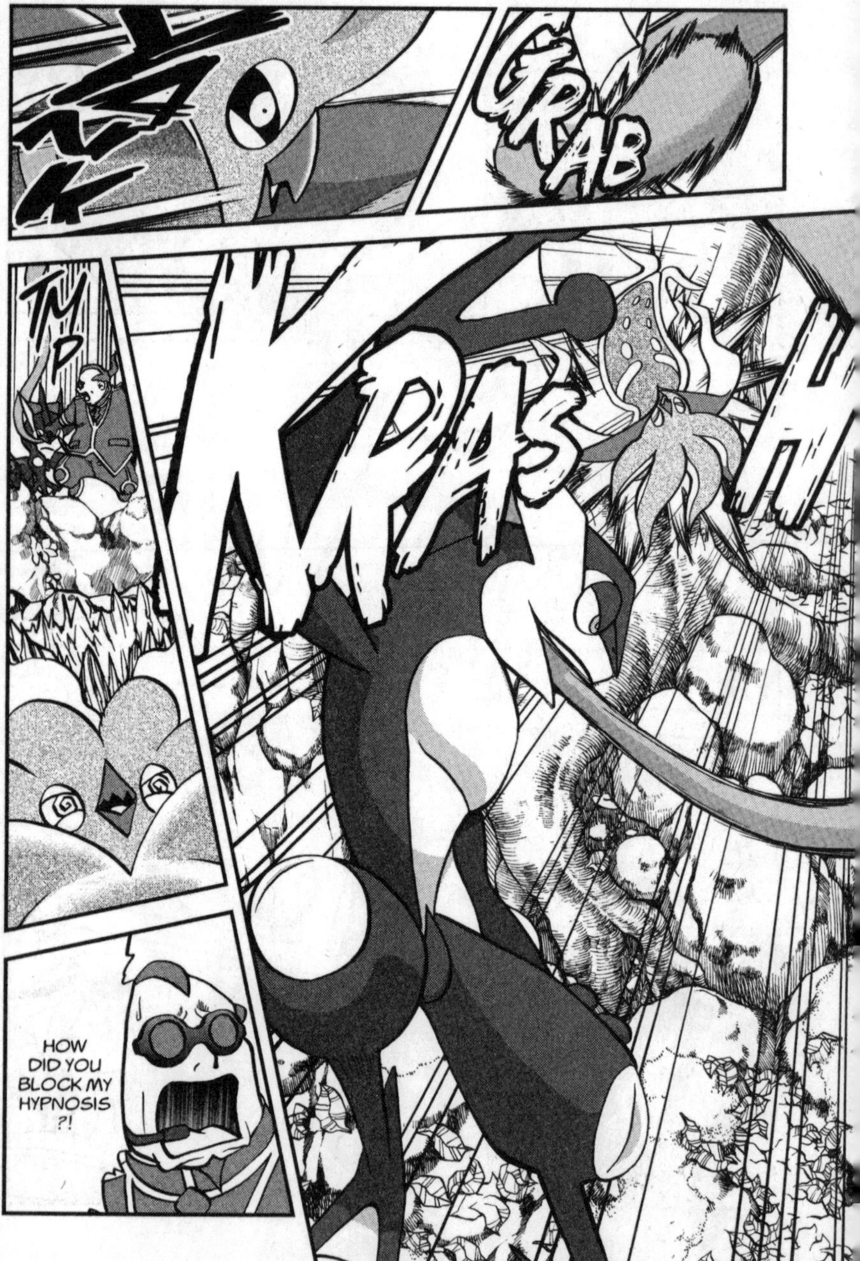
GRAB
KRASH
TMP
HOW DID YOU BLOCK MY HYPNOSIS ?!

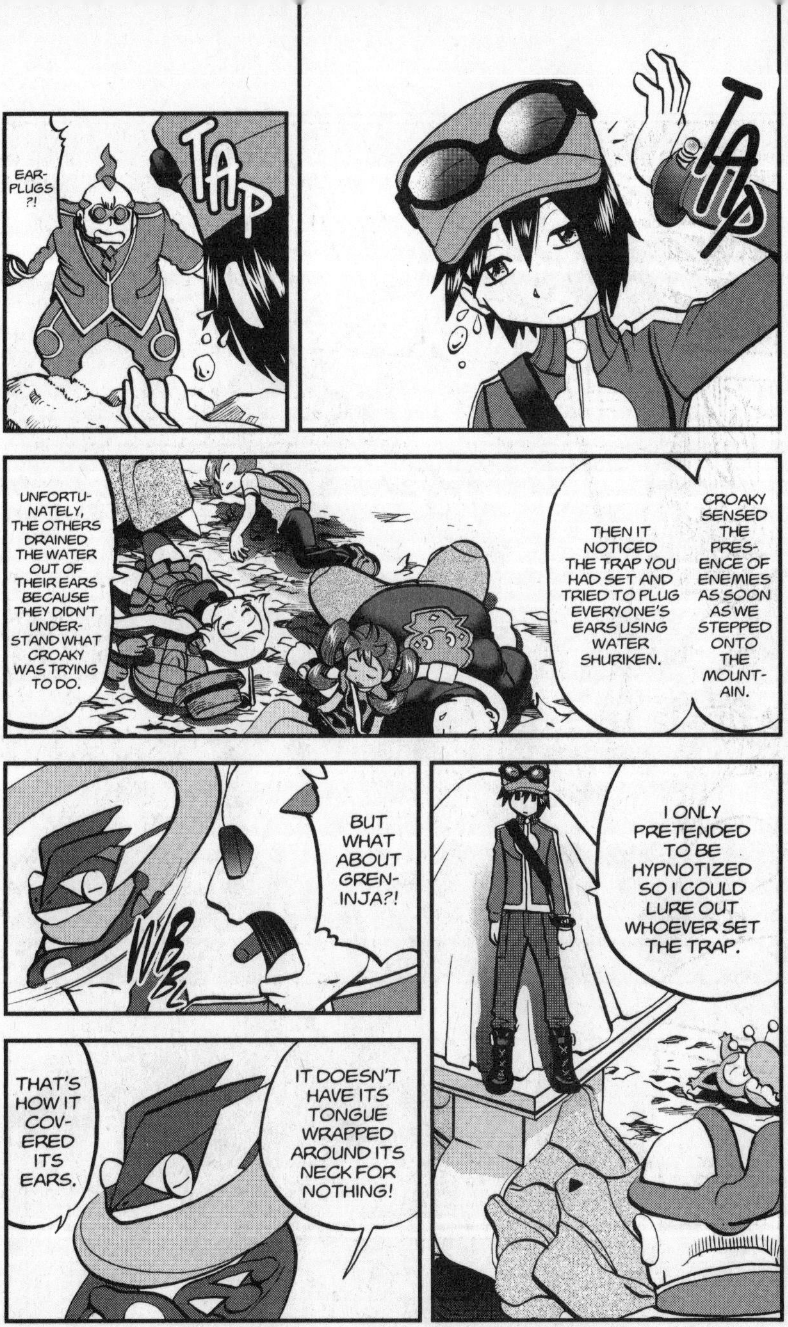
TAP TAP
EAR-PLUGS?!
TAP
CROAKY SENSED THE PRESENCE OF ENEMIES AS SOON AS WE STEPPED ONTO THE MOUNTAIN.
THEN IT NOTICED THE TRAP YOU HAD SET AND TRIED TO PLUG EVERYONE'S EARS USING WATER SHURIKEN.
UNFORTUNATELY, THE OTHERS DRAINED THE WATER OUT OF THEIR EARS BECAUSE THEY DIDN'T UNDERSTAND WHAT CROAKY WAS TRYING TO DO.
I ONLY PRETENDED TO BE HYPNOTIZED SO I COULD LURE OUT WHOEVER SET THE TRAP.
BUT WHAT ABOUT GRENINJA?!
IT DOESN'T HAVE ITS TONGUE WRAPPED AROUND ITS NECK FOR NOTHING!
THAT'S HOW IT COVERED ITS EARS.

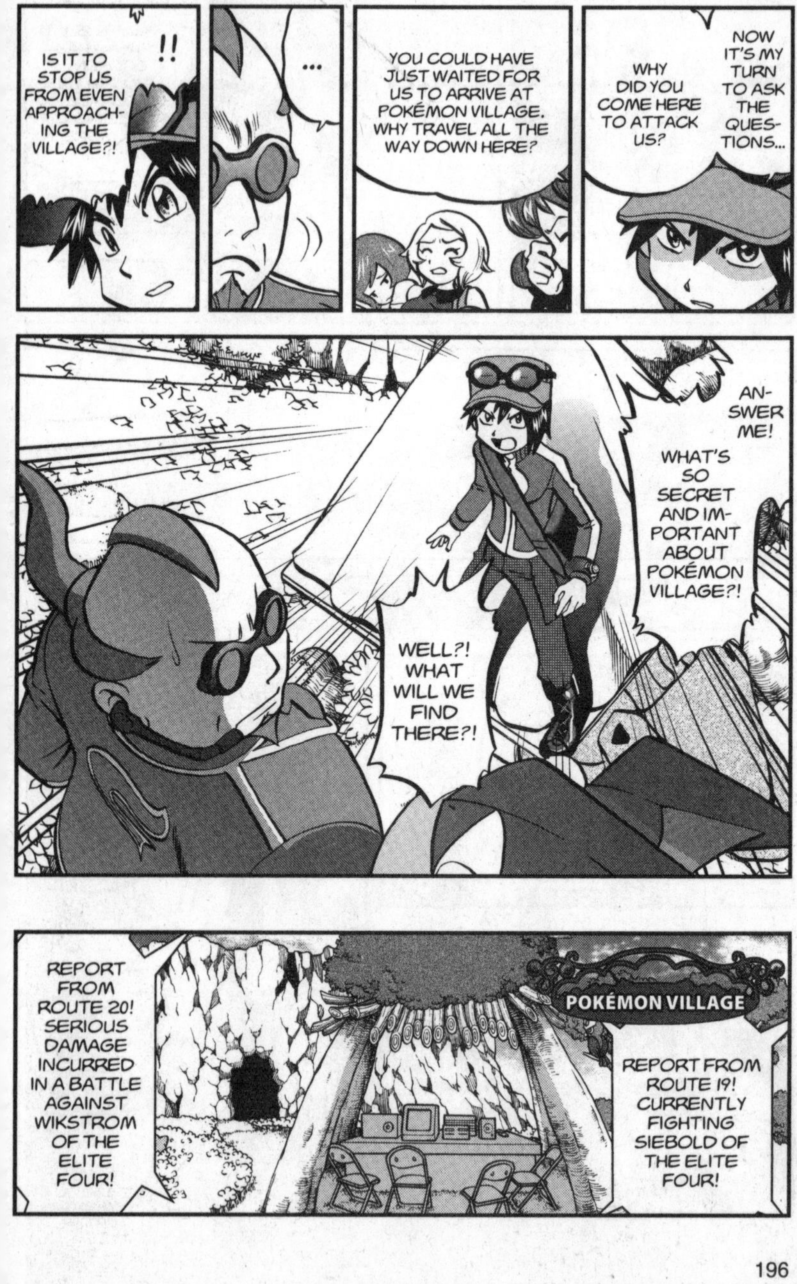
NOW IT'S MY TURN TO ASK THE QUESTIONS...
WHY DID YOU COME HERE TO ATTACK US?
YOU COULD HAVE JUST WAITED FOR US TO ARRIVE AT POKÉMON VILLAGE. WHY TRAVEL ALL THE WAY DOWN HERE?
...
!!
IS IT TO STOP US FROM EVEN APPROACHING THE VILLAGE?!
ANSWER ME! WHAT'S SO SECRET AND IMPORTANT ABOUT POKÉMON VILLAGE?!
WELL?! WHAT WILL WE FIND THERE?!
POKÉMON VILLAGE
REPORT FROM ROUTE 19! CURRENTLY FIGHTING SIEBOLD OF THE ELITE FOUR!
REPORT FROM ROUTE 20! SERIOUS DAMAGE INCURRED IN A BATTLE AGAINST WIKSTROM OF THE ELITE FOUR!

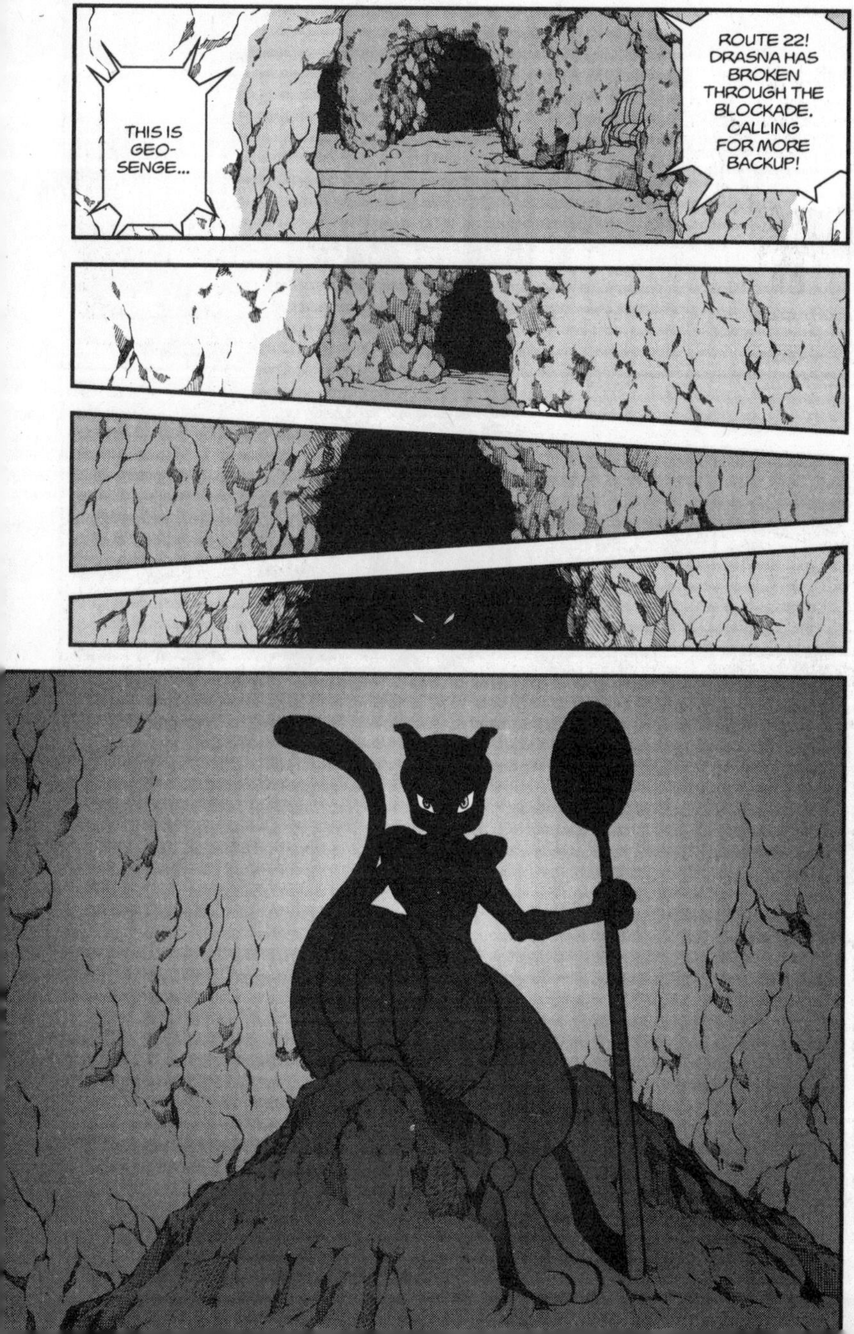
ROUTE 22! DRASNA HAS BROKEN THROUGH THE BLOCKADE. CALLING FOR MORE BACKUP!
THIS IS GEO-SENGE...

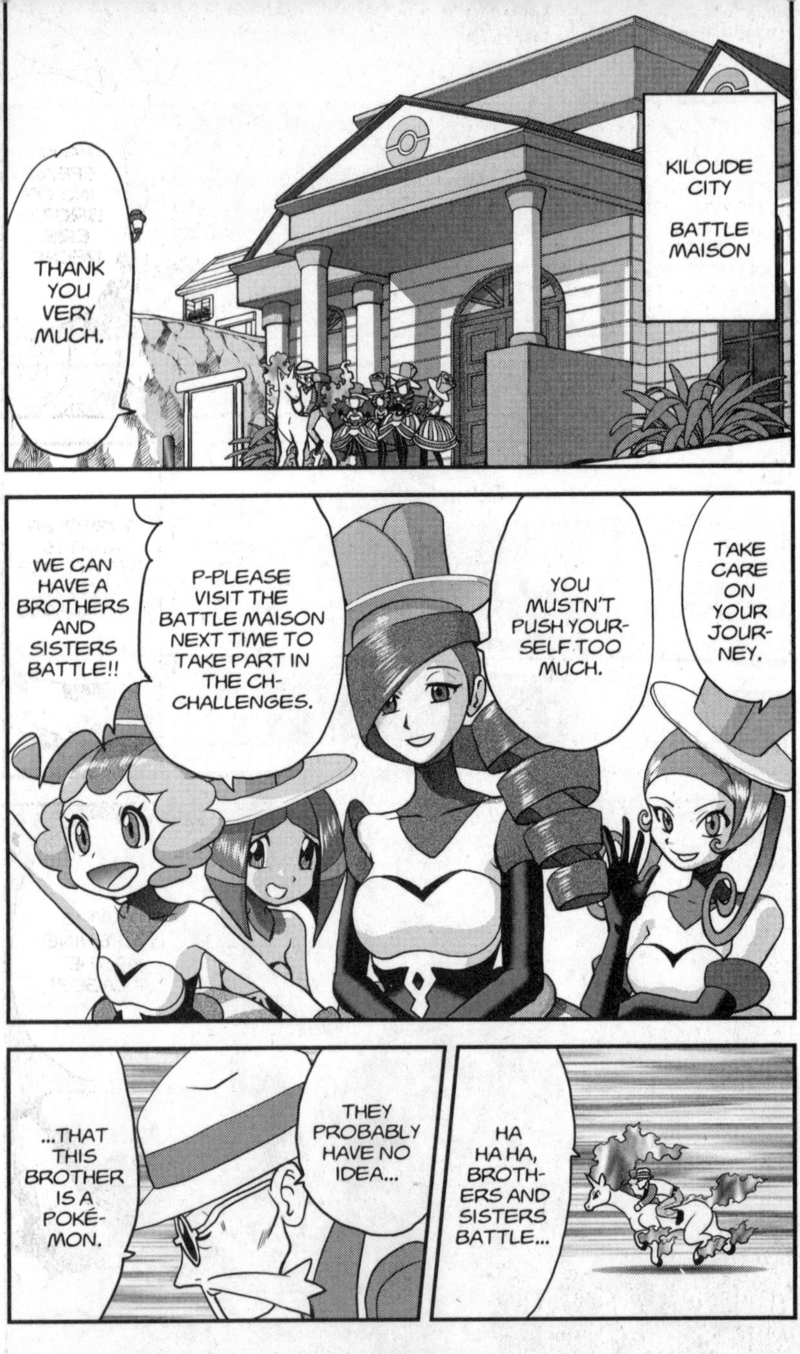
KILOUDE CITY BATTLE MAISON
THANK YOU VERY MUCH.
TAKE CARE ON YOUR JOURNEY.
YOU MUSTN'T PUSH YOURSELF TOO MUCH.
P-PLEASE VISIT THE BATTLE MAISON NEXT TIME TO TAKE PART IN THE CH-CHALLENGES.
WE CAN HAVE A BROTHERS AND SISTERS BATTLE!!
HA HA HA, BROTHERS AND SISTERS BATTLE...
THEY PROBABLY HAVE NO IDEA...
...THAT THIS BROTHER IS A POKÉMON.

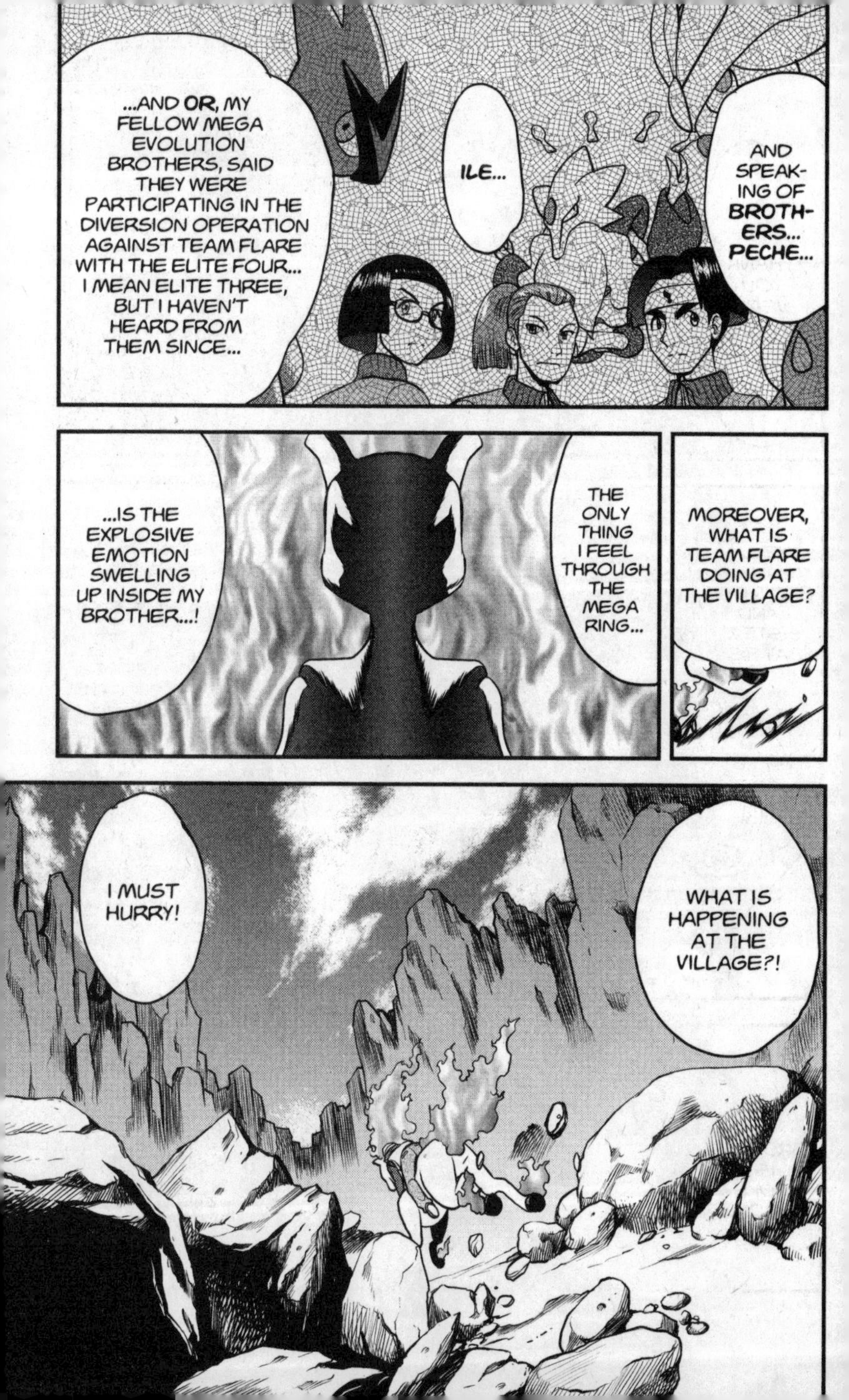
AND SPEAKING OF BROTHERS... PECHE...
ILE...
...AND OR, MY FELLOW MEGA EVOLUTION BROTHERS, SAID THEY WERE PARTICIPATING IN THE DIVERSION OPERATION AGAINST TEAM FLARE WITH THE ELITE FOUR... I MEAN ELITE THREE, BUT I HAVEN'T HEARD FROM THEM SINCE...
MOREOVER, WHAT IS TEAM FLARE DOING AT THE VILLAGE?
THE ONLY THING I FEEL THROUGH THE MEGA RING...
...IS THE EXPLOSIVE EMOTION SWELLING UP INSIDE MY BROTHER...!
WHAT IS HAPPENING AT THE VILLAGE?!
I MUST HURRY!

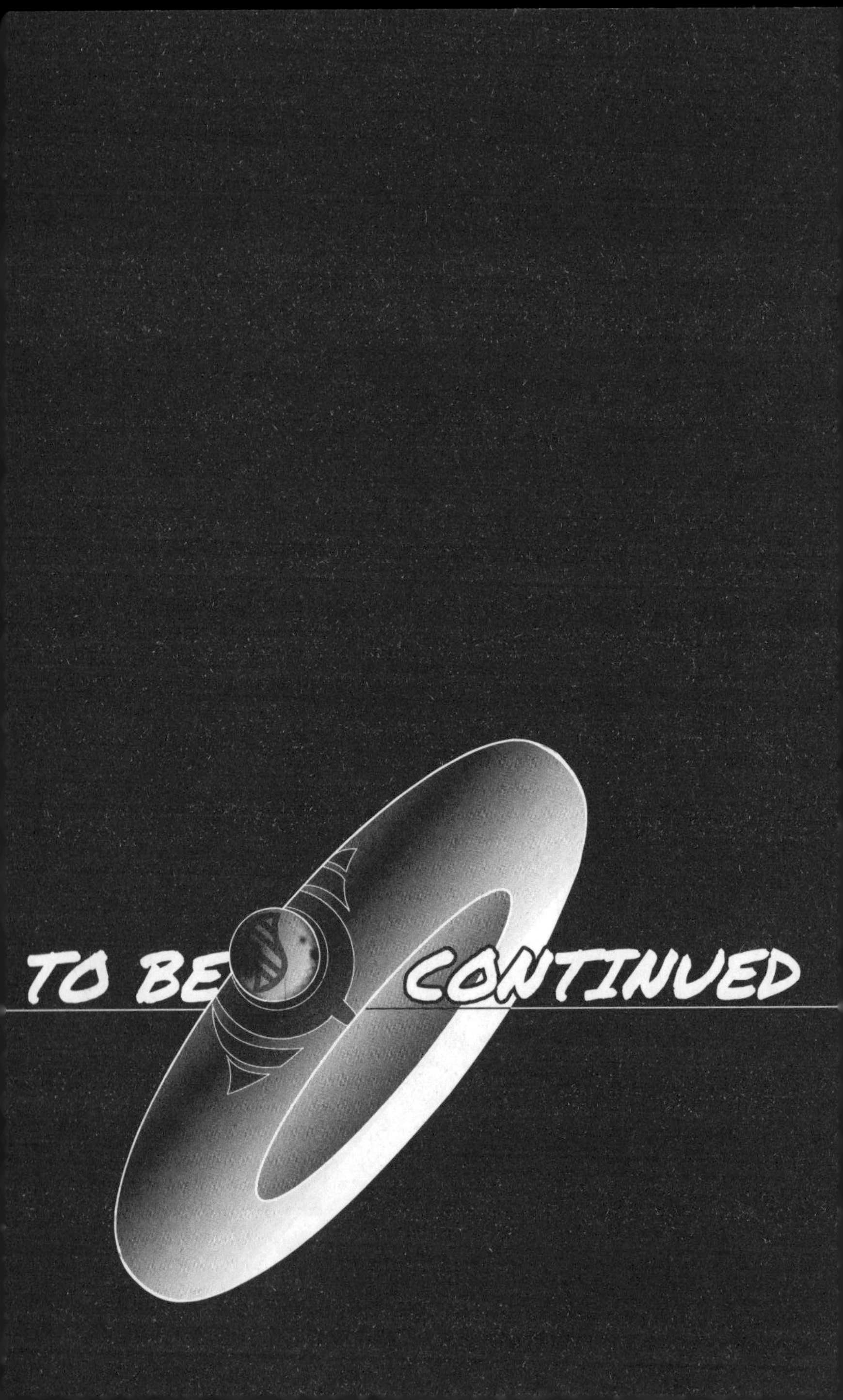
TO BE CONTINUED

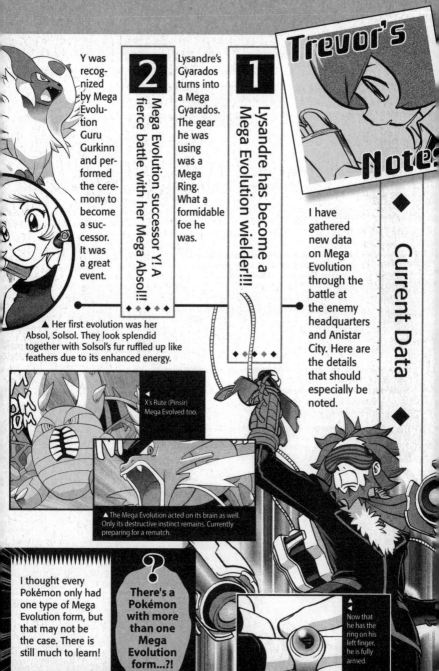

Trevor's Notes

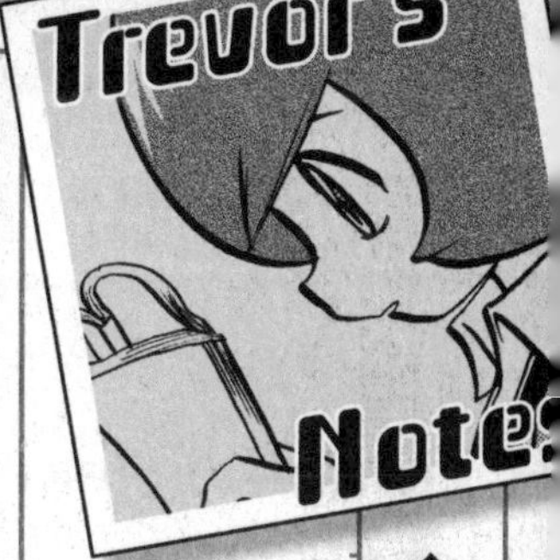

Current Data

I have gathered new data on Mega Evolution through the battle at the enemy headquarters and Anistar City. Here are the details that should especially be noted.

1 Lysandre has become a Mega Evolution wielder!!!

Lysandre's Gyarados turns into a Mega Gyarados. The gear he was using was a Mega Ring. What a formidable foe he was.

2 Mega Evolution successor Y! A fierce battle with her Mega Absol!!

Y was recognized by Mega Evolution Guru Gurkinn and performed the ceremony to become a successor. It was a great event.

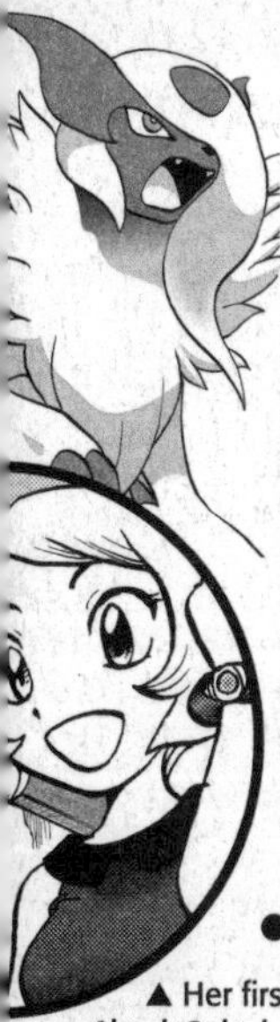

▲ Her first evolution was her Absol, Solsol. They look splendid together with Solsol's fur ruffled up like feathers due to its enhanced energy.

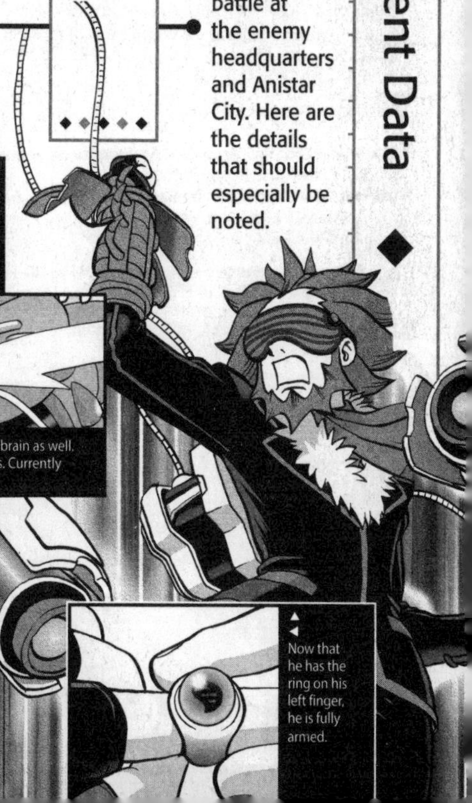

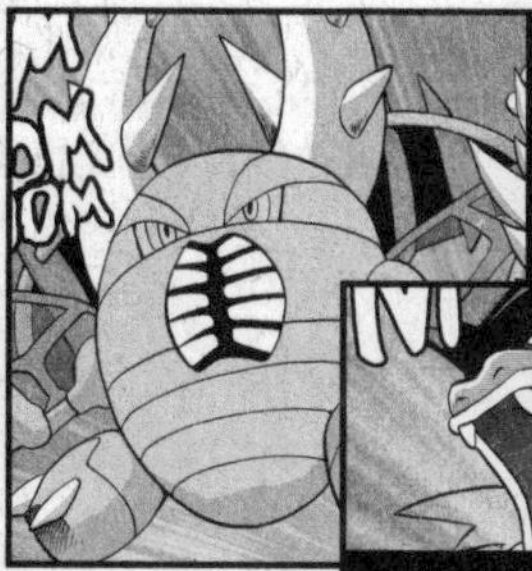

◀ X's Rute (Pinsir) Mega Evolved too.

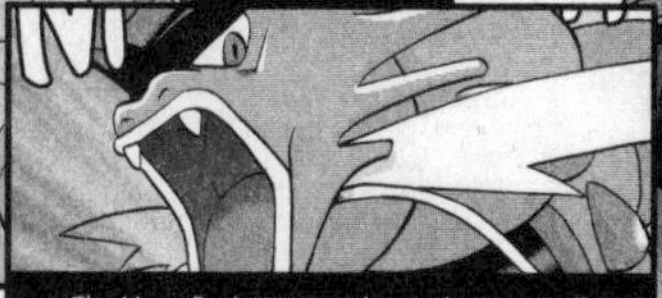

▲ The Mega Evolution acted on its brain as well. Only its destructive instinct remains. Currently preparing for a rematch.

▲ Now that he has the ring on his left finger, he is fully armed.

There's a Pokémon with more than one Mega Evolution form...?!

I thought every Pokémon only had one type of Mega Evolution form, but that may not be the case. There is still much to learn!

Pokémon ADVENTURES: X·Y
Volume 5
VIZ Media Edition

Story by **HIDENORI KUSAKA**
Art by **SATOSHI YAMAMOTO**

©2023 Pokémon.
©1995–2021 Nintendo / Creatures Inc. / GAME FREAK inc.
TM, ®, and character names are trademarks of Nintendo.
© 1997 Hidenori KUSAKA, Satoshi YAMAMOTO
All rights reserved.
Original Japanese edition published by SHOGAKUKAN.
English translation rights in the United States of America,
Canada, the United Kingdom, Ireland, Australia and New Zealand
arranged with SHOGAKUKAN.

Translation/Tetsuichiro Miyaki
English Adaptation/Bryant Turnage
Touch-Up & Lettering/Annaliese "Ace" Christman, Susan Daigle-Leach
Original Series Design/Shawn Carrico
Original Series Editor/Annette Roman
Graphic Novel Design/Alice Lewis
Graphic Novel Editor/Joel Enos

Special thanks to Trish Ledoux and Misao Oki at The Pokémon
Company International.

The stories, characters, and incidents mentioned
in this publication are entirely fictional.

Printed in the Canada

Published by VIZ Media, LLC
P.O. Box 77010
San Francisco, CA 94107

10 9 8 7 6 5 4 3 2 1
First printing, May 2023

viz.com

PARENTAL ADVISORY
POKÉMON ADVENTURES: X·Y is
rated A and is suitable for readers
of all ages.

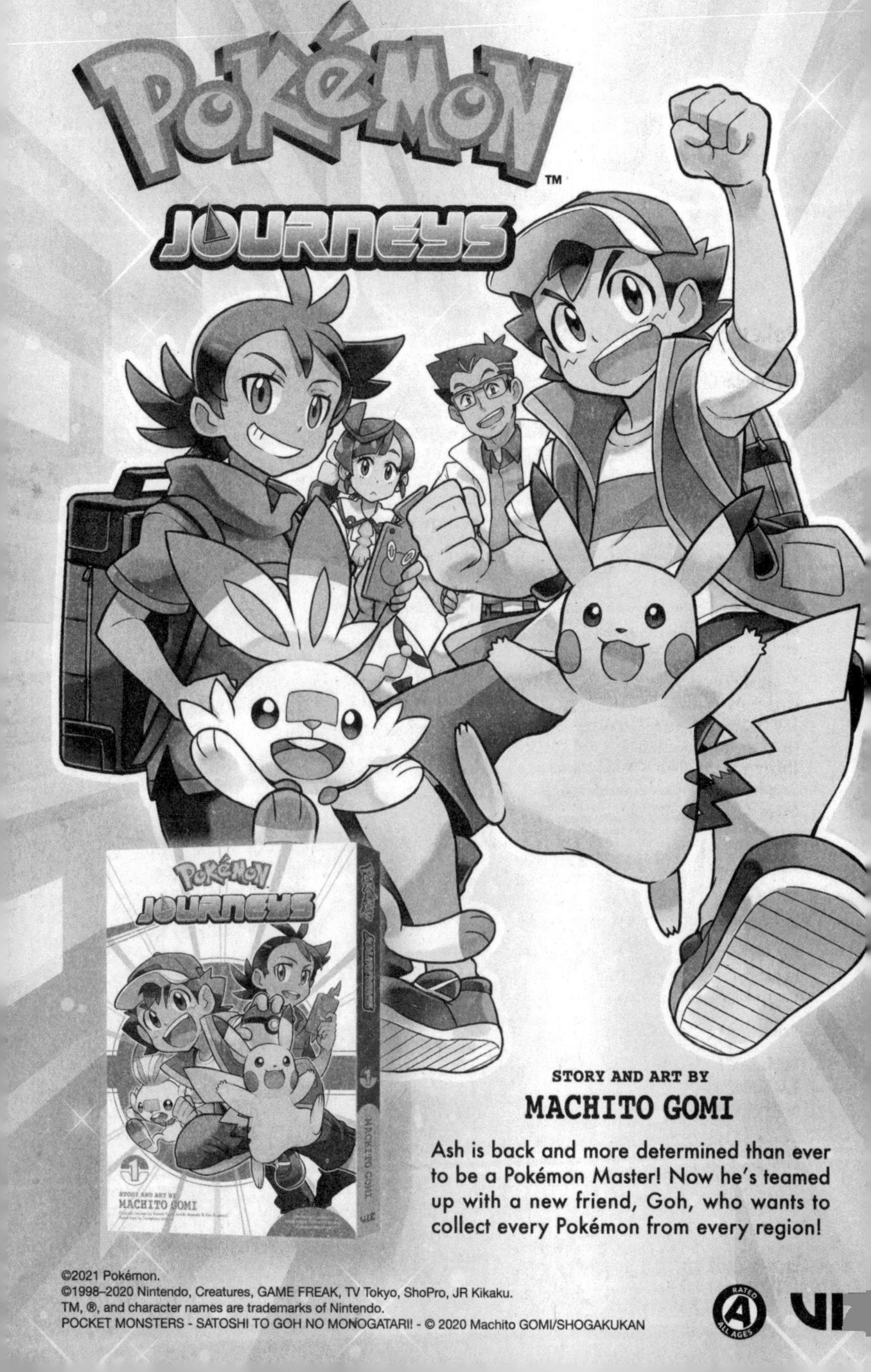
POKÉMON
JOURNEYS
POKÉMON
JOURNEYS
STORY AND ART BY
MACHITO GOMI
MACHITO GOMI

POKÉMON™

SWORD & SHIELD

Story by
Hidenori Kusaka

Art by
Satoshi Yamamoto

Awesome adventures inspired by the best-selling
Pokémon Sword & Shield video games
set in the Galar region!

 RATED ALL AGES

VIZ

ALL YOUR FAVORITE POKÉMON GAME CHARACTERS JUMP OUT OF THE SCREEN INTO THE PAGES OF THIS ACTION-PACKED MANGA!

POKéMON
ADVENTURES
COLLECTOR'S EDITION
Story by HIDENORI KUSAKA   **Art by MATO**

A stylish new omnibus edition of the best-selling *Pokémon Adventures* manga, collecting all the original volumes of the series you know and love!

POKÉMON ADVENTURES 20TH ANNIVERSARY ILLUSTRATION BOOK

THE ART OF

STORY AND ART BY
Satoshi Yamamoto

A collection of beautiful full-color art from the artist of the Pokémon Adventures graphic novel series! In addition to illustrations of your favorite Pokémon, this vibrant volume includes exclusive sketches and storyboards, four pull-out posters, and an exclusive manga side story!

viz.com

The POKÉMON COOKBOOK

Easy & Fun Recipes

by Maki Kudo

Create delicious dishes that look like your favorite Pokémon characters with more than 35 fun, easy recipes. Make a Poké Ball sushi roll, Pikachu ramen or mashed Meowth potatoes for your next party, weekend activity or powered-up lunch box.

VI
viz.co

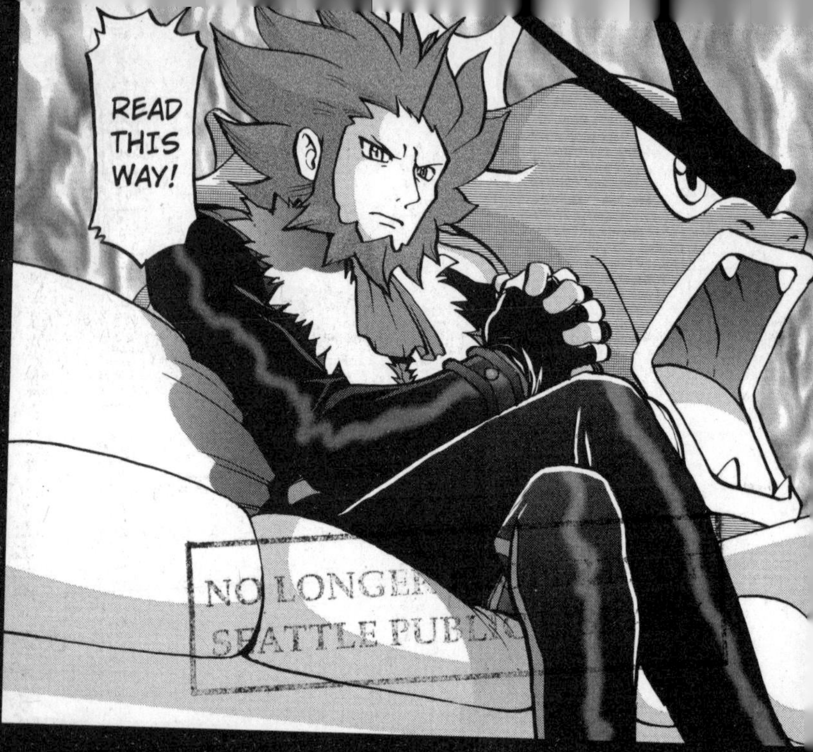
READ THIS WAY!

THIS IS THE END OF THIS GRAPHIC NOVEL!

To properly enjoy this VIZ Media graphic novel, please turn it around and begin reading from right to left.

This book has been printed in the original Japanese format in order to preserve the orientation of the original artwork.

Have fun with it!

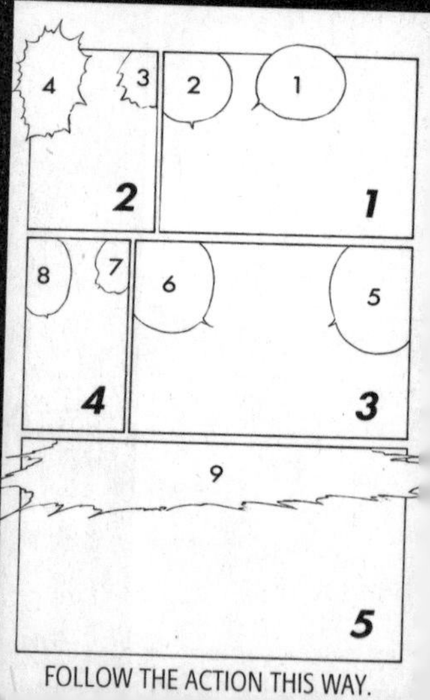
1
2
3
4
5
6
7
8
9
1
2
3
4
5
FOLLOW THE ACTION THIS WAY.